Praise for
## A Dream of Wolves

"White's emotionally packed novel delivers first-class examinations of morality, mixing strong supporting characters and unexpected plot turns, enveloping the reader in an extraordinary story."

—*Publishers Weekly*

"A marvelous evocation of place and character, right down to the flinty-eyed stare of the backwoods folk of North Carolina's Blue Ridge Mountains. A raw and powerful achievement."

—Anita Shreve, author of *The Last Time They Met*

"A wonderful novel, strong and tender and rich. I loved it. . . . This book deserves a big readership."

—Anne Rivers Siddons, author of *Nora, Nora* and *Up Island*

"Contains a fascinating collection of Southern customs. Its use of dialect is spare and elegant. . . . Male readers will recognize and sympathize with the doctor's timeless dilemma."

—*Washington Post*

"*A Dream of Wolves* recalls Faulkner's ability to create a plausible imaginary universe in which painful moral choices do not depend on health, wealth, or position."

—Jacquelyn Mitchard, author of *A Theory of Relativity*

Miriam Berkley

## *About the Author*

MICHAEL C. WHITE, who teaches at Fairfield University, is the author of the *New York Times* notable book *A Brother's Blood* and *The Blind Side of the Heart*. He was the founding editor of the annual fiction anthology *American Fiction* and currently edits *Dogwood*. He lives in Massachusetts with his wife, Karen, and two children.

Also by Michael C. White

*A Brother's Blood*

*The Blind Side of the Heart*

# A Dream of Wolves

a novel

## Michael C. White

Perennial
*An Imprint of HarperCollinsPublishers*

This is a work of fiction. The characters, incidents, and dia-
logues are products of the author's imagination and are not to
be construed as real. Any resemblance to actual persons, living
or dead, is entirely coincidental.

A hardcover edition of this book was published in 2000 by Cliff
Street Books, an imprint of HarperCollins Publishers.

HarperCollins books may be purchased for educational,
business, or sales promotional use. For information please write:
Special Markets Department, HarperCollins Publishers Inc., 10
East 53rd Street, New York, NY 10022.

First Perennial edition published 2002.

*Designed by William Ruoto*

The Library of Congress has catalogued the hardcover edition as
follows:

White, Michael C.
A dream of wolves : a novel / Michael C. White.
p. cm.
ISBN 0-06-019432-4
I. Title.
PS3573.H47447 D7  2000
813'.54—dc21
00-043114

ISBN 0-06-093236-8 (pbk.)

02 03 04 05 06 ❖/RRD 10 9 8 7 6 5 4 3 2 1

*For Caitlin Mary and Wesley Beattie,*
*mountain born;*
*and for my friends in Cullowhee,*
*North Carolina.*

*To write prescriptions is easy, but to come to an understanding with people is hard. . . . The doctor is supposed to be omnipotent with his merciful surgeon's hand.*

—FRANZ KAFKA "A Country Doctor"

# Prologue

*What I know* of death is how hard we work to deserve it and how little we appreciate it when it finally comes. We do foolish, reckless things. We throw caution to the wind and then have the audacity to be surprised when death comes calling. Take this old couple a few years back. They lived down in Cashiers, in one of those fancy new retirement villages. Florida people. They're the worst. You can spot them a mile away: the big cars and flashy clothes, those leathery melanoma tans, the rapacious look of children on vacation. We get a lot of them up here, especially the summer sort. They run from the crime and cold up north, take their dough and retire to some gated community down there, with a security guard and one of those beepers in case they fall. Then, with the first mugging or coronary-inducing heat wave, they pack up and run again, this time for the haven they feel these cool blue mountains afford. Here they allow themselves the illusion of feeling safe. Insulated from trouble. The hard-won lessons of a depression and a world war are forgotten; the wariness that comes of living in a dangerous world abandoned. They let their guard down is what they do. They commit stupid, impulsive acts they'd yell at their own grandkids for doing. They leave the door unlocked at night and don't remember to have the chimney cleaned. They go hiking in the mountains without a compass or their angina pills or a shred of common sense. They suddenly forget how to drive in snow because they think they're in the South, and with the first storm we'll find a Caddy with Florida plates at the bottom of some ravine, a couple of senior citizen traumatic arrests in the front seat. Cecil calls them shit-for-brains Yankees, and though I'm a former one myself, I can't say I disagree with him.

The way we had it figured with the Cashiers business, the old guy—
let's call him Harry—was taking a bath and must've had the radio on
the edge of the tub. Now our boy Harry had probably done it a hundred
times before. While he soaked his bones, he liked listening to the big
band station out of Asheville—Glenn Miller, Tommy Dorsey, Les Brown
and his Band of Renown—the sort of music my own father liked to listen to.  Harry was probably picturing himself in his GI uniform jitter-
bugging with some girl just before he was sent overseas. He'd lived
through Normandy and Guadalcanal, and forty tough years in some
battle zone of a place like New York or Detroit, so he felt he had old Mr.
Death's number. Why, he thought he could spot him coming a mile
away: cancer, Alzheimer's, some black kid with a gun. "You'll live to be
a hundred," his doctor had assured him, as long as he watched what he
ate, got some exercise. What Harry didn't know was that he'd invited
death into his home, placed it right by his shoulder. We found the radio
in the water with him, which happens more than you'd think.

Yet that was just your run-of-the-mill shit-for-brains stupidity. What
really took the cake was what the wife did. I'll call her Dorothy, or Dot,
since by the time I was finished I knew her well. Cecil and I found her
kneeling beside the tub, an apron on and her hands still covered with
flour from the apple pie she was making. The way I had it sorted out,
Dot's fixing dinner, hears him groan with the first surge of the 220 amps
snaking through his body, and comes running. If she were thinking she'd
have gone for the plug, but she wasn't thinking, of course. They seldom
do. Or she could have dialed 911 and waited a half hour for the EMTs
to get there from Glenwood Springs. But in that case, she might just as
well have called Childress Funeral Parlor up in Slade and saved everybody the trouble. Instead, what she does is reach into the water to try to
save him. Sticks her hand right in. Like I said, people do foolish things,
as if hell-bent on their own destruction. Yet put yourself in Dot's shoes.
There he was, the love of her life, the man she'd spent fifty years waking
up beside, calling to her from the abyss. What was she supposed to do?
What would you have done?

I had the damnedest time trying to pry her fingers off his wrist, as if
even in death she didn't want to let him go. Their faces frozen into those
startled, caught-with-your-hand-in-the-cookie-jar expressions. Harry in
his birthday suit, scrawny and shriveled, in his own excrement, his business standing at attention for the deputies and EMTs to snicker at. Not

exactly the way he'd pictured checking out. But then, how many of us really picture our own exit? And there was Dot with this worried, fretful expression that seemed to say, "We really screwed up this time, didn't we, dear?" I felt like taking them by the shoulders and giving them a stern lecture: Next time be more careful. It's dangerous out there. But, of course, there would be no next time for them.

# 1

*"Gotcha one, Doc,"* came Cecil Clegg's familiar twang on the other end of the phone. His voice syrupy-thick, urgent, slightly bovine, what I imagine an unmilked cow sounding like if a cow could talk. That chewing-on-cud hillbilly accent, the vowels all drawn out and masticated to hell.

Fuzzy-headed, I glanced at the bedside digital clock, which proclaimed, in letters so red they seared the darkness like a branding iron, 2:13. The familiar dream I was having when Cecil called still hovered uneasily nearby. Will. I'd been dreaming about him a lot lately. In it he'd had his own dream. A dream within a dream, like one of those Chinese boxes Annabel used to collect. As if in a Grimm fairy-tale, he'd awakened from a nightmare with wolves chasing him through some dark wood, and had run into our room and clambered into bed with us.

He'd gone through a period when he used to have bad dreams involving wolves. I'm not sure why. We don't have any in these mountains. Though there's a Wolf Knob and a Wolf Lake three miles east of here, wolves have been extinct in the southern Blue Ridge for more than half a century. Maybe it was some book we read to him or just his child's fertile imagination. In any case, wolves terrified him. Each night he'd insist I look under the bed to make sure none were lurking there, that his window was locked. Despite these precautions, he'd sometimes wake from a nightmare and make a dash for our room. He'd crawl between Annabel and me, smelling vaguely of urine and fear, his small heart beating like a drum. *A wolf was after me, Dad*, he'd say. *He had these big teeth*. I'd tell him everything was fine, that it was just a dream, as if that made his fear any less real. My own dream seemed so real I found myself patting the far side of the bed, as if searching for him. But it was empty, of course, the sheets cool as rubbing alcohol on the skin.

"Y'all there, Doc?" Cecil asked, interrupting my thoughts.

I felt an odd sensation in the back of my head, an unpleasant kind of tickle, as if someone were teasing my brain with a feather. I was still half asleep. I'd been at the hospital until eleven with a protracted labor, and, pooped but wired as I always am after such a birth, it was nearly one before two glasses of Scotch had induced sleep in me. What I wanted more than anything was for Cecil to be just a dream so I could crawl back into my other dream and lie there holding my son. But duty called.

"I'm here," I said at last.

"You *are* covering tonight, right?"

"I'm covering," I replied. "What's up?"

"For a minute I thought maybe I should've been bothering Dr. Neinhuis."

"No, you're bothering the right fellow. Rob went over to Charlotte to be with his in-laws for Christmas."

"I don't mind saying I prefer working with you anyway, Doc."

"'Preciate that, Cecil," I said, dropping syllables, which you tend to do after being here as long as I have. It's not so much an effort to fit in, plane the edges off my sharp New England accent, as it is pure contagion. Or sheer laziness. I'm not sure which. "What do you have?"

"Not that I got anything against Neinhuis, mind you," he said, ignoring me. "It's just his manner I don't take to."

"Rob's a little high-strung."

"I'll say. He lets you know right quick *he's* the doctor. And you're just some redneck peckerwood with a badge."

"So what's up?" I asked, growing impatient.

"Not like you, Doc. You're regular folk. Or almost," he added with a snicker.

"You didn't call at two in the morning to tell me I'm regular folk."

He laughed nervously. "Sorry. Got us a homicide."

He never liked to tell me straight out why he was calling. He had this exasperating habit of making small talk, giving it to me a little bit at a time, almost as if he feared that if he dumped it on me all at once, I just might hang up on him and go back to bed. Which I sometimes had a good mind to do. Yet I knew when Cecil Clegg, the Hubbard County sheriff, called in the middle of the night like this it could only mean one thing: He wanted me to pronounce somebody. *Pronounce,* the way you would a word, or two people man and wife. Only in this case it was saying they were legally, certifiably dead. Cecil wanted me to drag my butt out of a nice warm bed and accompany him to some sordid spot where death had left its signature. To drive out with him to a cold, dark stretch of mountain road or hoof it into the woods or climb down into someone's dank-smelling cellar. All those places people choose (if they're lucky) or have chosen for them (if they're not) as the spot where they'll breathe their last.

It might be some trucker, say, who'd fallen asleep at the wheel while hauling logs over to Knoxville. Or a girl who'd made the mistake of hitchhiking home after the high school dance and was just another face on a poster until some fisherman snagged her moon-pale thigh with his Rapala out at Glenwood Lake. Or a kid from the college who'd gone backpacking alone in the mountains, got himself good and lost, and what was left of him in the spring after crows and wild dogs got through with him would fit in a violin case. Or some poor slob who'd recently been laid off from his job at the paper mill in town and whose wife had taken the kids and left him; somebody who'd reached the end of his rope and found his only answer was to start up his new Jimmy pickup, the payments on which he could no longer make, pull it into the garage, slip a Waylon Jennings tape in the dash, and wait for things to simmer down in his head.

You see, I'm the medical examiner. Part-time anyway, two weeks a month and whenever Rob Neinhuis, the assistant ME, goes on vacation or is on call at the hospital. Rob's also part-time. Hubbard County, North Carolina, is too small to have need for a full-time ME. Neinhuis's day job is orthopedics, setting broken bones. But he's only a few years out of med school, still trying to get on his feet. He's got a young family to support, and even in a rough and often violent place like these mountains, there are not enough fractured fibuli to make ends meet. So he moonlights as an ME to pay off his student loans, save for his kids' college, and, for all I know, feed a coke habit (like I said, he *is* high-strung). My own day job is a comfortable OB-GYN practice in town, an irony I still find amusing. In that role I usher people into the world, while in my ME capacity, I work the other end of the line. I'm paid $22 an hour by the county to officiate at the "unnatural or suspicious" departure of people determined to throw off this mortal coil and discover that undiscovered country.

"What else?" I asked.

"Darryl says victim's a white male, late-twenties," Cecil explained. "Darryl and Butch is out there now."

"How did it happen?"

As odd as it may seem, I usually want to know the *how*, even before the *why*, which holds only marginal interest for me, and well before the *who*. I'm more concerned by the mechanics, how things work, or in these cases, stopped working. I guess it stems from my science background. First causes don't much concern me. I leave the *why*'s to God or whoever's in charge of things, and to the lawyers and judges to sort out. As for the *who*, I figure if it's someone I know, Cecil will tell me in good time.

"Twelve gauge, from point-blank range," Cecil replied, sounding for some reason vaguely annoyed. "Coupla blasts of double aught. Fellow took one in the head. 'Nother in the gut. Jesus."

"That'll do it."

"I reckon so. Won't be pretty, I 'spect."

"No, I don't imagine so."

"You still got yours, Doc?"

"My what?"

"Your Ithaca double barrel."

"I do."

"That's a right nice gun. Ever consider partin' with it?"

"Not really."

Cecil and I and a couple of other fellows used to hunt together, back before my knees got too bad to go traipsing up and down these mountain ridges. Several of us would go every fall: Cecil; Jim Bradley, who teaches biology at the college; Marty Bledsoe, a fellow who works on my truck; sometimes Drew Hazard, the publisher of the town paper. Jim had a camp over near Fontana Lake in Swain County. I wasn't like Jim and Marty, good, earnest hunters who got their deer every year; I was more a casual hunter, though I had a good shot and was possessed of the steady hands of a doctor who performs surgery. For me it was more that I liked the crisp, early mornings, the smell of coffee, the quiet camaraderie of the woods. It brought back pleasant memories of when I was a boy and my father would take us hunting up in Maine, one of the few times my brothers and I had our physician father completely to ourselves. The gun Cecil meant is a side-by-side twelve gauge, with nice engraving, Damascus barrels. A beautiful old gun. It used to be my father's pride and joy, and it became mine when he died, and of course I'd never consider parting with it.

"Any suspects?" I asked, trying to get Cecil back on track.

"We got us," he said, sucking hard, I could tell, on a cigarette, "one in custody. Only wisht they was all this easy, Doc."

"Who?"

"The fellow's old lady."

"His wife shot him?"

"Yes indeedy. It ain't gonna be pretty," he said again, already sounding reluctant. He had a delicate stomach, tended to get squeamish at the sight of human blood. Gutting a deer didn't bother him, but a little blood on a finger turned him to jelly.

"Where did all this marital bliss take place?"

"At their home. Way down near Tanavasee Lake."

"What the hell happened?"

"I told you. She blasted him."

"No, I mean, any reason?"

"Christ, Doc, you know how these things go. Maybe he's getting a little on the side or she is. Or maybe he come home liquored up again and laid into her and she got fed up. Take your pick. All comes to the same thing."

"I suppose. How'd you hear about it?"

"Was her called it in. She said he was dead and for us to come and fetch him. Like he was a damn suit she wanted picked up for cleaning. The hell's wrong with people anyway?"

"You're sure about him, right Cecil?"

"Whatcha mean by sure?"

"Sure as in we're not in any rush? That he's beyond our help."

"They's no question about that. Darryl says our boy's dead, then dead he is. He'd be the one to know."

Which was true. Darryl knew his way around dead people. Deputy Childress used to work as a mortician's assistant for his uncle Chilly, who owns Childress Funeral Parlor up in Slade.

"How long, he couldn't say," Cecil added. "That's your territory, Doc."

*My territory*, I thought. In my mind I saw one of those pull-down maps social studies teachers once used for teaching history, the reds and yellows and greens indicating various empires and kingdoms and invasion routes. I pictured a sprawling black expanse on one of those maps, a place called "Territory of the Dead, Stuart P. Jordan, M.D., Emperor and Sole Proprietor."

"Tanavasee Lake's out your way, Doc. I could be at your place in fif-teen minutes."

"Seeing as there's no rush, could you make that half an hour? I have to take care of something first."

"Don't see why not. Our boy ain't going nowhere. Hope I wasn't disturbin' nothing."

"It's 2 a.m. for Christ's sake. I was sleeping."

"'Course you were, Doc," he replied. I detected, though, the faintest edge of sarcasm mixed in with his soft, twangy drawl. What did he mean, hope he wasn't disturbing me? Was that supposed to be a crack about Bobbie and me, I wondered. Did he know? Or was I just being paranoid?

"You take care of what you got to do. I'll have coffee with me."

"That horsepiss you call coffee."

"Don't start," he said, and hung up.

I'd been out so many times with Cecil I guess I wasn't prepared that this time might offer something different, something besides the simplic-ity of death.

• • •

Swinging my white, old man's legs out of bed, I felt the grudging cold-ness of the house as soon as my feet hit the floor, which felt like ice. When I first moved out here to the mountains, I assumed the winters would be mild, as they had been in Durham, where I went to med school. Having grown up in New England, I was used to winters, real winters, serious and unforgiving as an old Puritan preacher. But also quite clear in their intentions. The southern Appalachians, however, have a sneaky sort of cold. A warmish Indian summer lulls you into a dangerous complacency. Then winter creeps in, promising more of the same, but all the while getting ready to spring on you like a predator. People, especially outsiders, don't take it seriously, and because of that they suffer the consequences. They don't have snow tires put on. They go hiking in the mountains in light clothes and get caught in bad weather. They don't wrap water pipes, and they find themselves in a mess of trouble. Take, for instance, this year. It'd been a pretty mild fall until around Thanksgiving. I'd put off cranking up the woodstove, get-ting by with using the electric heat, closing off unused rooms of the big old farmhouse. After all, it was just me. I could manage, I figured. But one morning I woke and my breath came out of my mouth in smoky billows. I looked out the frosted bedroom window and saw that the rugged peak of Painter Knob, the mountain due north across the valley, was covered with snow. Winter had sneaked up on me during the night and I wasn't prepared. I had to call Jack Potter and have him drop me off a load of firewood.

I dressed quietly in the dark, a doctor's on-call habit from all those years of trying not to wake a sleeping spouse. My joints were stiff with arthritis that got worse each year. My knees felt like tough pieces of leather, clicking with each step. They hurt whenever it turned cold, and it was cold now. Once dressed, I hobbled downstairs. I went into the den, opened the door of the stove, and with a piece of pine kindling poked the dying embers awake. I turned the damper, shook the ashes grate, and filled the firebox with bone-white ash, so the house would be good and warm for when I got back. I was figuring if it was as cut and dried as Cecil made it sound, I might even have a chance for a catnap before I had to be at the office for my first appointment at nine. I didn't need much sleep anymore, but I hated to get up much before daybreak.

I headed into the kitchen. I considered making instant coffee, but it wasn't coffee I was needing right then. Something stronger. From the cabinet above the sink, I grabbed the bottle of Glenfiddich and poured myself two fingers in an unwashed coffee mug. If this call had been a woman six centimeters dilated, I wouldn't have touched a drop. For those times you needed a steady hand and a clear head. But to go out and gaze into the mysterious vacuum of a dead man's eyes, it was just the ticket. I took a sip, let the Scotch sink its razor-sharp talons into me, the shock spreading throughout my sluggish system. Once acclimated, I downed the rest to get my blood moving and, I hoped, to drive that damn tickle from my brain.

Then I went into the bathroom and washed my face and brushed my teeth. In the mirror I glimpsed my old man—the same sharp features: the hawklike, intrusive nose and accusatory jaw; the down-turned, slightly frustrated-looking mouth; the broad, cool expanse of forehead. A cynical face, really, more that of an anesthesiologist than an obstetrician. Except for the eyes, a watery blue, which always seemed on the border of needing more sleep (they did) and therefore softening the overall effect. A tall and, except for a slight paunch, bony old man, what hair remained the same light brown as in his boyhood. Fifty-seven years old with bad knees and sleepless nights, living alone in a cold farmhouse up a steep mountain road the county didn't bother plowing in bad weather, and about to go pay a visit to a dead man. You stupid bastard, the face seemed to say back.

Though my beeper hadn't gone off, I nonetheless put in a call to the hospital, to check on my "living" customers. The one thing I am above all others is tediously conscientious. I got the annoyingly chipper female voice on the new phone system the hospital just put in. I pushed five for the maternity floor and was relieved at the contrast of Lucy Ballard's sandpapery voice. She was a nurse who worked nights up there.

"Hey, Doc," she said. "Y'all hear the one about the one-legged preacher and the one-eyed hooker? Dang it all. Wouldn't you just know I'd git it ass-backwards. It's a one-eyed preacher and a one-legged hooker. There we go."

"No," I said to both versions.

After Lucy finished her joke, I asked after several patients. There was Nora Bump, who was recovering nicely from a section for fertility-pill-aided triplets. Then there was little Sue Ellen McCreadie, fourteen, a pudgy girl who'd managed to keep her pregnancy hidden from her parents till she was five months along. When the jig was finally up, she decided the only answer was a handful of her mother's sleeping pills. She awoke not in some adolescent heaven of slim hips and singleness, but in the ER, still very much pregnant and having her stomach pumped. Luckily, she and the fetus were doing fine. And then there was my real reason for calling: Emmilou Potter. A mountain woman from out in Potter's Cove, she was gravida five with no children to show for all her effort: three miscarriages and a stillborn. This time around she was twenty weeks' pregnant and had already developed early signs of preeclampsia, unusual at this stage and all the more dangerous. I'd told her to rest, stay off her feet as much as possible, but the Potters were poor, and she couldn't afford the luxury of lounging in bed. She'd gotten up to milk the cow and had had a dizzy spell. She called a neighbor, who drove her to the hospital. I was just trying to buy some time for the baby, give it a fighting chance. This pregnancy, if it didn't kill her, would likely be her last shot at motherhood.

"How's Emmilou doing?" I asked.

"She's restin' just fy-on, Doc," Lucy replied. *Fy-on*, two syllables, was the way the locals pronounced *fine*. Days were *fy-on*. Children were *fy-on*. Pregnancies were often *fy-on*, except when they weren't. "Question is, wha'chall doing up at this hour?"

"Couldn't sleep pining away for you, Lucinda."

"Why, heck, Doc. You're all talk and no action." We often kidded around like this. Lucy was a hot ticket. Her husband, Tom, was the pastor of the First Calvary Baptist Church in Slade, and she sang in the choir and had a half-dozen kids. But she loved telling raunchy jokes and innocently flirting. "How long can you resist my charms, Doc?"

"What about your husband?"

"That old cuss."

"He'd like to take after me with a loaded gun."

"Then that'd be about the *onliest* thang of his loaded these days," she joked, breaking into ripples of laughter.

"If anything changes with Emmilou, make sure you page me. I'm going to be out with Sheriff Clegg."

When I got off the phone, I felt it again: that tickle. At the back of my brain, just brushing across my consciousness like a down feather. Annoying. Insistent. I had the sensation I wasn't so much forgetting something as I was just plain overlooking it. Like when you're hunting for your hat and it's already on your head. What? I wondered.

From the hall closet in the entryway, I grabbed my coat and my doctor's bag, although double-aught twelve gauge from close up made that superfluous. This wasn't going to be subtle. But there was always paperwork. Death was simple only for the dead; for everybody else it was a royal pain in the ass—a slew of forms and red tape, hoops to jump through and dots to connect. I decided to head out into the night to wait for Cecil, hoping the cold air would clear out that tiresome sensation in my head.

Above, the stars were little slivers of glass that would cut if you were dumb enough to touch them. The night was cold and still, except for the low, steady rush of the creek off to the right of the house, over near the woods—the noise like one's pulse, something felt more than heard. Down the mountain I could make out a light glowing in the kitchen window of John Wallenbach's place. John, a semiretired farmer, was my eighty-one-year-old neighbor. He told me how when he couldn't sleep he would sit at the kitchen table reading. Despite never having gone beyond grade school, he was surprisingly well read. He'd gone through all of Shakespeare and Dante and Homer, though his particular passion lay in ancient history. I could picture him sitting there now reading about Etruscans and Carthaginians, about old battles and long-ago invasions. The other morning when I was heading down our road, on my way to work, John was driving his tractor, hauling some hay. I stopped to say hello, as neighbors in this part of the country do. He started jabbering about a book he was reading on Hannibal. "Did you know, Doc," he lectured, with that imperious Southern challenge to his voice that he used with me, a neighbor and friend but a Yankee outsider nonetheless, "that fella's elephants served no tactical military purpose whats'ever. But they sure must of scared the bejesus out of them Roman legions when they seen 'em coming over the Alps."

After a while I saw the cruiser's flashers inching their way up Mason Hollow Road, the old logging road that leads up Shadow Mountain to my house. I could hear the out-of-breath whine of the cruiser's motor as it took on the last steep stretch of road just past the Wallenbachs' farm, straining the way Hannibal's elephants must have, sucking on the cold, thin mountain air.

There's no telling what a person will think about standing alone on a mountain in the middle of a frigid winter night, and what I thought about then was fear. Not in the abstract, not the *idea* of fear, but in its particular and homely manifestations. In my position, I saw a good deal of it, or at least its effects: what fear does to people, how it makes them selfish or foolish, petty or dangerous or mean, or, on those rare occasions, brave or generous, even noble. I wondered whether or not the dead man had been afraid before his wife let him have it. I wondered if she'd been afraid when she pulled the trigger or was just running on the pure white-hot surge of adrenaline it takes to do something like that. I thought of my own father, a well-respected GP in a small Massachusetts town, a man beloved by his patients though unknown by his own kids, someone I never thought was afraid of anything in this world, that is, until the Parkinson's turned his precious hands into his enemy, and then he was afraid of them. I thought about Emmilou Potter lying in a hospital bed, a brave, decent woman, someone who didn't fear for herself as much as for the fragile life she was carrying this time. Did the others, all those babies she'd cradled in her belly and then lost, come to her when she closed her eyes at night, like a family of half-formed ghosts? Did they appear to her in dreams, the way Will would come running to me, terrified by a wolf from which I was powerless to protect him.

Will, I thought. Then: Yes. Will.

I pressed the date button on my watch and the gaudy-red letters and numbers merely confirmed what I already must have known in my heart: DEC 23. Of course, I thought. That was it. That was the tickle in the back of my mind, the thing I couldn't remember earlier: Will's birthday. I didn't usually forget the day, though once, some years before, I had remembered so late that I might as well have forgotten. I would have to get some flowers and take a ride out there. To the cemetery. And then I did what I usually did on his birthday. I worked out the math. Like an aeronautical engineer, I computed the hypothetical trajectory of a hypothetical life that had barely lifted off the ground before it crashed. Fourteen years since he died, plus the five, almost six, he'd been alive: twenty. In college. I saw a tall, gangly, towheaded youth who had Annabel's mouth, my eyes, a boy standing on the cusp of manhood, aloof and sullen and distant as teenagers are, someone about to go out and make his mark in the world. The thought of his unfulfilled life, of the promise of the young man he'd never get to be, hit me like a punch in the gut as it always did on this day. I felt my heart contract into a small, hard, cold thing, like a stone at the bottom of a river, felt an involuntary shudder go coursing through me.

Yet it wasn't Will so much that occupied my thoughts right then. A former Catholic who no longer believed in much of anything, I believed at least he was out of harm's way. Knew he was at peace. Safe. What I mostly thought about was Annabel. I tried to picture how the memory of his birthday would come to her, wherever she was. Would it arrive in a dream, as mine had, about his fear of wolves? A tickle at the back of her mind? Or, more likely, would she feel her waters break as on that day twenty years ago? Perhaps a phantom pain in her cervix, the contractions coming faster. Would she wake today and experience a strange, leaden emptiness in her womb, a ghostly ache in the place where she'd once carried him, the way people do who've lost a limb yet continue to feel the pain?

# 2

The sheriff's cruiser turned up my long dirt drive, the siren off but flashers turning lazily to proclaim this official county business. As I got in the car, Cecil flicked on the dome light, so he could see to pour me coffee from a thermos.

"Here you go, Doc," he said. As usual, the car reeked of cigarettes, though Cecil refrained from smoking at least while I was with him. He knew I didn't like it. In addition to its professional capacity, the cruiser also served as his own personal means of transportation, which meant the backseat was littered with the typical family man's flotsam: stray toys, candy wrappers, baseball cards, athletic gear, underwear, his daughter's hairbrush, a crumpled teen magazine.

"Mm. Kenyan or Guatemalan," I joked, after sipping his coffee, which always put me in mind of the sludge at the bottom of an oil pan.

"Just Bi-Lo brand," he said humorlessly, even a bit testily. Our good-natured banter about the stunning dreadfulness of his coffee took us right up to many a crime scene. He shot me an ornery look. "You ain't crippled, Doc. You don't like it, make it your ownself."

There was an uncharacteristic irascibility to his voice tonight. Normally Cecil was as even-tempered a fellow as there was. He shut the dome light off, turned around, and angrily punched the gas pedal so the tires spit up bits of gravel as we bolted down the driveway.

"Just kidding, Cecil," I said. "Don't get bent out of shape."

"Same dumb-ass jokes. They get on your nerves after a while."

"I'll try to come up with some new ones then."

"You're getting awful fussy in your old age, Doc. Bad enough I can't light up."

"Just looking out for your health, Cecil." Figuring to change the subject, I asked how Ruth was.

"She had her that bug's going 'round. Laid her up pretty bad."

"How's she doing otherwise?"

"Fair. They put her on some new medication. Makes her dopey as hell."

"Prednisone?"

"I couldn't tell you. They's all the same to me. She's holding her own, I reckon." Then, hitting the plastic dash with his knuckles, he added, "Knock on wood."

Cecil's wife had lupus, a disease of the immune system. As diseases go, it wasn't a good one to have. It's one of those slowly debilitating illnesses that can't be cured, can only be managed, and Ruth was in and out of the hospital with lung and renal problems. Cecil had his hands full taking care of her and their four kids, as well as working full-time. Tell you the truth, I didn't know how he managed.

He was in street clothes, jeans and a bulky down vest, his big Colt automatic protruding from his hip like a tumor. Around fifty, he looked years older, with a full beard coming in now mostly silver gray; thick, greasy glasses that gave his eyes a slightly demented murkiness; and the quietly frustrated expression of someone who spent far too much time in hospital waiting rooms and perusing police reports. He was about five-eight but solid as a tank, a powerfully built man. It wasn't fat so much as the bulk of an ex-linebacker going to seed (he was all–Western North Carolina for Hubbard County back in the sixties, even played a couple of years for Appalachian State before dropping out, getting drafted, and finding himself running blitzes over in Nam). Besides being overweight, Cecil smoked like a chimney and drank way too much. Any sort of exertion winded him, and I could only guess at his blood pressure. I kept trying to talk him into letting me check it, but he refused. That's all he needed, he said. Get forced into a medical disability and have to live on that income.

"Everything all right, Cecil?" I asked.

"Just peachy, Doc. Got me three deputies out sick, another on vacation, a murder on my hands two days before Christmas," he replied sarcastically, as he turned onto Highway 7, heading south toward Tanavasee Lake. "On top of ever'thing, I feel lousy, like I just got run over by a Mack truck. Things couldn't be better."

"What's the matter with you?"

"Think I'm coming down with what Ruthie had. My guts is rumblin' like crazy."

"Is it any wonder, the way you take care of yourself?"

"And kinda achy all over. Right up in here," he said, rubbing his bull neck. "You're a doctor. What do you think it might be?"

"Pain in the neck is my diagnosis," I kidded. "Goes with the job."

"Pain in the ass you mean. Sometimes I think I'm gettin' way too old for this bullshit, Doc."

"*You?* I must have, what, six, seven years on you, Cecil?"

"It's different with you."

"How's it different?"

"Me, this is what I do. But you, you could walk away from this any time you've a mind to," he said, glancing over at me. "So why, then?"

"Why what?"

"Why the hell do you do this?"

"Must be I like your coffee," I joked, not wanting to get into a serious discussion of motives and career choices at this hour. Cecil wouldn't let it drop, though.

"No, really, Doc. The hell you do this for? Ain't the money, like with Neinhuis. A smart fellow like yourself."

It was a question I'd often asked myself, and more and more lately. The short answer was that it started out as a favor for a friend who was then the ME, Dr. Delvin Jamison, who did it all by himself. He went on vacation to the Yucatan and asked if I'd cover while he was gone. I reluctantly agreed. As luck would have it, he died of a massive coronary climbing some Mayan temple to the sun god. Troy Bumgartner, the DA, asked if I'd stay on until he found somebody else. He kept dragging his feet, telling me he was looking. Thirteen years and a hundred or so nights like this one later, I was still doing it, though I had help now.

The longer answer was more complicated, as longer answers generally are. I could say exactly why I'd become a doctor. Ever since I was a kid, it was all I ever wanted to be. I was simply following in the footsteps of a distant father I admired and I guess I sought to please, even though I wasn't aware of it and even though by the time I went to med school he was already dead, and pleasing him was beyond my reach. Later, I believed, with the naive arrogance of all interns, that I could help people: easing pain and suffering, bringing life into the world, the whole corny Hippocratic oath. But an ME? I couldn't help those people. And Cecil was certainly right that I didn't need the money. I had a comfortable practice. Oh, I didn't make the big bucks that my old med school colleagues raked in with cushy gynecology practices in high-rent suites in places like Charlotte or Atlanta. Then again, I didn't have their headaches or overhead. My house was paid for. I didn't have to worry about putting kids through college. My needs were modest. Unlike a lot of doctors I knew, I had no expensive hobbies or vices, no vacation house or boat, no addictive habits beyond a yen for well-aged single malt Scotch, and, for the past year or so, throwing for a room at the Skyline Motel over in Crawford City. But more on that later.

So why *did* I do it? Maybe at my age death was close enough to hold a certain morbid fascination, my *momento mori*. Or maybe having brought so many Hubbard County residents into this world over the past twenty-eight years, I felt a certain responsibility to see them out, like a gracious host after a dinner party escorting his guests to the door. Then again, as Bobbie Tisdale liked to say—she was the assistant DA and therefore someone eminently qualified to cut through false motives and reduce things to their unpretentious essence—"Who are you shitting, Doc? You just get a kick out of playing Sherlock Holmes." I have to admit to a certain fascination with constructing the "how" of a death. There's a satisfying mathematical elegance in arriving at causes, which, as I said earlier, appeals to some logical part of my brain. However, the simplest and probably truest explanation I can come up with is this: plain dumb inertia. As with many things in our lives, we doggedly continue along some course just because it would take more energy and more intelligence and more courage to stop than to go on with it. Routines. Habits. Nature abhors a vacuum, and I didn't know what nature would put in the place of that vacuum if I stopped going out with Cecil altogether. But these were not the sorts of questions one likes asking oneself at 2 A.M., when about to visit a man dispatched with a shotgun at point-blank range. You just do it and don't think too finely on things. Otherwise you'd stop doing it. So I shrugged.

"Like hell I'd be here if I didn't have to," Cecil said.

"And just what would you do with yourself?"

The expanse of such a thought, a Grand Canyon of leisure and time on his hands, left him speechless for a moment. Then he said, "No more of this bullshit, that's for damn sure."

We drove southeast along the winding, steeply banked Tuckamee River toward South Carolina. Tanavasee Lake was down near the state line. No one else was out at this hour, and the mountains just beyond the tunnel of our headlights loomed darkly above us like sleeping giants. Lulled by the steady rhythm the tires made over the pavement, we fell into an uneasy silence. We passed a mixture of hardwood and pine forest, whole mountainsides stripped bare by the Nantahala Paper Company. Hillsides choked beneath frost-yellowed kudzu vines. Broken pasture land. Nurseries and apple orchards. Hardscrabble farms with junk cars slowly rotting back into the earth. Sagging barns that a good wind would knock over. Dirt roads winding up into pitch-black "hollers." The occasional gas station or trailer or tarpaper shack with smoke billowing out a rusted metal stovepipe. Welcome to Appalachia.

In some places the highway rose a hundred feet or more above the river, and we skirted dangerously close to the edge. Oblivious to this fact, or defiant of it—hard to tell which—Cecil held his coffee in one hand and aimed the cruiser with the other. He drove well over the speed limit, gunning it on the straightaways, expertly negotiating the sudden turns of the road with experience that came from nearly thirty years patrolling these mountains. However, as we rounded a bend in the road, in the headlights, not fifty feet away, was the spectral form of a possum. The stupid creature had stopped in the middle of our lane, its tiny pink rat-eyes locked in our lights, as if daring us to put it out of its misery. We were headed right for it. My own foot reached for a brake that wasn't there as my heart slid into V-fib. I was well aware that people died in just such unplanned moments as this, moments when their own mortality seemed distant, unimaginable to them. But without showing the least alarm, Cecil casually swung into the other lane and around the stricken animal, the wheels squealing bloody murder yet without so much as spilling a drop of coffee—or blood. I glanced over at him, both impressed and a little angry.

"What's the big rush?" I asked. "You said yourself, our boy's not going anywhere."

"Stupid bastard," he cursed, and I couldn't say if he meant the animal or our boy out in Tanavasee. Something, I could tell, was bugging him. More than the usual, justifiable crabbiness that came with our sleep being interrupted and having to go out on nights like this. More than him feeling shitty or that he was short-staffed. Maybe Ruth was worse than he was letting on. Maybe it had something to do with where we were headed.

"So?" I said, when his silence had become oppressive.

"So what?"

"So how come you're so quiet?"

"What's there to talk about?" he said morosely. Cecil and I had been friends for ages. Not close friends. Not bare-our-souls-to-the-other sort of friends. He'd never even set foot inside my home, except maybe to wait in the entryway while I got my things. Nevertheless, there existed between us the sort of sincere camaraderie and natural bond that resulted from shared experiences of an unsavory nature. Besides hunting together occasionally, we'd been going out on nights like this for thirteen years. Usually we talked and kidded around while we headed out to the scene of a murder or accident. The easy, mindless banter of a couple of high school boys bombing around in their old man's car. I might tell him some joke Lucy Ballard had told me, or he'd talk about a nice eight-point buck he'd spotted. Or we'd debate the chances of Appalachian State beating Eastern Tennessee State. Plus we had one other thing that made us brothers of sorts: We both knew what it was like to have a sick wife.

After a while, he said, "Why do the stupid bastards have to be up at this hour?"

"Possums are nocturnal creatures."

"Don't mean them and you know it. I mean those *folks*. The ones shooting the hell outa each other. Why can't they just stay in bed where they belong?"

"That's not always the safest place either."

"If it wasn't for them, we could be in bed."

"Is that a proposition, Cecil?" I said, trying to joke with him, tease him out of this mood he was in.

He ignored me.

"Shit-for-brains," he said, after a while. That was one of his favorite expressions. In Cecil's book, people in general had shit for brains, as did all teenagers, possums and assorted other varmints who ran under your tires, slick lawyers and mollycoddling judges, some hillbillies, most drunks, almost all Floridians and Yankees (me being a notable exception), as well as the occasional doctor or deputy. In fact, sometimes it was a general lament for the state of the world. "Why can't they just go to sleep?" he said. "If they were sleeping they wouldn't be up to all this damn foolishness."

"'Sleep that knits up the raveled sleave of care.'"

"The hell you talking about, Doc?"

"Nothing," I said.

I could remember how Will, after one of his bad dreams, would say he was afraid to close his eyes, afraid of the wolves' coming back. How helpless I felt. And how for months after his death I couldn't sleep either. I'd wander the house. I'd go by his room, afraid to go in, afraid of what I'd find there. I'd sit at the kitchen table with a bottle of Scotch, even if I had a 6 A.M. surgery. Only dumb luck prevented me from hurting anybody. Sometimes I'd just lie in bed, though, awake, silent, beside Annabel. I could hear her breathing, the sort of measured breathing that suggested she wasn't sleeping either, that told me she had her own wolves to contend with. How many nights had we lain there side by side? How many nights had I wanted to whisper into the darkness, "I'm sorry. I didn't mean it. Can you forgive me?"

"So here we are freezing our balls off, Doc. And for what?"

"Come on, Cecil. What's really the matter?"

"I'm just fed up is all. These stupid bastards thinking a gun was always the answer. If they couldn't sleep, they could at least play cards. Or watch TV? Something. Even *screw*. They could always do *that*, couldn't they?"

"I suppose."

"No, really. If they were busy *screwing* their brains out, they'd be too worn out for *blowing* their brains out. Now what's so wrong with that?"

"Nothing," I said.

"I'm not kidding."

"Sounds like you're onto something, Cecil."

"I fuckin' *mean* it, Doc," he cursed, with anger that surprised me.

"You're absolutely right."

Expecting resistance and getting none, Cecil just seemed to implode into his own argument. He glanced over at me, deadly serious at first, but then, slowly, grudgingly, seeing the absurdity in what he was saying, gave in to a partial smile. "You damn right, I'm right."

"Cecil Clegg's new coitus therapy for violent thoughts."

"Whatever."

"Maybe you could write a book. Go on the lecture circuit."

"I reckon I could. Call it *How to Fuck Your Troubles Away*. How's that sound?"

"Now you're talking. You could hit all the talk shows. Go on *Oprah*. I could act as your impresario."

"My *what*?"

"Like your agent. Take my ten percent."

"Sure. We'd make a killing and then I could tell Troy Bumgartner to shove this goddamned job up his goddamned ass," he said, bitterness leaching slowly out of him. He wagged his large head and then laughed out loud. I laughed, too, the noise sounding forced even to me. "Fuck it all to hell, right, Doc," he cursed. "Five more years and I'm outa here anyway."

"That's the attitude."

I sipped my coffee. Bad as it was, it was exactly the sort of thing you needed to get out of bed on a night like this. It dawned on me Cecil hadn't told me yet who the victim was, and I was starting to get nervous. I was hoping it wasn't somebody I knew, at least not well, which is always a danger in a small town. I remember a couple of years back, I'd had to pronounce Vernadine Crenshaw. She'd been my patient for years; I'd delivered her three kids. She was a sweet lady, used to bring me in preserves she'd put up. They found her under the bridge north of town, raped, her skull stove in with a rock. I'd had to collect evidence— semen and pubic hairs—and it was ugly business all around.

"Who's our boy?" I asked finally.

"Roy Lee Pugh."

"Any relation to the Pughs over in Little Mexico?"

"Hell, all them Pughs are related, one way or t'other. This is Glenn W.'s youngest. They're bad news, that bunch."

"So I've heard."

The Pughs were the local bad boys, part of an almost legendary clan that lived so far back in the hills, a place called Little Mexico, that people joked the kids who lived there missed a whole grade just riding the bus to school. I'd been out there a few times, back when I used to make house calls. The locals used to warn me about going up here. Said the people of Little Mexico were a different breed from other mountain folks, more clannish and backward, that they didn't take to outsiders, and especially not to Yankees. Yet I'd delivered two babies at home up there and never had any problems.

Every mountain town had a clan like the Pughs, who were known to be violent and irascible and reclusive, even by hill standards, who were always getting into scrapes with the law. In the old days they were the type of hill-clan that made moonshine, take potshots at a "revenuer" who got too close to their still, kill a neighbor's prize hog over some personal slight. Now and then one of them would get tanked up and get in a fight at some bar over in Crawford City, cut somebody with a razor, shoot somebody in the leg.

You read about the Pughs in the paper, how this one was arrested for discharging a firearm within the city limits or that one had poached a deer on state land; how another had smashed some Jehovah's Witness's windshield with an ax because the woman had made the mistake of driving up to Little Mexico to try to convert them. For the most part, they were still small-time mountain hoods. Yet in recent years their criminal activities had grown and they'd diversified; they'd gotten into stealing cars, running guns, dealing drugs, you name it. Occasionally you'd see the Pugh clan in town, and people passing them on the sidewalk would avert their eyes and give them a wide berth. You didn't want any dealings with their kind. The locals spoke of them with an odd mixture of revulsion and fear and disdain, but also with a certain element of pride. They were part of a vanishing breed.

"Word is," Cecil explained, "they grow a mess of that wacky-tabacky way the hell up in the hills. DEA boys been after them for years. This Roy Lee fellow's spent time in jail for dealing."

"You think this has anything to do with drugs?"

"Never can tell. Hope not anyway. The less I have to do with them Pughs, the better I like it. They're backwoods mountain folk."

"What do you got against mountain folks?"

"Not a blessed thing. My grandpappy came down out of the hills during the Depression. Took him a factory job. No sir, I got plenty of respect for them. Most are hard-working, law-abiding people. Don't want no truck with me. Wouldn't take welfare if you shoved it at them. But then again, they's some just got bad blood. Too much inbreeding, you ask me. Like the Pughs."

When I first came here, I'm embarrassed to admit that the extent of my knowledge of the Appalachian people was *The Beverly Hillbillies* and *Li'l Abner*. To me, they were all mountain folk—hillbillies, backwoods, back*wards*. After finishing my OB-GYN residency in Durham and having just broken off a long engagement to a woman there, on a whim I moved out to the western part of the state. I'd driven through the mountains once or twice; I found their stark, rugged beauty alluring. They reminded me of Maine, only bluer, shrouded in a filmy haze that, except for a dryish autumn, never quite lifted, always gave you the sense of things unseen or only partially seen. And I was single, unattached, ready to try something new. I thought it might be interesting practicing rural medicine for a while, though I had no intention of staying forever. I guess I always believed I'd return someday to my New England roots.

But I found my work in the mountains challenging and rewarding, if more than a little daunting.

I was the first, and for many years the only, obstetrician, which meant seventy- and eighty-hour workweeks. After several years here, I began to settle in, to understand the mountain accent and the mountain ways, to accept the locals and in turn be accepted by them. Though it didn't come easily. Not by a long shot. I had two strikes against me: I was a Yankee, which meant I talked funny, as well as a nominal Catholic. An outsider in a part of the country proud of its stubbornly insular ways. But after a while, most finally came around. They placed their trust in me. They started calling me Doc Jordan, or just plain Doc. I liked walking down Main Street in Slade and having people say, "Right nice weather we're having, eh Doc?" Or "How 'bout them Tarheels?" Or "How's your boy doin', Doc?"

I learned the ways of the mountains, the sometimes subtle distinctions the locals themselves make. For instance, they weren't all hillbillies. There's the old-monied sort who affect the genteel mannerisms of the deep plantation South, the ones who live in the elegant Victorian houses in Slade, the county seat; or the new-monied professionals, the sort who take up residence in one of the ostentatious developments going up on the outskirts of town. Together, they're the ones who run things, who own the fabric mill or the Nantahala Paper Company or who teach at the local college; they're the doctors and professors, the lawyers and judges; the ones who drink wine with their meals and go to the symphony over in Raleigh, who say "you'uns" or "reckon so" with a self-deprecating smile, and who, consciously or otherwise, look down their noses on the rest of Hubbard County society. Several rungs below them on the social ladder are the townies: merchants or tradesmen or factory workers, locals, good ole boys like Cecil, the ones whose parents or grandparents came down out of the mountains on a mule or Model T to settle in modest ranch houses or double-wide trailers in town. They become the proud owners of forty-two-inch television sets and microwaves and satellite TV dishes in their backyards; they graduate from the regional high school and marry someone from a different gene pool; they're people who have been more than happy to trade their mountain heritage for a piece of the American pie.

Then there's the last group: the real, honest-to-goodness mountain folks. The hillbillies. People who are not only respected and revered by the others because they haven't sold out, haven't given up the old ways or their independence, but who are also ridiculed and scorned, perhaps because they remind the townspeople of the red-clay-dirt-and-hard-scrabble lives they came from. I learned that, around here, depending on how it's said and who says it, "mountain folk" can be either a compliment or fighting words. This last group is made up of large, tight-knit, isolated clans, like the Ledbetters and McClatcheys, the Coghills and Queens and Carters, the Tarbells in the next holler over from me. And the Pughs. Families that go back six or seven generations to the original settlers, people who live twenty winding miles up some holler, sometimes the only electricity supplied by a generator, their running water from a creek. People who are suspicious of outsiders and wary of change. Their menfolk are proud and stubborn, almost genetically prone to violence; they get drunk and shoot each other or beat up their wives or impregnate their cousins or nieces. Their rawboned kids take a bus an hour to school and arrive with head lice and ears set low on their skulls, and are teased by the townies or the professors' kids; they drop out of school in the ninth grade because their daddies promised them a Firebird or because they got some girl knocked up. And then there are the women. Oh, yes, the women. Those pretty, sad-eyed creatures, lovely and innocent mountain flowers at twelve, angry and desperate mothers by seventeen, and sunken-cheeked and resigned grandmothers by thirty; women who take snuff and don't have Pap smears and who, when they finally come into my office for "female problems," have metastasized breast or cervical cancer and there's not a thing you can do for them.

But it's also because of the people that I stayed all these years in Hubbard County. While they may be different, some narrow-minded or provincial, not a few racist rednecks or ignorant and superstitious hillbillies, they are, generally speaking, as decent and noble, as gracious and generous, as hopeful and brave and abiding a lot as you could hope to find anywhere in this country. Resourceful. Fiercely independent. Loyal. Though mountain folk may take a while to warm up to you, when they do they are the best friends or neighbors a person could ask for. Far better than the aloof and cold New Englanders I was used to. Mountain people will be there if you need them. Strangers stop if you have a flat tire. When someone in the family is sick, they come quietly and humbly to your door with food or sincere offers of help. They invite you to their houses for Sunday dinner, and even though you're a Catholic, they ask you to lead them in prayer. And for a doctor, they are also the most exasperating, trying, and stubborn of patients, which is another reason I stayed. Whereas in some comfortable suburb I would just be another OB-GYN doctor, with a cushy practice tending to middle-class women with neurotic middle-class health problems—hot flashes, frigidity, PMS—here I've felt needed. Here, I thought, I could make a difference. So I stayed.

• • •

"And the wife?" I asked.

"Don't know who'all she is. Darryl said she looked Cherokee."

Cecil slowed the cruiser and turned right onto Carter Hollow Road, which winds its way up to Tanavasee Lake, several miles away. I know because I had to deliver a baby out here once. One of the Carter clan. The woman had waited too long for her husband to drive her the thirty miles to the hospital, and by the time I got there the baby's head was already crowning, so I had to deliver it right in her bed, like they did in the old days.

I stole a glance at Cecil. He was staring grimly at the lit tunnel of road ahead. It was the way some men stare into their drinks, others at naked women they can't ever possess. A kind of bitter, amorphous craving, though its object remained elusive to them. Cecil didn't like any of this. People dying on him on cold, black nights. People getting out of bed when they should be sleeping and loading shotgun shells into guns, forcing us out of bed, too. He didn't like to contemplate an ugly shit-for-brains universe, one governed by chance, accidents, bad luck, mindless violence, intentional or casual cruelty. Where I got hooked on the *how*, Cecil was a *why* man. Why do things like this happen? Why is evil allowed to freely roam the world, striking people at random? Why does a nice old couple get zapped in a bathtub? Why does a sweet woman like his wife get a terrible disease like lupus? Why does a small boy wander off into the woods and get lost for no reason? For him, I guess, it bespoke some monstrous and malignant stupidity eating away at the very heart of things. And yet he wasn't naive, not someone inexperienced in the cruel ways of the world. He'd served a tour of duty in Vietnam and had been a police officer for almost three decades. So he had certainly seen as much as I the gnarled shapes men's souls can take, the randomness that can decide our fates.

But despite the grizzled exterior, the badge and the big gun, the combat in Nam, Cecil was at heart a docile, sensitive soul, someone who got physically ill at the sight of pain and violence and bloodshed. Take what happened up at Miller's Landing. A couple years back we had to go out on a homicide-suicide: the Ledbetter boy and Tanya Pressley. Her grandfather, Orel, had run the feed and grain in town; her mother, Dixie, was a patient of mine. I'd delivered all the Pressleys. Tanya was the only girl, a colicky, difficult baby, who, according to her mother at least, grew into a difficult child and then later a difficult young woman. She and the Ledbetter kid were boyfriend and girlfriend, though her parents didn't approve of her seeing him. They thought he came from white trash. The two kids had probably just read *Romeo and Juliet* for English class and took it to heart. We found them out at Miller's Landing, a lovers' lane a few miles north of Slade. They were dead in his Firebird, as if hoping to rise from its ashes. The boy had used a deer rifle, doing his girlfriend first in the heart and then himself, sticking the gun in his mouth and tripping the trigger with his toe. A 30.06 220-grain hollow point discharged in a human mouth is not one of life's more pleasant sights, believe me. Poor Cecil took one look and went belly up, passed out cold. It was just me and him at first, so when he came to he swore me to secrecy. Who would ever want a sheriff queasy about blood? He was a decent man, one who'd like to think the world was a decent, orderly, forgiving place. Problem was it's not, and at fifty years old, he woke up one morning and found himself stuck in a job whose purpose was to sweep up after the stupid, messy mistakes of others. He'd had his bellyful of death and violence, of *why*'s he had no answers for.

Not that I cared much for it myself. Though I'd been doing this for thirteen years and had been to a couple dozen murder scenes in that time, I've never actually grown accustomed to seeing a homicide. Maybe you *never* do, even if you worked in a big city and saw a thousand. It's not the physical fact of death; that doesn't bother me so much. As an obstetrician I'm no stranger to the physicality of the dead. You can't work for nearly thirty years as a physician without losing some patients; it comes with the territory. Yet the handful of deaths I'm confronted with in my practice have to do with disease, with bad luck or bad technique, with poor judgment or flawed genes, and no one certainly means for it to happen. It's sad and heart-wrenching when a child is stillborn or dies shortly after birth from complications or when a woman dies of cervical cancer. Sad but natural. Murder, on the other hand, is a different story. It's the epitome of *un*natural. It always comes as an affront to one's fragile beliefs in order and harmony existing in the universe to see someone lying there dead by another's hand.

Unlike some men—Cecil, for instance—I don't concern myself with large notions, like whether harmony exists in the universe or not, the question of evil, if there's a heaven or hell waiting for us at the end of the line or just a hole in the ground. You might think that to see death up close as I do, I would have had to come to an understanding of such looming questions, that I'd need to subscribe to a grand scheme that shapes our lives and gives meaning to our ends. Yet the plain truth is I haven't. The murder victim holds no lessons for the observer, even for the professional observer. I've read some of those glitzy books by prominent coroners—the Naguchis and the Badens and Lees—and they speak of the dead as if they were a repository of all this hidden meaning. What they are really talking about is the body: It can tell you how it ended, but that's all it can do. Nothing more. It's silent about the really important questions, like where the soul slithers off to after it peels off its pale skin of mortality. A dead man's eyes proffer no profound truths, no hidden meanings. They are as silent and dumb as stones.

I sometimes think I lost any belief in large things when my son died, but the truth is I'm not sure I ever held them. Some people simply don't have a largeness of soul in them. Such people make quite capable scientists and accountants and medical examiners, occasionally even very skilled and caring physicians. They are good "how" people; they are the sort who tend to the boring details of running the world's affairs. But the *why*'s of things are quite beyond their scope. This is the case with myself. Maybe that's the reason I make a good ME: I deal with facts. I connect the dots reasonably well and can sleep nights with the picture they form.

"Darryl said the girl's not saying squat," Cecil offered.

"How come they didn't bring her in?"

"Ran into a little problem."

"What kind of little problem?"

"You'll see. I told 'em to sit tight till we got there."

"She called it in, you said?"

"Yes indeed. She even gave me directions, on account of most people couldn't find the place."

"That was thoughtful of her," I said.

"Oh, she's just a very thoughtful gal, that one."

# 3

*When we got* up near the lake, a slick black mirror set between stands of hemlock and white pine, we came to a wooden sign nailed to a fence post, saying OLD CARTER SETTLEMENT, with an arrow pointing up the hill. Cecil swung the cruiser onto a steep washboard road, and we started climbing, following the power line up the mountain. The rear wheels began to slip, kicking up a flurry of stones against the car's undercarriage.

"They keep promising a four-wheel," Cecil said, meaning the county. "I ain't agonna hold my breath."

"We should've taken my Blazer," I said.

Cecil shrugged.

For these mountain roads you really needed a truck. The cruiser lurched forward, bucking and pitching. Sometimes the tires spun free, revving into an angry snarl like a cat whose tail has been stepped on—*reowwwww, reowwwww*. After several miles, the mountain ridges opened up into a clearing, what the locals call a cove, though we were four hundred miles from water. In Hubbard County there were hundreds of such coves: Copes Cove, Magruder's Cove, Buford Cove, Queen's Cove, Carter Cove. Most were named after the original Scotch-Irish settlers who had come down through the Cumberland Gap two hundred years before and hacked lives from the teeming wilderness, carving these tiny sheltered inlets out of the inhospitable sea of surrounding mountains and forests. The ones who came first got the rich bottom land, while the rest took to the hills. They cleared the land and farmed it as best they could, put down roots, got married, had children, and finally, after fighting the poor red soil for all their lives, surrendered themselves to it.

We drove past a small cemetery with moss-covered stones; an abandoned farm with a boarded-up house and dilapidated barn; a rusted, metal-tired John Deere tractor lying on its side like a discarded child's toy; and assorted other broken pieces of farm machinery littering an open field. It almost seemed as if the farmer just gave up one day, took the clothes on his back, and went west. Just beyond the field, Cecil turned left up a narrow dirt tote road, deep ruts now frozen into axle-breaking grooves. When the path ended abruptly and the woods opened up into a clearing, we found ourselves in what looked like an automobile graveyard. Scattered about were various automobile parts—axles, engine heads, transmissions, fenders, and bumpers—as well as half a dozen complete junk cars of various vintages dating back to the rotted-out husk of a 1956 Ford Fairlane, their windows shattered and doors pockmarked by bullet holes; a favorite pastime of local kids was plunking cars. Off to one side, the hulking ghostly white corpse of a refrigerator shone in the headlights, while nearby a weather-beaten doghouse squatted in front of some bushes. Over toward the back of the clearing was a brown, vinyl-sided double-wide. In front of the trailer were the two cruisers Darryl Childress and Butch Slocum, the other deputy, came up in, as well as a late-model Chevy pickup truck. Already draped around the trailer was the gaudy yellow crime-scene tape, which Butch had gone a little wild with as usual. It was strung from the door handle of one of the shot-up cars on one side clear to the clothesline pole on the other, a hundred and fifty feet away. It gave the trailer the appearance of a huge Christmas present wrapped with a bright yellow bow.

"He's like a little kid with that goddamn stuff," Cecil said.

From the doghouse, a pair of hungry red eyes glinted out from the dark maw of the doorway. On seeing us, the animal moved cautiously out of its shelter a little way, its chain scraping wood. The thing bayed once, a sharp but plaintive howl. It was a mottled-gray bitch, some sort of hound. She'd recently finished weaning a litter, her dugs hanging withered and low between her back legs, her ribs pressing sharply against her coat. The thing stared at us, her head held low between bony shoulders, her broad gray muzzle nosing the air for our scent.

Cecil cut the engine. He grabbed his big police flashlight from the seat and got out of the car. He walked over toward the doghouse and squatted.

"It's okay, girl," I heard him murmur. The dog retreated into the house, but turned and poked its head out from the doorway. The animal let out a low belly growl, full of sinister intent. Cecil removed his ciga-rettes and lit up. I remained in the car for a moment. As I sat there, I tried to firm up the muscles in my stomach. It was something I did. A habit. A little trick of mine. Like right before I have to tell a woman her Pap smear isn't good news, I'll sit in my office for a minute trying to make my flabby middle tight and hard. It has something to do with the diaphragm. It makes my voice firm and resolute, filled with confidence where there is only doubt, so I can say what I have to say. Bad news is part of the job. Part of *both* my jobs. The thing with the stomach was something they didn't teach you in med school. You picked it up along the way.

Cecil stood and relieved himself, steam rising up around him. When he was finished, he walked around to the trunk of the cruiser and re-moved the Polaroid and the little black attaché case he brings to crime scenes. With my doctor's bag in hand, I got out and headed over to join him. A lumpy blackness coated things like creosote, giving the night a matte finish and seeming to soak up what little light there was.

"Sooner we get this over with, the sooner we can go on home," Cecil said. Which, I had to agree, was sound advice.

I followed his wide sloppy butt up to the trailer. The night was quiet and still and close as a low ceiling. When we reached the trailer door, however, a muted yet very distinct cry injected itself into the night like a hypodermic needle into flesh. A raw, outraged noise, defiant, yet at its core impotent and filled with immeasurable sadness. The hoarse whim-per of a sick animal beyond help.

"What the hell's that?" I exclaimed.

Cecil turned and stopped me with a hand in the middle of my chest.

"Doc, we got us kind of a situation here," Cecil said. "That woman's got her a baby and she won't give it up."

"Is that the little problem?"

"Yep. I guess when they got here she was nursing, so they let her fin-ish. Then she wouldn't let them touch the baby. Darryl thought she wasn't firing on all eight. I didn't want things to get out of hand, so I told them to baby-sit her till we got here."

"Where's social services?"

"Called 'em. Got a damn recording. Some lady said to call back at nine tomorrow."

"What are you going to do with the baby?"

"The hell I know. This's all I fuckin' need."

"How about the emergency shelter over in Crawford City?"

"No answer there neither. With the holidays and all, I reckon."

"Jesus," I said.

"I ain't give him a try," Cecil said.

I wondered if this was what had put him in a bad mood earlier.

As soon as Cecil opened the trailer door, the smell inside seemed to leap out at you, like a wild thing cooped up in its own filth for too long and just wanting to get loose. The lingering stink of cordite hung in the air, as well as the human stench of sweat and urine, of anger and fear, and of the release of bowels. And under it all, the raw, fetid odor of co-agulated blood: a trapped, secretive smell like the insides of a turkey. The smell of unnatural death, of violence, almost as if blood gives off a different scent if it's spilled by another's hand, tainted by evil motives. What Cain must have smelled. Darryl slouched against a wall, while Butch Slocum sat on a chair in the kitchen and puffed on a cigarette.

"What took you so long, Chief?" Darryl said jovially, relieved to see us.

Ignoring him, Cecil said to Butch, "Put that damn thing out in here," the way a father would scold a son he'd caught smoking in the basement. "This's a crime scene." The young deputy took on a wounded look as he crushed the cigarette on the floor. Butch, who'd only recently joined the sheriff's department, was a pudgy, baby-faced kid just two years out of high school. I think Cecil saw in Butch something of himself thirty years before, and he seemed unconsciously annoyed that the young man was making the same mistake he had. He never missed an opportunity to chastise him publicly.

"I want you to drive back down to the highway and wait there for Slim Jim."

"You don't need me here?"

"What did I just say? When he gets here, you show 'em the way up. And remember, no smoking in county vehicles."

Butch, disappointed that he wasn't going to get to stay at the scene, sullenly slunk out of the trailer, got in his cruiser, and headed back down the mountain.

"What do you say, Doc?" Darryl offered. Darryl Childress, the other deputy, was in his mid-thirties, tall and gangly, pasty-looking from too many night shifts. Like I said, he used to work in the funeral home business but he found that depressing. So he took the test to be a deputy. Go figure.

"How are you, Darryl?" I said.

"No sense complaining, right?"

"What's going on?" Cecil asked him.

"She's finished nursing but that young'un keeps crying," the deputy explained. "Betcha he's got the colic. My sister's used to get that and she give 'em paregoric. Ain't that s'posed to work, Doc? Paregoric."

On a ratty sofa in the dollhouse-small den, a woman, who appeared hardly more than a girl really, sat rocking a howling infant. The mother was dark-skinned, appeared to be a full-blood Cherokee. She had long hair that was pulled back into a single tight braid like a black snake and eyes as hard and impassive as roasted chestnuts. She was wearing jeans and a dark blue T-shirt that advertised a rock radio station from Johnson City, up in Tennessee. Her thin exposed arms were covered by track marks, the scars old by the looks of them. Her lower lip was split and puffy from a recent blow, and above her right eye the flesh was contused, the skin broken, dark blood angrily scabbing over a nasty-looking gash. Already I was making inferences, connecting the dots, drawing conclusions, which is what you're paid to do. As a doctor you try to find out what's wrong and fix it. Blame isn't a factor. As an ME, you try to find out not only what went wrong but whose fault it was that it did.

The Indian girl didn't look at any of the people now standing in her house. It was as if we didn't exist for her. She stared off to her right, seemingly at a half-empty bottle of Jack Daniels on the small kitchen table. Near it was a single plate of food, untouched, fried ham and potatoes and gray biscuit gravy hardened into cement. The remains of a shattered beer bottle were strewn across the linoleum, with urine-colored liquid splattered over a wall. On the floor a wooden chair lay in a broken heap. An end table was overturned. More glass shards here and there littered the floor, so you had to watch your step. In the corner of the kitchen sat a kerosene space heater glowing red. Despite the heater, the place was chilly, damp feeling.

Methodically the girl rocked the baby back and forth, almost as if she were in a trance. Nonetheless, the child continued to cry, though it obviously didn't have its heart in it. More just crankiness now, crying because the poor thing couldn't stop itself, like with hiccups. The baby was dressed in a blue sleeper with spit-up milk staining the front. The child was dark-skinned, like the mother. About three months old and, judging by the hands, I'd say a girl, despite Darryl's *he* reference. She was solid, with pudgy, dimpled cheeks and a perfect circle for a face. Her eyes were wide and clear, and from time to time she took a break from her howling to peer curiously at the strangers encircling her.

Cecil said to Darryl, "She still wouldn't give up the young'un?"

"No sir."

"You Miranda her?"

"'Course," the deputy replied, offended Cecil would think he'd forget something so elementary. "And I secured the scene."

"I saw your tape job."

"That weren't me, Chief. Butch done that. I told 'im to go easy with that tape but he don't listen. Murder weapon's over yonder. Winchester pump, twelve gauge. Three shells fired. I already bagged 'em. And don't worry, I didn't *touch* nothing."

"She say anything?"

"Ain't opened her mouth, 'cept to snarl at me when I got near her baby. I think she's mental. What do they call it, Doc? Psychotic."

"Where's . . . ?" Cecil began.

Darryl motioned with a flick of his thumb toward the back of the trailer. "Victim's down thataway. Hope you ain't just had dinner, Chief."

"What?" Cecil said.

"It's the gawd-awfulest mess I ever seen."

"You keep your eye on her and let me worry about the mess. Doc, whyn't you see if you can get the baby to simmer down," Cecil said, throwing a look my way.

From the attaché case, Cecil took out a pair of surgical gloves and put them on. Then, armed with the camera, he passed through the tiny kitchen and down the narrow hallway to take pictures of the victim.

"Chief's sure got a bug up his hole tonight, don't he?" Darryl said.

I winked at him, then went over and knelt in front of the mother. Though youngish in appearance, she had old-looking eyes, could have been anywhere from fifteen to forty. They—Indians, that is—had this funny way of evading our—the white man's—means of assigning time, especially the women. It's as if they existed outside our time, beyond it, disdainful of it; they got old or stayed young according to some internal clock which had nothing to do with our months or years. Though they had their own clinic over in Cherokee, I'd sometimes see them in my office in Slade: wrinkled and dried-up women who looked fifty but were still in their twenties; others whose sweet, innocent faces looked ten but who were already menstruating or gravida two. Except for the eyes. The eyes even of Indian girls always somehow managed to look old, wise, and filled with knowledge well beyond their years, as if having seen way too much way too soon had spoiled them somehow. Up close, this one, if I had to say, looked about twenty-three, though it wouldn't have surprised me to learn she was thirty, thirty-five.

"I'd watch it if I was you, Doc," Darryl advised. "Like I said, she's loco."

"I'm Dr. Jordan," I said to the mother. "How old's your baby?"

She remained silent, rocking back and forth, back and forth, absently looking over my left ear, down the hall that Cecil took. She had dark spatters of blood on the knees of her jeans. Her black, burnished eyes didn't move, didn't even blink; they were the flat, fixed, remorseless eyes of a doll. Her skin was pockmarked from a bad case of chickenpox when she was young. It was a shame, because she was a striking-looking girl otherwise. You could tell this in spite of the swollen lip and laceration of her eye. Her braided hair made me think of Annabel's when she was young and kept it long. Like this woman's, Annabel's was jet-black and coarse, shiny as a piece of coal. Bunched in your hand it felt substantial as a rope.

I'd never seen mother or daughter before. They'd probably gone to the clinic on the reservation, that is, if they'd ever even been to a doctor. Despite it being the nineties, way back in some of these hollers there were still people who managed to be born, live, and die without ever seeing the inside of a hospital or clinic, without ever requiring the services of a doctor. Many of these little coves still had their own midwives as well as their own herbalists and old-timers versed in mountain cure-alls. Goldenseal was supposed to work on ulcers. A slippery elm poultice healed a cut. A drop of asafetida or kerosene in milk was good for the colic. Some really out-of-the-way places even had their own churches, which dispensed their backwoods brand of health care. Tiny cinder block structures with names like "Most Holy Church of Signs with Jesus Following." Way out in the boonies, where they still handled copperheads, fell down when filled with the Holy Spirit and spoke in tongues, where they fought against ovarian cancer or sterility or AIDS with prayer and the laying on of hands. Faith healers could supposedly stop bleeding or draw out a burn, cure the "yaller thrash" just by reciting a certain line from the Bible. If all else failed, they had their own cemeteries, too, named after the clan who'd first settled in the holler.

I know this because, as I've already said, when I started to practice out here, I made house calls to places just like this. One day a week, I'd leave the sterile safety of my office in Slade and drive for miles up some dirt road that wound its way into the hills, penetrating some holler carved so deep into the mountains that its residents saw the sun for only a few hours a day. I'd be there to check on a fifteen-year-old eight months along who'd never had any prenatal checkups, who smoked Camels and drank Co'Cola all day. I was appalled at the living conditions I found. Here I was, somebody who'd grown up in a picture-postcard New England village an hour's drive from Harvard Square. I thought it was just a cliché. You know, President Johnson sitting on some coal miner's porch among a half-dozen dirty kids as a photo-op for his War on Poverty. Bad teeth and bad genes. Ignorance and incest. Just a stereotype, right? My *own* ignorance, I figured. But for every stereotype, it's not the unexpected that comes as the real shocker; it's the grain of truth you find in the heart of every cliché. I'd see entire families crammed into a three-room trailer or rough-hewn log cabin on cinder blocks. Once even a tent in the middle of winter. There would be hogs and chickens and guinea fowl rooting around in the front yard. No indoor plumbing. Open cesspools. Drinking water infected with *Giardia* and typhus. I saw women nearly die of puerperal sepsis, "childbirth fever"; others who were septic from D&Cs performed by some old lady using a piece of bailing wire. I saw kids with worms and rickets and scurvy, some with diabetes left untreated so it caused blindness or brain damage. I saw babies born with rare diseases or exotic syndromes I had to search my textbooks for, because of the inbreeding. Most of the Coghills had six toes. Epilepsy was rampant in the McClatchey clan over in Roane Hollow. Third world, I swear.

Things had certainly changed in the nearly thirty years I'd been in practice here. Health care was decidedly better, prenatal conditions vastly improved. But despite the progress, it was still pretty backward by American standards, especially way back in the hills. Teen births and low fetal weight. Bad nutrition. Incest was still a problem. Fetal alcohol syndrome. And now the influx of drugs. Like the inner cities or Indian reservations, the Appalachian mountains continued to be a place most Americans didn't know about, didn't want to know about either. And as bad as it was for poor whites, it was usually worse for the few blacks we had. And, of course, for the Indians.

"Mrs. Pugh, how old is your child?" I asked again.

"Littlefoot," the girl replied, the first words she'd spoken.

"What?"

"It's Littlefoot, not Pugh. We weren't married. She'll be three—no, four months come next week."

"*She,*" Darryl said. "No wonder she was pissed at me."

"Is she hungry?" I asked.

"I don't know," she replied, still not making eye contact with me. Her voice had an uneasy, affectless quality to it. "She's usually a good eater."

As I made to touch the baby, the girl drew back, curled around the baby to protect it.

"Easy," I said, holding up my hands. "I'm not going to do anything, Miss."

"You need a hand, Doc?" Darryl asked. "Want me to hold her or anything?"

"No, that's okay." Then to the girl I explained, "I just want to help."

"It's my baby. You understand?" With this, her eyes met mine for the first time. They suddenly came to life, turned from flat and opaque to sharp and fierce and filled with a kind of desperate fury. I sensed she'd claw my face off before she'd let me take her baby away.

"I'm a doctor," I said, holding up my bag as proof. "I just want to take a look. Make sure she's all right."

"She's mine," the girl repeated. "Don't think you can pull something on me. I know what's what."

"I'm not going to pull anything, Miss Littlefoot. I promise. I just want to see if your baby's okay. Does she have a fever?"

She shook her head. "She don't feel hot to me."

"Can I see? I just want to help. Please."

The mother interrogated me with her eyes to make sure I meant no threat, that I wasn't trying to trick her. Slowly, I reached out and touched the baby's cheek with the back of my knuckles. Maybe a little hot but nothing serious. You always wondered when drugs were involved. Yet other than being exhausted, the baby appeared healthy enough. In fact, well cared for. She already had the mother's thick black hair and those same dark, impenetrable eyes, eyes like stones that had been in a fire.

"She might still be hungry," the girl said. "She nursed for a while, but I don't reckon as she got much with all the commotion."

Commotion? I thought. Was that all this was to her, a little commotion?

"You want to try again?"

"Is it all right?" she asked, looking over at Darryl.

"Why don't you give it a try?" I said.

She lifted up her T-shirt—she wasn't wearing a bra—and placed a small but swollen breast against the baby's mouth. Though thin, she had a slightly distended belly. A little young for cirrhosis, but I'd seen twenty-five-year-old Indian women with bellies already bloated from booze. The baby rooted around for the nipple, latched onto it, and began sucking hungrily. Coughing, Darryl said, "You look like you got things under control here, Doc. I'll see if the chief needs any help."

The baby worked at the nipple, but after a couple of minutes she seemed to lose interest and took to whining again.

"I'm not sure she's getting none," the girl said. "My breasts are hard, but I don't know if I got any milk left."

"Have you any formula?"

"No."

"Any regular milk?"

"Some. I think it's gone bad though."

I got up and walked over to the small refrigerator. I took out a plastic gallon of milk and smelled it. The sour stench nearly knocked me over.

"*Whewph*!"

I went back over and squatted in front of the girl, my knees already starting to throb.

"Is she teething?"

"She might be."

"Is it all right if I take a look?"

"I guess so."

She propped the baby on her knees, facing toward me. I probably could've snatched the child from her but decided not to chance it. I poked a finger around in the baby's mouth. In the front I felt two small nubs, about to break through. I opened my bag and removed a bottle of Ambesol, put a drop on my little finger, and rubbed some along her gums. She puckered her face at the taste, and like a fish with a hook in its mouth, she tried to spit my finger out. While I was at it I figured I'd take a quick listen to her chest. After all, this might be the first checkup she'd had. I got out my stethoscope, rubbed it between my hands for a moment to warm it.

"Mind?" I asked. The Indian girl lifted her shoulders cautiously and let them drop. I listened to the baby's heartbeat, rapid but strong, then percussed her lungs. They sounded pretty clear. Then I took out the oto-scope, because at this point I was figuring ear infection. But her ears looked fine, too.

"Has she ever been to a doctor?"

"Not since she was born."

"How about her shots?"

"I been meaning to bring her," she said, apologetically. "She's been right healthy, though."

"How long have you been clean?"

She glanced down at her arms.

"'Bout a year, I reckon. Since I learned I was pregnant."

"Nothing since?"

"No. Maybe a joint or two."

"Have you or the baby been checked for HIV?"

She shook her head. "But I ain't never used anybody else's needle. I was always good about that."

"I ought to have a look at that eye."

She didn't say no, so I put on rubber gloves. From my bag I took out a sterile pad and some Betadine, and started in cleaning up the wound. She winced but didn't make a sound as I worked. I knew it had to hurt. Under normal circumstances, it probably could've used a couple of stitches. But I settled on a Steristrip bandage for now.

"He do this before?"

"Only when he got liquored up," she replied; she thought about it for a moment, then added, "which was mostly."

After a while, Cecil and Darryl came back into the living room. Cecil's heavy face was coated with a sheen of sweat, like a glazed Christmas ham, and his complexion was pallid. Looked like hell. He had to steady himself with one hand against the wall. "Doc, whyn't you go back there and have you a look-see."

"You all right, Cecil?" I asked.

"Yeah."

"You sure?"

"I *said* I'm all right. Just gonna grab me some air. Keep an eye on her, Darryl."

I stood up, the pain in my knees ratcheting up a couple of notches, and hobbled stiffly down the narrow hallway to the bedroom. The metallic stench of blood grew as I approached, becoming overpowering, rank and foul as a meat-packing plant. Just inside the door, this fellow was lying on his back. A big guy, a broad trunk, must go well over two hundred pounds, I figured. One leg was straight out in front of him, the other bent at an odd angle that made me wince. Darryl was right; it was a goddamn mess. Carnage. Slaughter. No other words would do the scene justice. Blood and pieces of whitish brains everywhere. The guy's shirt and pants, the surrounding floor, even the bedspread behind him were slathered with blood, black and slick as ink. I saw that he had long reddish hair and oddly delicate features, a thin nose and sharp chin, a mouth fixed into a grayish-blue sneer. The top right hemisphere of his skull had been blown away, from the hairline back and down to his ear. His skin was the nothing-color of trout that's been kept too long in a freezer. The right eye had taken a couple of pellets, and the resulting hemorrhage had ballooned it a ghastly red; the other was fixed and dilated, seemed to be gazing with annoyance at something on the ceiling. This Pugh fellow looked like he had an itch he couldn't get to, a craving he couldn't satisfy. Don't talk to me about the dead looking at peace or serene, or any of those pleasant lies you read about dead people. Hell, they never do. They usually have a surprised or greedy, angry or sullen or brooding look, or quite often simply the discouraged expression of somebody who finished second in a very long and difficult race, just glad it is over.

I wondered what happened this time. Another domestic dispute that spiraled beyond their control? Like Cecil said, maybe he'd come home drunk again. Maybe he didn't like what she made for dinner or the baby's squawking. Maybe he'd forgotten to bring home the milk. There were words, curses, the usual threats. A fist shot out. I saw plenty of abused women in my practice: the bruises and scars they didn't want to talk about; the old broken bones they'd gotten from being so "clumsy"; the lacerated vaginas from a husband or boyfriend who "got hisself all sexed up and done it a mite rough, Doc. No need to git the police involved." But something different happened tonight. Perhaps she'd taken the last punch she was going to and said this was it. This was where it stopped. Something in her snapped, and things ended the way they did.

I went through the motions of making my investigation, knowing it wouldn't take a rocket scientist or even a medical degree. The head wound was from the front, the powder burns on the cheek telling me from up close, no more than a foot or two away, probably a downward shot because of the pattern of blood spatters and the bone and brain fragments fanning out on the surrounding floor. But there wasn't as much blood as there ought to have been from a head wound, which suggested to me it wasn't the first shot. Next, I lifted the bloody shirt, loosened the belt, unzipped the zipper. The clothes were saturated, heavy and greasy and cold with blood. Even through the latex it felt unctuous, slippery as the sides of an eel. Below the guy's belly button there was another entry wound, a rough perforation about the size of a ripe apple. Part of the large bowel was hanging out. This shot was from a little farther away, say, four or five feet. Generally speaking, shotgun pellets fan out about an inch for every three feet they travel. These are facts, things you can count on.

After that, I rolled him on his side. No exit wounds, of course, not with a shotgun. The telltale lividity of the torso was distinct and permanent when touched, his back a deep cabernet color. Rigor was also pronounced, the arms stiff and the muscles hard. Our boy had been dead a while. I began to connect the dots, to create a picture of what had happened. They're fighting. He punches her and things escalate. Somehow she gets her hands on the gun, and I'm thinking, because of the close range of the shots, maybe he comes at her. She tells him to stay back, but he doesn't listen, and she lets him have it, the first shot to the belly. On purpose, out of fear, just an accident—who knows? Months from now, in a cool, sterile courtroom that doesn't smell of blood and anger and booze, they'll argue her motivations; they'll parse out her actions, try to crawl inside her heart and look around. But right then it's all heat and confusion, I'm sure. The first blast slams into him, the scalding double-aught pellets burning a white-hot message of pain into his gut, and he crumbles.

She's still not in over her head. A good defense lawyer can do a song and dance around that. She was abused. She was afraid. She was just protecting herself and her baby. If she'd stopped there, she might not even serve a day in prison. Meanwhile, our boy is lying there bleeding like a stuck pig from a wound he'd probably die from eventually. But he isn't dead. Not yet, anyway. He's in a world of hurt. More pain than he's ever known in his life. If there's a hell, being gut-shot must be in the vicinity of it. He's begging for his life. Talking about how much he loves her, how he'll never lay a hand on her again. She's debating whether to believe him, whether it's too late to turn back. Maybe she goes over and pours herself a drink or picks up the screaming infant. Minutes pass. Her life stretches out in front of her while she waits. That's why there's so much blood from the belly wound; he's had time to bleed out, to get white and scared and maybe go into shock. He's praying or pleading with her. But she's heard it before and she's tired of his talk. What if he does recover? Imagine what he'll do to her then. She's had it up to here with waiting for him to change. She figures she's gone this far, she might as well go all the way. What's she got to lose? She pumps another shell into the chamber, raises the gun, sights down on him, says, "So long, you bastard," and sends him packing. It's this shot, where she stands over him and calmly, deliberately blows away half his head—that's the one she's going to pay for. Manslaughter, if she's lucky. Worse if Bumgartner, the DA, has a bug up his ass.

Roy Lee Pugh was cold to the touch already, but I still had to take his temperature. Ninety-two rectal. All things being equal, the body loses about one degree an hour. Another fact. The facts are the frame on which you hang your theory, the outline you color in with instinct and feel and gut reaction. Which meant he'd been dead about five or six hours. Christ, I thought. What did she do all that time? Did she consider taking the baby, getting in the truck, and making a run for it? Or maybe hiding the body, burying it in the woods someplace? In these mountains, somebody wouldn't be missed for a long time. Or did she just sit here with that baby squawking its head off and him lying just down the hall?

I looked at my watch, then took out my notepad and jotted down a couple of things: time, position of the body, blood splatters, types of wounds. The usual things they would want for court. Under cause, the death certificate would say something fancy like *fatal derangement* or *penetrating cerebral wound* or *injury event: multiple gunshot wounds,* but it would all amount to the same thing: He was dead and somebody had very much wanted him to be. Later, I'd have to type up a report, but my job here was done. Everything was falling into place. It'd be a piece of cake even for someone as thoroughly incompetent as our district attorney, Troy Bumgartner. Cecil would ship the body over to Chapel Hill for an autopsy. Oh, in a pinch Rob Neinhuis or I might help Chilly Childress do one over at his funeral home; say, if we just wanted to rule out foul play or if it was something Bumgartner wanted to handle locally and didn't want to get the state boys involved. But mostly we knew our limitations. This wasn't some big-city crime unit. We'd none of those hi-tech forensics you see on television. Let's face it, I was just some hick obstetrician masquerading as an ME, somebody who signed the death certificate saying this guy was no longer among the living.

There was one thing, though, that didn't sit right.

"Hey, Darryl," I called. "C'mere a minute."

"Yeah, Doc?" he said, sticking his thin homely face into the doorway. He resembled his uncle Chilly, the same toothy grin and gaunt undertaker look to him.

"You said there were three shots?"

"Found three spent shells."

"Where?"

"Right here on the floor."

"The thing is I can only come up with two hits. One to the belly and the other to the head. Where do you think the other shot went?"

He smiled so his teeth broke through his mouth like a bone jutting through a compound fracture. "Looky up there, Doc," he said, pointing above my head.

There I saw a fresh hole ripped in one of the ceiling tiles. The hole continued through the thin metal skin of the trailer roof and out into the dark night. I glanced from it to Darryl and then to the dead man, who seemed actually to be staring at the hole.

"How do you figure?"

"A bad shot," he offered.

"This close?"

"She was scared. Could've been a warnin'."

Which was how I was leaning. *Stay away*, she might have said to him and shot once to show she meant it. Yet that close to him, close enough so he could lunge at her, I wondered if she'd have wasted a warning shot. Would she have had the presence of mind to warn him? Or the time to chamber another shell? And given how she'd later coolly blow away half his head, would she have been in a warning frame of mind? Then again, maybe there had been a struggle and the gun had gone off. That was possible. But she was a small, thin woman. How had she managed to wrest the gun from someone as large and beefy as Roy Lee Pugh? Adrenaline can explain a lot of things, and maybe it could plug the gap here. You see, no murder investigation is ever perfect. There is always something. Even in the best of cases, cases where I could sleep nights after helping to put somebody away over in Raleigh for life, there were always rough edges, pieces you had to make fit, whittle down. Pieces you sometimes needed to ignore altogether. Life was messy, so why should we think death would be any different? Just an errant shot. Don't make an issue where there is none, I said to myself. It was late and I was beat, and if I was going to grab an hour or two of sleep, I didn't need to get picky.

With that I closed my bag and left the mess for the EMTs.

"So what do you think?" Cecil whispered to me in the kitchen.

"Two shots. The first was the one in the belly. The second was the head shot. It came later."

"That's what I was figuring. How much later?"

"Hard to say? Five, ten minutes. Maybe more. He bled a lot from the belly wound."

"Jesus. I guess she wanted him dead."

Cecil went over to where the girl sat holding her baby. He looked down at her and said, "You'll have to come with us now, Miss. But don't you worry none. We'll take good care of your daughter."

The mother didn't make any sign that she'd heard him. She stared straight ahead, her gaze a curious mask of calm surface detachment beneath which lingered that same fierce intensity. Her dark, feral eyes had seemed to relax a bit, grow resigned. They made me think of a trapped wild thing that had decided to stop fighting and, at least for the moment, give itself over to its confinement. The way a rattlesnake might go limp in a bag—until you reach your hand in.

"You listen here now," Cecil said. "You got to hand over that young'un."

More silence.

"You don't want your baby in a jail cell, Miss? That ain't no place for a baby."

Still nothing.

"They's three of us and just the one a her," Darryl said. "What in Sam Hill we farting around for?"

"Just shut up," Cecil told him. "Look, Miss, I been more'n patient with you. But I'm starting to lose my patience. You need to come with us and you need to come *now*," he said, taking a step toward her.

I don't even know where she got it from—under one of the couch cushions, I guess. But there it was suddenly, like some sleight-of-hand trick: a wooden-handled, serrated steak knife pressed against her own throat. She kept one arm wrapped around the child.

"*Whoa,*" Cecil said, freezing in his tracks. "Easy now, Miss."

"Don't you come near me," she cried. "I'm warning you, I'll do it."

"Told you she's crazy," Darryl said.

"You don't want to do nothing you'll regret," Cecil advised.

"I only regret I ain't done it already."

"Just relax and put the knife down, Miss."

"Stay back! Stay the hell back!"

"We're staying back," the sheriff explained, raising his hands as if in surrender. "Think of your baby."

"I *am* thinking of her. She'd be better off without me."

"No, she wouldn't," I offered. "She'd be all alone in the world."

"She's gonna be that anyway. I should a done us both when I had the chance."

"Don't talk like that," I said. "She's got her whole life ahead of her."

"Some life," she said. "What's going to happen to her now?"

During this, the baby had stopped crying and stared around the room, as if sensing some fundamental change in things. Her eyes seemed to light on the gun on Cecil's hip.

"We'll find her a good place," the sheriff said. "Don't you worry none, Miss."

I could see her debating with herself, could tell that she was serious enough to actually go through with it but that she hadn't yet made up her mind completely. The knife was pressed hard against her carotid artery. I was thinking how if she cut, cut deep enough, she could bleed out on us real quick. I'd nearly lost women on the operating table from hemorrhage due to something like *placenta accreta,* and that was with a full staff and plenty of blood handy.

"Mind if I sit?" I asked. "My knees aren't so good anymore. I promise I won't try anything. You have my word." She remained silent, so I took that as a yes, and I cautiously sat on the other end of the couch.

"You want a cigarette?" I asked.

She hesitated, then said, "Yeah, okay."

I looked at Cecil and he fumbled for his pack. He took one out, lit it, and cautiously held it out to her. With both hands occupied, she warily accepted the cigarette with her mouth. She inhaled deeply.

"Do you have any kinfolk you could leave the baby with?"

She shook her head.

"Nobody over in Cherokee?"

"My old man," she replied, out of the corner of her mouth. "But him and me, well, we don't exactly see eye to eye." She glanced down at her track-ridden arms. "Besides, he's kinda poorly."

"What about some of those Pughs?" Cecil interjected.

"Them!" she said. "No way."

"How's about I give 'em a call and see?"

"Listen, Mister, it'll be a cold day in hell before I give her over to them. And anyhow, like I said me and *that one*," she explained with a toss of her head toward the bedroom, "we wasn't married."

"The baby's still their blood," Cecil said. "Pughs take care of their own."

"Not here they don't."

"Can't hurt to try," Cecil said.

"Ain't no *fuckin'* way I'm gonna leave my baby with their kind. You understand?" she yelled, pressing the blade against her throat so it lightly creased the skin, made a thin line of blood appear almost magically.

"Easy, Miss," Cecil said. "All right, we won't call the Pughs. Just don't do anything crazy."

"How about any friends?" I asked. "Just for tonight?"

The girl looked down at her baby and shook her head. She suddenly seemed so lost and desperate, so all alone. I expected her to break down and start balling on me as most girls would in her shoes. Like the ones I saw in my practice, the ones who were pregnant and whose father would kill them if he found out. Like Sue Ellen McCreadie, a tough little cookie who broke down and sobbed in my office when she had to tell her parents. But this one didn't cry. She was too angry still to give in to tears, or still too much in shock. Or perhaps like her breasts, everything was bound up tighter than a clenched fist inside her.

She turned toward the bedroom and cursed, "Damn him."

"Listen," I said to her, "if you can't think of anybody to leave her with, they'll stick your baby in some foster home. Till the courts can straighten it out. That's what they'll do. If we don't come up with some other plan, that's what going to happen. Trust me."

"Trust you?" she said, looking over at me. "Why should I trust you?"

"Who else do you have?" I asked.

She seemed to ponder that for a moment. "How about you then?"

"How about me what?"

"Would you take her?"

"Why, of course," I said. "I'll see that she's placed in good hands."

"No. I mean, would *you* take her? Look after her."

"Me!" I exclaimed with a nervous laugh. I saw she was dead serious, though. Why this struck me as odd, after what she'd already done, I couldn't say. But for some reason it did. "I . . . I couldn't possibly take her."

"Please, Dr. Jordan," she said, somehow remembering my name.

"But Miss Littlefoot . . . "

"Rosa," she said. "It's Rosa."

"All right, Rosa. I'd like to help. Really, I would. It's just that there's no way I could take your baby. There must be somebody else?" I asked.

"There's nobody. Please, Doctor. Couldn't you take her? Just for a little while."

"I'd like to. Really, I would. It's just . . . "

"I got nobody else. Please. I'm begging you."

Cecil cleared his throat. "Doc," he said, "can I have a word?" I got up and walked over to him. He led me down the hall, out of earshot.

"Look," he whispered, "tell her you'll take the kid."

"I can't do that."

"Doc, don't get on your high horse with me. I'm tired and I feel like warmed-over shit, and I just want to go home and take a nice hot bath. Tell her whatever she wants to hear. But just get that young'un from her before somebody gets hurt. Y'hear, me? We can sort it out later."

I hesitated for a moment, then realized the soundness of what he was saying. We could sort it out later.

I returned and sat down on the couch next to her. "All right. I'll take your baby."

"You promise?" she asked.

"I promise."

"You're not tricking me, are you?"

"No, I'm not tricking you."

"Don't you worry, Miss. Doc here's as good as his word," Cecil tossed in. I felt like slugging him.

"Swear it then," she said to me.

"What?" I exclaimed.

"*Swear* it. Swear you'll take care of my baby and you won't let nothin' happen to her."

"All right, I swear it."

Perhaps I said it too quickly, without enough conviction in my voice. She stared at me, her sharp, black eyes like diamond-tipped drill bits burrowing to the core of my mendacious heart.

"You a churchgoing man, Dr. Jordan?"

"I'm not," I replied.

"What do you hold sacred then?"

"Sacred?"

"You know, what's the one thing you would die for?"

"I don't know. There's not a whole lot I'd die for."

"You got any children?"

"I had a son. He died."

"Did you love him?"

"Why, of course," I said. "Yes."

"Then swear on his grave."

"What?"

"Do it. Swear on your son's grave you'll take good care of my little girl."

This is crazy, I thought. This is going too far. I glanced over at Cecil, but he only raised his eyebrows while screwing up his mouth. *Just do it*, his look said. The night was getting stranger by the second.

"All right, I swear."

"On your son's grave. Say it."

"On my son's grave."

"So help you God."

It sounded like I was reciting a prayer. It made me think of when I was an altar boy back at St. Carmel's and I would repeat the lines of the Kyrie after Father Morelli. *Lord, have mercy. Lord, have mercy. Christ, have mercy. Christ, have mercy.*

"So help me God," I said.

She stared at me for another second or two, still debating whether to believe me or not. At last she said, "I'm trusting you?" It was part statement, part question, all of it a desperate plea. Only then did she drop the knife on the floor and give her daughter over to me. She shoved the child into my chest, gently but firmly, the way you would a handoff in a close football game and you were on the opponent's three-yard line. She stood up and offered her slender brown wrists so Cecil, stunned for a moment by her sudden change of heart, could put the cuffs on her. He gave Darryl instructions to put her in the cruiser and bring her along to the jail in Slade.

"Book her," Cecil told his deputy, sounding like Jack Lord used to in Hawaii Five-O. "Have Henry put her in cell two. It's closer to the radiator. She'll be warmer there. And 'cept for a lawyer, if she wants one, she's not to see anybody. You hear me? Tell Henry I'll be along directly. After I drop Doc off, I'm going to head out to the Pughs' place and break the news to them. When Travis and G.T. report for duty, tell Henry to have them get on down here and have a look around. And have them bring Fritz along, too." Fritz was a drug-sniffing German shepherd that the sheriff's department had recently received through a state antidrug grant. "Can you remember all that?"

"'Course."

When Darryl hesitated, Cecil scolded, "Don't stand there with your thumb up your ass. Gw'on, *git!*"

Before she was led out the door, the girl turned to me one last time. "You'll take good care of my baby, won't you, Dr. Jordan?"

I nodded halfheartedly and glanced over at Cecil. When the two were out the door, he said, "Nice work, Doc. Christ, you could talk a coon out of a tree."

"I didn't like doing that to her."

"What you talking about? You done her a favor."

"Some favor."

"Besides, it was her own fault. The hell she want to go and do something like that for when she's got a kid to worry about? Two days before Christmas, too. Damn."

I glanced down at the child in my arms. She stared back at me with her mother's glistening black eyes. Poker eyes, I thought. Eyes that give nothing away, that hold everything in.

"I doubt she was thinking that far ahead."

# 4

*Shortly after Darryl* left with the girl, Slim Jim Dyson and Lakesha Hicks pulled up in the ambulance to pick up the body. I'd run into both many times at the hospital. Slim Jim, as his nickname implied, was a skinny guy, sunken-chested, with a bad smoker's hack. Right off the bat, he tried to bum a cigarette from Cecil. "Buy your own," Cecil told him. Lakesha was a young black woman, big-boned and hefty, but she moved with catlike agility as she negotiated the stretcher through the trailer's narrow door. I'd delivered Lakesha, as well as her twin younger brothers, Tyrell and Buster, back in the days when it was hospital policy not to allow blacks to use the same labor and delivery room as whites. The hospital had a small room down the hall they designated as the "Colored Labor and Delivery." Cherise Hicks, Lakesha's mother, worked in the kitchen at the hospital, and she birthed all three of her babies in that room.

"Colder'n a witch's tit, ain't it, Doc?" said Slim Jim, blowing into his hands.

"Over yonder," Cecil said to Slim Jim, indicating with a nod of his head that the body was down the hallway. I was sitting on the couch holding the baby. Lakesha squatted in front of me to have a look at the child, who was now all but asleep. She still didn't quite let herself go completely. Her body remained tense, wary. The poor little thing kept fighting sleep, her eyelids heavy but jerking wide open every time she started to nod off. She no longer trusted people.

"She all right, Dr. Jordan?" Lakesha asked.

"I think so. Just flat-out exhausted."

"She sho is cute, ain't she?"

"Yeah. How are you doing, Lakesha?"

"Just fy-on. Still takin' courses for my nursing degree," she replied.

"Good for you. And the twins?"

"Tyrell doing good. Got himself a job at the mill. It's Buster who's the problem." Then, looking over her shoulder to make sure Cecil wasn't in earshot, she whispered, "He be doing all that crack nonsense. Always was a dumb-shit nigger." She wagged her head sadly. "Give my poor momma nothing but heartache and grief since the day you brung him into this world."

The entire ER staff knew Buster Hicks. As did Cecil and his deputies. He used to show up in the emergency room when I was there with a woman in labor. He'd be drunk or high, or looking for drugs.

"Sorry to hear that," I said to Lakesha. "Say hello to your mother."

"Will do."

Slim Jim came back into the kitchen then and announced, "That's a holiday scene if they ever was. Who's the lucky fellow?"

"Roy Lee Pugh," Cecil replied.

"One of *the* Pughs?"

Cecil nodded. "Glenn W.'s kid." He pronounced the W as *dubya*.

"Sweet Jesus," Slim Jim said, rolling his yellowed lunger's eyes. "Gonna be trouble."

"They ain't gonna be no trouble," Cecil snapped at him.

"Shee-it. I surely wouldn't want to get on the wrong side of that bunch. No sir, I would not. Why, they're meaner'n a stepped-on rattler. What was it, six, seven years back, Cecil? They sent up one of them Pugh boys for murder. Ike, I think."

"It was Glenn Junior."

"You sure? I thought I heard tell it was Ike Pugh."

"Who the hell's the sheriff around here? It was Glenn Junior," said Cecil, annoyed. "The oldest boy."

"It don't make a rat's ass of a difference, though I still think it was Ike. Anyways, he was over to Knoxville making a dope deal or something. And this city fellow there thought he was gonna pull a fast one on a dumb hillbilly. Don't recall all the details. Cecil here could tell you, if he didn't have a hair up his crack."

"Get you a move on," Cecil told him. "I wanna be out of here sometime this year."

Ignoring him, Slim Jim continued his story. "Well, this Ike or Glenn or whoever the hell it was got riled up and took a ballpeen hammer to this fellow's head. He's up to Brushy Mountain now punching out license plates till the year two thousand and eighty or somewhere's about. Yessir, there'll be hell to pay when them Pughs find out somebody kilt their boy."

"Ain't gonna be no trouble," Cecil repeated. "Now stop your jawing and get a move on."

After Lakesha and Slim Jim had bagged the body, carted it out to the ambulance, and headed for Chapel Hill, I went down the hall and into the bedroom. Careful where I was stepping—the floor was a mess—I looked around for something to put the baby in against the cold night. Near the bassinet was a bureau. The two top drawers proved to be empty, not a stitch of clothes, but in the bottom one I came across a baby blanket and some other things. I spread the blanket on the bed, laid the baby on top of it, and wrapped it snugly about her. While her eyes remained wide open, she was lethargic and didn't have the energy to so much as whimper. She just stared up at me, in a place beyond resignation. On a shelf I noticed a picture of the Indian girl and what must have been the dead fellow. They were at a lake somewhere. He was wearing cutoff jeans and she had on a yellow two-piece, and they had their arms around each other. They were smiling, happy. She was pretty, and he wasn't a bad-looking guy either. In fact, they made a nice-looking couple. I wondered how love could turn out like this, but of course if I knew the answer to that one, they wouldn't need MEs.

"Doc, whyn't you take that young'un and wait in the cruiser?" Cecil said. "I got to take care of a few more things. Here's the keys. Warm the car up." While Cecil finished up his examination of the crime scene, I headed out and waited in the cruiser. The baby started to fuss again, so I put the tip of my little finger in her mouth. She latched onto it and began to suck, though without much energy. I found myself humming a lullaby to her. She gradually settled down and finally drifted off to sleep in my arms. "Atta girl," I whispered to her. "Go to sleep, little one."

It was almost five o'clock now and the darkness had thinned, faded to a vaporous blue; the amorphous night shapes were slowly becoming articulate. I could see stiff clothes hanging over a nylon rope strung between a pair of tulip trees, while nearby a large, console TV set, whose picture tube had been smashed, lay on its back facing the night sky, conjuring up in my mind the dead man staring blankly at the ceiling. Off to the right a ways, a chain hoist dangled from a broad hickory limb, and suspended baitlike at the end of a hook was a rusted V-8 engine block, as if to lure the gaping maw of a hungry car.

I kept hearing the Indian girl's voice rattling around in my head: *Swear on your son's grave you'll take good care of my little girl.* She'd been desperate. She'd just wanted some reassurance that her baby would be safe, in good hands. Not necessarily *my* hands. And *you*, I said to myself, you were just trying to calm her, ease her fears. Cecil was right. You were doing her a favor. You weren't lying. Or if you were, you were only doing it to help out. Sort of like when you told a woman with a lump in her breast it was probably just a fatty tumor, nothing to worry about, even when you suspected otherwise. You were just calming her down. Comforting her. Despite all that, I heard my reply, reverberating in my mind like a metal door slamming irrevocably shut: *I swear.*

After a while, Cecil emerged from the trailer carrying something. It was the plate of food from the table. He walked over and set it on the ground at the edge of the dog's chain-run. I heard him whistle, say, "Here you are, girl." The dog peered out warily from the doorway but didn't move. The sheriff then bent over and vomited on the ground. I could hear him retching several times. Finally, he stood up and came over and climbed into the cruiser.

"You all right, Cecil?"

"Just peachy," he said. He placed his hands on the steering wheel, leaned forward, and rested his head on his knuckles for a moment. He glanced over at me. He was breathing hard, wheezing. You could hear the damage the cigarettes had done to his lungs. He looked pale, his eyes slippery as olives beneath his glasses, and he was holding his face the way you might in a strong wind, the muscles tensed, as if fighting some formidable external pressure. The night had pushed Cecil over a line beyond which a man shouldn't be called on to cross, certainly not for the sake of a mere job. "Shit for brains, eh Doc? Shit for fuckin' brains."

"Yeah." I placed my hand on his shoulder and said, "You want me to drive, Cecil?"

"No, I'm all right. Let's get the hell out of here."

He turned the cruiser around and we headed back down the holler.

After we reached Highway 7, we drove north in silence. The baby fortunately continued to sleep. I felt her body gradually relax, her arms grow less rigid as she sunk deeper into her exhaustion. My mind continued to replay what the Indian girl had said to me: *I got nobody else . . . I'm begging you . . . promise me.* Of course, she hadn't really expected that of me any more than I could expect it of myself. She had to have understood that. We both understood that. I was lying to protect her, and on some level she knew it and accepted my lie. She was scared and confused, and I said what I did for her peace of mind. That was the unspoken bargain we'd struck, the deal we'd made.

"What's going to happen to her?" I asked after a while, softly, so as not to wake the child.

"I suppose Bumgartner'll arraign her on murder charges when Superior Court meets next week."

"No, I mean the baby."

"Oh. I don't know," Cecil replied. "Christ, I ain't thought that far ahead."

As we entered Turner's Crossing, a small hamlet along the Tuckamee, Cecil slowed and turned off into LeBeau's convenience store, open now for coffee and donuts, cigarettes and lotto tickets, for all the factory workers heading north for first shift at the mills in Slade.

"I got to make some calls," he said. "See if I can work something out for the kid. You want a coffee?"

"No. Maybe you ought to pick up some formula if they have it," I advised him. "And a box of diapers."

I watched as Cecil made a half-dozen calls on the pay phone outside, chain-smoking cigarettes and looking up numbers from a small address book. He waved his hands about, imploringly, angrily, and with each call, more frantically. I could almost read his lips at times: *That's your job,* and *What the hell am I supposed to do?* and *I got nowheres else.*

Turner's Crossing was a small village, one of a couple dozen spread out all over Hubbard County. At the foot of every holler or the junction of every stream flowing into a river were clustered a few houses, a store or two that catered to the people way back in the hills. This hamlet amounted to a handful of rundown houses and trailers, a post office, two churches, a welding business, a second-hand clothing shop, and LeBeau's. After the last call, Cecil slammed the phone into its cradle, and with a steel-toed boot aimed a kick at thin air. He headed inside the store and returned in a few minutes carrying a sack of groceries. He stuffed the last of a Twinkie in his mouth as he got in the car.

"You want one?" he asked, holding a yellow sponge cake out to me.

"No," I said. "I thought you don't feel good?"

"I don't. But I eat when I'm nervous."

"We all set? With the baby?"

"Set? Oh, hell, yeah," he scoffed. "We couldn't be any more set, Doc."

"What's the matter?"

"I called half a dozen places. County social services. The youth hot-line. Christian Ministries. You name it. Same story. The shelters are filled to bursting already. On account of it being so close to Christmas."

"There must be some place. Did you try the Good Shepherd down in Farley?"

"Yep. No openings. The best the county social worker could come up with tonight was a foster home over in Raleigh."

"Raleigh! That's more than five hours away. There's nothing closer?"

"Nope. They'll have a bed in the Crawford City emergency shelter but not till day after Christmas. And they can't even bring her over to Raleigh tonight. They had another emergency up in Cold Springs, and they're having to find places for seven kids as it is. Woman told me I'd have to find a way to get her over to Raleigh myself."

"What are you going to do?"

"I sure as hell ain't gonna drive all the way over to Raleigh. I'm short-staffed as it is. I reckon I could call on the Pughs. They're next of kin. Let them worry about her."

"The mother didn't sound too thrilled with the child going there."

"Well, ain't that too damn bad. She should've thought of that before she blew her old man's head off."

"I'm just saying she may've had her reasons."

"And *I* may have my reasons, too." Cecil lit up a cigarette and I didn't object, figured I'd cut him some slack. "I'd bring that little one over to the Pughs' right now 'cept I don't like dealing with that bunch if I don't have to. Only other option is to bring her home with me."

"With you and Ruth not feeling well?"

"You got any better ideas, Doc, I'm all ears."

He looked over, expectant as a dog waiting for a table scrap. But I kept my mouth shut.

Dawn had cracked like an egg, and a viscous light was oozing down some of the higher peaks to the west, a watery yellow. The baby's breathing was steady if a bit congested, her mouth puckered into a fleshy O. It wouldn't hurt you, I thought. Just a day or two. Until they came up with a placement. Help the poor bastard out. But then I re-minded myself I already had a full dance card. I had to be at work in less than three hours. The morning was booked solid with women wanting a clean bill of health before giving themselves over to holiday cheer: the usual prenatal visits, pregnancy tests, GYN exams, worrisome breast lumps, urinary tract infections, change-of-life complaints, menstrual cramps, PMS. In addition, I had a scheduled C-section in the afternoon as well as hospital rounds. Plus, there was no telling with Emmilou Potter; she could get into trouble in the blink of an eye and I'd need to be there. I also had a ton of paperwork to catch up on—insurance forms, lab reports, discharge summaries—not counting my report on the shooting, a preliminary version of which DA Bumgartner would expect on his desk before the end of the day. On top of everything, I needed to get out to the cemetery. No, I thought. Don't. I had my own problems.

We climbed Shadow Mountain and pulled up my driveway. In front of my house, Cecil put the car in park, though he left the motor running. He reached under his seat and took out a pint of Old Grand Dad. He passed it to me and said, "Here you go, Doc." I shook my head, not wanting to drink when I was going to be seeing patients in a few hours. But he said, "G'won and have you one. You earned it tonight." So I took a nip, hoping perhaps to drive that raw stench of blood from my nostrils.

"What are you going to do about her?" I asked, passing the bottle back. He took a halfhearted sip, then chased that with a serious one before replacing the pint under the seat.

"Sensible thing would be to drop her off at the Pughs' when I'm out that way."

"I don't know, Cecil. She seemed dead-set against it."

"They *are* next of kin. Whether we like it or not, they got rights, too."

"I don't have a good feeling about it."

"Now, Doc, you and me both know we don't got nothing to go on 'cept her word—and I wouldn't bet the farm on that."

"You said yourself they were trouble."

"Some of them are, yeah. A few bad apples don't mean they're all bad. I know for a fact the mother, Ada, is a churchgoing woman. Besides, I don't have no other choice, do I? *Do I?*"

He glanced over at me again with that hang-dog expression on his puffy face.

"No way," I said.

"What?"

"Don't 'what' me, Cecil. I can see the wheels turning. No way I can take her."

"You're the one so dead-set against placing her with the Pughs."

"That's right, I don't think it's a good idea. But that doesn't mean *I* get stuck holding the bag."

"Not even just for a little while?"

"No!"

"Just till social services can come up with something else. If nothin' turns up in a day or so, I'll drive her over to Raleigh myself. Whadya say, Doc?"

"How the hell am I going to look after her? I have to be to the office in a couple of hours. I have patients to see. Today's going to be *very* busy, Cecil."

"Couldn't you bring her with you?"

"Bring her with me? Who's going to watch her there?"

"You could have Stella or one of them gals in your office look after her."

"They're busy. They're not baby-sitters."

Cecil scratched his beard.

"I tell you one thing for sure," he said. "That girl ain't agonna like it when I tell her I had to place her baby with the Pughs. No siree. Especially not after what you promised."

"*Me!*" I said angrily. "Now you just hold on a minute."

He laughed, trying to make a joke of it. "Easy, Doc. I'm just kidding."

"Don't you pull that with me, Cecil. I made that promise under duress. And it was just to help out your sorry ass."

"I know, Doc. I know. It's just that I'm out of options. What if I was to take her home? The way that little one's been carrying on tonight and with Ruthie and me not feeling so good. I'd sure hate for her to get what we got. On top of everything else, have her get sick on us? Why, I'd feel a whole lot better if she was with somebody that had, well, more training. A professional."

"A professional, my ass."

"I mean, who's got more experience with young'uns than you, Doc?" Cecil's mouth hinted at a smile, but he held it in check. I looked down at the baby. She was sucking on her two middle fingers, the way Will used to. Away from the stink of death in the trailer, I could smell her for the first time. A slightly sour odor of urine but also that characteristic smell all babies had, of hair and new skin and freshness. The smell of potential, I suppose. I felt something inside me shift, move ever so slightly. Something that had been still and dormant for so long I'd forgotten it was there.

"Doc, I know it's way beyond the call of duty. Believe me, I do. And I wouldn't normally ask you. It's just that I'm up shit's creek without a paddle. Christ, I don't even got a boat." He laughed nervously. "It'd only be for a little while. No more'n a coupla days. Monday the latest. I give you my word. Whadya say, Doc?"

I did feel sorry for him. He was a decent man with a sick wife and a job that was slowly killing him. Nights like this had to take their toll. Yet when I finally relented and agreed to take the baby for a couple of days, I had a sneaking suspicion I'd been had. That he knew when he called me it would turn out exactly like this and that I'd end up taking the child off his hands. I saw a glimmer of canine cunning in his eyes.

"But just till you can find another placement. We clear on that?"

"Absolutely. Thanks, Doc. I owe you one."

"I'm going to hold you to that, don't think I won't," I replied, grabbing my doctor's bag and the grocery sack in one hand, while balancing the baby in the crook of my other arm.

"Need a hand, Doc?"

"I can manage."

Before I got out, however, I remembered something from earlier.

"By the way, when you called tonight. You seemed to think you were disturbing me."

Cecil shrugged. "Just an expression, Doc."

"That's all it was?"

"Yeah . . . why?"

Just by the way he said it, I knew he knew more than he was letting on.

"All right. What did you hear, Cecil?"

"Hear?"

"Don't play dumb. Remember, you owe me."

"Come to think of it," he said, smiling coyly, "I do seem to rec'lect a little birdy whispering something in my ear. About a doctor who shall remain nameless and a certain DA of the female persuasion."

His smile turned into a hairy, carnal laugh.

"What little birdy?"

"You know I can't divulge my informants. Got my professional standards. Besides, Doc, a thing like that don't stay quiet long 'round these parts. You oughta know that."

"Is it common knowledge?"

"No, I wouldn't say common. More on a need-to-know basis now. By the time it gets to be common knowledge, Drew'll put it in the *Messenger*." He was referring to Drew Hazard, the publisher of the *Slade Messenger*, the gossipy weekly rag of a newspaper.

"Well, do me a favor. Keep it under your hat. For Bobbie's sake."

"Sure thing, Doc. Ain't none of my business anywho. Word to the wise, though. Watch yourself, y'hear? I don't want to be getting called out some night to check on an unresponsive-white-male-with-suspected-MI, found buck-naked in the Skyline Motel."

He let out with a laugh.

"Very funny."

"But seriously, Doc. An old fart like you chasing after a pretty young thing like Bobbie Tisdale, y'all only asking for trouble. And her being married, too. Not that I fault your tastes in women, mind you. No sir, that Mrs. Tisdale's a looker, all right. But hell, you don't watch it, you'll end up just like that Nelson Rockefella, have himself the big one plunking some young thang half his age. If'n her old man don't shoot your balls off first. You watch yourself, y'hear?"

"Just find a placement for the baby, Cecil. And damn quick, too."

"It's priority one," he said.

I got out, and he backed up, turned the cruiser around, and gunned it heading out, already forgetting me. In a minute he was out of earshot and, save for a mourning dove's melancholy *who-ee who-who-who*, the mountain resumed its cathedral-like quiet. I headed up onto the porch. The early-morning air was crisp and had a vaguely ciderish flavor to it from the wild crabapple trees up in the woods. Though ominous steel-gray clouds hovered to the northwest, it looked as if it might be a clear day once the sun got high enough in the sky. Now, though, there were still elongated blue-gray shadows stretching from east to west down in the valley, called Mason's Hollow after the Mason clan who lived down near the highway. Smoke drifted from the Wallenbachs' chimney as well as from the houses farther down the mountain: the Isleys', the Breuers', the Masons'. Mists hung in gauzy strips above the Tuckamee River, which churned white and fast as it roared out of the spillway below the dam for Little Bear Reservoir. A mile down-river, behind the cluster of trailer homes and low-lying pasture land and the Baptist church, the water slowed, spread out into shallow pools used by both fly-fishermen after trout and preachers fishing for souls. In nice weather you'd see some minister out there baptizing his followers into everlasting life.

I paused for a moment, savoring the breathtaking view. It was what sold Annabel and me on the place when we bought it more than twenty-five years before. On a fine, clear day, you could see northwest all the way to the Smokies, northeast to the Blue Ridge Parkway, south to the humpbacked hills of Georgia and South Carolina. The mountains rolled on and on into the hazy distance, like the waves of a rough sea, getting lighter and lighter blue until they became indistinguishable from the sky. Annabel loved to paint them. Her mountains, is how she thought of them. A local girl, she knew each peak and gap and ridge by heart: Doubletop, Coward Bald, Needle Mountain, Hornyhead, Standing Lady, our own Shadow Mountain. Just across the valley loomed the five-thousand-foot Painter Knob (ironically, *painter* had nothing to do with artistic pursuits, it being only the local term for panther, something as extinct as wolves in these hills). She knew the Indian names, too, the ones that flowed off the tongue like warm honey: Ottaray (the Indian name for all the western mountains), Cullowhee Gap, Mt. Toxaway, Nantahala Ridge, the Watauga Range, Cullasaja Peak.

Annabel loved hiking up into the hills behind the house or driving over to the Blue Ridge, where she'd find some quiet spot, a scenic overlook with a panoramic view, set up her easel, and spend the day working. But most of the time she'd paint right from the front porch, especially after Will was born. She painted brilliant sunsets over the mountains. Rhododendron in bloom during May. Autumn leaves and snow-covered peaks. In early morning, mist-enshrouded hills undulating like a blue sheet snapped in the wind. I used to like spying on her as she worked. *Do you have to watch me?* she'd say. *You make me nervous, Stu.* Nervous. Sometimes her hands would shake so badly she could only make incomprehensible slashes of color on the canvas. But other times she painted beautifully, at least it seemed so to me. Annabel considered her own work just "tourist schlock," yet it was good enough that the shops in Slade were always after her to display her paintings in their windows for the summer Florida crowd.

Suddenly my lack of sleep kicked in, and I hungered to shut my eyes, even for just a few minutes. Once inside the house, though, the baby commenced to fussing again. I took the blanket off her and realized she'd wet through her diaper. I figured I'd better change her. I spread the blanket on the floor in front of the stove and lay her on it. As I unzipped her, she looked up at me with those dark cryptic eyes of hers, unsure about this character hovering above her. I got a diaper from the box Cecil bought and began to change her. She had a pretty bad rash, her bottom red and sore. I thought of the home remedy for diaper rash one mountain woman told me about when I first moved out here: dirt from a bird's nest. *Took care of a young'un's bottom right quick*, she'd told me. Since I didn't have a bird's nest handy, I had to settle for the tube of A&D ointment in my bag. She felt a little hot, so I checked her temp while I was at it. It was 101.8. I gave her a Tylenol suppository, then finished changing her.

Her fussing continued to escalate, however, becoming more urgent. "I bet you're hungry. Is that it?" I said to her, only then realizing I didn't even know her name. "What's your name, little one?" She stared at me with a slightly contemptuous look, as if to say, *What's it to you, buddy?* "I'll be right back."

I went into the kitchen. I tried to think where Annabel would've stored the bottles, unused since Will was a baby. I was pretty sure she wouldn't have given them all away or thrown them out, as I would be inclined to. She was a pack rat. She was sentimental and would have saved all of his baby things, carefully packed them and squirreled them away someplace, as if against some future need. I checked in the cabinets over the stove, then got down on my hands and knees and looked under the sink. Nothing. The baby was flat-out squawking now, demanding some chow. Think. Where would she have put them? Next I searched in the pantry, even way up on top where there were little-used cooking utensils and an odd assortment of canned goods, pitted with rust. Still no luck. I was considering the attic, but that would have required replacing the bulb I should've replaced last time I was up there. Then I remembered: the storage closet in the basement. Recently I'd been down there hunting for my college yearbook, when I came across a box filled with baby stuff. I checked there and *bingo*, I hit the jackpot. Several glass bottles in a cardboard box containing an assortment of baby things—blue sleepers and blue hooded sweaters and matching blue receiving blankets, still folded, everything neat as a pin—as well as other baby paraphernalia: a vegetable grinder, juice cup, pacifiers, rattles, bibs. I brought the box upstairs and set it down in the den.

I scoured a bottle, then cracked open a can of formula. I filled the bottle with the sweet, yeasty-smelling liquid and put it in a pan of water on the stove. Funny how it all came back to me, especially the smells of a baby. While it was heating, I returned to the den.

"It's coming, little one," I said, stroking her soft brown belly with my knuckles. She paused in her crying for a moment. "*Unh unh*," she said. From the box of baby things I grabbed one of Will's blue sleepers and put it on her. She was swimming in it, but it'd have to do for the time being. When the bottle was warm, I looked in the box of baby things only to find there were no nipples. So I improvised, which is what mountain people were famous for. From my doctor's bag I removed a rubber glove. I'd used this trick in a pinch before. I tied the glove to the top of a bottle, so just one finger was sticking out, and made sure it was good and snug. With a scalpel I made a tiny slit in one finger.

I headed back into the den, where I picked the baby up, sat in the rocker, and began to feed her. It took her a little while to get the hang of it, to fall into a steady rhythm, but when she finally did she went at the chow like a construction worker at an all-you-can-eat buffet. Her plump cheeks worked fiercely, her jaws pumping, her hands grasping at the bottle in front of her. When she finished, I laid her over my shoulder and burped her. She spat up on my chest and I could smell that sucrose fragrance of undigested milk. "Atta girl," I said. I rocked her back and forth. After a few minutes, her belly full, a dry diaper on, she drifted off to sleep once more. The poor thing. She'd been through so much already in her short life. I considered just staying like this. It was a nice, pleasurable feeling, holding a sleeping baby against your chest. In the past dozen years I'd probably delivered a couple thousand babies, though I couldn't recall the last time I'd held a child like this. But I knew my back would be killing me if I slept in the chair.

So I carried her upstairs. I debated about which room. I thought about the guest room at the end of the hall, where Annabel used to stay when she came back. What had once been her studio. In fact, the closet still held her supplies: her tubes of paint and brushes still flexible, canvases neatly rolled up and held by twine, a metal easel, her paint palette. But the bed here was too narrow for both of us and too far away from the heat of the stove. Next, I considered my room, but for some reason I couldn't put my finger on, I decided against it, too.

At last I settled on Will's room, feeling a little like Goldilocks trying out each bed for the right fit. It was a pleasant room really, airy and bright, with a stenciled border Annabel had painted of mountain flowers: trillium, larkspur, toothwort, flaming azalea. She used to take Will for walks in these hills, teaching him the names of the flowers, trees, and birds. The room faced northeast, with a nice view across the valley, and in summers it received a cool breeze off the creek that passed by the house. After Will's death we kept everything the way it was, the room exuding the morbidly still, fragilely sacred air of a museum. I've heard of other parents who've lost children keeping their child's room like a temple, as if awaiting his return. For the longest time after Will died, I couldn't bring myself to set foot in here. I just couldn't bear to. It was like jabbing an exposed nerve. In time, though, I'd got so I could come in, usually late at night and secretly, as if I were doing something illicit, touch his things; I'd run my hands over his toy cars and fire engines, his teddy bears, his little plastic action heroes, a stiff baseball glove I'd got him for his fifth birthday and which I could not recall our ever having used. I would open his drawers and grab a handful of his clothes, his underwear and socks, the things closest to his body and which therefore most retained his smell, and guiltily, hungrily, bury my face in them. I'd breathe in his scent, which got fainter with each passing month: part soap, part smelly socks and sweaty hands odor, a young boy's sweet-sour fragrance. Will's scent. The smell of his things used to bring a burning, ragged knot to my throat, as if I'd swallowed a shot of ammonia.

Then six, maybe seven years back, Annabel left me for nearly a year. I hadn't so much as a word from her. I thought this time, perhaps, she was gone for good. One day, on an impulse to clear away my past, I gathered up most of my son's things and brought them to the Goodwill box in town. *Good Will*, I thought. I felt I needed to get on with my life, and Will's things would help some poor mountain family clothe their living child. When my wife eventually did return and saw what I'd done, she was inconsolable. She broke down and sobbed: *How could you get rid of his things, Stu?* she'd cried. *Our baby's things?*

I laid Rosa Littlefoot's child gently on top of the covers. I took hold of the Jacob's-ladder-pattern quilt at the foot of the bed, one Annabel had made for our son, and spread it over her, tucked in the far side to keep her from rolling off. I figured only to rest for a bit, close my eyes for a few minutes. Just to take the edge off my exhaustion. A light sleeper anyway, I was used to catching a few winks in the doctors' lounge at the hospital while waiting for a mother's labor to progress. An internal clock always kept me ready, prepared for anything. Since there wasn't much time, I didn't bother undressing. I had no plan for what I was going to do with the baby. None. Figured I'd worry about that when I got up. I slid under the quilt, turned on my side so I was cradling the baby against my chest. I lay there shivering, trying to draw some of the baby's warmth from her. I was struck by the irony of it all, as if there were a meaning in the meaningless chaos of the night: Here I was lying with some stranger's baby, a murderer's child who had, as in some biblical story or German fairy-tale, been thrust into my hands, both of us lying in my son's bed, on the very day he was born twenty years before. A scientist and physician, I am not normally a believer in signs or omens, which I think can only lead to unfulfilled hopes or unfounded fears, but I must confess I was hard-pressed to slough this off to mere chance.

While I was dead tired, I held out against sleep's strong gravitational pull. In some way I couldn't put my finger on, it seemed that there was danger in giving in to it. It felt as if I was dangling from a rope, suspended above a dark pit, holding on for dear life. My mind raced with the night's crazy goings-on, a cacophony of unsavory images and sounds and smells. I could hear the plaintive, hollow-lunged cry of the baby. I could smell the bitter smell of cordite and the rancid odor of curdled milk, and that raw stench of blood infusing the trailer with its rankness of death and violence. I saw a man with half his head blown off, one eye bloated red, the other flat and dull and fixed on the ceiling with a dogged curiosity. And, last of all, I saw Rosa Littlefoot, her dark, bruised face, her hard yet milkless breast at her baby's mouth. I saw the way her eyes pleaded with me as she was led out of the trailer. And I heard her ask one last time, *Swear on your son's grave you'll take good care of my little girl.*

My son's grave, I thought. At last, my strength at an end, I gave up fighting, surrendered, and felt myself tumbling headlong into the beckoning, perilous darkness below me.

# 5

*I had one* of those textbook Freudian dreams, the sort that's so trans-
parently symbolic you wonder if it can be *that* obvious. It was about a
woman who stood naked in a raging river. She held something in her
arms, though from where I stood on the bank I couldn't tell what it was.
She called out suddenly to me, as if in danger. I hesitated at first, fearful
of the surging water. Finally, I threw caution to the wind, jumped in the
river, and started making my way toward her. The water, heavy and fast
and brutally cold, clutched at my thighs, trying to suck me under. Nearing the woman, I saw that she was sharp-featured with raven-black eyes
and dark, flowing hair that spilled down over her thin, angular shoulders. Her lips were a pallid shade of blue. And I saw that what she was
holding was a child, pressed to her breast. She held the baby out to me,
as if beckoning me to take it. Before I could react, though, she shot me
an accusatory stare, and then she and the child slipped beneath the dark
waters. *Wait*, I cried out. But she and the child had vanished.

A phone call yanked me out of the dream like a fish on a steel leader.
I jumped out of bed and hurried into my room to get it. I could feel my
heart pounding fiercely from the dream as I picked up the phone.

"Dr. Jordan! Where y'all at?" came Stella Plumtree's voice. Stella
was my receptionist and office manager. "It's a madhouse here."

I glanced at the clock on the nightstand: 9:48.

"Damn." I'd overslept, which wasn't like me at all. I was normally
conscientious to a fault.

"Mrs. DeForest been here since nine and she's madder'n a wet hen.
Got a bad pain in her belly, or so she says. And they's a waitin' room full
of grumpy people. Oh, and that Mrs. McCreadie's here to speak to you
about Sue Ellen."

I started mentally to triage.

"I'll call Mrs. DeForest's prescription in to Green's. Tell her she can go down there and pick it up." Mrs. Jillian DeForest, one of *the* DeForests whose family owned the textile mill, usually wanted pain medication for some vague and ever-changing "female" complaint. She was one of the "genteel" addicts every small-town doctor has to put up with. "What's Mrs. McCreadie want?"

"She wants for you to put her daughter on the pill."

"Pill! Sue Ellen's pregnant, for heaven's sake."

"I told her that." Then in a whisper, Stella added, "Kinda like shutting the barn door after the heifer's already out," and laughed.

"Tell her I'll call her."

"What about the rest?"

"Is Cheryl there?" Cheryl McClain was my office nurse, who'd been with me almost as long as Stella.

"Now, Doc, you know well's I do she took the week off."

"Oh, that's right. I forgot."

"Want I should have Gladys handle what she can?"

Gladys Dills was my PA—physician's assistant. She was a bright, capable young woman, but she'd only been with me a year, and I didn't want to let her get in over her head. Have her miss something potentially serious. If Cheryl, a battle-hardened OB-GYN nurse, were there, I'd have felt a whole lot better. She was as good as most doctors I knew.

"Yes. Tell Gladys to take the well prenatals. Schedule the rest for next week. If anyone is presenting with something more pressing, squeeze them in for tomorrow."

"But that's Christmas Eve. Besides, you're already booked solid."

"It can't be helped, Stella. Something's come up."

"Having to do with that murder, I bet."

"Where'd you hear that?"

"It's all over town. Stopped at the Pancake Barn for coffee. That's all Raylene and them was a-yakkin' about. Course Raylene knew on account of Cecil getting the food for the prisoners there. She was saying that Indian girl was higher'n a kite when she gunned down one of them Pugh boys. That true, Doc?"

"You ought to know better than to believe everything Raylene tells you, Stella. Any calls from the hospital?"

"No. You're supposed to do Mrs. Titus's section this afternoon, don't forget?" she lectured, as if I was a grade-school student going to be late with my assignment.

"I won't."

"What about me? I could take the afternoon off and catch up on some Christmas baking."

"Actually I'm going to need you today, Stella. Just sit tight. I'll be in later."

"By the way, that Mrs. Tisdale called looking to speak to you." When I didn't say anything, she added, "You know, the prosecutor lady."

"I know who she is, Stella. Did she say what she wanted?"

"I s'pect it's got to do with that murder. What else would she be calling you for?"

I didn't catch the faintest note of irony in Stella's voice. I took that as a good sign. For gossip, her ears were usually more sensitive than a stethoscope. If Stella hadn't heard about Bobbie and me, then maybe the cat wasn't out of the bag yet. Or at least didn't have more than a paw and a few whiskers showing.

"You're probably right," I said.

"Oh, I almost forgot. Your . . . " Stella offered, hesitating. "What I mean is, you got a letter from Annabel Lee."

"Annabel?"

"Yessum. I kinda opened it before I knew it was personal."

"What did she want?"

"It was mixed in with the office mail. 'Course, I didn't read it. Not when I seen it was for you."

"Of course not, Stella," I replied, going along with her.

"Just gave it a quick eyeball, if you know what I mean."

"From what you could make out, did she say if anything was wrong?"

"I don't believe so."

"She need some money?"

"No. Far as I could tell—and like I said, I just eyeballed it—she was writing about . . . well, about your boy, Doc, I think."

"I'll be in shortly," I said to her and hung up before she could give me her opinion about my personal life.

Stella had known Annabel even longer than I had. They were both local, born and raised right here in Slade. Annabel's family, the Brysons, lived just one street over from the Tinsleys, Stella's family. They went to the same Methodist church, and it was Stella's mother, a seamstress, who had made Annabel's bridal gown. Stella had told me how she could recall the two Bryson girls, daughters of Professor Bryson, who taught at the college, walking by on their way home from grade school. The older one, Lenore, was pretty, blond, and tall and elegant, with the carriage of someone who'd gone to finishing school; the younger one was dark-haired, awkward, all elbows and knees, "a scrawny bit of a thang," Stella would say. "She sure was a feisty gal, that Annabel Lee. Had a mind all her own."

I wondered at the coincidence of Annabel's letter, how within the span of a few hours we'd both been thinking about the other. But then again, I should've expected to hear from her today, of all days: *December 23*. It wasn't any coincidence. Coincidences were random things. This was a rational event, one in a line of other events, a dot connecting other dots and leading inexorably toward a logical conclusion. It made all the sense in the world that I'd hear from her today. It was, after all, Will's birthday. She usually wrote or called. Not always but often enough that when she didn't I was a little surprised. I wouldn't hear from her for months. But on December 23, I half came to expect a letter in the mail or a message waiting on my machine when I got home from work. "Just thinking about you, Stu," she'd say. Or "Sorry I haven't been in touch . . . ." Or "Remember the time he . . . ."

Once or twice, she even showed up at the house on his birthday. One time, she stood there on the cold dark porch like a ghost, or the shadow of one. "Can I come in?" she asked, as if she actually expected me to say no, as if I *could* say no. Yet I hadn't heard from her for months, not since that time she called to ask if I could send her some money. There'd been a problem. I didn't ask what it was this time. I just sent her a check. And I hadn't seen her in person for nearly two years, that time she was sick, summer before last. So, while I probably should have been expecting her to contact me today, it nonetheless came as a surprise, sort of like when you're standing at someone's door ready to knock, and they open it just as your knuckles are about to strike, and your hand falls on empty air.

• • • •

The baby was still sound asleep, pooped out from last night's goings-on. So after tending to the fire, I had a chance to shower, shave, and get dressed. I put on a pot of coffee and fixed myself some breakfast. I found I was starved now and wolfed down two bowls of Cheerios, some toast, and an overripe banana. The pain in my knees had been joined this morning by a dull headache, a tightness in the back of my neck which scurried along the base of my skull like a lizard. I washed a couple of Advil down with coffee. Then I put in a call to the hospital, to check on my patients. Luckily things were quiet. After placing a bottle of formula on the stove to warm, I headed upstairs to get the baby up. Though she was sleeping soundly and I hated to wake her, I had to get a move on.

"Good morning," I said as I lifted her off the bed. She woke with a start, her body stiffening, her back arching. She stared at me, her dark eyes wide with alarm, and commenced to crying. "*Ssh*. It's okay. You hungry, little one?" I lay her over my shoulder, jiggling her till she quieted down. "Atta girl." Despite a wet diaper, she had that sweet baby fragrance to her, like biscuits warming in the oven. I brought her downstairs and into the den. I placed her on a blanket on the floor in front of the stove and began to change her. In the light of day, I noticed a small, dark, eggplant-colored bruise on her pudgy thigh. It could've been perfectly benign but, given everything, I couldn't help but be a little suspicious. The diaper rash had improved some but was still inflamed, and I applied some more ointment. She stared up at me, no longer afraid so much as just plain curious now. Who is this guy? she was thinking.

"How are you this morning?" I asked. I tickled her, made clucking noises, but she steadfastly refused to smile. She was a serious, sober little thing.

I finished dressing her, left her there for a moment, and headed into the kitchen. The bottle still wasn't quite warm, so I poured myself another cup of coffee and stood at the kitchen sink, gazing out the window. The day had changed its mind and turned overcast, the sky a mottled lead-pipe gray, dull and absorbing light like a sponge. My property extended level and clear for several hundred feet behind the house before angling sharply up toward the summit of Shadow Mountain. At the creek that fed the water cistern, the woods took over: dense, tangled thickets of rhododendron and mountain laurel interspersed with hardwoods like ash and hickory, beech and tulip poplar, some chestnut suckers. The cold had shriveled the leaves of the rhododendrons into tight green cones, and a hard frost made everything gleam dully. In front of the cistern was a small plot of ground, now wildly overgrown, where

Annabel used to raise vegetables; in fact, standing in the middle of it still was the raggedy, skeletal remains of a scarecrow, wearing one of my old coats. Next to that lay what was left of the flower garden Annabel started when we first moved out here.

Annabel had loved to garden. Every year she sent away to a place called Spring Hill for bulbs and seeds. Our neighbor, Kay Wallenbach, and Annabel would argue good-naturedly over who had the prettiest roses and hydrangeas. I could recall summer evenings coming home from work and standing at this very spot, secretly watching her out there on her hands and knees, pruning, digging, planting things, coaxing life from the barren, red-clay mountain soil. Sometimes Will would be out there, her little helper. As with her painting, I knew that when she took an interest in her garden, things were fine. Funny how the garden seemed to mirror her moods. Vibrant and orderly, teeming with health and vitality when she was; wild and unkempt, going to seed when she wasn't.

Now, left mostly untended for years, the garden had slowly reverted to its natural state; it had been invaded and taken over by the encroaching woods. What the deer and rabbits hadn't gotten to, an army of attacking kudzu had, overrunning most of it, strangling everything in its cancerous grip. Spindly tulip tree and hickory saplings grew from the garden floor while wild rhododendron bushes had muscled their way in and pushed out the more delicate azaleas and roses, the hostas and burning bushes, the bleeding hearts and keys of heaven Annabel had planted. It was no longer really a garden now but merely a tangle of unrestrained growth, brownish in winter.

My thoughts were on Annabel, when I caught a dark figure emerging from up in the woods. For a moment I thought it was nothing more than a trick of the morning light, a passing shadow. But he was real enough. He came plodding right through the garden, stepping on things as he approached. He jounced along, loose-limbed, his movements revealing he was accustomed to negotiating the uneven terrain of these hills. He climbed onto the back deck and walked over to the sliding doors. Instead of knocking, he put his face up to the glass and cupped his hands around his eyes to peer in. I was standing no more than ten feet from him, but evidently he didn't see me. He was a large man, about six feet, broad through the chest and shoulders. He wore a grease-stained army jacket, unzipped despite the cold, an Atlanta Braves baseball cap, and gum-soled hunting boots. He was clean-shaven, with a broad, uncomplicated face and a loose-fitting mouth whose primary emotion suggested impatience.

What the hell? I thought.

I was pretty sure I'd never seen him around here before. Nobody lived above me on the mountain, though the old tote road, almost impassable beyond here, did meander up through the woods and over the ridge. Sometimes boys on all-terrain vehicles or dirt bikes or hunters with dogs in the backs of their trucks would pass by on their way up and over the mountain. Or kids would go parking up in a little clearing just above my place. And a couple of families, the Tarbells and McAteers, did live on the other side of the ridge, in an isolated holler called Harlan's East Branch. Maybe he was one of them. Or it might be someone needing the services of a doctor. Some husband coming to get help for a laboring wife somewhere back in the hills. That had happened more than once before. Then again, maybe he wasn't even from around here. Perhaps he was lost and looking for directions. Outsiders often got lost driving up these long, poorly marked dirt roads.

I remained motionless, watching him to see what he was going to do. I had another thought then: What if he's a robber? Somebody who thinks nobody's home? I'd had one break-in a few years before. They took a stereo, a few other things. So when the man tried the door, jiggled it to see if it would open, something tightened in my chest. Fortunately, the door was locked. Maybe if I don't answer, he'll just go away, I thought. But then he knocked on the glass, at first lightly, but when he didn't get an immediate response, more insistently.

"Hello," he called. "Y'all home, Dr. Jordan?"

When he said my name, I decided somehow he wasn't a threat.

Opening the door, I asked, "Can I help you?"

"You Dr. Jordan?"

"Yes? Is somebody sick?"

"No. Nobody's sick. I'm Tully Pugh."

"Who?" I asked, the name at first not registering.

"Pugh. My brother was Roy Lee Pugh. The fellow . . . "

"Oh, right. Right," I said. "I'm sorry for your loss."

"That's mighty decent of you. Me and Roy weren't what you call close. But we were still blood."

"What is it I can do for you, Mr. Pugh?" I asked.

"Tell me, Doc, did my brother suffer much?"

"Not too much," I said. A lie, of course. The shot in the belly would have been pure agony, not to mention the time it took for him to bleed out and for her to decide his fate. But why tell him that now? It would come out at the trial anyway.

"Thank God. That's something at least. Our momma will sure be glad to hear his passing was quick."

"Is that all you came up here for?" I asked.

"Well, no. You see, I come to fetch Maria on home."

"Maria?"

"Roy Lee's young'un." It was the first time I'd heard her name. Maria, I thought. Then I wondered how he knew she was with me, but of course news traveled fast in the mountains. Maybe Cecil let it slip when he went out there or they'd heard it on the police frequency. "I'm here to take her off your hands," this Tully Pugh said to me.

"You want to take her?"

"Yessir. I want to thank you for lookin' after her and all. We're much obliged. If there's a bill we got to pay for your services, you send it along and we'll square up with you, Doc. We pay what we owe."

"I'm paid by the county."

"Well, thank you anyway. If you'll just get her for me, I'll be on my way."

I recalled how upset Rosa Littlefoot had gotten at the mention of her child going to stay with the Pughs. And I thought about the bruises on her face, not to mention the one on the child's leg. And what Cecil had to say about the Pugh clan, their run-ins with the law. How one of them was serving time for murder. They didn't seem like the sort of family you'd feel comfortable handing a child over to. I'm not a man who usually bases his decisions on gut instinct. I feel more comfortable with facts. But I just had a bad feeling in this particular instance.

"I'm afraid I can't," I told him.

"Can't?"

"She's not here."

"She's not? I heard tell she was."

"That's true, she was. But social services picked her up already."

"Is that so?" the man asked.

"That's right. They came by earlier and took her."

"You know where they brung her?"

"You'll have to call Sheriff Clegg. He'd be the one to talk to."

Tully Pugh stood there for a moment, appraising me, wondering if he should take me at my word. Finally, he said, "I guess I won't be bothering you no more, Dr. Jordan. Thank you for your time."

Before I could get the door closed, however, the baby happened to let out with a squawk. Damn, I thought. It wasn't a loud cry, and for a moment I was hoping Pugh hadn't heard it. Yet he stopped in his tracks, glanced over his shoulder at me, a faint smile playing about his impatient mouth.

"I thought you said they done picked her up already?"

The game was up. No use lying anymore, I could see.

"I've been asked to look after the baby for a while."

"*You!* What do you got to do with it? You ain't kin."

"And neither are you. Legally that is. They weren't married."

"They were common-law. Everybody knows that. That young'un in there is my niece. She's blood, Dr. Jordan."

"That may be true. But I've been asked to look after her for the time being."

"Who asked you? We didn't."

"For one, Sheriff Clegg. And for another, Rosa Littlefoot."

"*Her!*" he said, forcing a sardonic laugh, which drew his loose lips back over his teeth. His were surprisingly white, not the usual sort possessed by backwoods mountain people who still thought fluoridated water a communist plot. "She ain't got no say in this. And with all due respect, neither do you. She ain't your'n, Doc. So if you'll run along and fetch her for me, I'll be leaving."

"She's still the mother," I said.

"And I'm the kid's uncle. That woman murdered my brother in cold blood, Dr. Jordan. I'm not saying Roy Lee was a saint, mind you. He had himself a right bad temper. Still, he was blood and that woman took him away from us. And now she's aiming to take our kin from us. She ain't got no right to do that."

"I'm just trying to do what's best for the child."

"What's best for her is to be with her people, y'understand what I'm saying?"

I could feel myself getting sucked into something I didn't want to, pulled against my will the way you might in a strong current of water. I thought of that river again, the one in the dream. Getting pulled under its cold and deadly surface. I could almost taste the water in my mouth. Sometimes, it didn't matter how good a swimmer you were, the water was going to do with you what it would. The best course of action was to go with the flow for a while and hope to change direction later on.

"I'm sorry about your brother, Mr. Pugh. But I don't have the authority to just hand her over to you. We'll have to let the courts sort out where she's going."

"The courts got diddly-squat to do with this," Pugh said. "This is family business. And you, Dr. Jordan, you ain't family."

"It's a little more complicated than that, I'm afraid."

"It ain't complicated a'tall. It's real simple. You got my brother's kid and I'm here to fetch her on home. Now if you'll 'scuse me, Dr. Jordan," he said, moving toward me. He put one foot on the sill and a hand on the door and made as if to slide it open. But from the other side I held the handle. He pushed with more force against the door and I managed to resist his challenge. Our faces, straining, were no more than inches apart. I could smell him now, a heavy, dense odor like axle grease. And this close I could see the resemblance to the dead man, at least from what had been left of his brother's face. Tully Pugh had his brother's sharp, pointy chin, the almost delicate features. He was a handsome man, with gray-green eyes and long lashes, and with unusually straight teeth for somebody from Little Mexico. He stood there for a moment staring at me. Though I was a couple of inches taller, he probably had thirty pounds on me, and I had thirty years on him. I tried not to let him see I was breathing hard or to allow any sign of the tightness in my chest, which had grown to a painful knot right behind my sternum, to betray itself in my expression. I could see what he was thinking: He's an old man and a Yankee to boot. How hard would it be to push him out of the way and go in and take what I come for? Yet for some reason, he didn't.

"I got no quarrel with you, Dr. Jordan," he said, letting go of the door and taking a step back. "People around these parts have always spoke highly of you. They say you're a decent fellow. No need you getting yourself mixed up in this. I just want Maria."

"I'm sorry. I just can't let you have her."

"This *ain't* your concern."

"Unfortunately, it is," I replied. "For now, anyway."

He stared at me for another moment, debating what to do.

"Have it your way then," he said at last. He turned and headed down the steps, making for the woods. With his back to me and not bothering to turn around, he called, "You're gettin' into something you don't want to get into."

# 6

*Sipping coffee, I* drove north on Highway 7, following the river as it snaked its way through the mountains. The Tuckamee, Cherokee for "blood of the mountains," did resemble a major artery, starting up in the Smokies and coursing down through the very heart of Hubbard County. Ice had formed along the shore while frost glistened hoary-white on the kudzu choking its banks. For a while, an osprey glided above the river, almost level with me. I could see its yellow, razor-sharp eyes hunting for a meal below. I had the radio tuned to the Slade station to see if they had anything about the murder. They didn't. Only the morning livestock prices and the weather, which called for the cold spell to continue though they weren't predicting a white Christmas. In the back, the baby was strapped in the car seat I'd borrowed from Kay Wallenbach, who kept one handy for her grandchildren. The baby made soft gurgling noises. Maria. The Pugh fellow had told me her name was Maria. A pretty name. *This ain't your concern*, he'd said. *This is family business.* I wondered what I would've done if he'd been determined to push his way into my house? I was glad I didn't have to find out. I'm not by nature a brave or reckless man. I'm the sort who prefers things quiet, the kind of man who would like to die in his sleep at ninety.

I came over a rise near the new Wal-Mart plaza, and below sat the small town of Slade. It was situated at the juncture of two rivers, the Tuckamee and Little Addie, in a narrow alluvial valley gouged between the Cowee and Plott Balsam mountain ranges. Clouds of yellowish smoke belched from the Nantahala Paper Company, the town's largest employer, flattened out like batter on a hot griddle, and hung suspended just above Slade. The downtown had one of those self-consciously quaint, Hopperesque main drags, which catered to the horde of Florida tourists descending on us each summer. There were gift shops which shamelessly peddled hillbilly-motif souvenirs, a pharmacy with a soda fountain, a barber shop sporting a working barber pole, a five-and-dime that had a fortune-telling scale out front, as well as several trendy newer restaurants and shops appealing to the more sophisticated tastes of the tourists with money in their pockets. Not to mention the array of real estate offices with pictures in their windows of "getaway" mountain retreats and "cozy" summer homes. Traffic flowed one way down Main, west to east, presenting the best face to most coming to town for the first time, before doubling back along the seedier Mill Street, behind the squalid, grimy backs of stores. South of Main were the large and stately Victorian homes belonging to the town's old-monied elite, including the residence, now a museum, of Judge Clayton Slade himself. Slade had founded the settlement in the early 1800s, having confiscated the land from the Cherokees after they'd been driven out. A half-mile to the north, up on a hill, was another new shopping plaza with a Bi-Lo and a Kmart and a four-screen cinemaplex, as well as Pancho Villa's, a restaurant I sometimes ate at after work. Just up the road, on the way to the Interstate, was the seventy-five-bed regional hospital where I practiced.

Slade had that smug, self-righteous air a lot of small towns have, particularly small Southern towns, the sort of take-us-as-we-are-or-get-the-hell-out attitude. Its civic and business leaders tried hard to cultivate an image of smallness and tradition, and down-home, saccharine-sweet wholesomeness. A sign on the bridge as you entered the city limits proudly proclaimed this as "God's Country, USA." On the town green there was a whitewashed bandstand where in the summer cloggers or bluegrass bands performed. There was Mountain Festival Days in the fall, with its parade down Main and its floats of fiddlers and bagpipers and old ladies in bonnets quilting away. Each summer brought the big tent revival meeting in the vacant lot between the now-defunct Catamount Theatre and the offices of the *Slade Messenger*, where preachers in white suits yelled and sweated and were filled with the Holy Ghost, before heading down to the Tuckamee River to baptize their flock.

At exactly 11:30 each morning, the local radio station broadcast hymns and sermons by the fiery Reverend L. B. Stevens, who chastised people both for sins actually committed and for those only imagined, while at noon, accompanied by creepy organ music, L. B. recited eulogies of our dearly departed brethren, sponsored by the Childress Funeral Home, "a familiar face in your time of bereavement." In the unfortunate event no one passed on, you were treated to a straight hour of Beulah Sowerby, the Calvary Church organist, plunking away tunes such as "Bringing in the Sheaves."

But Slade, like most of the new South, had been rapidly changing, sloughing off its small-town, Bible-thumping, good-ole-boy skin. It was the nineties, after all. We even had a smooth-talking cracker in the White House. Besides its McDonald's and Burger Kings and Pizza Huts, the town now boasted Italian, Mexican, Indian, and Chinese restaurants. Slade had its Wal-Marts and Radio Shacks run by people from Charlotte, its convenience stores and motels owned by dark-skinned families with unfamiliar accents. It sported tanning salons, health clubs, and video arcades, not to mention an adult movie shop and even a leather and tattoo parlor down near the river. The hospital was the proud owner of new CT scanning and MRI equipment, had a state-of-the-art trauma center, and was staffed by Pakistani, Korean, Iranian, and Jewish doctors. Slade even had a tiny synagogue. Though still small, the town had more than doubled in size since I came in the sixties. Housing developments were popping up all over the county: summer homes for the wealthy, retirement villages for seniors, country living for young professionals tired of the crime and congestion in places like Knoxville or Charlotte.

But with the growth came problems. Hubbard County used to be dry, though of course there was always white lightning to be had for those who knew where to go. Now, however, it had one of the highest alcoholism rates in the state. Where drugs were almost unheard of thirty years ago, we now had our share of addicts and overdoses, drug busts and drug-related crimes, our own local chapters of AA and Al-Anon. Just this past Thanksgiving, I'd had to pronounce a young black woman who'd OD'ed on heroin up in the Hobbstown section of Slade, what used to be called, without batting an eye, "Niggertown." And the year before, a senior at the college had snorted too much coke and gone into cardiac arrest. Drive down Mill Street after dark—no one walks it anymore when the sun goes down—and you would likely see people sleeping in doorways or dealing drugs, dirty needles and empty crack vials in the gutters. Thanks to the big gambling casino they built over on the reservation, we now had prostitution and organized crime, graft and corruption, just like in the big cities. Violence, too, had escalated. We were seeing more domestics, more fights, stabbings, shootings, rapes. It used to be the county got maybe one homicide a year, if we were lucky.

But for the past half-dozen years it's been running three or four, and that was in addition to suicides and accidents. In my own practice I saw more sexual and physical abuse, more STDs, more cases of HIV, more crack mothers and crack babies. Though it was a late bloomer, Slade, "God's Country, USA," had come of age.

Today, two days before Christmas, the town was decked out in reds and greens and fake white snow; only a few of the higher mountain peaks surrounding the town had snow yet. Plastic holly was draped around the street lights, and banners and ornaments were in all the store windows. At the west end of Main, perched on a high knoll overseeing everything the way a stern librarian would watch her quiet domain, was the whitewashed Hubbard County Courthouse building. It was one of those impressive edifices of late-nineteenth-century southern jurisprudence, squarish and stately, with columns out front and a dome covered in gold leaf, whose imposing image was intended to humble those hillbillies foolish enough to let themselves be brought before it. Besides the Superior and Civil courts, it housed the recreation department, the dog warden's office and sewage department, the county water authority, the Slade town police and county sheriff's departments, the prosecutor's offices up on the third floor, as well as the county jail in the basement. It was there, at this very moment, Rosa Littlefoot sat in a five-by-ten-foot cell awaiting her arraignment for murder.

I parked the Blazer in front of my office on Main Street and removed Maria from the car seat.

"How are we doing, sweetie?" I said to her. Her wide brown eyes casually took in the Christmas decorations gracing Main without the slightest reaction. I couldn't much blame her. The day after her mother had blown her father's head off, Maria viewed the world with a curious disinterest.

"Who belongs to that?" Stella asked when I came in. Stella Plumtree was in her sixties. She had wispy blond-gray hair and a permanently flushed face, as if she were recently embarrassed by something. The right side of her face drooped a little from the small stroke she'd had a few years back. She'd been with me nearly since I'd first hung out my shingle. Without resorting to the files, she could tell you to the penny how much a patient owed us or who the second cousin once removed was of another. And in a pinch she could fill me in on medical histories or even offer a prognosis. ("All them Queens is small-hipped," she'd explain. "So you might's well go ahead and schedule a section right now, Doc, and be done with it.")

Though she was as nosy as a cat and was forever trying to introduce me to some nice "widow lady who knows her way around a kitchen," Stella had her good points, one of which was a fierce canine loyalty.

"Say hello to Maria Littlefoot," I replied, heading by her and into my office.

"The child of that murderess?" Stella asked, following me in.

"The woman who's *accused* of murder."

"Same difference."

"Where's Gladys?"

"She's looking at a patient in room one. Ain't she got purty eyes," she said, hovering over the baby, cooing to it and pinching her cheek. "What's you'all doing with her?"

"Cecil had nowhere to bring her last night. So I got volunteered."

Stella laughed.

"What's so funny?"

"You tending to that woman's baby."

With one hand, I began leafing through my mail, sorting through the envelopes, bills, lab reports, and pharmaceutical flyers.

"It's in your top drawer," Stella advised, reading my mind. "Give that child here." She took the baby from me and started tickling her with a knuckle at the edge of her mouth. Maria smiled at her, the first time I'd seen her do that. At least I now knew she was capable of it. Stella's own children were grown, and she loved nothing better than holding the babies of mothers who came into the office. I took out the letter, and before opening it, I glanced at Stella.

"I'll be outside," she said.

I sat down at my desk and opened it, immediately recognizing the handwriting—a beautiful calligraphy, the long-tailed, swirling *g*'s and *s*'s, but also the shakiness of a slight tremor she'd developed, most likely a side effect of the Haldol she took. Handwriting that was both artistic and pathological at once, creative and destructive. The return address was new, not the previous one I'd been sending the checks to. Annabel tended not to stay in the same apartment very long, though she had been living in Asheville for the past few years. I recognized the street as being down near the French Broad River, a rundown section of town. *Dear Stu*, her letter began.

> *Sorry I've not been better about keeping in touch. You know me though. I dreamed of you and Will the other night. You were shaving and Will was watching you. You let him put shaving cream on*

*and pretend to shave. He had it all over his face. It was a nice
dream. When I woke up, though, I lay in bed in the dark trying to
remember his mouth. But for the life of me I couldn't recall it at all.
Couldn't see him talking or smiling or anything. And yet the harder
I tried to remember what his mouth looked like the less I actually
could. Pretty soon I had to get out a picture of him. Do you ever
forget what he looked like? The smell of his hair? The softness of
the skin on the back of his hand. Maybe it's a blessing after all. I've
read someplace that the mind can't remember what pain feels like.
Just the idea of pain. Then again, it seems like forgetting is just another kind of pain. That it's just trading one sort for another.*

*It doesn't seem possible, does it? Fourteen years. It's hard to pic-
ture him as a grown man now, shaving and having a girlfriend.
Have you ever thought of what he might have turned out like? Of
course, you have. I sometimes play this game with myself. I'll see
some boy somewhere, with blond hair and gray-blue eyes, like his.
Like yours. Maybe he's sitting with some pretty girl in a park. Or
just walking down the street. And I'll make believe that it's him.
Our Will. I'll say to myself, That's what he'd look like, right there.
Other times, usually late at night, when everything is still and my
mind slows down a bit, I'll hear his voice. Talking to me. Calling
me momma. Asking for something. To tuck him in. And it sounds
so real. The pain in my heart feels like a dagger then, but I wouldn't
trade it for the world. It's the sweetest sort of torture. Sometimes I
think the pain is the only thing I have left of him, the only thing
that keeps me going.*

*I've been meaning to get out there—to see you and to visit the
cemetery. In the meantime, say a prayer for him for me, would you?
And while you're at it, one for me. You're still that much of a
Catholic, I bet. Hoping this letter finds you well.*

    *Love,*

    *Anna*

Annabel's contacts were, to say the least, infrequent, sporadic, usually coming after months, occasionally even a year or two, where I
didn't hear a word from her. And then it would often be some problem.
A call from an emergency room where she'd landed after a full-blown
manic episode. A landlord wanting rent. A scrape with the law and she
needed to make bail. At least that's what she'd tell me, for I had long

since stopped pressing her about specifics. I didn't want to know the details of her life; I found it easier to think of her in a vacuum, suspended in my memory as a specimen in formaldehyde. When she'd show up at my door, suitcase in hand, she'd be looking for a place to stay, appearing exhausted and strung-out. Other times I'd get a call late at night, a jukebox blaring in the background and her talking a mile a minute, wired, rambling, incoherent, in the midst of one of her manic phases. Still other times, there would be a stony silence on the other end so I knew who it was even before she said, "It's me, Stu," her voice dull, affectless, hammered flat by the lithium or Haldol or whatever sedative some ER doc had prescribed for this agitated street person, just to get her out of his hair. The last time I'd heard her voice was the previous summer. She was living in Asheville, waitressing part-time, the sort of job she usually got. She was at work when she called from a pay phone; there were voices, men's voices, and loud aggressive laughter in the background.

"Are you all right?" I asked. "Do you need anything? Money?"

"I'd appreciate it if you could send some. Something's come up."

"Sure."

"Are the rhododendrons in bloom up on the mountain?"

I told her they were. I told her how pretty they'd come in that year, a brilliant splash of whites and pinks and lavenders scattered across the hills. I said she ought to come back and paint them. She laughed, I recall, her voice light yet tinged with ache and sorrow. She hadn't, of course, painted in years. Couldn't paint anymore, she'd told me, not only because of the shakiness of her hands but simply because she had, as she put it, no more inclination.

She hadn't been back here in a long while. More than a year at that point. The last time was two summers ago. And then she hadn't actually come back voluntarily. I'd gotten a call from an ER up in Johnson City, Tennessee. Annabel hadn't been taking her lithium and she'd had a severe episode of mania; she was delusional, combative, and had to be tied down with restraints. The police had arrested her for shoplifting but had brought her to the hospital when they saw how crazy she was acting. By the time I arrived, they had her pretty well doped up and she was calm, her fury spent, a small, childlike figure curled in a fetal position in the bed. She looked a mess, bone-thin, her lips cracked, her cheeks sunken and hollow, her complexion ashen. She was dirty, hadn't bathed in days.

I agreed to pay for what she'd stolen, and the store manager dropped the charges. I put her in my truck and headed for home, as I had so many times before. She slept the entire way back to Slade, except for one moment, when she sat bolt upright, looked over at me, her eyes filled with a wild, scary gleam. "I talked to him the other night, Stu," she said. I didn't have to ask who she meant. Now and then she carried on conversations with our son, especially when she was ill. "Do you remember," she continued, "how he used to be afraid of wolves? How he used to crawl in bed with us?" I didn't say anything. What was the point? "Well, he told me he's not afraid anymore. He said he's all right now. That he doesn't have those bad dreams anymore." I nodded, kept driving. After a few minutes, when I looked over at her she was sound asleep again.

At home I put her in the tub and cleaned her up. She had bruises on her body, and her feet were blistered and bleeding, as if she had walked a great distance. I gave her some penicillin so the blisters wouldn't get infected and a shot of Seconal to sleep. I helped her get into a clean nightgown, and then, as she was so weak, I carried her upstairs and put her to bed. She slept for a day and a half, and ended up staying on for several weeks. During the day she would sit on the front porch sipping tea and staring at the mountains, vacant-eyed, an old quilt she'd made wrapped around her thin shoulders. In the evening she headed upstairs and into the spare bedroom, where she usually stayed when she came back. When I got up in the middle of the night, I'd see her light on, spilling out from under her door. When I made her food, she hardly touched it. When I asked how she was feeling, she would shrug and say fine. If I so much as hinted at the possibility of her going to see somebody, getting some help, she nearly bit my head off.

"I won't go back to that place," she hissed. "You hear me, Stu?"

"Just to see somebody. I know this new doc . . . "

"And have him ship me off to Cedar Crest? Like hell! I won't go there. I *won't*!"

"Someplace else then. Just to get checked out."

"I don't need *checking* out," she cried. "Why don't you say what you really mean? You just want me gone."

"That's not true. I'm just worried about you."

"Bullshit. You'd like nothing better than for them to haul my ass off to the loony bin. Like all those other times."

"Anna, that's not fair and you know it."

"If you don't want me here, why don't you at least have the guts to tell me straight out. Don't say you're doing it for my benefit."

I tried to reason with her, though when she was like this there was no reasoning with her. But that time I didn't have to do anything, didn't have to talk her into seeing anybody, have her committed voluntarily or, as a last resort, involuntarily. One day while I was at work she took off again on her own. She left a note on the kitchen table that said, "Thanks for letting me stay, Stu. Take care of yourself." She didn't leave any forwarding address. Just did her usual vanishing act. I'd long ago stopped trying to keep her here or search for her. I knew better. It was like holding back the wind or digging a hole in water. That was the last time I'd seen her.

• • •

I slipped the letter into my coat pocket and went out to Stella's desk, where she sat bouncing the baby on her knee.

"What you fixin' to do with her, Dr. Jordan?"

"I don't know. She didn't say she needed anything."

"No, not your wife. I meant this here little one."

"Oh. Just looking out for her for the time being."

"Her daddy was a Pugh? The one that was kilt?"

"Yes."

"Must be one of Ada's boys. Lordy, that woman's had nothing but calamity her whole life. One boy in prison and now another dead. And the rest of 'em no-counts and criminals. Ain't her, I blame. It's that husband of hers. Glenn W. was always a wild, mean-spirited sort. Even as a boy. Ada comes from good stock. She was a Buford. Her daddy was a preacher. How she ever got mixed up with them Pughs I'll never know." She glanced at me. "You look beat, Doc. Whyn't you lay down in the back room and get you some sleep? You got a couple of hours before you got to be at the hospital."

"I have some errands to run. Could you do me a big favor though? Would you mind watching her?"

"Would I mind!" she said, kissing the baby's head. "You don't watch it, I'll steal her for my ownself."

I headed down the hall and into the supply cabinet. I grabbed a sales rep sample of Enfamil and then hunted around for a breast pump. I returned and handed Stella the can of formula.

"For when she gets hungry," I said.

"I think I know how to do for a young'un. What's that for?" she asked, meaning the pump.

"Her mother might need it. I got to go over to the courthouse. Tell Gladys I'd like her to do a complete physical assessment on Maria. And she should go ahead and give her her shots. DPT, the works."

"Don't s'pose she's got *in*surance. Who should I bill it to?" she asked. A mother hen, Stella was always looking out for the office's financial interests.

"Don't worry about it. And could you take a ride over to the Bi-Lo and pick up some groceries for me? Baby food, anything else a baby might need. Use some of the petty cash. Also, stop at Shuster's and buy some winter clothes for her. Have them bill the office."

"How long you fixin' to keep her anyway?"

"Not long."

"Poor thing don't have a father nor a mother now. They's no kinfolk to look after her?"

"I guess not. Listen, I got to run. I'll be back after surgery."

"Don't forget, that Mrs. Tisdale called."

I waved as I headed out the door.

I got in my truck and headed over to the courthouse. As I drove along Mill Street, I happened to glance at the homeless people hanging out in the small park down near the river. During the tourist season the Slade police would roust them out of the park, but in the middle of the winter they let them congregate there or in front of the Christian Ministries food pantry on Center Street. Some were wrapped in sleeping bags against the cold, while others were picking through a dumpster. Like any place, we'd always had our town drunks. But they used to be people you could point to by name, knew a history of: Big Earl Tate, who took to the bottle after his wife died, or Crazy Bob, one of the Reece clan who lived over in Luther's Cove. Now, most of them were strangers from someplace else, drifters, and not just winos but drug addicts, many of them kids on the run and some of them infected with HIV. I thought how it wasn't so long ago that the local ministers would get up in the pulpit and preach that AIDS was the Lord's vengeance, something "big city faggots" deserved for disobeying His will. Then the drugs started coming into the county, first heroin, then crack, from Knoxville and Asheville and Atlanta, and junkies in Slade started contracting HIV, as did blacks from over in Hobbstown, Indians from the reservation, even poor mountain people. Yet it was only when it started hitting closer to home—the gay son of a prominent minister, the philandering husband of a school principal, even a blue-haired DAR member who sang in the choir and happened to be a hemophiliac—only then did people around here start to change their tune.

While waiting for the stoplight at the corner of Center and Mill, I saw a woman standing apart from the others in the park. She wore a dirty pea coat with the collar turned up, and from time to time she would look up Mill Street as if expecting someone. Her long, dark, greasy hair hung limply around her waxen face. She puffed on a cigarette and shuffled from foot to foot trying to stay warm. She could have been anywhere from twenty-five to fifty, had the bleached-out, wired demeanor of a druggie looking for her next fix. As I watched her, I thought, *Annabel*. Yes, it could have been. Except that my Annabel was shorter, frailer, and even from a distance I saw that this woman's eyes were different. Annabel was prettier, too. At least, had been. Still, seeing this woman made me recall suddenly all the times I'd searched parks just like this one, or bus stations, street corners, back alleys, bars, honky-tonks, from here to Charlotte.

As I had many times before, but especially these last few weeks, I thought about writing to Annabel. Telling her about Bobbie and me, as Bobbie had been urging me to and as I myself wanted to. But each time, something held me back. It seemed gutless to tell her in a letter, yet the idea of driving over to Asheville and telling her in person wasn't something I looked forward to. I told myself it would upset her. Maybe push her over the edge again. Which it very well might. So I put it off, promising myself I'd do it soon. When the right moment presented itself. The light turned green and I continued on, though I found myself watching the woman grow smaller in my rearview until she was just a dark speck.

As I turned up the courthouse road, I heard the Childress Funeral Hour being broadcast on the radio. "Today we mourn the passing of our brethren Roy Lee Pugh. We pray that Roy Lee is with our Heavenly Father . . . ."

# 7

"*Is Mrs. Tisdale in?*" I asked the secretary in the district attorney's office on the third floor of the courthouse. She must have been new; I'd never seen her before. She looked young, just out of high school. A pile of reddish-brown hair cut in a Farrah Fawcett shag, still fashionable in the hills, cascaded down over her bony, thin shoulders. She was pretty in the way of mountain girls: sharp, birdlike features, with deep-set eyes and a hard, pinched mouth that looked like a badly sutured wound. By the time she'd had her third child, her face would be caved in, all nose and chin.

"She's awful busy," she explained. "Y'all have an appointment?"

"I'm Stu Jordan, the medical examiner. She wanted to see me."

"Tha's different, I reckon." She got up from her desk and went down the hall, teetering awkwardly on high heels, like a little girl playing dress-up. When she came back she said, "Mizzus Tisdale says for you to g'won in."

Troy Bumgartner, the DA, happened to come out of his office then. He used a cane and moved gingerly, like someone afraid of breaking something.

"Myrna, sweetheart, could you run these down to the clerk of courts for me?" he said, handing the young secretary a large yellow envelope. She gave him a blank look. "Remember, that's downstairs."

"Oh, ry-ot," she said.

As she walked away, Troy's sleepy eyes casually followed her behind. He glanced at me; I'm sure he thought about winking, then decided I or the girl's behind wasn't worth the effort. Instead he said, "Why, Stuart, you ole sum'bitch," slapping me on the shoulder as he always did, as if we were good buddies, which we weren't and never had been. I was never quite sure whether he knew that and his show of camaraderie was intended as ironic, or if he actually considered me a friend. He had this perpetually phlegmatic expression, so that it was hard to get a read on what went on behind those sleepy eyes. A heavy man with small fleshy eyes, Troy had a mouth on him that always looked like it was chewing on bad news. He'd recently thrown out his back, which was the reason for the cane.

Obliged to play along, I asked, "How's the back, Troy?"

"I tell you, it's hell to get old. First the prostate and now this." He leaned close to me so I could catch his cigar smell and whispered, "They had me in a damn diaper for near onto six months. Picture that. Couldn't even perform my husbandly duties."

"Sorry to hear that. I'm sure things will work themselves out."

"Oh, I'm back in the saddle now," he said, feeling free now to offer me that wink, a leering man-to-man sort accompanied by a hearty laugh. "Better'n ever in that department—that's what the old lady says anyway. Can't keep her hands off me. Now it's this durn back of mine. Going under the knife pretty soon. That Neinhuis fellow's doing me. He any good?"

"Yeah, he's good."

"Oughta be. He a Jew, ain't he?"

"Dutch Lutheran, I believe. You know his work, Troy."

"With dead bodies. Which I don't plan on becoming. Anyways Neinhuis says I should be back on the links before summer. I'll have to take you out and whup your Yankee ass, Stu."

I'd known Troy Bumgartner for years. He and I were both "Blue Devil boys," as he was fond of saying (he went to Duke law while I attended med school there, though we didn't meet till I'd moved out here). That was about the only thing we had in common. He was a local boy, his father having been sheriff back in the good ole days when sheriffs could crack somebody up the side of the head, no questions asked. Troy's politics were a shade to the right of Jesse Helms's, and when it came to his professional ethics, he was about as meticulous as a pig at a trough. He was one of those small-town southern DAs who ran the office as if it were his own private fiefdom, who thought of the Bill of Rights and the Supreme Court and the Miranda decision as annoying Yankee impositions on Southern autonomy. If some hillbilly was caught with a joint in his car, Troy would look to send him away to the state pen in Raleigh for ten years. Or if some black kid from Hobbstown stole a pack of cigarettes, he'd throw the book at him. On the other hand, if one of his golfing cronies, who just happened to be on the zoning board, was caught taking a bribe from a land developer, Troy usually looked the other way or at worst gave him a slap on the wrist.

"Ugly business out in Tanavasee Lake last night, eh Stuart?"

"Yeah."

"I get your report yet?" he asked.

"I haven't exactly had a chance. It's coming."

"Hell's bells, so's Christmas," he said, as he always said, before realizing it *was* almost Christmas. "Shouldn't take you too long. I mean, she couldn't have made it easier for us. Superior Court meets next week. Just get it to Bobbie as soon as you can. I'd like everything in order for her before I go under the knife."

"I will."

"Have a merry Christmas, Doc," he said, turning and hobbling back into his office. Over his shoulder, he added, "Or maybe I'd better say X-mas on government property or someone from the damn ACLU'll have my ass in a sling."

I found Bobbie sitting at her desk, eating one of those brown high-energy bars.

"Hello, counselor," I said, shutting the door behind me.

"Hey, Doc," she greeted me, without looking up. She was busy reading something and marking sections with a pen. Her short, frosted blond hair fell to her green eyes. On the end of her nose she wore a pair of half-glasses, and something she was reading made her frown and screw up her mouth. "Sorry, but I'm kinda in a rush here. Supposed to be back in court in fifteen minutes."

"I could come back."

"No, that's all right. I can always spare a minute for my favorite gynecologist. Sit your butt down. What's up?"

"You called. I assume it was about the shooting?"

"Well, I wanted to talk to you about that, too."

"Will you be prosecuting Rosa Littlefoot?"

"Me or Troy. But he'll probably give it to me seeing as he's going in for his 'surgery.'" She hooked her red-fingernailed fingers into double quotes. "That's all I've been hearing about, his damn back. And before that his prostate. How he couldn't pee or . . . you know. Why do men think women got nothing better to do than hear all about their plumbing problems?"

"Pretty open and shut, I imagine."

"Huh?"

"The Pugh murder."

"Oh." Raising her eyebrows but still not looking up, she said, "Y'all went out with Cecil. You saw her handiwork."

"What about self-defense?" I asked.

"What about it?"

"Couldn't she say she was just protecting herself?"

"Are you kidding?" Bobbie replied, glancing up at me for the first time. "Lordy. You look like shit, Doc."

"I didn't get much sleep. Pugh beat the daylights out of her."

"This isn't Cambridge, Massachusetts. Heck, it's not even Durham. This is Old Testament, eye-for-an-eye country. You know that as well as I do. Most folks around here might buy her getting mad and splitting open his head with a baseball bat. Or if he was two-timing her, which from what I hear he was, they might even condone her cutting his doohicky off like that gal up in Virginia. But not what she did. Shoot, Doc, she executed the sucker."

"They were fighting. It got out of hand. She's just a scared kid."

"Kid, hell. She's twenty-nine."

"Twenty-nine?" I said, at once surprised and yet not surprised. Like I said, Indians had little regard for looking their age. Time was a white man's invention they didn't much concern themselves about.

"She's been around the block a time or two," Bobbie said. "I've looked over her file." She explained how Rosa Littlefoot had had a rough childhood, been shuttled from foster home to foster home growing up. Juvenile detention. One run-in with the law after another. A record as long as your arm. Drugs, prostitution, theft. Assault, too. She cut one of her johns with a knife and robbed him of several hundred dollars. "We're not talking about some sweet innocent Pocahontas type here."

"She looking at manslaughter?"

Bobbie shook her head, went back to reading.

"Second degree?" I asked.

"Bumgartner's talking murder one."

"What! It's a domestic. A nasty one, I'll grant you that. But no way it's first-degree murder."

"That's what he's saying anyway."

"Where's he get off going for first degree? Have you seen her face? And it's not the first time either."

"You know Troy, Doc. He doesn't like it when women get uppity. Besides, he thinks he's got a good shot at being appointed to the bench after the next gubernatorial election, and he doesn't want to look soft on crime. He still remembers the flack he took with the Blevins case."

Katie Blevins lived with her mother over in Pumpkintown Gap. Her mother was dying of cancer, and Katie, an RN at the hospital, a sweet, churchgoing woman, had helped her mother along with a cocktail of morphine and Valium. This was a few years ago, and Neinhuis, who was still fairly new at the time, made the mistake of requesting an autopsy. That's when the shit hit the fan. They discovered the unusually high level of morphine in the bloodstream. Some of the big-city papers in Charlotte and Raleigh picked up the story and made it a cause celebre for mercy killing. The fundamentalists took up the issue. Reverend L. B. Stevens and that bunch made a big stink. According to them, only God and the State of North Carolina had the right to terminate a life. For once, that weasel Bumgartner did the decent thing and decided not to prosecute Katie. But he caught holy hell from the Christian right for going easy on her, and he almost didn't win the next election as district attorney. So he was still licking his wounds and trying to play local politics to his advantage.

Bobbie looked up at me again. "In defense of Troy, though, there are some things that just don't fit a simple domestic."

"Such as?"

"Such as she wasn't too scared to wipe the gun clean."

"It was clean?"

"Mostly. Cecil said they were able to lift a partial thumbprint from the barrel. Which just so happens to match Littlefoot's."

"I still don't see how you get premeditation from that. In the heat of the moment she thought about covering her tracks. So what? Anyone might have done the same thing in her shoes."

"There's more. This morning when the sheriff's deputies were down there investigating the crime scene, the dog led them to one of the junk cars out in back of the trailer. In the trunk, they found a suitcase packed with clothes—a woman's and an infant's."

So that's why the bureau drawers were mostly empty, I thought.

"What's that prove?" I said. "She probably panicked, threw some things together, and thought about taking off. That fits with her wiping the gun clean."

"But it doesn't make sense, Doc. Just think about it. If she did it *after* she shot him, why hide the suitcase? I could see her packing some things and jumping in the truck and taking off. But why hide the suitcase when he was already dead? Who was she hiding it from? That doesn't make a lick of sense."

"All right. So she wasn't thinking rationally."

"In the suitcase, they also came across several hundred dollars in cash. She was rational enough to think she'd need something to get by on. And rational enough to wipe the gun clean." I was about to interject, but she held up her hand like a cop directing traffic. "Wait. Here's the kicker. They also found some bags of heroin with a street value of a couple of grand."

"*Humph*," I said.

"*Humph* is right."

"So how are you figuring it?"

"Hard to say right now. One thing looks pretty clear: This wasn't a spur-of-the-moment kind of thing. Littlefoot had her escape all planned out. If I had to guess, I'd say she'd stolen the smack and the money, and Pugh found out. They could have fought. He beat her up and she went for the gun."

"You could still look at it as self-defense."

"If you're of a charitable disposition. Or as a fight over drugs."

"But why did she call the police then? I mean if she had this all planned out like you're suggesting, why didn't she take the money, get in his truck, and make a run for it?"

"Who knows, Doc? People have a change of heart after doing something like that. Maybe she realized she wouldn't get very far with a baby in tow. I tell you one thing for sure. It's not just some abused wife who was fed up and after a little payback. And on top of everything, she shot the poor bastard twice. If it were just self-defense, the first shot to the belly was enough to incapacitate him, wouldn't you say?"

"More than enough."

"We'll give her that one. Cecil said you thought the first shot and the one that finished him were spaced a little ways apart."

"I believe they were, yes. Based on how much he bled from the belly wound."

"There you go then. She had some time to reflect on her actions. Before she executed him in cold blood. That's premeditation."

"He probably would've died from the first blast."

"We don't know that for sure, Doc. And neither did she. I'm not saying Pugh was any sweetheart. He'd been in and out of jail himself. The usual—trafficking, assault with a deadly weapon. He put some guy over in Carson City in the hospital with a fractured skull. Hit him with a hammer, which seems to be the Pughs' weapon of choice. Maybe he did deserve killing. Hell, if he'd been doing to me what he did to Rosa, I'd probably have tattooed him with some buckshot myself. I'll give her the first shot. It's the second one I have a hard time swallowing. Besides, the drugs complicate things. Troy's looking at it as a homicide involving drugs, which means capital murder. Anyhow, what's the big interest in her case?"

"I'm just trying to figure it out. Do *you* think she deserves a first-degree murder charge?"

"My own opinion—probably not. But what I think doesn't count for squat around here, and you know that as well as I do. Bumgartner says first degree, then it's first degree. Any way you cut it, though, she's looking at a long stretch over in Raleigh."

"Has she confessed to anything?"

"Hunneycutt's advised her not to say diddly."

"Hunneycutt's representing her?" I asked.

"Yeah," she said, shaking her head.

"Too bad." Lewis Hunneycutt was an attorney in town who took on indigent clients, people nobody else wanted: blacks, Indians, gays, poor mountain people. He was as hard-working, honest, and dedicated a lawyer as you could find. The only problem was he wasn't a particularly good lawyer. He'd gotten his law degree from some "floating" university, and, as Bumgartner put it, didn't know a tort from his tush. You'd see his name in the paper representing tribal rights against the government or suing some big company on behalf of a worker who'd lost an arm through faulty safety procedures. Though he put up valiant fights, his clients invariably lost.

Bobbie said, "What's this I hear about you looking after her baby?"

"Oh. Yeah. Cecil couldn't find a placement. He was in a bind, so I agreed to watch her till social services could come up with something."

"Where's the child now?"

"In my office. Stella's looking after her."

"Littlefoot doesn't have any family?"

"At least none she can turn to. And she didn't want to place the baby with his side of the family."

"Ah, the infamous Pughs," Bobbie said, rolling her green eyes. "Can't say's I blame her none."

"You've had dealings with them?"

"Enough." She recited a brief history of her experience with the Pughs: She'd prosecuted Vern Pugh, a cousin, for raping a twelve-year-old retarded girl from down in Glenwood Springs; then there was Ike Pugh, who was tried for assault and battery with a deadly weapon when he blew off some fellow's kneecap because the guy had "made eyes" at his woman; and of course Glenn Junior, who, before he was sent up for that murder over in Tennessee, had been locked up for various and sundry offenses. Not to mention assorted assaults and disturbances of the peace and trafficking charges involving other members of the family. And especially the head of the clan, Glenn W. Pugh, who had a long record of arrests and convictions. "They're cowboys, those Pughs," Bobbie said. "Hillbilly mafia, some folks call 'em."

"Could they sue for custody of the child?"

"If they wanted to they could petition the court for a custody hearing. They are blood, and that counts for a lot around here. Given their history, though, most judges wouldn't be exactly eager to hand the child over to them. But first off, there's the ICWA to consider."

"What's that?"

"The Indian Child Welfare Act. It's a federal law that stipulates that preferential consideration be given to Indians in the placement of Indian children. Unless circumstances preclude that."

"What sort of circumstances?"

"The parents' wishes for one."

"You mean if the mother wanted the baby placed with someone, the court would honor that?"

"They'd take that into consideration. That is, if the placement seemed in the best interest of the child, and the Cherokee council approved it. If custody were contested, though, they might order social services to do a preplacement investigation first. There might be a hearing. A trial even. It could get quite involved. Why? Did the mother name anybody she wanted the child to stay with?"

"Yeah. Me."

"*You?*" she said, leaning back in her chair and laughing that snorting laugh of hers. She had this habit of wrinkling her nose, rolling her green eyes way back in their sockets so all you saw were the whites, and letting out with this boisterous, snorting guffaw that welled up from her belly. "Good Lord. Why you, Doc?"

"I guess I have a trusting face," I said, adding my own laugh.

"You don't know her, do you?"

"Never saw her before in my life."

"And you agreed?"

"Didn't have much choice." I explained about the knife and our concern she might do something crazy. How Cecil thought it was the only thing to do at the time. I didn't say anything about Rosa Littlefoot making me swear on my son's grave.

"Look, Doc, it was a really sweet gesture and all, but as soon as they come up with a placement, it's not your worry anymore."

"I know. But . . . "

"But what?"

"I sort of promised I'd look after her kid."

"Promised?" she asked.

"For a little while."

"You and your damn promises. When are you gonna learn, Doc?" Bobbie said, shooting me a look full of meaning. "You know what she is? I'll tell you what she is. She's a sneaky little bitch who's just taking advantage of you. Playing you for a sucker. You don't have to keep a promise under those conditions. Anyways, you don't want to get mixed up with that Pugh bunch. Just stay clear of them."

I thought of telling her about the visit Tully Pugh had paid me that morning. But I knew if I did, it would only support the logic of her advice. Which I knew was sound and which I also knew I was probably going to disregard.

"Mind if I see the mother?"

"What for?"

"She had a cut over her eye. I'd like to take a look at it."

"All right. Just don't talk about her case."

When I stood as if to leave, Bobbie got up and came around her desk. As always, she looked nice. Her hair was done just so and her makeup, though extensive, had a certain casual ease to it, not so much something tacked on but a natural extension of herself. She wore a dark suit, which flattered her runner's figure, high heels, a dark shimmery blouse open at the neck, a gold necklace. A tall woman with broad shoulders, Bobbie moved with the toe-out, jaunty stride of an athlete. She could hit a golf ball about two hundred yards, straight down the fairway. As she approached, I got a whiff of her perfume, White Shoulders. Its aroma made me aware of a certain looseness in the region of my knees, the way a whiff of booze would turn a drunk's legs to rubber. As Cecil had said that morning, Roberta Tisdale was a very attractive woman, not to mention nearly eighteen years my junior. Sometimes when I saw her in public, walking down Main, say, or standing in front of me at the Bi-Lo checkout, I had to convince myself that this very desirable, very *married* woman and I were lovers. Bobbie came up to me, put her arms around my waist, pulled me forcibly to her, and kissed me hard on the mouth.

Surprised, I said, "We throwing caution to the wind here, counselor?"

"Relax, you old fuddy-duddy. Who's going to see us?"

I considered telling her about Cecil's comment that morning, that some may already know about us. But I didn't feel like spoiling the moment, one of the few good ones I'd had in the past twelve hours.

"I missed you, Doc," she said, her breath smelling sweet from the candy. This close, I could see how the light khaki green at the edge of her eyes shaded to a deep avocado at the center, like a whirlpool getting darker at its vortex. Her left eye had a faint yellowish arc in the iris, shaped like a quarter moon. "What's it been, two weeks?"

"Twelve days," I replied, kissing her back. "But who's counting?" Then I kissed her hands, first one, then the other. I loved her hands, could have, if time permitted, lingered on them slavishly. After that, I buried my face in the sweetness of her neck, gave her several hungry, marauding kisses down her throat to the delicate swelling of the sternal angle at the top of her breastbone. I paused there a moment, my lips picking up a rumbling deep in her chest. Beneath the White Shoulders I could detect Ivory soap, and beneath that just the familiar scent that was Bobbie. Her hips began moving against mine, and I felt myself responding. It was crazy, crazy and dangerous, doing that right there in her office. What if Troy walked in on us, which he was liable to do? He didn't know about things like knocking. Besides, here I was with a mess of obligations and duties and headaches stretching dully out in front of me like a blistering Kansas highway in August. What I was tempted to do, however, was give in to it, take her right there, on her desk if need be. *Geronimo*, I felt like yelling. That's what Bobbie said I should do more often—yell Geronimo and just jump in, give myself over to the moment. Not think about things so much, which I have a bad tendency to do. She was capable of making me feel and behave like a brainless teenager whose hormones dictated his every action. But just then there came a knock on the door.

"Mizzus Tisdale," called her secretary, "oughtn't you to be getting on back to court now?"

"I'm coming, Myrna," Bobbie said as we separated. She hurriedly grabbed her briefcase from a chair and shoved her notes into it. Then she reviewed herself in the full-length mirror on the back of her office door. "The other reason I called. I have some good news. Well, it's not really good. In fact, it's bad news. Paul's mother has had another stroke. A pretty severe one this time. They don't know whether she'll pull through or not. I feel bad because she's a nice lady. I always liked her, though I can't say the same for her son. So the long and short of it, he's going down to Gainesville for a couple of weeks to be with her and his family. And I'm going to meet him down there next week after Rosa Littlefoot's arraignment."

"That's the good news?"

"I'll be gone for a few days. But I told him I had too much work here, especially now with the Littlefoot case, and that I'd have to come back early. So that's partly why I called. I was wondering if you had any plans for New Year's."

"Last I looked I was pretty free," I said with a smile.

"I could come over. Stay the night if you'd like."

"Do you think that's a good idea?" Not counting one brief encounter late one night in her Volvo out in the courthouse parking lot, we were always discreet, went someplace safe, where no one knew us. We never went to my house, fearing that in a small nosy place like Hubbard County someone might see her car. So we always left town, usually heading over to the Skyline Motel in Crawford City, where you could rent a room by the hour.

"Geez Louise, Doc, none of this is a good idea," she said. "But if you'd rather not."

"No, no. It's just . . . please, I'd love you to come."

"Then it's settled." She kissed me again lightly on the cheek, then said, "I'll call you when I get back. By the way, remember what we talked about last time?"

"How could I forget?"

"Well, have you said anything to her yet?"

I thought of Annabel's letter, resting at that moment in my coat pocket. Only moments before, it had been crushed between us in our embrace.

"No, not yet."

"You said you would."

"And I will. I will. I just wonder if you've thought it through. You have a lot more to lose than I do."

"Don't worry, I've thought it through. I'm going to tell Paul as soon as things with his mother are . . . well, settled. The question is, when are you going to tell your wife?"

"Actually, I'm going to try to see her tonight." The fact was I found myself making that decision on the spot, as it were.

"And you'll tell her about us?"

I nodded.

"Doc, it's the right thing to do. For you. For us. For her, even. She deserves to know, too."

"You're right. I'll tell her."

She stared at me for a moment, searching my face to see if I was telling the truth. Then she led me to the door. As we passed her secretary, who was busy typing, she said, "Dr. Jordan, I'd appreciate a copy of your ME's report as soon as possible."

"Of course, counselor," I replied, both of us assuming the postures we took with each other in public. If I passed her on the street, I would nod and say, "Good morning, Mrs. Tisdale," and she would reply, "Isn't it a lovely day, Dr. Jordan?"

Before I left, though, and with Myrna right there but not looking, Bobbie affectionately patted my tush and winked me out the door.

# 8

*Roberta Tisdale and* her husband had moved to town a few years before from Winston-Salem. An assistant prosecutor in the city, she took a position in the Hubbard County DA's office. Since I was sometimes called on to testify in murder cases, I'd had the chance to work with her a few times. I liked her right off. She was friendly and easygoing, had a good sense of humor, which you needed not only for working homicide but for putting up with Troy Bumgartner. At the same time she was a bright and able prosecutor, tough but fair, confident without being cocky. While hardly a novice, she was still idealistic enough to think of herself as a public servant whose business was to ensure that justice—and not simply her own career—was served. Unlike Troy, for whom the job was just a step toward a cushy judgeship he'd had his eyes on for years. Though I did have to agree with Troy on one thing. Shortly after he'd hired her, I'd asked him how the new assistant DA was working out. "She's one of them independent-type gals," he complained. Then, leaning toward me he said confidentially, "But she sure ain't hard on the eyes, I'll give her that much, Stuart."

One evening Roberta Tisdale and I were working late in her office, preparing for a trial. It was an ugly case. A six-year-old girl had died of a skull fracture. I'd been the ME on the case, and the stepfather's story about how she'd "fallen" out of the bed of his pickup truck didn't sound right. The injuries weren't consistent with a fall, and besides, the autopsy determined the child was being sexually abused. After some questioning, the mother finally broke down and gave up her husband, and he was indicted for murder. As Bobbie went over my ME's report, I caught myself staring at her hands. She had lovely hands, long-fingered, strong, capable-looking, the nails plain, cut short in a no-nonsense way; at the same time her hands were feminine, supple and smooth. The sort you wanted to take hold of and, for no reason you could explain, put to your lips and kiss. I'd noticed how she was always touching people with those hands: rubbing the back of the dead child's mother, alighting on someone's wrist while laughing that peculiar laugh of hers. Some men are leg men or ass men or breast men. While I like those parts well enough, I guess being in my position, where a woman's body can be considered more work than pleasure, I've come to appreciate the more subtle offerings of a woman. Her earlobes. Smile. Hands.

After we'd finished our work, I was gathering up my notes.

"I don't know about you, Dr. Jordan," she said, "but I could eat a horse. You want to grab something?" I hesitated for a moment, thinking about some work I had back at the office. "I hate to eat alone," she added.

Finally I said, "Sure, why not?"

We went to Pancho Villa's, a new Mexican restaurant in the plaza over near the hospital. I sometimes ate there after work rather than going home and throwing something together. After a difficult delivery, I might stop in the bar for a drink—or two or three—and catch a ball game. Hector, the Cuban bartender, was, like myself, an outsider, as well as a big sports fan, and we'd watch the Braves on the cable station. He liked the Oakland A's because they had Jose Canseco, a fellow Cuban.

Bobbie and I sat in the dining room. She ordered a margarita, while I got a Scotch on the rocks. Each table had a small cactus wearing a tiny sombrero and buttons for eyes, like one of those old Mr. Potato Head figures.

"These sorts of cases suck," Bobbie said, taking a sip of her drink. She had an indeterminate Southern accent. Not the tinny, nasal twang of the mountains nor the broad, lilting vowels of the deep South. An accent that suggested she'd been around, especially during her formative years. She also had a mouth on her that sometimes raised eyebrows in this staid little town. "A murdered child. An accused family member who was sexually abusing her. It's all fucked up."

"Not exactly my cup of tea either," I said, noticing how she folded and unfolded her cocktail napkin.

"I wouldn't think so. Being in your line and all. Tell me, Doc—mind if I call you Doc?"

"Not at all. Most people do."

"How does an obstetrician wind up dealing with dead folks?"

"Good question. It wasn't something I planned on," I said. "I was filling in for a colleague and he up and died on me, leaving me holding the bag."

"How inconsiderate of him. I hope he was your first customer," she replied, laughing. She had a ready laugh and that peculiar habit of rolling her pretty green eyes way back in their sockets, her lids fluttering rapidly as if she were going into some sort of seizure, while at the same time snorting loudly. It was the most unfeminine laugh I'd ever heard on a woman. Somehow, though, when Bobbie did it, it seemed perfectly natural, even charming. "But you stayed on?"

"Yes. Been doing it thirteen years. I guess some part of me finds it interesting."

"I can imagine it does have its moments. May I ask a personal question?"

"Sure."

"What sort of man goes into, well, you know . . . gynecology?" she asked with a serious expression. She held that look for a moment, then her eyes turned suddenly playful and she laughed. "Just pulling your leg, Doc," she added, reaching across the table and tapping my hand. "But why a doctor?"

"My father was a doctor. I never really pictured doing anything else."

"Was he proud that you followed in his footsteps?"

"He never lived to see it. He died when I was a kid. He was only fifty-four."

"That's young."

"He had Parkinson's. But that's not what killed him. When the disease got bad he drove our Buick into the garage and shut the door. My mother found him. The whole town turned out for his funeral. People loved him."

She paused, then asked, "And you?"

"I'm not sure. I guess I did. What I knew of him. You see, he wasn't there a lot for us when we were growing up. His family took a backseat to his patients."

"Doesn't every doctor's family suffer the same fate?"

"I suppose." I stared at her hands, at her wedding band. "Does your husband mind eating home alone, Mrs. Tisdale?"

"Please, call me Bobbie. Paul's not home. He works for the paper company and has to travel a lot for his job. So I don't bother with cooking when he's gone. The plain truth is, I'm not much of a cook even when he *is* home." She did that thing with her eyes and snorted again.

"I thought all Southern women could cook. That it was something in the genes."

"Just one of those pernicious stereotypes of Dixie womanhood, I'm afraid," she said, running a finger around the rim of her glass and then sucking on the salt. "I was more of a tomboy, an only-child army brat. My mother left us when I was young, and my daddy raised me. We moved around a lot, me and him. I never quite fit in. I wasn't one of those chirpy cheerleader types whose ambition was to snag a man, get myself pregnant, and spend my days contentedly cutting out recipes. In school I was pretty much a jock. I played a lot of sports, tennis and field hockey. Some of those little pom-pom types used to call me a lesbian 'cause I didn't date much and never wore lipstick back then."

"A lesbian?"

She nodded, smiling ruefully. "Tell me, Doc, do I look like one to you?"

"Why, no," I said.

Our meal came then. Bobbie had gotten the burrito grande, and she dug in and ate with gusto. Most of the women I knew in Slade took little birdlike pecks at their food, especially in front of men, as if an appetite were an outward sign of some inner moral decadence.

"I just was never into all that girly-girl stuff. My daddy used to take me to the firing range on the base," she continued. "I qualified as a marksman with the old M-1 carbine when I was twelve. When he went off to fight in Vietnam, I stayed with my Aunt Vera, down in Mobile. Now *there* was a real Southern belle." Bobbie fluttered her eyes and laughed. "Good Lord. She used to have these afternoon teas for her DAR lady friends. She wondered to what conceivable use a girl could put a knowledge of firearms. She taught me, or tried to anyhow, the finer points of domesticity: how to make black-eyed peas and corn pone and chicken-fried steak, how to sew and cross-stitch and darn, how to make"—here Bobby's voice slipped sarcastically into a deep South drawl— "a *ma-yan* happah. The whole nine yards. Told me if I was fixin' to catch myself a ma-yan I'd bess learn right quick how to fill up his stomach with vittles. 'Otherwise, Roberta Lynn, y'all are gonna end up an old spinster, I do declare.' Unfortunately I wasn't a very apt pupil. Was never very into the home arts."

"Yet you didn't end up an old maid."

"Let's just say Paul didn't marry me for my Betty Crocker skills."

"What *did* he marry you for?" I asked.

She stared across the table at me and, with a straight face, replied, "He always said I gave him the best blow job he ever had."

I almost choked on my enchilada, which goes to show how old-fashioned I was in some ways. Here I could look up women's crotches all day long, but blushed like a schoolboy when one said she was skilled at fellatio. She paused for a moment, then burst out with that guffaw again, laying a hand on my wrist. It was, I'd later learn, the sort of thing Bobbie liked doing. She would shock you with an offhand comment, nonplus you with some bold act, like the kiss in her office. I felt my face redden.

"Why, I do declare," she said, laying on the drawl again. "I think I've embarrassed the straitlaced Dr. Jordan."

"I'm just not used to women around here being so . . . "

"Blunt? Well, you asked for it."

"I suppose I did." Changing the subject, I inquired, "You have any children?"

"Nada. I was always too busy with my career. Some career! An assistant DA out in the boondocks. It's not that I don't like kids. I guess they just weren't in the cards." Then she added, "Besides, Paul's enough of kid. But don't get me started on that subject."

Over dinner that first time, she didn't talk about her marriage, which I later found out was far from a happy one. Instead, she spoke about her childhood. About a father she obviously loved, but who was gone a lot and distant when he was home, a stern soldier not quite up to the task of raising a daughter by himself. About having to avoid sinking down deep roots because she knew wherever her father was stationed, she wouldn't be staying long. About having to become self-reliant since she spent much of her childhood alone. She said she'd gotten very good at being alone.

"It's a real talent. Knowing how to get along by yourself is a lot more useful than knowing how to cook. Wouldn't you agree, Doc?"

"Actually, it seems like it would come in handy. You always get to eat, right?"

"I was talking more about being a kid all alone. Why, do you like to cook?"

"Used to. I don't do much anymore."

"I'd imagine knowing your way around a kitchen would be a plus for a man in your shoes."

"My shoes?"

"I mean, someone who's single. A bachelor and all."

I hesitated to correct her, finding myself in that awkward position I sometimes did with people who were new to town or didn't know me. The problem was my marital status didn't fit readily into one of those nice neat, taxable categories: single, married, divorced, widowed. I wasn't any of these. Many times, I wasn't even sure myself what I was. I could pretend that I'd never married, that I was some crusty, small-town bachelor set in his ways, which had more than an element of truth to it. Or I could simply say I had been married once and leave it for others to draw whatever conclusions they were of a mind to. I'd made the mistake of doing that with a woman I'd been seeing several years back.

Madeline was a pediatric resident I'd met at the hospital. I hadn't dated much during the time Annabel and I had been what I came to think of simply as "apart." Oh, there was the occasional "nice widow lady" Stella had fixed me up with or a dinner I'd have with a nurse from the hospital. But I didn't really consider them dates. More just casual get-togethers. And besides, after getting together once or twice, we'd both quickly realize it had been a terrible mistake. One woman, I recall, as I dropped her off after an evening spent mostly talking about Annabel, told me, "You look me up soon's you got her outa your system." Or if things did progress further, as had happened once or twice, I'd get a call from Annabel and I'd have to drop everything and go and bring her home; there's nothing like a spouse reentering the picture to put a damper on a relationship.

Madeline was the first woman I'd gone out with in any serious way. When she and I started seeing each other and the subject of my "status" came up, I simply said I'd been married once and left it at that. I figured I'd tell her the rest at some convenient point, if and when the need arose. Madeline was a very proper Southern woman. She went to church. She never swore or drank hard liquor. I don't think *blow job* was in her vocabulary. We'd been seeing each other for a few months. We enjoyed each other's company. She was pretty, intelligent, well educated. We both liked listening to blues, and of course we shared professional interests. It wasn't a grand passion certainly, but we were friends, and given the right conditions, things might have gone beyond friendship. I even sent a letter to Annabel, explaining how I was seeing someone. I sent it to the last address I had of hers. I hadn't heard from her in months. I didn't hear back from her after sending the letter either; in some ways I didn't expect to. Then one night Madeline and I were at my place. She was the first woman I'd had out to the house. I'd made dinner for her. We were just sitting down to eat when, out of the blue, Annabel showed up. There she stood at the door, a battered suitcase in one hand, looking lost and pathetic as always, like a refugee child who'd just wandered through some war-torn country. Her hands trembling, her eyes red-rimmed and wild looking.

"I catch you at a bad time, Stu?" she said.

"Didn't you get my letter?" I replied.

"Letter?" she said. I couldn't say if she was telling the truth or not, though I suspected she wasn't. I had the feeling she'd come back exactly *because* of the letter. There was an awkward scene as I tried to explain to Madeline who this strange-looking woman was. The next day Madeline came storming up to me in the doctor's lounge at the hospital. "That was your *wife*?" she cried.

"I can explain," I pleaded.

"Explain? You *lied* to me, you bastard!" she said, slapping me in the face. (I'd never been slapped by a woman before—or since; I wasn't the sort of man to evoke that kind of passion in women.) Once more I tried to explain that I hadn't, technically speaking, lied. But she wasn't in any mood to listen to semantics. She broke things off between us, and a month later she took a job down in Atlanta.

With either version of my story, an outright lie or the partial truth, I felt I resembled in certain respects that stodgy character in *Jane Eyre*, Edward Rochester, a man with a secret wife he kept hidden from public view. On the other hand, I could do what I sometimes did—tell the whole truth. All of it. Which would mean a long, convoluted story, one people usually got tired of well before I reached the end, which wasn't really an end at all, but simply a convenient place to pause and allow my listener to politely squirm out of hearing the rest.

For some reason I offered to this Bobbie Tisdale the latter. "Well, actually I was married. *Am*, I should say. At least legally."

"You're *married*? But I thought . . . "

"That's what a lot of people think."

"Where's your wife?"

"Last I heard she was living in Asheville."

"Last you heard? You mean you don't know?"

"We're sort of . . . separated. She doesn't stay in one place very long."

"How long have you been separated, if you don't mind my asking?"

"We've been apart for nine, ten years. Mostly apart."

"Mostly?"

"She comes back every so often."

"Ten years. That's what I call a long separation," she said, her gaze falling into her drink. I was perfectly ready to drop the subject entirely, let her off the hook. I pictured her suddenly glancing at her watch and saying, "Would you look at the time!" Yet when she finally looked up at me, she said, "I have a confession. I knew about your wife."

"You *did*?"

She nodded, offering up a guilty smile. "Troy told me. I was just being coy, pretending I didn't know. Forgive me."

"Oh, don't worry about it. But what did Troy tell you?" I asked.

Now I was the one being coy, pretending I didn't already know what people in town whispered about my wife behind my back. *Annabel Lee Jordan sure went off the deep end after their boy died.* Or, *She was always a strange duck, that gal, long before the business with their son.* Or, *Ask me, I think it was that daddy a hers, the way he brung her up.* Those were the sorts of things they whispered to each other, the bits and pieces I picked up, overheard when people didn't know I was around. Like that big-mouth Raylene Huggart over at the Pancake Barn, confiding to a customer within earshot of me once: *Why, I heard tell the po-lice picked her up sleeping down yonder under the bridge. Can you b'lieve that? And her being married to a doctor and got that big fancy house up on the mountain.* Or another time, while standing in the checkout line at the Bi-Lo, I overheard the woman in front of me say to another: *Never guess who I saw over in Asheville. That Annabel Lee Jordan. Goodness gracious. Hardly recognized her. She was looking terrible.* Her voice drifted off when the other woman noticed me standing there and gave her a nudge. Another time, a woman in my office was talking to Stella and I heard her ask: *How come he never divorced her, young feller like that?* But to my face, of course, they were too polite, too decorously Southern to bring it up. With me they maintained a courteous masquerade when it came to the indelicate subject of my wife. Bobbie, however, wasn't one to mince words, or hide behind Southern civility. Besides, she was an outsider, without prejudices one way or the other.

"He said she had a nervous breakdown after your son . . . after his death, I mean. That's what he said anyway."

"It's a little more complicated than that."

"You don't have to talk about if you don't want."

"It's not that. It's just . . . well, it's hard to explain."

"Forget I asked. Sometimes I can be a royal pain in the ass. I take my prosecutor's role a little too much to heart."

She pursed her lips and frowned. The skin at the corners of her eyes crinkled, turned fragile as tissue paper. It made her look older, a woman closing in on forty, and sadder, too, another person whom happiness had managed to elude. At the same time it turned her all the more lovely, the way sadness and affliction and unfulfilled longing can. Suffering has a way of making certain women look hard and fearful, their eyes filled with cynicism and regret, their mouths held in a certain desperate way; for others, however, heartache has the opposite effect. The lines and wrinkles and experience leave them even more beautiful, their beauty refined and distilled, like a well-aged bottle of Scotch.

"I just don't want to bore you with my life's story," I said.

"No, I'd like to hear it. Really. That is, if you feel like telling me."

I hadn't told anyone in a long time. Had no need to, you see. People from town already knew the story about my wife and son, and those who had just moved in found out through the grapevine. Of course, now and then some new resident or nurse at the hospital would innocently ask about my wife, and I'd tell them some abridged and sanitized version. Or a friend who knew all about it, someone like Cecil Clegg or Stella Plumtree, would ask me how "things" were going, especially in those first few years after Will's death. And I'd say "things" were going fine and leave it at that. I'm basically a private person. My problems are my own. It's that Yankee in me, I suppose. But one of the benefits of living in a small nosy town is that people already know your business and so don't have to ask you directly. Most knew all about my "situation," and what they didn't know they were quite willing to make up on their own. As the years went by, my personal life gradually ceased to be a topic of more than passing interest to most folks, which is how I preferred it.

Yet I found myself telling the story of my son's death, as well as the aftermath of it, to this woman I hardly knew, a woman whose job it often was to extract the truth from people unwilling to give it up. Perhaps that was part of it—she was used to getting what she was after, ferreting out the whole story. Perhaps, too, it had something to do with the booze lubricating my tongue. But mostly I think it was the simple fact that I wanted to tell her, *needed* in some way to tell her, to tell someone. And this Bobbie Tisdale proved to be a good listener: patient, interested without seeming to pry, occasionally nodding sympathetically or reaching out and touching my wrist lightly with those lovely hands of hers. She had the sort of face that invited you to bare your soul, eyes you wanted to jump headfirst into, like into a cool mountain creek on a blistering day.

And so I told her. All of it. Leaving nothing out.

# 9

*The day we* lost Will was a warm, clear autumn day, the last of Indian summer. The sun had burnt off the lingering mists, leaving the skies high and sharp and burnished, a fine cerulean blue, the mountains ablaze with color. It was a Saturday, and we'd made plans to drive up along the Blue Ridge Parkway for a picnic, something we liked to do when I could get away. Wanting to take advantage of the beautiful day, Annabel had packed her art supplies: her brushes and paints and canvases. She would set up her easel on a scenic overlook and spend a couple of hours painting. While she worked, Will and I would go off by ourselves, exploring the woods. He loved picking out a stick and pretending it was a sword and he a warrior, slaying imaginary dragons and monsters as we went. He was still light enough for me to carry on my shoulders when he got tired. We were already out the front door when my beeper, which I should've left behind but hadn't, went off. Old Doc Coombs, a GP who was covering for me, was with a patient of mine who was having a difficult labor. It was a partial breech, and he wanted to know if I could come in and just take a quick look. It was my weekend off. I didn't have to go. And it wasn't that Doc Coombs hadn't delivered his share of babies. But he was in his seventies and set in his ways, and I, in those days at least, tended to look down my professional nose at small-town GPs. Like a lot of doctors, I was overly possessive about my patients. I felt no one could give them the care and attention I could. A form of vanity, one that used to annoy Annabel.

"They don't need you every single damn second, Stu," Anna scolded me. We were standing on the front porch. Will was waiting in the car, watching us argue.

"I know. It's just . . . "

"Doc Coombs has been delivering babies since before you were born."

"What if he needs a hand?"

"What if *we* need a hand? For Christ's sake, Stu."

"Don't be mad."

"That's just great. We made plans. This was supposed to be *our* time together."

"I know."

"Forget about me. What about him?" she said, glancing out toward the car. Will made an impatient wave of his hand. "He's counting on you going."

"Tell you what. How about if you take the car and go on ahead, and I'll meet you up there later with the truck?"

She shook her head.

"This always happens. What about *us*?"

"I'm sorry. I'll come as soon as I can. I promise. How about if we drive over to Asheville afterward and have dinner? The three of us."

She wagged her head, but finally relented. We agreed that I'd meet her up at Black Mountain, a spot we'd been to a few times before.

The labor proved to be longer and more difficult than Doc Coombs had let on. I didn't get out of the birthing room until late in the afternoon, and by then I figured I might as well just head home, get washed up, and try to make it up to them with dinner in Asheville. I thought Anna would already have realized I wasn't coming and returned home, but when I got there the house was empty. I was getting dressed when the phone rang. I thought it might be Annabel calling but instead it was Cecil Clegg.

"Something's happened, Doc," he said. "It's Will." He explained that he'd had a call from the Haywood County sheriff's office saying that Will was missing, that he'd gotten lost up in the mountains and they were searching for him.

"Lost?" I said.

"In the woods."

"How?"

"I don't rightly know. Evidently, the boy wandered off."

"Where was . . . I mean, where's Annabel?"

"She's fine. She's up there still. They got some folks looking for him. Probably find him by the time we get up there."

I met Cecil in town and we drove up to Black Mountain in his cruiser. When we arrived, they still hadn't found him, and it was getting on toward twilight. They already had a bunch of people scouring the woods. There were police cars and first-aid vehicles and search-and-rescue volunteers in a small clearing just off the parkway. When I saw them, the coordinated seriousness of their presence, something in my gut turned like a jagged piece of metal. Annabel got out of one of the police cars when we showed up. She was barely managing to hold it together. Her face was pale and she'd been crying.

"Where were you, Stu?" she asked. "We waited and waited."

"I got hung up. What happened?"

"I don't know."

"Where did he go?"

"I told you, I don't know," she snapped. "I was over there," she said, pointing at her easel. It sat facing out over a broad vista of valley and darkening mountains. "I was painting and well . . . ," she tried to explain, but her voice broke and she began to sob. "He was *right* here one minute and then . . . I don't know. He just . . . wandered off."

Annabel had a scared, childlike look of desperation in her eyes, a look that asked nothing more than forgiveness, a simple reassurance that things would turn out all right, that Will would be returned to us safe and unharmed, that her negligence was a small thing that would have no large consequences. I should have taken her in my arms and said, "Don't worry. They'll find him." I should have said, "It wasn't your fault," or "He'll be back." Instead, before I knew it, before I even had a chance to think, I blurted out, "Why the hell weren't you watching him?" I wanted to grab the words that hung foully in the air between us, wanted to stuff them back into my throat. I saw the brutal recognition come quickly into her dark, frightened eyes, saw her recoil from it the way a woman will when I have to tell her that her breast cancer has already spread, gotten into bone or brain and there's not a thing we can do. That drawing back from the terrible doom of truth. I knew even then my words would haunt me—us—forever. I knew no matter what I did later, how hard I would try to mitigate their damaging effects, neutralize their poison, they would spread, cancerlike, into every part of our lives, radiating outward, metastasizing and eating away at our marriage. I knew all that as soon as the words left my mouth.

"Dear God, Stuart," my wife cried. "I'm sorry."

"It'll be all right, darling." I tried to comfort her, taking her in my arms at last. I scrambled to recover the lost moment, repair damage that was irreparable and already growing worse. "It'll be all right, I promise." I sensed even then that things would not be all right, that my promise was empty, that disaster and misery lay ahead.

"I wouldn't worry, Mrs. Jordan," Cecil offered. "You know boys his age. Off exploring. He'll come back soon's he gets good and hungry."

They searched until dark, then broke off and waited for morning. Though someone offered us a place nearby to stay, Annabel wouldn't leave the spot, so we waited out the night in our car, drinking coffee the volunteers provided and trying to keep our hopes up.

"We'll find him," Cecil kept saying.

Neither Annabel nor I slept, and though we must have spoken, I can't recall a single word that passed between us. We sat there quietly, waiting for daybreak, our insides dry as dust. It turned cold that night, the way it can at five thousand feet. A hard frost formed on the windshield. Will had been wearing only a T-shirt and shorts, a pair of sneakers. Still, the rescuers tried to reassure us that a healthy boy could survive the night. As long as he stayed dry and got in out of the wind, he had a fighting chance. More than a fighting chance. I tried to believe them, tried to put aside my knowledge of the human body, its frailty, what it was susceptible to, especially that of a five-year-old. And I tried to imagine how he felt: cold, alone, afraid. I couldn't help but think of his fear of wolves, how he would run into our bedroom at night. I remember praying, asking God to watch over him, to keep him safe. It was the last time I'd ever pray, at least the last time with the sense that somebody was actually listening.

At first light the search resumed. The sun stayed hidden behind a damp gray sky. By this time most of Slade had heard about Will being lost, and dozens of people showed up to help in some way or other. Like I said, mountain folks are close, tight-knit. Marty Bledsoe and Jim Bradley, men I hunted with, brought Marty's dogs along to help search the woods. Women who were patients of mine, neighbors, even complete strangers, came with coffee and food, with quilts to keep us warm against the cold night, as well as prayers and encouragement. Stella showed up to help. Kay Wallenbach, who had often baby-sat for Will, arrived with John. She took Annabel in her arms and said, "He'll be along by and by, don't you fret none. I know that young'un. He's got a good head on his shoulders. He wouldn'ta gone fer." The police brought in professional trackers and bloodhounds and locals who knew the mountain well. They had a forest fire plane trying to locate him from the air.

They searched all that day, too, but without success. We tried to keep our hope alive. We tried to hold onto the slender belief that Will would come back to us. Annabel, though, was beside herself, alternately sobbing, then staring vacantly off into the woods, then chattering nonstop.

"I know I should've been watching him," she said.

"Don't talk like that," I reassured her. "They'll find him."

"I just wanted to get it right. Before it slipped away."

"Before what slipped away, Anna?"

"The light. It was so perfect, Stu. You should've seen it. Like gold."

She went on and on about the damn light. Something about how it was her soul, and she had to get it down on canvas or her soul would slip away. Rambling, talking too fast, the way she got sometimes when she was getting sick. She'd been fine for a long time, hadn't had any episodes. But now I could see the stress getting to her. I had somebody local fill a prescription for Valium, and I gave her a shot so she could get some rest. She finally dozed off in the back of one of the police cars. At sunset I got out to stretch my legs. It had stayed damp and chilly all day. I headed over and stood by myself in a small clearing in the woods, near where Annabel's easel still remained propped up, overlooked in the commotion. The coffee can that held her brushes was on the ground, the brushes scattered about, their bristles stiff with paint. The canvas she'd been working on remained on the easel. It was a nearly finished picture of the mountains. There were overlapping scallops of various shades of blue: dark, gunmetal blue in the foreground, then progressively lighter hues, dissolving, the color leaching out of them as they unfurled toward the horizon. The light, I thought. She had to get it down before it slipped away.

I was staring at the picture when I felt something brush softly against my cheek, like the touch of a child's cool finger. At first I didn't recognize what it was, then I thought, Dear God. No. It had started to snow. Lightly at first, a few delicate flakes appearing as if out of nowhere, alighting on the mountain. But it soon picked up, was coming down hard, collecting on the ground, covering whatever trail Will had left for the dogs to pick up. I remember Annabel waking later and gazing in horrified disbelief out the window.

"It's *snowing*?" she asked. "Oh, my God. He'll be so cold, Stu." She started to sob. I already felt the curse of having said what I had. Annabel's guilt wouldn't allow her eyes to meet mine. They called off the search again, and this time we waited out the night in a forest service cabin not far away. The last of our hope faded as the snow swirled about outside.

At dawn the next day, they resumed looking for him, but by then I think the awful truth had, like the snow, settled coldly upon us. The mountains blazed brilliantly in the morning sunlight, light that was sharp and unforgiving as a scalpel poised over flesh. Sometime before noon, Cecil took me aside. His face was pale with what he had to tell me.

"What, Cecil. What is it?"

"Got us some bad news, Doc," he said. One of the tracking dogs, he told me, had found a sneaker. It turned out to be Will's. Not too long afterward they found him huddled under some bushes. Smart boy that he was, he'd crawled there, had tried to cover himself with leaves. He was lying in a fetal position, curled up tight, which is how most people who die of hypothermia are found: conserving heat, instinctively protecting the vital organs. I tried to find comfort in the fact that he would've become lethargic, disoriented, would have drifted slowly off to sleep, that he wouldn't have felt much pain—or fear. But it wasn't much comfort. My son was two months shy of his sixth birthday.

•  •  •

That was the easy part of the story to relate, a child's death. It happens to families all the time. The natural order reversed, the parent outliving the child. I see it in both my occupations: stillborns, birth defects, an umbilical cord wrapped snakelike around a neck, a difficult labor some doctor bungled, as well as premature ends of the more violent sort, drownings, car accidents, the foolish things young kids are capable of, even the occasional murder. The part that was harder to tell because it was less clear to me was what happened afterward. To my wife. To me. To *us*. Sometimes families survive the death of a child; the hurt heals over into a permanent knot of a scar that they touch gently and reverently from time to time, just to remember that it's there, that they haven't forgotten their child. Yet they somehow manage to pick up the jagged pieces, put them together in some semblance of a life, and go on.

Sometimes the pain even makes them stronger. But over 80 percent of families who lose a child don't make it. Those are the facts. For them, the wound doesn't heal; it festers and turns septic, and the family doesn't survive.

As best I could, I tried to explain the aftermath to Bobbie. How I'd desperately tried to protect Annabel from her own guilt and from the guilt I'd heaped upon her. How I'd attempted to shield her, keep her from dwelling on Will's death. And how my wife had blamed herself, took on the guilt, wrapped herself in it like a shroud. How for months afterwards—eating breakfast, getting ready for bed—she couldn't look me in the eye. How my cruel words that night up on the mountain did indeed come back to haunt us; they colored our every word and gesture; they sat between us always like a terrible smell, the stench of decay and death and, above all, betrayal.

Of course, well before Will's death, even before his birth, Annabel had not been well. Though not diagnosed as manic-depressive until we were married and she was in her late twenties, she'd been having "spells," as they euphemistically put it in these parts, most of her adult life. She'd been seeing quack doctors who put her on bed rest with the curtains drawn or who prescribed various tonics or had her wrapped in cold, wet sheets. When we first started seeing each other, while her behavior at times struck me as peculiar, I wanted simply to chalk it up to who she was. Her unconventional, artistic nature, which was what I loved about her in the first place. Of course I noticed those wild flights of imagination, those frantic periods of hyperactivity, where she would talk nonstop or want to do five things at once. Or the sudden mood shifts, from smiling and cheerful one moment, to angry the next, to dejected and miserable after that. Even early in our marriage, the signs were there—the frenetic cleaning of the house, the feverish painting up in her study, the nervousness of her hands—if I'd wanted to recognize them. For instance, the time we had a party at the house for some of the doctors and nurses I worked with. She had baked a dozen pecan pies, and when someone made an offhand comment that he didn't like pecan pie, Annabel broke down sobbing in the kitchen. Or the other times, when she'd suddenly seem to run out of gas, slide into what her sister, Lenore, had referred to as her "blue moods." When she wouldn't get out of bed all day, wouldn't eat or comb her long black hair, wouldn't paint or take the slightest interest in her garden or anything else for that matter. It usually only lasted a day or two. Then, just as quickly as it had come upon her, it would leave, and Annabel would get out of bed and go back to what I came to think of as her "normal" energetic self.

Though I was a doctor and should have recognized the symptoms, for the longest time I denied anything was really the matter with her. I tried to protect her from others, from herself, tried even to keep from admitting the truth to myself. When someone told me something odd Annabel had said or done, I would dismiss it, make up excuses, cover for her, or simply chalk it up to the petty minds and vindictive hearts of a small town that refused to accept someone like Annabel. When Darlene Vickers, from over at the bank, called me once to say my wife had been in and acting "mighty strange," talking to herself and making odd noises, I said only that she'd been taking an allergy medication which put her "out of sorts." Once I got a call from Aaron Shuster of Shuster's Department Store in town that Annabel had charged several hundred dollars worth of shoes. I came home to find boxes and boxes of shoes: fancy dress-up shoes, pumps with stiletto heels, open-toed espadrilles, penny loafers, this despite the fact that Annabel never got dressed up, never wore anything but jeans and boots or sneakers. I simply paid the bill and explained to Aaron that we were donating them for a charity ball. When she was first arrested for shoplifting in Crawford City that time, I went over to the jail and picked her up, quietly settled things without having to go to court. She'd tried to leave a store over there with some underwear hidden under her coat and was caught by a security guard.

On the way home I asked her, "For God's sake why, Anna?"

"I don't know," she said. "They were pretty."

"I would've bought them for you. You know that."

Or take the times she would change from the sweet, easygoing country girl I'd married to a belligerent and nasty shrew. Screaming at people she thought cut in front of her at the checkout line of the Bi-Lo. Swearing obscenities at a gas station attendant because he had failed to wash her windshield. One time, I recall, fat old Mrs. Lorrelei Watson came storming into my office to inform me that Annabel had a serious "mental imbalance." The woman, one of those blue-haired, pearls-and-white-glove dilettantes small-town culture is famous for, was the president of the Hubbard County Arts Council, an organization to which my wife, not normally a joiner of civic groups, belonged. The Arts Council decided which local artists received funding and whose work was good enough to be displayed in the courthouse rotunda during Mountain Festival Days. She and Annabel were always at loggerheads over artistic issues. Annabel thought of her as a big fat cow who wouldn't know art if it came up and bit her on the ass. Anyway, Lorrelei Watson explained how she was holding a meeting of the Council when my wife stood up and starting carrying on, and when she, Lorrelei, told her she was out of order and to kindly have a seat, my wife took to yelling at her. "Frankly, Dr. Jordan, I've never known a lady of any character to use such shocking profanities," Lorrelei explained. "Though I'm certainly not a professional, I would say your wife has a mental imbalance of some sort, sir." I knew, in the way people with an awful secret in their family know, that something was terribly wrong with Annabel—which is to say I turned the other way and hoped it wasn't true.

What finally brought things to a head was Annabel's first disappearance. She vanished. I came home from work one evening and she wasn't there. Her car wasn't in the driveway, yet there wasn't a note saying where she'd gone. She hadn't packed any clothes—I'd checked that first. When it got late and she still wasn't home, I started calling around. Friends, people we knew in town, her sister down in Spartanburg. But no one had heard from her. Hours passed. Finally, in the middle of the night, I called the sheriff's department. Some fool deputy there told me not to worry, that she'd probably just gone somewhere and forgotten to tell me.

"But you don't know my wife," I barked at him. "She wouldn't just *go* somewhere without telling me."

"Maybe it's *you* don't know her," he said; that was more true than he could possibly have realized.

By morning I was worried sick. I spent the next two days thinking something terrible had happened: that she was in an accident, that somebody had hurt her. Finally, I got a call from the Asheville police. They had her locked up over there. She'd been arrested and charged with vandalism and public indecency, and with assaulting an officer. They'd found her on a school playground, just wearing her pretty underwear, the ones she'd stolen, though it was winter then. One of the officers tried to get her to come along peacefully with him. She slapped him, and as he tried to handcuff her, she bit him on the arm. Along one side of a school building, she had started to paint a huge mural, a frightening nightmare scene like something out of Hieronymus Bosch, complete with skeletons copulating and devils with pitchforks. When I picked her up she was still out of it, ranting about how she was going to sue the police for violating her rights. "Tell 'em, Stu," she cried. "Tell the bastards this is a free country and I can paint anywhere I goddamn well please."

With that, I could no longer deny what should have been apparent all along, that she was ill, seriously ill, and needed more help than I could give her. That's the first time I had her committed to Cedar Crest. A psychiatrist I knew over in Asheville, Dr. Higgins, examined her. It didn't take him long to diagnose her as manic-depressive. Right away he put her on lithium and an antidepressant, and she responded fairly well. I read up on what I would come to consider the enemy: mood disorders such as bipolar I and II, rapid cycling, the phases of the illness and the various treatment regimens and the expected prognoses. I did research on lithium carbonate and anticonvulsants, on Haldol and Thorazine, on side effects such as tardive dyskinesia, on antidepressants like monoamine oxidase inhibitors and tricyclics. The medications, I soon learned, wouldn't cure her, would never, in fact, *cure* her. Even with the drugs, she would always have her bad times, her relapses, her wild manic periods, her moments of depression and despair. But the medication, especially the lithium, did have a large palliative effect on her mood swings, lessening the extremes, moderating the excesses. What was more, we learned, the way families with a chronically ill member do, to make adjustments, to compensate, to avoid certain things the way a person who's allergic to chocolate learns to avoid it. In short, we learned to live as best we could in the relatively calm periods in between the dizzying heights of her mania and the abysmal lows of her depression; these times were like a small, sheltered cove between jagged mountain peaks.

We'd been married almost five years when Annabel became pregnant. The doctors had warned us that any sort of stress, like having a child, might have a deleterious effect on her. So while we both wanted kids, Annabel and I had discussed the topic and agreed that it wouldn't be a good idea. We'd always been careful, using birth control. Still, somehow she became pregnant. Maybe she did it on purpose—I don't know. I tried to talk to her about whether we should go ahead with the pregnancy, but she wouldn't even consider an abortion. I prepared for the worst, though my fears proved unfounded. She did just fine during the pregnancy. In fact, she seemed to bloom like one of her roses. She smiled and laughed more than ever before. She was happy and excited about having a child. When Will was born she did have a mild postpartum depression, but it lasted only a short time. After that, now and then she had bad spells, and Kay Wallenbach would have to look after Will. Or her sister, Lenore, would come up from Spartanburg to stay with us until Annabel was feeling better. Mostly, though, Annabel did just fine. More than fine. She adored our son, threw herself into being a mother. She became almost conventional. She drove Will to a play group in town. She went to lunch with other mothers. She joined clubs. She acted more "normal" than she ever had. Will's coming seemed to provide a steadying ballast for her life. It was as if she didn't have time to be sick. The five years he was with us, she was the healthiest and happiest I'd ever seen her.

• • •

Will's death sent Annabel reeling, made her sicker than I'd seen her before. The accident pushed her over a precipice and into a dark abyss, one that had always been there, I knew, lurking, waiting to destroy us. She would suddenly stop taking her lithium, saying it made her dull or fuzzy-headed, sick to her stomach, feel fat or ugly, or that she simply didn't need it. Before Will's death, while it was hard to predict the exact path of her illness, her manic cycle usually lasted anywhere from a few weeks to a few months, during which time she'd cruise at ninety miles an hour, hardly stopping, sleeping but a few hours a night, if at all. This was usually followed by a brief but intense period of depression, where she wouldn't get out of bed, wouldn't eat or bathe or take the slightest interest in things. Now, however, especially when she stopped taking her medication, her moods swung erratically, often day by day, sometimes even hour by hour. One moment she'd be happy and laughing; the next angry, screaming some foul obscenity at me or anyone else unfortunate enough to get in her way; and the one after that depressed and sobbing in utter despair. She had episodes where she was psychotic, subject to hallucinations. She was hospitalized dozens of times. She was in and out of ERs, psych units, halfway houses. She'd been admitted to Cedar Crest six or seven times. She'd been on various drug regimens, with only moderate success. I'd taken her to countless psychiatrists and therapists, counselors and psychopharmacologists. She'd had several sessions of ECT, also known as shock therapy. Nothing worked. That's when the drinking began and the drugs, the speed or Valium or cocaine, all of which exaggerated her behavior: inflated the highs, deepened the lows.

She tried to take her own life twice. One time, Kay Wallenbach had stopped by to see how Annabel was doing, and when she didn't answer the door, Kay went in and found her unconscious. She'd overdosed on barbiturates. A note by the bed said she hoped her death would at last set us both free. Another time she'd jumped into the Tuckamee River, but as she later confessed, she couldn't go through with it, couldn't find a way to swallow that cold water and end her misery.

At about this time, several years after Will's death, she started taking off more and more frequently. Leaving me. Yet I don't think it was really me that she was running from. Or at least not *just* me. I think it was as much that she was trying to get away from herself, maybe from this place and the memories it held for her. That's one of the symptoms of people with manic-depressive illness. When they get in a bad manic state, they do reckless things, things they wouldn't normally do: They spend money wildly, abuse alcohol and drugs, become promiscuous. Take off on a whim, without any plan or destination. My wife would get in her car and just go, without leaving me a note or any indication where she'd gone. She would usually come home after a day or two, reeking of booze and cigarette smoke and the musky scent of other men, a scary, half-sated look in her dark eyes. When I'd press her about where she'd been, she say, "It's none of your damn business, Stu." Other times, though, she'd show up back at the house contrite, sobbing, telling me how sorry she was, begging my forgiveness, like a frail, hurt little girl. And I'd open the door and ask no questions at all.

Sometimes she'd be gone for days on end, even weeks. If she ran out of gas, she'd catch a bus. If she had no money, she'd hitchhike. Her illness became chronic, overwhelming, devastating, like a ferocious, hungry beast let out of its cage. Every few months, she'd just up and vanish. I'd call the police. Cecil Clegg, a deputy in those days, would tell me he'd keep an eye out for her, and he'd contact the surrounding counties. Pretty soon, it got to be a regular occurrence. After a few days, I'd usually get a call from him or some other police officer saying they'd picked her up sleeping in the park, or that she'd been involved in a little "disturbance" at a bar over in Crawford City, nothing serious, but could I come and get her.

As Annabel's illness deepened, she started straying further afield—to bars in Knoxville or Johnson City or Greenville—and doing crazier and crazier things. Once I got a call from a night clerk at a motel down in Columbia, South Carolina. He said he'd found my number in my wife's pocketbook. He said there'd been some trouble. Annabel, he explained, had been in a fight and was at the moment passed out drunk. He said there had been some damage to the room and wanted to know who was going to pay for it. When I arrived at the seedy motel in a rundown part of the city, I found her curled up on the bed, unconscious, a sheet draped over her naked body. Besides being drunk, she had been beaten to within an inch of her life. She had a swollen jaw, which later proved to be broken, bruises on her face and neck. I knew what it was then to hate, a violent, monstrous hatred that recognized no bounds. With my bare hands I could've killed the man who had done that to her. I could have reached into his chest and pulled out his heart. I brought her home and admitted her to the hospital. She stayed for several weeks that time, slowly recovering from the beating, before taking off again.

That became the pattern of our marriage, if you could still call it one. She'd drift in and out of my life. Now and then when she'd come home, things would actually go fine for a while. Our life would almost begin to feel normal again. We'd do the regular, normal things a husband and wife do: go shopping, rake leaves, watch television, even occasionally make love. She might work in her garden or take long walks in the woods. I'd think, Maybe. Maybe this time. Then, often without warning, she'd take off. I wouldn't hear from her for weeks. I'd call around to places she'd been to before, bars or bus stations or motels. Or I'd look up some old friends she used to hang around with in Asheville from before we got married, ask if they had seen her. Sometimes her sister would call me, saying that Annabel had shown up in Spartanburg. And I would drive down and get her. Yet the last time she dropped in at her sister's place, Lenore said to me, "I won't take her in anymore, Stuart. I can't. You oughta have her put away someplace permanent-like. She's just going to pull you down." But I would place her in the truck and take her home. Other times, I'd have to stick ads in newspapers or put up posters with her picture, like those kids on the milk cartons: "Have you seen this woman?" In the evenings after work, I'd drive around Asheville looking for her, cruising up and down the streets, the way men would who were looking for a woman to buy for the night. Sometimes, if I was lucky, I might find her in a bar or sleeping on a park bench. But most times I didn't.

Once, after not hearing from her for nearly two months, I hired a private detective. Even he had no luck. Mostly, I'd just have to sit tight and wait for her to turn up, hoping, as I had with Will, that she'd come home safe, that she wouldn't turn up dead. In the mail one day I might get a bill for a room she'd charged in Charlotte. Or a phone call from the police station in Boone, where she'd been picked up for buying drugs or solicitation. My wife, the woman I loved more than anything in the world, picked up for selling her body to buy drugs! Or someone from an ER would contact me saying they had an Annabel Lee Jordan there, and I'd drop everything and go and get her. I'd call Stella and she'd cancel my appointments, make up some excuse for me. Or when I absolutely couldn't get away because of my work, I'd send her a bus ticket or wire her some money. Sometimes she'd call herself, from a motel room or highway truck stop, not having the slightest idea how she'd come to be there, sounding confused or high, crying, asking if I could come and get her.

Her appearance would always come as a shock. Wild-eyed and manic, not having slept for days. Dirty, grubby looking, foul smelling, like any other street person, which is exactly what she'd become. I would try to nurse her back to health. I'd take her in and get her cleaned up. I'd shoot her up with vitamins. I'd make an appointment to have her teeth looked at. I'd enroll her, or at least try to, in yet another detox program, get her admitted to yet another psychiatric facility, have her see yet another doctor. Sometimes she'd go along with it. Those times she seemed actually to be getting a little better, to *allow* herself a certain measure of forgiveness. Her hands would stop their trembling, her eyes would momentarily lose that distant, glassy look of theirs and actually seem to *see* what was in front of her. And while I warned myself not to, I'd begin to let myself think she was over the hump. That *we* were over the hump. Despite losing Will, we'd get through this, somehow or other. Maybe we'd even have another child. We were still young enough to start a family again. But of course that was just wishful thinking. Annabel couldn't even take care of herself, let alone a child. It didn't matter. I just wanted her back, the woman I'd fallen in love with.

While she might be good for a few weeks, sometimes even as long as a month, sooner or later I'd sense her starting to drift again, to slip away from me. Eventually she'd stop taking her medication. I could tell. I'd notice the symptoms returning: the way her hands would start to get antsy, that faraway look in her eyes at the breakfast table, the odd behavior. The normal frenzy of activity ratcheting slowly into a full-fledged manic episode. The paranoia. The delusions returning. The merely quirky behavior turning into out-and-out craziness. The sudden free-fall into depression. The fickleness of her moods. One minute gay and cheerful, the next despondent, the one after that angry and belligerent, picking a fight over nothing. Once she accused me of cheating on her when she'd been away. I swore to her that I hadn't, yet she started ranting and raving, saying she could smell when a whore had been in *her* house. Another time, I remember coming home from work and finding her upstairs in her studio. She was sitting there dressed in her bathrobe, sobbing inconsolably. On the easel I saw she'd started a sketch of Will, but when she'd almost finished it, she'd taken a pair of scissors and slashed the canvas to shreds.

When things started to get bad again, I would try to talk her into going to the hospital. I would try to reason with her, convince her it was in her best interest, beg her, plead with her, *anything*, to let me get her some help. But she'd usually refuse to go, saying nothing was wrong with her. Or that I just wanted to get rid of her, have her put away so she'd be out of my hair. Her descent into madness was like watching a tornado approaching, getting closer and closer, feeling the windows start to rattle, the impending doom in the air. Several times I ended up having to bring her, or have her brought, to the ER in the middle of the night, or over to Cedar Crest. She hated going, fought me or the EMTs, kicking and screaming until they had to restrain her and give her a sedative.

I recall once she hadn't slept in about a week. She was really bad, wild-eyed, hallucinating, carrying on conversations with her dead father or Will, prowling the house at night, sobbing or talking incoherently. Finally, I decided she needed to be checked into a hospital. I made the mistake of driving her to the emergency room in Slade myself. Halfway there, she attempted to open the door and throw herself from the truck. I had to grab her by the arm.

"Anna," I yelled.

"Let go, you fucking bastard," she cried, as I pulled over to the side of the road. She managed to break loose from me, got out of the truck, and rushed down toward the river. I was able to catch her in time, before she flung herself into the swift-moving Tuckamee.

"Let me go. You want to get rid of me so bad, I'll leave you. For good, too."

"No," I said. "I just want to get you some help, Anna."

"Help!" She turned on me those dark accusatory eyes, now glazed over with the filmy bluish sheen of a gut-shot deer. "You always blamed me, you bastard," she cursed at me.

"What? No, I didn't."

"Yes, you did. You never let me forget it was my fault. Never. You've always hated me for what happened."

"No, I haven't."

"You wish I were gone. You wish I were dead and buried."

"Stop it! Don't say that."

"Why? You know it's true. You'd be better off without me. We both know that."

"No," I said. "That's not true."

"Isn't it? You wouldn't want me dead and out of your life once and for all?"

"No! No!"

"You're just saying that. One of these days you'll end up leaving me. You watch."

"No," I said. "I won't leave you."

"Yes, you will. You'll leave me. And I deserve it, too."

"I won't," I said, hugging her thin quivering body to mine. "I promise I won't."

She looked up at me. She had calmed down enough to let me put her in the truck and drive her to the hospital.

But mostly I didn't have to resort to having her put away. Mostly I just waited and she would leave on her own. Sooner or later, I'd come home and she'd be gone. Sometimes a note. Other times nothing. No sign she'd even been there. Except for this ragged hole she'd ripped in my heart, as if some wild animal had torn it with its fangs. Eventually the hole closed, and I learned over time not to hope, not to expect her to return—at least not the Annabel I'd loved. I had my work, my patients. And as time wore on she stayed away for longer and longer periods, came home less frequently. Sometimes an entire year or more would slip by, and I wouldn't hear from her. I would start to think she was gone for good, that she was out of my life completely. I would let myself believe she had met someone else, had started a new life; I even wished that for her. Sometimes, in the middle of the night, I'd wake up and find myself picturing her dead. Yes, dead. She was right after all about that. In my mind I saw her as one of the bodies I had to deal with as the ME. I imagined her dead a dozen different ways: frozen to death in some alley, an overdose, hit by a car. Part of me, I must confess, even *hoped* for that, hoped she'd die and I'd be released from the life I found myself locked into as in a prison. I'd let myself imagine an existence without her. I could put her behind me finally, grieve for the woman I'd loved, bury her beside Will, and get on with my life. Then, out of nowhere, I'd get a weepy call on Will's birthday. Or a letter in the mailbox saying she needed something, money, a place to stay. Or unannounced, she'd just arrive at my door. "Look what the cat dragged in, Stu," she'd say, smiling her still-girlish smile. And I'd take her in once more. What else could I do?

I suppose I realized that things couldn't go on like this forever, that sooner or later I'd have to put a stop to it, for I knew that she wouldn't. In my head I knew the rightness of this. But in my heart I couldn't bring myself to leave her, to sever ties completely with the life we'd had together.

# 10

When I finished my story, Bobbie didn't say anything for several seconds. She just stared down into her drink, screwing up her sweet mouth, in that way she had. I knew I'd gone too far, dumped my pathetic story on someone I hardly knew. I'd bored this kind woman with my troubles.

"I'm sorry," I said.

"Why?"

"You didn't want to hear all that."

"No, I did. Really," she replied, looking across the table at me. Her green eyes, I could see, had misted over. "What a sad story. You must've really loved her."

I nodded.

"I feel so bad for being nosy. But I am glad you told me," she said, sniffling. I offered her my handkerchief and she blew her nose. "Don't you get lonely, though?"

"Sometimes. I have my work," I replied. "The ME stuff keeps me busy, too. And like you, I guess I got pretty good at being alone."

"Sometimes people get too durn good at that. You said she's in Asheville now?"

"Last I heard."

"How long since you heard from her?"

"It's been a while."

"Since I've been this nosy, I might as well go whole hog. Whyn't you'all ever get divorced?"

I took a sip of my drink, letting the Scotch settle things in my stomach.

"I don't know. I kept hoping it might still work out. That there was still a chance for us. Then later, when I knew we were finished, I guess it was more out of a sense of guilt. Obligation, too, I suppose. I'd started more than one letter to her with the intention of asking for a divorce, saying we both needed to get on with our lives. Yet I never sent them. I just couldn't bring myself to abandon her."

"Sounds to me, she was the one who abandoned you."

"It wasn't her. It was her illness doing that. I couldn't break things off completely. I wanted her to know I was here if she ever needed me."

"It's commendable what you did, Doc. But shoot, fourteen years is a long time. Don't you owe it to yourself to get on with your life?"

"Funny, that's what Annabel says."

"She's right, you know."

"I suppose."

"Is it that promise you made her? That you wouldn't leave her?"

"Maybe a little. I figured I owed something to her. I can't help thinking if I'd been a better husband, if I'd thought more about my own family than I did my patients, things wouldn't have turned out the way they did."

"But you're a doctor. That's what a doctor does, thinks about his patients. Isn't that what your father did?"

"Yeah, he did. But he also had a family he should've paid more attention to. It's hard not to think that if I'd been with them instead of going to the hospital that day, maybe Will wouldn't have wandered off. Maybe he'd still be alive."

"You can second-guess yourself till the cows come home, and it won't do any good."

"I know. Or if I'd . . . "

"If you'd what?"

"If I hadn't said what I did. The night our son got lost. I still can remember the look on Annabel's face."

"Why, shoot, anybody might've said the same thing. You were upset. Scared. You can't blame yourself for saying something under those circumstances."

"But I felt that way, too. In my heart, I guess I blamed her for his disappearance. And when I wasn't blaming her, I was blaming myself."

"You want some advice, Doc? Stop beating up on yourself. It was an accident. A terrible one but an accident nonetheless."

Bobbie reached out and took hold of my hand. Her grip was strong, firm from all the tennis she played. What I wanted to do more than anything was to take her hand and place it against my cheek. I wanted the comfort it seemed to offer. But of course I didn't. She was a married woman and I had no right.

"It's too bad," she said, smiling wistfully.

"What is?"

"I didn't run into you a long time ago. Anyhow, I guess I should be going."

"Thanks for listening. See you in court, counselor."

Over the next several months, I had to work with Bobbie on other cases. We'd meet occasionally for dinner or a drink after work. Each time it would be under the guise of a professional meeting, and yet each time we would end up talking mostly about our lives, our marriages, our pasts and our presents. Then one evening, a Saturday in late fall over a year ago, I was alone in the bar at Pancho Villa's. I was having a drink and watching the Charlotte Hornets get their asses kicked by my old team, the Celtics. I'd just delivered a nine-pound baby girl for a woman who'd been in labor for twelve hours. I was dead tired. My plan was to have a couple of drinks, order something to eat, watch the game, then go home and collapse into bed. I had the next day off; Dr. Issacson, a young internist, was covering my patients. Hector, the bartender, came over and, though I hadn't ordered one, placed a Scotch next to the one I was already working on.

"From your lady friend, Dr. Jordan," Hector said with a wink.

I glanced toward the other end of the bar. Bobbie Tisdale sat there smiling.

I took my two drinks and moved over to where she sat. "*Gracias,*" I said.

"Howdy, Doc," she greeted me, belting down a shot of bourbon and chasing it with a beer, the way a person does whose objective is to get seriously drunk in the shortest period of time.

"Your husband away?" I asked.

"Yeah. And good riddance." She sighed, ordering another shot. After Hector had refilled her shot glass, she made a toast to Paul. "Here's to the bastard. May his dick rot off and be eaten by buzzards." She said it loud enough that a man and woman at a table near the bar looked over at her. Bobbie dispatched that shot just as quickly as the first and ordered yet another.

"You ought to go easy," I warned.

"I don't want easy. Not tonight."

She explained that they'd had a fight, which, I'd learned over the past few months, wasn't that uncommon. They fought a lot. I found out that this was her second marriage, the first having ended in divorce. Her current husband, Bobbie confided to me, had his problems with the concept of fidelity. Most anything in a skirt would turn his head. She'd thrown him out several times already, but each time he'd come crawling back asking her forgiveness; she'd end up feeling sorry for him and letting him return. The last time was after an ugly affair with a woman back in Winston-Salem. They had agreed to come out here and give their marriage a last try. That morning she'd just found a pair of panties in his suitcase.

I'd seen her husband a few times around town. He was a tall, good-looking fellow with eyes that never seemed to light on any one thing for very long. One look, and you could tell he didn't have any problems getting women. He was the sort that collected them like pelts.

"The stupid bastard," Bobbie cursed. "It was almost like he wanted me to find them. He promised he was through tomcatting around. What kills me is almost anything will do. I could see if he took up with some pretty young thing. But hell, the one back in Winston-Salem had a puss on her like a catfish. How is that supposed to make me feel?"

"Why do you stay with him?" I asked.

She screwed her mouth up, gathered it into that ball on one side of her face.

"I guess for the same reason you stayed with your wife. Dog-dumb loyalty. I loved the prick once and I kept hoping he'd change. I guess I ought to admit I'm a miserable failure in the area of holy matrimony. Maybe my aunt was right," she said. "The way to a man's heart is through his stomach and not his tallywhacker."

She smiled, trying to make light of it. But it was obvious she was hurt and angry.

"Like you told me, don't beat up on yourself too much."

"Look at me, Doc," she said, leaning toward me so our faces were only a few inches apart. She took my hands in hers. "I'm not such a bad-looking woman, am I? I run. I play tennis. I work out. I watch what I eat. Yeah, I got some wrinkles and I'm not as young as I used to be. But who the hell is?"

"For what it's worth," I offered, "I think you're a very attractive woman. Beautiful even."

"Well, shoot, Doc. You don't have to lay it on *that* thick. I'da settled for wouldn't-toss-you-outa-bed-on-a-cold-night sorta pretty."

She rolled her eyes back and laughed, this time meaning it.

"No, I do. I think you're beautiful."

"Y'all certainly know how to sweet-talk a girl, doncha," she said, patting my hand. "If I didn't know better . . . ," she added with a smile.

She tipped her head back, finished her third bourbon, and ordered another. The more she drank the more her Southern accent seemed to grow, as if she normally held it in check by a force of will, fearing that she'd sound like an uneducated cracker.

"Hector, *por favor*. Give one for my good friend here, Doctor Doolittle."

"Sí, señora," he said. "One for the good doctor."

"Don't you think you ought to slow down a little?" I said to her.

"Watch me. I'm just gettin' my motor revved up."

We sat at the bar and talked for a long time. We had more drinks. We laughed. Several times Bobbie leaned toward me on her bar stool, resting her hand on my arm, letting me inhale her fragrance. I had nothing to get home to, just some articles in a medical journal. The Scotch loosened a knot in my shoulders, and it felt good being in the company of an attractive, vibrant woman. There passed between us the sort of innocent flirtation that two unhappy people offer each other when they've had a few too many drinks and their unhappiness acts as a kind of aphrodisiac to them, in part because they don't think their flirtation will go anywhere, *can* go anywhere, so they feel safe playing their little game. It was late when we left.

Hector winked and said, "Take care of her, Dr. Jordan."

The autumn night was crisp, smelling of leaves and burning wood, and of the sickly sweet odor of the paper mill. The sky was a dark concave shape, like being inside a huge bell, with the darker ring of the mountains circling the lights of the town below. As we headed for our cars, Bobbie, weaving slightly, leaned into me and put her arm around my waist for balance. I got a heady whiff of her perfume. Near her car, we stopped. "So now what, Doc?" she said. Before I had a chance to interpret her question, she put her arms around my neck and tried to kiss me. She'd had way too much to drink and her aim was bad. She ended up kissing my chin. We both laughed nervously.

"You get the general idea anyway," she said.

"I think so."

"So what do you say, Doc?"

"I say you've had too much to drink. I'd better give you a ride home."

"Drink's got nothin' to do with what I'm feeling. I didn't just bump into you tonight by accident, y'know."

"You didn't?"

"Heck, no. I thought you might be there."

"What about your husband?"

"He's out of town."

"I don't mean tonight. In general."

"In general he's a low-down slug. We haven't slept together in a coon's age and I'm horny as hell. Shoot, Doc, I'm not proposing marriage or anything. Just a little mutual comfort is all. I thought you took some sort of oath to ease people's pain and suffering."

"I'm almost old enough to be your father."

"Don't gimme that bull-ticky. We both know what was going on in there. I may've had a few but I'm not drunk."

"I won't deny I'm attracted to you. I am."

"Then what's stopping us from offering each other a little plain old solace?"

"Is that what this is, solace?"

"Solace is a start. You know what your problem is, Doc?"

"No, what?"

"Your whole life is slipping by you while you sit on your duff feeling sorry for yourself."

"I don't feel sorry for myself."

"Like hell. And the thing is, you can't even see it. You throw yourself into all this other stuff—your patients or the ME business. Helping people. Being good ole Doc Jordan. But that's just your way of hiding."

"From what?"

"How the hell do I know? Maybe what happened to your son. Or the guilt you feel over some dumb thing you said one night years ago. Or some promise you made. And like a pig in shit, you just love wallowing in it."

"You don't even know me."

"I know you well enough to see you're afraid of moving on with your life. Getting hurt again. Living in the past is easy. There ain't no risk in that."

"I thought you're a prosecutor, not a shrink."

"I don't gotta be a shrink to know that. You think way too much."

"I *think* too much?"

"That's right. You let *this*," she said, touching my temple, "tell you what's right. Instead of *this*." She placed her index finger against the middle of my chest, above my heart. "Sometimes, Doc, you just gotta jump in with both feet and yell Geronimo!"

"You think so."

"I *know* so."

I stared at her for a moment. "Maybe you're right."

"No *maybe* about it. So what's it gonna be? Here I am offering you a slightly drunk but otherwise intact female who's looking for a little solace. You can take me. Or you can g'won home and back to whatever life you got there. Your choice, Doc."

She stared up at me with those beautiful green eyes of hers glittering in the lights of the parking lot, her mouth loose and sensual from the booze. Whatever qualms I might have had quickly dissipated.

"Geronimo," I said, and we both laughed again.

"Hell, Doc, you gotta say it louder than that."

So right there in the parking lot, I shouted at the top of my lungs, "*Geronimo!*"

"Now you're getting the hang of it."

We headed over to the Skyline Motel in Crawford City and rented a room under the name of Mr. and Mrs. Bovary, Bobbie's idea of a joke. The old Pakistani guy who worked the desk didn't even look up from his small portable TV.

Once in the room I confessed to Bobbie, "I'm a little nervous."

"Nobody's going to see us."

"It's not that. It's ... well ... been a while. I'm a little out of practice." It had been years since I'd made love to another woman, the last time being with Madeline.

"Relax. It's like riding a bicycle. A bicycle built for two."

As with so many things, she turned out to be right about that, too.

Since then we continued our affair, fitting each other in where and when our busy schedules allowed. On Wednesdays, I only made rounds at the hospital, had the rest of the day off, so we'd often meet at noon when Bobbie could get away for an hour or two. Other times we'd sneak off in the evening when Paul was out of town. Except for Madeline, I'd never been seriously involved with another woman. I guess I'd never *let* myself be. And even with Madeline, I always felt myself holding something back, as if not wanting to allow myself a chance at happiness. Maybe Bobbie was right. That I was hiding behind my pain. Feeling sorry for myself. Afraid to get on with my life. With Bobbie, things were different. I let myself jump in with both feet. Maybe it was because she was married and therefore in some way unavailable. Or maybe it was just because of who she was. Besides being beautiful and passionate, she was honest, irreverent, funny. I had a good time when we were together. I never laughed so much as I did when I was with her. She wasn't like most women in Slade; in fact, she wasn't like any woman I'd ever known. I looked forward to seeing her, spending time with her. Not just in bed, though that was certainly part of it. She startled you with the frankness and urgency of her passion. Yet more than the physical part, she made me feel reckless and on edge again; she made the blood pulse in my veins when I waited in the room for her to come; she made me feel ready and willing to allow myself to be in love once more. To be happy. For a long while, we never spoke about our future, about *us*. She was married, and in a way so was I. We accepted what we had now and clung to it for dear life.

After a while, I noticed a change in things. In Bobbie. In me, too, I suppose. She spoke more and more about how unhappy she was at home, saying there was no sense staying married to a man she didn't love. She talked about getting a divorce, about quitting her job as prosecutor and taking a position with a friend who had a law practice over in Crawford City, so she could start fresh someplace. And she seemed less cautious about concealing our affair, as if she didn't care if people found out anymore, as if, in fact, she actually welcomed them knowing. I happened once to run into her at Pressley's Dry Cleaning, on Mill Street. She and I made polite small talk until Mrs. Pressley went hunting for a suit I'd dropped off. As soon as she was gone, Bobbie kissed me and slid her hand down the front of my pants and grabbed hold of me. Right there. Anybody could've walked in on us. And one night when Paul was away, she asked me to come over to her house. I said I didn't think that was such a good idea. Besides, I felt that making love to a man's wife was one thing, sleeping in his bed, another. I still had some scruples left.

As for myself, I found I was becoming more and more possessive of her. I became greedy; I wanted her for more than just a few hours in some motel room a couple of times a month. I wanted her with me *all* the time. I wanted people to know she was mine. When Troy Bumgartner would say confidentially to me, "What you reckon she's like in bed, Stuart?" I had all I could do to keep from smashing his teeth in. And though she'd assured me that she and Paul didn't sleep in the same room anymore, the mere thought of her husband touching her, making love to her, both angered and depressed me. Sometimes I couldn't sleep nights picturing the two of them in bed. Several times I dialed her number and then hung up when Paul answered.

Things sort of came to a head the last time we were at the Skyline Motel, a couple of weeks before. I sensed something was wrong. She was uncharacteristically quiet, didn't laugh at all, wasn't her normal playful self. And her lovemaking, usually uninhibited and demanding, was halfhearted and uninspired this day. We seemed to go through the motions, like a couple married for twenty years. Afterward, lying in bed, we exchanged, as planned, Christmas gifts with each other. She'd gotten me a tie, and I'd given her a pair of earrings, plain gold hoops I thought she could've passed off as a gift from a colleague in the DA's office.

"Do you like them?" I asked.

"Yes. They're . . . lovely," she said distractedly.

"What's the matter?"

"Nothing," she replied, staring at the earrings in her hand. "Just that, where in the hell am I ever going to wear them besides . . . *here*? In this crummy room."

"Is that what's wrong?" I asked.

"I'm just sick and tired of the way things are," she said. "Hiding and sneaking around like this."

"Don't you think I am, too? Except what can we do about it?"

"We can decide to be together, that's what we can do. You and me." She rolled on her side so she was facing me. "I was all set to leave Paul. Even had my bags packed."

"What happened?"

"His mother just had a stroke. He's down in Florida now with her. They were very close and I just didn't have the heart. But I've decided to leave him. It's just a matter of when."

"Are you sure it's what you want to do?" I said.

"As sure as I can be," she replied. "It's just not working out. And anyways, I've been thinking more about us."

"Us?" I asked.

"Yes."

"That shouldn't have anything to do with your decision to leave your husband."

"What the hell are you talking about?" she scoffed. "My leaving Paul's got *everything* to do with us."

"What I mean is, it's just that sometimes people jump into one relationship because they're running from another."

"I'm not running from anything. Look, Doc, I never put any pressure on you. I never talked about there even being an *us*. I know about your ... *situation*."

"My situation?"

"You know, with your wife. I went into this with my eyes wide open. If all this is is a good fuck and some laughs, that's fine by me. I'm a big girl. It's just ... "

She started to cry. I leaned toward her and wrapped my arm around her shoulder, kissed her on the throat. Her skin was cool, tasted slightly salty. I could feel her shiver.

"You know that's not true," I said. "You know how much I care about you."

"Then what's the matter, Doc? I thought you'd be happy I was leaving him."

"I am. Of course, I am. I'd love for us to be together. It's just that ... I don't want you to make a mistake."

She probed my eyes for a moment. "What's a mistake is staying with someone you don't love. That's the real mistake."

"Then you should leave him, if that's what you want to do."

"Shoot, Doc, for a smart fellow, you're pretty thick sometimes. I'm not talking about me and Paul. I mean you and your wife."

"Huh?"

"That's what this is all about, isn't it?" she said, anger rising in her voice. "You saying you don't want me to make a mistake. When what it's really about is that as long as I don't leave Paul, you don't have to make a decision about Annabel."

"That's silly."

"Is it?"

"It's just that I feel responsible for her. I don't know how she'd do on her own."

"What do you think she's been doing all these years, Doc?"

"I mean, *all* alone. Without me there if she ever needed me."

"Is that all it is? A responsibility?"

"Yes, of course."

"And what about that promise you made to her?"

"It was just something I said."

"And you didn't mean it?"

"Well, I meant it at the time. But that was before I met you."

"Does she even know about us?"

"Does Paul?"

"It's not the same thing. We're still living together. Have you told her about us?"

"You know I haven't even heard from her in months."

Bobbie paused for a moment. She looked at my chest, then glanced up and into my eyes.

"Do you still love her?" she asked. "Is that it?"

"What? Of course not," I said. "I mean, I care for her. For what we had. But I love you. You know that."

"Do I?"

"Yes."

"Then prove it. Look, as soon as the situation with Paul's mother is resolved, I'm going to leave him. So we can have a future together. Are you willing to make the same commitment?"

I hesitated for just a moment, and Bobbie found my answer in that. She turned away from me and got out of bed. She started grabbing her clothes, getting dressed with that amazingly cool efficiency women have when they're angry. A flurry of fingers and buttons and zippers. When she was finished, she said, "I got to be back in court at two." She grabbed her purse and headed for the door.

"All right, I'll tell her," I said at last.

She paused at the door. With her back to me she said, "When?"

"As soon as I have a chance."

"And you'll ask for a divorce?"

"Yes. When can we see each other again?"

"I don't know. I'll call you," she said and then slipped out the door. I heard her car start up and take off.

I continued to lie in bed for a while, thinking over what she'd said. She was right, of course. I knew in my heart I needed to make a decision about Annabel, one I should've made a long time ago. It's just that every time I made up my mind to leave her, to ask for a divorce, the moment never seemed to be the right one. Something always seemed to happen. I'd get a call from her in the middle of the night—she was sick, needed money, needed my help. And I'd drop what I was doing and go to her. Or she'd show up out of nowhere, as she had when I was seeing Madeline. And I would take her in, nurse her back to some semblance of health, all the while saying that as soon as she was well enough, strong enough, I'd do it. I would tell her I wanted a divorce, that we both needed to get on with our lives. Hadn't she said as much herself? Yet when she was feeling better and the moment of truth arrived, I wouldn't have the heart to do it. I couldn't just leave her. Though I knew, now more than ever, it was the right thing to do. For both of us.

That was a couple of weeks ago.

# 11

"*Hell, Doc, you* look about like I feel," Cecil said, as I entered the sheriff's office in the basement of the courthouse. He had his butt planted on an old steam radiator, and he was hunched over, cradling his paunchy middle.

"That seems to be the general consensus," I said. I headed over to the coffee machine and picked up the pot.

"Bryce just put that on," he said. "Macadamian nut or some such. He likes all them flavored deals."

He sneezed once, then took out a handkerchief and made a big production of blowing his nose. Being as it was in the basement, the sheriff's department always smelled of dampness and mold, and of the candy-apple-sweet odor of insecticide. In a corner near the locked shotgun case stood the most sorry-ass-looking Christmas tree I'd ever seen: spindly, turning a yellowish brown as if some animal had been using it for a fire hydrant. Beneath it were the canned goods the sheriff's department donated every year to the food pantry for needy families. Bryce Clayton, the dispatcher, sat in a glass-partitioned room near the door to the prisoner's lockup. He gave me an exaggerated salute when he saw me.

"Got some good news," Cecil said. "Fellow over to the emergency center in Crawford City is s'posed to call me right back. Thinks he might have us a bed after all."

"Really?"

"Told you I wouldn't let you down. Where's she at? The baby."

"She's over at the office."

"I sure do 'preciate what you done, Doc. The way I'm feeling. Last night I think I got me a good chill in my bones on top of ever'thing."

"Take some Tylenol and go to bed."

"Yeah, *right*. Plus, another deputy called in sick. Something's going 'round."

"Mind if I see Rosa Littlefoot?"

"Bumgartner give his okay?"

"Roberta said I could check on her eye."

"Oh, well. If'n Mrs. Tisdale says it's okay, that's good enough for me," Cecil said, with stagy emphasis. He glanced over at Bryce, then at me, a hint of a grin sealing our little secret.

"Heard you found her suitcase," I said.

"Yes indeedy. Had herself all ready to scoot."

"You're thinking she killed Pugh over the drugs?"

He shrugged. "Could of."

"C'mon, Cecil. You saw what he did to her. Did she look to you like a cold-blooded killer last night?"

"She looked pretty cold to me. And anyhow, it ain't my call to make. That's up to Bumgartner. I just lock 'em up."

Passing by where the dispatcher sat, Cecil said, "I'm letting the doc into cell two." Bryce jotted down something in a logbook.

"Heard y'all had yourselves quite a night," Bryce said to me. He was a small man with a large shaved head, soft doughy features, a boyish smile. Rumor had it he was gay. Cecil wasn't overly fond of him, but if someone were to make a snide remark about Bryce, the sheriff would tell him Bryce was a good dispatcher and what he did on his own time was nobody's business but his own.

"Yeah," I replied.

From a jangle of keys at his hip, Cecil selected one and opened the door to the lockup. Before we headed down the hall to the cells, I said to Cecil in an undertone, "You didn't tell the Pughs I had the baby, did you?"

"Of course not. Why?"

"Somehow they found out. Tully Pugh came around my place this morning looking for her. And when I wouldn't give her to him, he tried pushing his way into my house."

"He *what*! Why, that stupid redneck sum'bitch," Cecil said, scratching his beard. "I should've known. When I went out there this morning to tell 'em about Roy Lee, Glenn W. asked about the baby. I explained how, for the time being anyway, she was going to be placed in state custody, and the old man near'bouts blew his stack. He carried on, saying that she was his grandchild and we didn't have any right, blah blah blah. I finally told him he'd have to take it up with the authorities. Anything happen? With Tully, I mean."

"Not really. When he saw I wasn't just going to hand her over, he turned around and left. What I was wondering is, should I be worried?"

"I doubt it. They're crazy, them Pughs, but they ain't stupid. They know if they was to pull something, the law'll be all over them like shit on a hog. And that wouldn't be good for business."

"So why did he come to get her?"

"My guess is they figured to scare you once and that'd be the end of it. It had to be the old man's idea. His boys don't fart without Glenn W. telling 'em to. Still, if you want I could take a drive out there and have a talkin' to him. Say I'll tho his goddamn cracker ass in jail, he tries something like that again. Just to show 'em who's boss."

"Maybe it'd just be better to forget about it."

"That's probably a good idea. But if they try anything else, you let me know. Anyways, once this fellow calls me back, we can hand the baby over and it won't be your worry no more."

"Let me have a couple cigarettes."

"Since when do you smoke?"

"They're not for me. And matches."

He took out his Winstons, and I snatched the entire pack from him.

"The hell, Doc, I just bought those."

"I keep telling you these'll kill you, Cecil."

• • •

Rosa Littlefoot was lying on her side, facing the wall.

"Got a visitor," Cecil called, unlocking the door. "You need me, Doc, give a yell."

The Indian woman rolled over and sat up when I entered her cell. She rubbed her eyes, squinted up at me. Overhead, from inside a small wire cage, a harsh 150-watt bulb poured caustic light down over the cramped space of the cell. The woman's sleepy eyes were reddish slits, like razor cuts, except for the puffy swelling above her battered right eye.

"Oh," she said. "Dr. Jordan."

"Did you get any sleep?" I asked, sitting down on the cot next to her, the only place available. As I sat, the mattress gave off the rank odor of stale urine and vomit and unwashed feet.

"A little."

"You hungry?"

"No. They already fed me."

"How they treating you?"

"Got no complaints."

"Here's some cigarettes," I said.

"Thanks." She removed one from the pack, lit it with a match, and took a deep drag.

"Hunneycutt representing you?"

"I reckon. He stopped by earlier."

"He's a good man," I offered. "He'll give you all he's got."

"He seemed nice enough. Though I don't suppose it matters much one way or the other."

In the uncompromising overhead light, she appeared all of twenty-nine and then some, as if just being in the cell for a few hours had transformed her, aged her, the last vestiges of youth leaching out of her and into the dank concrete walls. What was left was the shell of another burnt-out druggie, like the woman I'd just passed in the park. Her face had hard lines around her mouth, and the whites of her eyes looked slightly more jaundiced in this light. I was thinking hepatitis. The bruises from the tracks on her arms looked more recent, too, and I wondered if she'd lied to me about when she'd last shot up. Her long beautiful braid had come undone, and the black hair lay about her face tangled and ungoverned, giving to her the appearance of a wild woman who had come down out of the mountains. Her right eye was swollen almost shut, the aggrieved flesh turning a gaudy purple. Whereas last night she contained within her the fierce power of a cornered animal, now she seemed merely an exhausted and beaten one.

"Can I take a gander at your eye?"

"It don't hardly hurt now. But go ahead, you want."

I put on some rubber gloves, lifted the bandage I'd put on the night before, and gave it a look.

"That should have a couple of stitches. Otherwise you'll have a bad scar there."

"If you think so."

I got some things from my bag: Betadine, a suture and needle. "This is gonna hurt a little." She didn't move as I sewed her up, just stared straight ahead, her eyes distant and unfocused. She gave off a sour smell of sweat and rancid milk.

"There," I said when I'd finished. "You need anything?"

"I could use a change of clothes."

She still wore the same jeans and black T-shirt from last night, but in the light they looked grubby, the bloodstains a gaudy reminder of the night before. Over each breast, I noticed, too, a darker circle, wettish looking.

"I'll see what I can do. I thought you might want this," I said, taking out the breast pump from my doctor's bag.

She stared at it, uncertain of its purpose. I told her what it was, how to use it.

"They been hurtin' real bad. I pumped 'em best I could." She glanced over at the sink in the corner. "I don't know why nothing was coming last night."

"You were nervous. It happens."

She glanced at me, her eyes suddenly filled with alarm. "Where's Maria at?"

It was as if she'd temporarily forgotten about her child, or through an act of will had been consciously avoiding thinking of her, like someone starving would avoid the thought of food. Almost as if by not asking about her, none of this was real. Not the jail cell or the blood on her pants or the night before. But now, having thought about milk and having invoked her daughter's name, everything came tumbling down on her. I saw her mouth wince, the lips drawn sharply across the too-large front teeth in an attitude of revelatory pain.

"She's at my office," I reassured her. "A woman there is looking after her."

"Has she taken food for you?"

"Yes, she's eaten."

"How is she? How's my baby, Dr. Jordan?"

"Don't you worry. She's doing just fine."

"*Ka-ma-ma*," she said, I guess something in Tsalagi, the language of the Cherokee Indians. Her voice was oddly uninflected, devoid of emotion. She stared straight ahead for several seconds, her face still drawn into a hard mask of defiance, anger, desperation, suffering. Then she cursed, "Damn him," just as she had the previous night. She leaned forward, put her face in her hands, and broke into sudden, jagged tears. Her bony shoulders quaked, and her ragged cries tore from her lungs, came from some deep, secret place inside her. In the same way her breasts had been dry last night but were now leaking, the tears burst forth as if from a dam that had suddenly given way. They slipped between her fingers and fell to the concrete floor. The change was so unexpected and complete, it took me a little by surprise. I reached out and put my hand on her shoulder.

"It's okay."

"Oh, my little *ka-ma-ma*," she cried, her voice cracking in her throat.

"Easy," I said, feeling her shoulders convulse with sobs. "Take a deep breath."

She sucked in a mouthful of air, held it for a moment, then blew it out.

"Now another." She did it several times. Trying to gain control of the pain the way a woman in labor does, hoping to define it, limit it, enclose it in some unfeeling space inside her. And in a sense the Indian woman was giving birth: to the fully formed idea of what lay in store for her. "Better?" I asked.

She nodded. I gave her my handkerchief and she blew her nose.

"It'll be all right," I said.

"I don't reckon it will," she replied. "I didn't mean for things to turn out like this."

"Why didn't you just leave him?" I asked, knowing already the answer to that. All those girls and women I saw in my office, the ones with the bruises and broken teeth, the battered faces and frightened doelike eyes. All the futile reasons they gave for staying with men that hurt them, with men that brutalized and enslaved them: fear, loyalty, children, money. And love, too—that always figured into it. Love so twisted and bent out of shape as to be unrecognizable.

"I asked myself that a thousand times. Roy wasn't so bad when he wasn't liquored up." She fell silent, her stare as empty as the shells we picked up from the trailer's floor.

"And he got you your drugs, right?"

She shrugged, then nodded. "I was really trying this time. I was off the needle. I'd put back some money. I wanted to make a new start for me and my baby. I thought maybe this time I could turn things around."

Though Bobbie said I wasn't supposed to talk about the case with her, I asked, "Is that why you had the suitcase packed?"

She glanced at me, surprised that I knew.

"They found it," I explained. "And the heroin. Were you going to use that for your new start?"

"I guess so."

"Did you fight over the drugs? Is that what happened?"

"No. I mean . . . Hunneycutt says I'm not supposed to say nothing."

"Sure, I understand. Is there anything else I can do?"

She sat up straight, lifted the bottom of her T-shirt to wipe her eyes. I had a glimpse of her small, slightly swollen belly. She had old track marks there as well.

"You already done enough," she said. "About last night, Dr. Jordan. I had no right to ask you what I did. I was in a bad way. I wasn't thinking straight."

"You were just looking after your baby."

"I didn't know what else to do," she replied. "But now I can see it wasn't right of me putting that on you. I just didn't want Maria going with his people."

"What do you have against the Pughs? I mean, besides their troubles with the law."

"They're no good. Me and them never got along. They didn't like that Roy Lee and me was living together. They thought I was dirt. Just a stinkin' Indian. The old lady wasn't so bad. And Tully, he was decent. But the rest, hell, I wouldn't give you two cents for."

"Tully?" I asked, remembering what he'd said to me that morning about blood loyalties.

"He was okay. When Roy Lee was serving time for dealing, he used to stop by. See how I was doing. If I needed anything."

"So he helped you?"

"Some. He'd give me some money when I had nobody else to turn to. Helped out in other ways, too."

"What did Roy Lee think of that?"

"He never found out. There'd a been hell to pay. You see, Roy has himself a right bad temper," she said, unconsciously touching the spot where I'd just put in the stitches. Then, remembering things clearly, she added, "*Had.*"

"The Pughs want custody of the baby," I said.

She looked over at me, some of that fire returning to her eyes.

"Over my dead body!" she hissed. "I know I'm no saint, Dr. Jordan, but I don't want Maria going with their kind. I want better for her than I had."

"Nobody over on the reservation you could leave her with?" I asked.

She thought about it for a moment before shaking her head.

"Dr. Jordan, you don't owe me nothing. Not one damn thing. I won't hold you to anything you promised. Could you just see to it that Maria finds a good home is all?"

*Don't,* I warned myself. *Don't do it. This wasn't your concern. Last night was one thing. This was something else entirely.* I knew I'd regret what I was going to do. But I also knew I'd regret it more if I didn't at least offer.

"Tell you what. How about if she stays with me until we see how things play out?"

"Play out?"

"Over the next few weeks. With your case."

"You don't have to."

"I know. But for right now anyway it might be the best thing for Maria. This way I could bring her in and you could see her now and then. She's going to need you. And you're going to need her, too. Would you be willing to sign papers making me her temporary guardian?"

"Well . . . sure. I guess so. Yeah."

"I'll get in touch with Hunneycutt then. See if he can arrange it."

"You sure you want to?"

"I'm willing to give it a try. We can see how things go."

"Thank you, Dr. Jordan," she said, beginning to cry again. She wiped her eyes with my handkerchief. "*Ga-li-e-li-ga.* How can I ever repay you?"

"Let's not worry about that right now. Listen, I have to go," I said, standing. I walked over to the door. Before calling for Cecil, I said, "One other thing. How many shots were fired?"

"Shots? I don't know. A couple. Why?"

"They found three spent shells."

"Then I reckon it must a been three."

"Two hit Pugh. What about the third?"

"How should I know? It wasn't like I was counting. Besides, what difference does it make? Roy Lee's just as dead whether it was one shot or a dozen."

For the first time, I had a funny feeling she wasn't telling the truth, or at least not all of it, that she was holding something back.

"It's not important. You take care of yourself."

On the way out of the sheriff's office, Cecil said, "Well, we're all set, Doc. They got a bed over in Crawford City. Social services can send somebody by to pick her up and bring her over there this afternoon. Told you I wouldn't leave you hanging out to dry."

"If it's all the same to you, I think I'll just keep Maria with me. For the time being."

"*What?*"

"I talked things over with Rosa, and we both felt it might be best for the baby to stay in town. That way the two can still visit while she's waiting for her trial."

"That might be a couple of months or more."

"I know."

"I wouldn't feel obligated to her, if I was you. I mean about . . . well, her making you swear and all that business, Doc."

"It's not that. Not now anyway."

"You sure you know what you're gettin' yourself into, Doc? What about the Pughs?"

"You said yourself you wouldn't worry about them. That they weren't stupid enough to try anything."

"Still, there's no telling about that bunch."

"It's just for the time being. We'll see how things go."

"I feel awful bad about getting you mixed up in this."

"Don't worry about it. I know what I'm doing," I said. Though I wasn't at all sure why I was getting myself into this or where it would lead.

"Suit yourself," Cecil said, disappointed. "I'll call and tell 'em we don't need the bed after all."

·  ·  ·

After leaving the courthouse, I still had some time before I had to be in surgery. I decided to drive over to Calby's florist shop, which was across from the bus station. I bought a poinsettia plant. Then I drove the two miles out to Laurel Branch. Just past the Methodist Church Annabel used to go to as a girl, I pulled into the cemetery and parked. I picked up the plant, got out of the truck, and started walking toward the back. A raw wind blew out of the northwest, and steel-gray clouds gathered in ripples like smocking over the Plott Balsams due north of town. The ground of the cemetery was frozen hard, the brittle grass making a crunchy sound like broken glass beneath my shoes. It was an old cemetery, with moss-covered stones dating to well before the Civil War. At the back, a row of tall cedars tried to maintain the tranquillity of the place, which was in danger of being disturbed by the new housing development going in up the branch. It was prime real estate with a beautiful view of Balsam Ridge. Florida people and young professionals were buying up the lots. Will's stone lay under a towering, bone-white sycamore near the creek, next to that of his grandparent, Edward Tyler Bryson, Annabel's dad, and her mom, Ida Mae Bryson. I'd never really known him; he died before we were married.

I hadn't been here in a while. For the longest time after Will's death, I came every Sunday morning, instead of going to church. Sometimes with Annabel, but more often alone. Now I came on his birthday and whenever I got around to it. I glanced down at his stone: *William Avery Jordan.* My father's name. Both dead. My father and my son forming parentheses around my life. Both dead by unnatural causes, both gone before their time. *Swear on your son's grave you'll take good care of my little girl.* Rosa Littlefoot's voice still echoed in my mind. I'd given her my word. I knew I didn't need to concern myself with this, but an oath was an oath.

I squatted and set the poinsettia plant near Will's headstone. I removed the pot of dead geraniums I'd placed there months before. When I visited, I usually didn't say anything. Words seldom came to me, and it seemed somehow theatrical and contrived to force them. So usually I just waited silently, the way I used to wait in his room at night when I'd get home late from work. I'd stand above his crib watching him sleep, listening to his breathing, taking in the sweetish aroma of his small body. The difference, of course, was that back then the future—his, ours—stretched out in front of us like these blue mountains on a perfect spring day. Endless. Everything possible. No choice irrevocable, no moment fleeting. We had all the time in the world. If I had to miss his third birthday party because I had to stay late at the hospital, there would be other birthdays; if I couldn't see him in the kindergarten Christmas pageant because I was working, I'd see the next one; if my patients had to take precedence over my family, there would be time to make it up. There would always be *time,* I'd felt. Of course, it was, as it always is, just an illusion. When I looked back, entire weeks and months of the precious little time we had him slipped by me, whitish blurs in my memory, like cataracts in one's vision. I thought about what Annabel had said in her letter, about forgetting what his mouth looked like. How I knew that feeling! The fourteen years since his death sometimes seemed like a million; it seemed as if our son was just some pleasant dream from long ago. I knew what it was to forget parts of him, to keep losing him a bit at a time, week after week, year after year, his image slowly eroding in my mind; not to recall his voice, what his hair smelled like, the dimples when he smiled. The subsequent, small, daily deaths.

Out of instinct, I mumbled a prayer, asked a God I no longer believed in to keep him safe in a place I could no longer picture. I'd been raised Catholic, though I hadn't gone to the small Catholic church in Slade for years. In fact, I wasn't sure what I believed anymore. Was he in the arms of angels? Did his spirit rest in the sheltering bosom of these hills? Annabel didn't believe in a heaven or hell, at least not the usual fire-and-brimstone and God-in-the-clouds sort. She believed that our souls made long arduous journeys from ignorance and pain toward wisdom and enlightenment. She used to say that Will was in a place beyond suffering. I guess the Catholic in me wanted to believe that, too, but the only thing I could say for sure was that I missed him, even now, all these years later. I couldn't touch his toys or stand above his gravestone without a small, hard lump forming in my throat.

After Will died, I had thrown myself into my work and into the work of caring for my wife. Her pain kept me from feeling my own, I suppose. Worrying about her was like an anesthetic for me. I remember once, a couple of years after Will's death, when Annabel had taken off. I searched everywhere for her. On a hunch, I finally came here. I found her lying on his grave, asleep, an empty bottle of Jack Daniels nearby.

"Come on. Let's go home, Anna," I had said, picking her up and carrying her to my truck. She was drunk, slobbering, her hair matted from the dew. She smelled of booze and sweat, mixed with a vaguely metallic odor I knew was other men. She looked wild, half crazed with the mania, the booze, her own guilt.

"It was my fault," she cried.

"Stop that."

"No! You were right, Stu. I should've been watching him. If I had, he'd still be alive."

"Ssh! Try to forget about it."

"I can't forget. I *can't*!"

"It's all right. You're home now."

"I'm so sorry, Stu. Can you ever forgive me?"

Who was I to forgive anybody?

# 12

*At the hospital* I scrubbed for the scheduled C-section of Mrs. Sally Titus. Sally was a heavy woman, late twenties, gravida four, a two-pack-a-day smoker whose babies tended to be on the small side. I'd delivered the first three, all girls, vaginally, and I'd expected to do the same with this one. But about a month ago, on a routine prenatal visit to my office, the ultrasound showed the fetus was breech. I'd held out the hope that nature would step in and turn the baby on its own, but on Sally's last visit I confirmed it was still breech, so we scheduled a section. Dr. Chung, a GP who'd been in town several years, assisted me. I made a horizontal slit into the uterus, and lemon-colored amniotic fluid spurted out. I reached deep into Sally's womb and felt for something to get my bearings, finally recognizing the heel of a tiny, eel-slippery foot. I lifted the baby, a premie-sized boy with a full head of glistening black hair, out and into the light of day. For several gut-wrenching seconds, the baby lay flaccid and silent. Chung went to work suctioning mucus and meconium from the infant's nostrils, and soon Raymond Allen Titus II let out with an outraged howl, pissed off, as any reasonable soul would be, at having his nine-month nap so rudely disturbed.

"He do fine," Chung said in his heavy accent. "Not to worry."

As I washed up, I thought how in a little over twelve hours, I'd pronounced a man dead, took on the responsibility of his child, heard from my wife for the first time in months, visited my son's grave, and delivered a baby boy—all on about an hour's sleep. Though I should have been beat, I felt myself shift into high gear, as I usually do after the adrenaline-surge of delivering a healthy baby. Even my knees no longer hurt. When obstetrics was bad it was downright awful, but when it was good, there was no better feeling than placing a newborn in a mother's anxious arms.

After that I checked on Nora Bump and her triplets. She and the babies, two girls and a boy, were getting along just fine, so I went ahead and discharged her. I next looked in on Sue Ellen McCreadie, the pregnant fourteen-year-old who'd tried to overdose. I was keeping her, as doctors like to say, for observation, which means covering your ass legally. And what I was observing now was a sullen child lying in bed watching one of those late-afternoon talk shows where the guests holler at each other. Sue Ellen was a pudgy little girl with stringy auburn hair and the doughy features of her mother. A tray of uneaten food lay on the nightstand.

"How you feeling?" I asked.

"Food sucks around here. Like to make me barf."

"It's their way of getting you better real quick."

"Any chance I could get a cheeseburger? I'm starving."

"A friend works in the kitchen. I'll see if I can pull some strings, but only if you behave yourself."

"When can I go home? There's nothing to do here."

"A day or two. You got to promise me you're not going to pull another stunt like that."

"Which one? My mother's more concerned about the stunt I pulled six months ago."

After I'd checked her out and was satisfied she and the baby were doing fine, at least physically, I paid a visit to Emmilou Potter.

Emmilou was thirty-six, normally a pale, thin woman with the gaunt, high-cheekboned features of true Carolina mountain stock. Now, though, she was bloated with early signs of preeclampsia. Her face was swollen, and her fingers were puffy with edema, resembling sausages. She could barely contract them into a fist. When she came in the hospital two days before, her blood pressure had spiked to 180/110, and when I ran lab tests I found that she was putting out protein in her urine. I was now mostly afraid of damage to her kidneys. This was her fifth pregnancy, without a child to show for it.

I liked Emmilou. She had grit. She never whined or complained, even when she was really sick, never asked why she couldn't bring a child to term, was always cheerful and pleasant. She and her husband, Jack, were dirt-poor. He logged for a living, delivering wood to the paper mill, while Emmilou cleaned houses, took in laundry, and sold eggs to make ends meet. They didn't have insurance, and yet, like many mountain folk, they were too proud, perhaps too stubborn, to take a handout or go on welfare. So they did what used to be far more common in the old days of doctoring; they paid me in kind. Before she got sick, Emmilou cleaned my house and did my laundry, brought me fresh eggs. And Jack Potter would show up at my house with his dump truck filled with three or four cords of well-seasoned firewood. That, along with the occasional twenty dollars in cash, was how they paid me.

"Hey, Dr. Jordan," she said spiritedly.

"How are we today?"

"Purty good. The dizziness is near'bouts gone."

"I'm glad to hear that."

I did a DTR exam—deep tendon reflexes—checked the fetal heartbeat, took her blood pressure. Emmilou's ankles were badly swollen, the skin mottled a pinkish gray like underdone pork. The flesh pitted deeply when touched, another bad sign. The prognosis wasn't good, not this early in the pregnancy. I had her on Aldomet to lower her blood pressure but wanted to avoid using a diuretic as long as I could, so as not to harm the fetus. I was hoping to buy some time. Another sixteen weeks would've been good, but I'd have settled for a dozen. I wasn't optimistic, though. Her body had been telling us in every way it could that it wasn't cut out to carry a baby to term. We were paddling furiously upstream against Mother Nature's strong, remorseless current.

"How's it looking, Doc?"

"I'm a little worried about your kidneys, Emmilou. I'm going to run some more tests."

"Am I gonna lose this 'un, too?"

"We're going to do all we can."

"I shouldn'ta got out of bed, is what. Poor Janey though."

"Janey?" I asked.

"That's our cow. She was a-mooing her head off 'cause her bag was full and Jack was off cutting somewheres. You hate to see a poor dumb animal in pain."

"Next time let Janey wait," I said.

"I will, Doc," she said with a chuckle. "How long you reckon I got to stay in the hospital?" She didn't say anything about the money, but I knew that's what she was getting at.

"We'll have you out of here as soon as we can, Emmilou. In the meantime, I want you to get plenty of rest. And remember to lie on your left side as much as possible."

"You got any clothes need tending to, I could have Jack bring me in my iron and do some whilst I'm just a-settin' here."

"I want you to take it *easy*. You hear me? This is serious."

A mischievous smile played across her bloated face. Like I said, my patients were the sort a doctor would certainly find exasperating. Not following your advice. Not taking the medicine you prescribed. Not taking their illnesses seriously. Suspicious of doctors and their newfangled ways. Still favoring the old ways, preferring to leave things in the hands of the Lord. Prayer over technology. It made you angry. It made you want to shake them and say, *I'm trying to help you*! Yet it also made you want to protect them, the way you would children from harming themselves. I was going to do everything in my power to see that she went home with a healthy baby this time.

The December night was as cold and clear as a mountain stream, the air pungent with the smell from the paper mill. As I passed Pancho Villa's, I was tempted to stop for a quick one. Though I hadn't eaten a thing since breakfast, what I craved more than food was a single malt Scotch, straight up, sipped patiently while sitting in a warm bar filled with people and watching a game whose outcome I didn't much care about either way. Shooting the breeze with Hector. But of course I couldn't; I still had things to do. I thought of them, the women whose lives I'd somehow influenced: Sally Titus, who was now nursing a healthy baby boy; Rosa Littlefoot, sitting alone in a jail cell, pumping her breasts and pouring the milk down the sink; Sue Ellen McCreadie, just a kid who'd made a mistake, who was more interested in a cheeseburger than the child she was carrying; and Emmilou, a woman who was dying—literally dying—to have a baby and her body wasn't cooperating. All of them depending on me, counting on me, putting their faith in me. I mostly liked the feeling: People placing their lives and the lives they were carrying into my hands. As corny as it sounds, that's why I'd gone into OB-GYN in the first place. But sometimes, like now, I almost wished I'd gone into something simple and uncomplicated, like dermatology, where at the end of the day you could go home and not worry about it. Skin can take care of itself.

I thought of my old man again, something I was doing more and more of late. Maybe because I was now about the age he was when he took his own life. I was the youngest of three boys, all of whom my father had had late in life. I thought about how much he loved being a small-town doctor. Not that it was all rosy. There were the long hours he put in. The nights and weekends. Being on call. Away from his family. Still, he loved it. It wasn't so much a job or a profession as it was a way of life, who *he* was. At the dinner table he would speak of his patients with the same sort of paternal pride or annoyance, concern or disappointment, that parents do of their own children. For in a sense they were his children. Some obedient to him and grateful for his help, others rebellious and unappreciative, abusing their health and causing him to worry. But *all* of them his concern. His headache.

Once when I was a boy and on school vacation, I'd accompanied him to his office on Main Street, above the Montgomery Ward store. He let me watch as he took a patient's blood pressure or percussed an infant's chest. "You gonna be a doc like your old man?" asked ancient Mr. Balise, who lived up the street from us and had bad emphysema. I remember nodding and my father looking at me with pride. It was never anything we spoke about; in fact, we didn't speak about much at all. He was a man of few words, fewer emotions. But it was nonetheless silently understood by both that I would follow in his footsteps.

I remembered when the Parkinson's got so bad his hands trembled and he could hardly hold a stethoscope. He'd spill the food onto his lap and my mother would have to feed him like a baby. I recalled how it shamed him to be rendered helpless, especially in front of his children, my older brothers and me. Though he had loved to hunt and fish, the thing he missed the most was touching people, laying his hands on his patients and easing their pain. That feeling of being useful, of being needed, even at times abused by patients. That's what he regretted most about getting sick—not being able to tend to his patients. I remembered the night he took his life. I was fourteen. My mother found him out in the garage, the Buick still running. Half the town came to his funeral. I recalled feeling proud that I was his son, that so many in town had loved and respected him. Yet, at the same time, I recalled feeling cheated and angry and bitter: for having had to share him with all the others, for his having spent so much time with his patients and not enough with us.

Yes, I thought. I'd followed in his footsteps, all right.

. . .

Normally, Main Street was deserted by seven o'clock on a weeknight, but this close to Christmas it was still busy, and I had to park a block down from my office. I spotted Drew Hazard coming out the door of the *Slade Messenger*, and I tried to duck into my office without his spotting me. He was someone I liked personally but whose weekly paper was little more than a gossip sheet. He was always trying to pump me so I'd let slip who in town was pregnant or who'd had a hysterectomy, or something relating to my capacity as ME.

"Oh, Doc," he said. "Hey, Doc. What can you give me about the shooting?"

"What shooting?"

"Real funny. The one down at Tanavasee Lake."

"Ask Bumgartner."

"Already did. He won't say a word. Can you tell me anything at all?"

"The deceased is one Roy Lee Pugh."

"I *know* that, for crying out loud. A rumor's going around that it had to do with drugs."

"No comment."

"C'mon, Doc. I need some facts to write a story."

"That's never stopped you before, Drew."

"And there was a kid, too, I heard."

"Sorry. Can't help you. Have a merry," I said, and headed into my office.

I found Stella sitting on the couch in our small lounge in back. She was eating a pot roast sandwich. The baby was lying next to her on the couch, sound asleep.

"*Ssh,*" Stella whispered, a finger to her lips.

"Sorry I held you up. Howard will be getting hungry."

"The man ain't crippled. Besides, it's his night to play cards."

"How's she been for you?"

"She's a right easy baby. Gladys looked her over from head to toe. She's fit as a fiddle," she said, then added cryptically, "'Cept of course that bruise on her leg."

"I think they were having their problems," I explained.

"Her? Or was it that Pugh fellow done it?"

"My guess, it was him."

I bent close to the baby. She stirred in her sleep, her eyelids fluttering. She raised her fat, dimpled hand to her mouth, found her two middle fingers, and commenced to sucking on them.

"Ain't she just the most precious li'l thing, Dr. Jordan?"

I nodded.

"Had me four healthy boys, and I wouldn't've traded a one of 'em. Most of the time anyway," she said, with a laugh. "And I know there's some, like the Potter girl, don't even get to have one. So I ain't complaining. Still, I always wish I'da had me a little girl. Dress her up and put bows in her hair. I reckon you'd have to be a woman to understand."

"No, I can understand. Annabel always wanted a girl, too."

Stella fell silent. After a time she glanced over at me, her droopy eye exaggerated the way it became when she was overtired.

"Look at you, Doc."

"Me?"

"Why, you got bags under your eyes. And I can tell you ain't been eating right."

"I eat just fine," I said, patting the small paunch I had as proof.

"Why, you ain't got no meat on you a'tall. What'd you put in your mouth today?"

"Two bowls of cereal."

"See. A grown man can't get by on two bowls of cereal. Lordy. Here, take you half of this sandwich." When I protested, she said, "G'won and take it."

I took the proffered sandwich and started eating. Only then did I realize just how hungry I was. I devoured it, the pot roast melting in my mouth.

"What y'all doing for Christmas dinner, Doc?"

"I'm on call."

"You still gotta eat, doncha? You come on over to the house for dinner. The boys'll be there with their families. You ain't seen them for a spell. Lyle's coming over from Murphy. He's got him a new baby girl, just about this 'un's age."

"We'll see."

"I won't take 'we'll see' for an answer. I'll set a plate for you, y'hear."

"All right," I said at last.

"Come by about two. By the way, I picked you up some baby things. Got a snowsuit on sale down at Shuster's. Thirty percent off."

"Thanks. Would you know anybody interested in doing a little baby-sitting?"

"When was you looking for?"

"Tonight. I have to go out."

"You should get you some sleep, Doc."

"I have something to take care of first. I need somebody to look after the baby while I'm gone."

"She could come home with me."

"I've already inconvenienced you enough, Stella."

"What inconvenience?"

"You sure?"

"I'm just settin' home by my lonesome. Howard's down to the Legion Hall. Figure to do some Christmas baking. She could keep me company."

"I might not be back till late."

"If I fall asleep just rap good and hard on the door."

"What would I ever do without you, Stella?"

"Only wish Howard would say that ever' onct in a while. Best I get from that one is a grunt if he likes what I fixed for supper. Leastways he don't go bothering me with his needs nomore. That's one thing to be grateful for, I suppose," she said with a dry cackle. She thought about it for a moment and then blushed.

I helped Stella get the baby into her new snowsuit, which was pink, with a white fur-lined hood that accented the dark oval of her face. Maria woke, looking quietly up at us.

"She's got right pretty eyes," Stella said. "Darker'n a skillet bottom. What's gonna happen to her momma?"

"They'll try her for murder."

"The poor thing," she said. I wasn't sure whether she meant the baby or her mother. "You leaving now, Doc?"

"No, I have some paperwork to catch up on here. You go on home."

With the baby in her arms, she headed over to the door. She stopped and said, "You be sure to say hey to her for me."

"Who?" I asked, thinking for a moment she meant Rosa Littlefoot.

"Why, Annabel Lee. That's who you're a-fixin' to see, ain't it?"

"How'd you know?"

"You getting her letter today. Plus, it being your son's birthday and all."

"You remembered?"

"'Course. I can still remember Annabel showing up here with that little feller. And later, when he was bigger, how you used to bring him to the office. Remember that?"

"Yeah," I replied, though the truth was I couldn't remember.

"He was about my grandson Tommy's age. Such a purty little boy. He favored you, except for the mouth. Which I think he got from Annabel. You think she's ever coming home, Doc? To stay, I mean."

I shook my head.

"I don't mean to be sticking my nose in where it don't belong. Just that after all the two a' you been through, it's a shame things worked out like they done. A cryin' shame."

"Yeah," was all I said.

"I sure do miss that gal. I know some folks hereabouts thought Annabel a bit peculiar, high-strung. But I always liked her. She had spunk, that girl. Didn't matter to her what people said. And the things that'd come outa that child's mouth, I swear. I remember one Halloween she come to our house trick-or-treatin'. She was in some getup. A sheet wrapped around her and wearing some kinda crown. My momma asked her if she was supposed to be the Queen of Sheba. And Annabel, she couldn'ta been more than nine, she says, 'Why, Mrs. Tinsley, don't you know I'm Helen of Troy?' Like any fool should have known. So my momma goes, 'Any kin to the Troys up in Green Mountain Fork?' Annabel, serious as all getout—you know how she always was—says, 'No, this Troy's in a book. The Greeks launched a thousand ships to bring Helen back.' 'Is that a fact, young lady?' my momma said, near to busting a gut. I'll never forget that. That poor gal's had her share of troubles and then some. You tell her hey for me, would you?"

"I will," I said.

"And don't worry none if you're late."

After she left, I got the bottle of Scotch I kept in my drawer and poured myself a drink. I felt I deserved one. With Emmilou Potter in mind, I skimmed a couple of articles on early preeclampsia, on natriuretic peptide levels as a predictor for gestational hypertension, on platelet angiotensin II binding measurements. Then I took out my notes and started writing up my ME's report on the shooting. Maybe Bobbie was right. Maybe Rosa Littlefoot was just a cold-blooded murderer. She'd shot him not once but twice, the second blast long after he could have hurt her and long after she'd had a chance to calm down and think over what she'd done. Not to mention the packed suitcase and the dope. And, of course, she'd wiped the gun clean. I had to admit, it all didn't sound like your run-of-the-mill domestic. Maybe she *had* planned it all out, waited for him to come home, and then killed him, planning on taking the dope and making a run for it. But if that was so, why hadn't she gone through with it? Why not take his truck and go? Why did she call the police? That didn't make sense either. Those two halves didn't fit together at all. The other thing that didn't fit was that shot in the ceiling. It was a small thing, I suppose, yet all day it had been chafing against me like a pebble in my shoe, rubbing, irritating, raising a blister before you knew it. What did that third shot mean? A warning? Had there been a struggle and the gun simply went off? The extra shot ran counter to some need in me for clean factual order, for a tying together of loose ends. I appreciated the symmetry of facts, one leading surely and confidently to the next. Yet I knew all too well that our lives had all sorts of loose ends, things that never got tied together. Things that remained ragged, asymmetrical, unexplained. And the same was true with our deaths. People died in strange and unimaginable ways, rough-edged, messy, with little thought for tidiness or order or logic. As I wrote up the report, something else kept rubbing me the wrong way, distracting me from finishing. I thought about what I was going to tell Annabel tonight. About Bobbie and me. I couldn't put it off any longer.

When I was finished I turned out the lights and locked up. I went outside and walked the two blocks to the bank and took some money out of the ATM machine. Then I headed for my truck. As I was about to get in, a voice called out, "Dr. Jordan."

I turned to see somebody crossing the street. He was a slight man, with narrow shoulders, and he walked with a noticeable limp, moving with a jerky crablike gait. Though it was cold, he wore only a white short-sleeved dress shirt and a string tie. When he got close enough, he extended his hand in greeting.

"If I could have a minute of your time, Dr. Jordan," he said, vigorously pumping my hand. His hand was cool and smooth, like the scales of a black snake. I think he expected me to know him, but I didn't. "I'm Glenn W." As an afterthought, he tacked on "Pugh."

So this small, gimpy fellow was the infamous Glenn W. Pugh, I thought.

"Hello, Mr. Pugh," I said. "My condolences about your son."

"Thank ye. Roy Lee was headstrong. Always was. Ever since he was little. Don't matter though. He was my boy and when you lose a young'un you lose part of yourself. I already got one might as well be dead to me. Sometimes I think it's the good Lord's judgment on me, I surely do."

Glenn W. Pugh's voice was pure mountain twang, squeaky as a rusty nail being pulled from wet cedar. Yet he spoke deliberately, choosing his words with care. Up close I saw that he had small, deep-set, liquid-gray eyes that seemed to coolly appraise me the way they might a tree for felling, trying to decide which way would present the least difficulties. His mouth was fleshless, a thin, jagged line, turned down at the corners, his chin prominent, like that of his boys. He was in his late sixties, I'd say, balding, though his face was smooth and without lines, making you think of something unnaturally young. Despite being slight of build, he gave the impression of being formidable in an indistinct way, of possessing hidden reserves of strength or tenacity or something which would make him a substantial opponent. It might have been in the set of his jaw or in those impassive gray eyes, but there was, unmistakably, something about Glenn W., a coiled-spring intensity lurking just beneath the placid surface. As if he were filled with the potential for danger in the same way a live round of ammo or a can of gasoline can be considered potentially dangerous.

"What can I do for you, Mr. Pugh?" I asked.

"Sure is a cold one," he said, blowing on his hands. "Can I buy you a cup of coffee?"

"No, thanks. I have to get going."

"Well, I'll make it short then. I want to thank you for all your trouble. Taking in Maria like you done."

"It was no big deal."

"All the same, it was mighty decent of you. And I want to apologize for my son coming by your place this morning. Tully don't always look before he jumps in. But he was upset about his brother."

"I understand. No harm done. Is that all you wanted, Mr. Pugh?"

"Truth is, I come to speak to you about my grandchild. The way I figure it, blood ought to be with blood. Don't you think that's only right, Dr. Jordan?"

I didn't want to bring Rosa into this if I could help it. So I said, "I believe Sheriff Clegg already explained the situation to you. If you're looking to get custody, you'll have to take up with the court."

"Which is exactly what I'm fixin' to do—*if* I have to. But I never did like having any truck with lawyers and all. For my money, they's nothing but hogs feeding at the trough. I was figurin' you and me could settle this thing like reasonable folk and save everybody a lot of headaches."

"I'm afraid it's not my decision to make." Which was, I knew, only partially the truth. I could have gone along with Cecil's idea to place Maria with the Pughs.

"But you're the one looking after the child, right?" he said, gazing past me into the truck.

"For now."

"You needn't get yourself mixed up in family business, Dr. Jordan. Busy man like yourself. I'm sure you got plenty better things to do."

"I just want what's best for Maria, Mr. Pugh."

"That makes two of us then. I can assure you, Dr. Jordan, we'd take good care of the child. Raise her up right, in a God-fearing family."

"I have no doubt you would," I said, trying to keep the irony out of my voice.

Pugh placed his hand on my arm and leaned toward me, as if to tell me something in confidence.

"Then what's to stop you from just handing her over to me? Maria'll be with her kin. You can go about your bidness. Ever'body's happy and we don't have to mess with them good-for-nothing shysters." He tacked on a little conspiratorial chuckle.

"I can't do that."

"Why?"

"Because she's not mine to give away."

"It's on account of her, ain't it? That Indian whore."

"No."

"Did she go bad-mouthing us to Clegg? Is that what this's all about?"

"She *is* the mother, Mr. Pugh. She had some . . . concerns."

"*Concerns?*" he said sarcastically, fixing me with those gray eyes. "And what in the name of Jesus were her *con*cerns?"

"Let's just say she wasn't comfortable with Maria going to stay with you."

"Is that so? And you'd take her word over mine? The word of a murderer and a junkie and a goddamned whore."

"Listen, Mr. Pugh . . . "

"No, *you* listen, Dr. Jordan," the man said. Though there was anger in his voice, his expression didn't change in the least. Not a single muscle moved in his face. Only those gray eyes altered slightly to show that he was angry. They appeared to shimmer, to change color and even shape almost, like globules of mercury that had been prodded. "I just come back from *i*dentifying what was left of my boy. What that bitch . . . " He paused while tears slid quietly down his cheeks. "What she done to him. Now she's gonna say *we* ain't fit to raise Roy Lee's child. Lord Jesus. Let me tell *you* something, Mister. She weren't nothing but a street whore turning tricks to support her habit when Roy Lee met her. My son took her in, put a roof over her head. Tried to make an honest woman of her. Christ, he even looked the other way when she had them fellers coming around, the whore she was. Me, I'da shot her dead and not shed a tear. Not a goddamned tear. But Roy Lee had him a softness about him." Glenn W. paused to wipe his eyes. "He loved her, Dr. Jordan. Lord knows why, but he did. And this is the way she repays him. Guns him down like a cur dog, and now she's aiming to keep his own flesh and blood away from his kinfolk. It ain't right, Dr. Jordan. No sir. And I won't abide it. Do you hear me? Maria's all I got left of my son, and I'll be damned if'n I let anybody take her away."

Despite his bluster, it was hard not to feel his pain.

"Mr. Pugh," I said, "I understand."

"I don't reckon you do, Dr. Jordan," he tossed at me. "But that don't matter a rat's ass. What would it take to change your mind?"

"What do you mean?"

"How much?"

Pugh reached into his pants pocket and pulled out a thick roll of bills. He licked his thumb and started counting them out, mostly hundreds and fifties.

"Just name your price," he said. "I'm willing to make it worth your while."

"Mr. Pugh, it's not a question of money."

"It's *always* a question of money. Just a matter of how much is all. Five thousand?" I just stared at him. "All right, whatsay we make it seven then? Seven thousand dollars cash to take her off your hands. No questions asked."

"Mr. Pugh . . . "

He smiled at me, his youthful-looking face turning gnomish and perverse. "Tell you what. I ain't agonna nickel-and-dime you. I'm a fair man. Let's make it an even ten grand. For all your troubles? 'Course, I don't have it all with me tonight. I could bring it over to your place tomorrow morning. My word's good."

He's changing tactics, I thought. His son had come by to scare me, and since that didn't work, now he was trying to buy me.

"For God's sake, Mr. Pugh, she's not a piece of property."

"Then what I got to do?"

"I told you. It's not my call to make. We'll have to leave that to the courts."

As if the subject of his grandchild's custody was right then under discussion, Pugh glanced up Main Street, toward the brightly lit courthouse on the hill. He sucked in a quick breath, then drew his mouth into a tightly zippered circle of anger.

"I know what people say about us. That we're just no'count hillbilly trash. They's nothing I can do about that. But I got rights, too. I just lost me a son, and now y'all are trying to take my granddaughter away. She belongs to us."

"The child will stay with me till they decide where she goes, Mr. Pugh. That's not up for debate."

"It ain't, huh?"

"No, it's not."

"Who in the hell put you in charge?" he cursed at me. With his index finger, he tapped me lightly on the shoulder. "You think you're some big important man, Dr. Jordan. Some Yankee come down here to tell all us redneck crackers how to run our lives. Bullshit. You hear that—*bullshit!*"

"I only want to help."

"Help. We don't need your goddamn help. Feller like yourself goes and sticks his nose in where he's got no bidness, he's liable to get it bloodied. Yes siree."

"What's that supposed to mean?"

"Just telling you how things is, *Doctor* Jordan."

"Is that a threat, Mr. Pugh?" I felt my stomach tense up, like it did when I'd had to pronounce one of his sons and keep his other son from pushing his way into my house. I was hardly aware of my hands curling into fists at the ends of my arms.

"Ain't no threat," he said, smiling cruelly.

"I already told the police about your son coming by. You stay away from me or I'll have you arrested. Do you hear me?"

"Good evening, Dr. Jordan," he replied with exaggerated politeness, before turning and limping across the street. He scampered up into a red Ford pickup, brand new looking though the rocker panel and fenders were thickly coated with ochre-colored mud. It had a cap over the bed and tires the size of small hippos. He started it, backed out onto Main, gunned the gas, and went screaming off down the street. I stood there for a moment watching him go, wondering if I should be worried.

# 13

As I drove east on the Interstate heading for Asheville, I had plenty of time to mull over what Pugh had said: that I was sticking my nose in where it didn't belong, asking for trouble. Maybe he was right. Maybe I should just stay out of it. Let social services handle things. After all, who was I to say what was best for Maria Littlefoot? Perhaps she would be better off with family, even one like the Pughs. Besides, what did I really know about them, beyond the stories people told, the rumors that circulated about the infamous Pugh clan? Only that and what Rosa had told me: that she didn't want her baby going there. And how could I believe her? A murderer and a junkie, just like old man Pugh claimed. What sort of mother was she that gave her any right to say where her daughter went? I thought about something else Pugh had said: Maria was the only thing he had left of his son. I could understand his wanting to get her back to hold onto something of his son's. I could certainly understand that.

Right after I crossed the French Broad River, I got off the highway. The small downtown part of the city, perched on a hill, sparkled gem-like, brightly illuminated for Christmas. Driving by Pack Square, I saw people window shopping for last-minute gifts, couples arm-in-arm as they emerged, smoky-breathed and laughing, from upscale restaurants and trendy cafés. The city had changed some in the past two decades, had become yuppified, as Annabel put it. Still, it made me think how we used to come here weekends, before Will was born. We'd go out to dinner or take in a foreign film Annabel had picked out. Go to an art gallery or a poetry reading.

Annabel loved Asheville, thought the small city charming and cosmopolitan, with its art deco and gothic buildings, its cafés and music and artsy, bohemian culture: a free-spirited sort of place which offered things she couldn't find back in the straitlaced, stifling confines of Slade. Back home they'd always thought of her as odd, an eccentric child of an equally eccentric father; later, they saw her as a woman possessed of peculiar notions and quirky ways. The way she dressed, almost always in black. How she acted. The way she didn't fit in, didn't even make an attempt to. And that was when she was healthy, before her moods became exaggerated as the manic-depression kicked in, subjecting her to the critical eyes of a small Southern town that frowned on people being different. But in Asheville she could blend in. She had a few friends here, people with whom she felt some sort of kinship based on their differentness. Hippies or musicians or artists, gays or blacks or Jews. That's why I think when she started taking off she would usually gravitate here. Unlike Charlotte or Atlanta or Knoxville, Asheville wasn't so big as to overwhelm her or so far away that she couldn't, if the mood struck her, catch a bus or hitch a ride with a friend and be home in a couple of hours. She felt safe here. The eccentricities of her personality and of her illness weren't so noticeable in the city. I sometimes wondered if things would have turned out different if we'd decided to move here instead of staying in Slade.

    In fact, it was in Asheville that I'd first met Annabel. While I'd dated some women from town, the truth was my job didn't allow much in the way of a social life, and even if it had, there wasn't a whole lot to do, especially for a bachelor who was not much given to attending church socials or square dancing at the VFW or judging pie contests. So sometimes when I wasn't on call, I'd slip out of town and drive over to Asheville, where no one knew me, and where, for a few hours at least, I didn't have to conform to the upstanding, wholesome image I'd somehow gathered around me. It was, after all, the sixties then, and while I was already past thirty and beginning to settle into the growing responsibilities of my practice, every once in a while I still felt the urge to get out of Slade, to escape its smug parochial attitudes and redneck provincialism. In Asheville, I'd go out to some restaurant and have a good bottle of cabernet with my meal, get a little drunk, take in a movie, maybe go to a club called the French Broad, named after the river that ran through the city. The French Broad had good bands that played blues and bluegrass and folk. It was a pretty eclectic place, daringly progressive for the hills back then. There were aging beatniks and young hippies, blacks and whites, professionals in Brooks Brothers suits sitting next to leather-clad bikers or hillbillies in coveralls. I'd have a drink or two, listen to somebody singing like B. B. King or Joni Mitchell, back before they'd become big names, and then head home to my "other" life.

One night I was at the bar in the French Broad, nursing a drink. I had surgery the next morning, and I made it a habit not to have more than one when I was on duty the following day. I'd come all the way this night to listen to some guy who played a lot of Dylan and Seeger and Joan Baez songs. Seated near me at the bar were two women and a man. The woman next to me was a loud, buxomy blond who smoked long, dark cigarettes. The man, who sat farthest away, was black, with a full Afro and bib overalls. Between them, the other woman was thin and pale, with a long black braid that snaked down her back all the way to her waist. During an intermission, they struck up a conversation with me.

"You don't sound like you're from these parts," the blond said.

I confessed that I wasn't, told them why I'd moved to Slade.

"Way out in the boonies," said the black guy. "That's real hillbilly country."

"Why, they're so backwards out there, you give 'em a toilet and they wouldn't know to shit in it," joked the blond, elbowing the other woman. "Ain't that right, Annie?"

"Us'n doan even wyar shews, Lorraine," the black-haired woman said in an exaggerated mountain accent.

"It's true. I been out there. Idn't it?" Lorraine said to me.

"It's a little backwards," I replied. "But the people are friendly."

The blond did most of the talking. As she spoke, I glanced over her shoulder at the dark-haired woman seated behind her. She didn't have much to say, would only frown now and then at something her friend said, sip her beer, stare off into space. I couldn't tell if she was stoned or aloof, or what the story was with her. She had a narrow face, with delicate features that gathered themselves into a wan expression. Her most striking feature was her eyes: deep-set, a smoky brown behind wire-rim glasses. Searching, ethereal sort of eyes. She wore a black leather jacket with a peace sign sewn on the back, black T-shirt, black jeans. Everything about her was black, which, combined with the fact that she wore no makeup at all, only accentuated the pale cool glow of her skin. She was pretty in a defiantly plain, ascetic sort of way. For some reason she made me think of a nun who'd just renounced her vows and was as yet

unaccustomed to being in the world, negotiating its unexpected free-
doms, moving about in a body suddenly emancipated.

After the last set, I said I had to get going, that I had a hysterectomy
to do in the morning.

"That must be a bummer," Lorraine commented.

"Say," the black guy asked, "any chance our friend here could catch
a lift back with you? Since you're going that way. She lives in Slade and
it would save me a trip."

"Don't see why not. You from Slade?" I asked the dark-haired
woman. I'd never seen her around town and I would have remembered
if I had.

She nodded, offering up an expression that was part-smile, part-
frown: One side of her small mouth turned up, the other down, as if it
couldn't decide what it wanted to do.

"You sure you don't mind?" she asked.

"Not at all." I offered her my hand. "I'm Stuart."

"Annabel Lee," she said, shaking my hand. "Glad to meet you."

That's how I met Annabel Lee Bryson. On the ride back to Slade, she
sang softly to herself, "It Ain't Me, Babe." We stopped at a roadside café
near Balsam Gap and had a coffee. I found out it wasn't that she was aloof
or stoned; she was just plain shy. As she grew comfortable with me, she
opened up, and then I saw a different person. This one was friendly and
outgoing, chattering nonstop, a torrent of words and opinions and nervous fluttering laughter. I found out she was born and raised in town but
was hardly your typical mountain girl. Well educated and articulate, she
was the daughter of Professor Bryson, who taught literature at the college
and was considered something of a crank. He smoked cigarettes in a cigarette holder and wore an ascot and a white linen suit even to the Bi-Lo.
After graduating from Bryn Mawr, Annabel had gone off to live in Green-
wich Village for a while, before coming back South and settling in
Asheville. She was older than she appeared, her girlish face belying the fact
that she was twenty-five already, with a degree in art. She said she didn't
consider herself an artist, just a dabbler who painted landscapes, an occasional portrait. She said she was brought up Methodist yet hadn't gone to
church for a while, that she'd been reading books on Buddhism and other
Eastern religions. "Exploring the alternatives," was how she put it, smiling that odd half-smile of hers. She said she practiced yoga and medita-
tion, and was against the eating of animal flesh, because it polluted the
temple of the body.

"You should know," she told me earnestly. She said most things with a disarming earnestness. "You're a doctor. It brings out a lot of bad karma. Like anger and lust."

"What's wrong with lust?" I joked. Her face remained serious. "You don't sound like most women I've come across in Slade."

"I suppose not."

"Are you back in town for good?" I asked.

"No," she said, stirring her coffee. "I just came home to help momma out. You see, my daddy took sick and I'm giving her a hand."

"I hope it's not serious."

"Actually, it is. He's got cancer. They can't do anything for it. We're just trying to keep him comfortable now."

"Sorry to hear that."

"Thanks. I figure to hang around while she needs me."

"Then what?"

"I'll leave."

"Don't you like the mountains?"

"It's home. There've been Brysons in these hills for years. Supposedly we got some Indian blood way back." She stared out the window for a moment, past her own reflection, out at the expansive darkness of the mountains. "It's just that folks in Slade want you to be just like them. And if you're not, if you're a little bit different, why, their tongues start to wagging."

"But they're not all like that."

"No," she conceded. "Not all."

"Annabel Lee. That's a pretty name."

"It's from a poem by Poe," she explained. She smiled, a bit reluctantly, her smoky dark eyes suddenly gleaming. She had a nice smile. Straight white teeth, a small but full, sensual mouth. Up close, her skin was pale and smooth, flawless as porcelain. Her hair, by contrast, was thick and coarse, darker even than her eyes, a glistening black like a lake in the moonlight. You wanted to touch her hair. You wanted to undo the braid and let it spill through your fingers like flour.

"You should smile more," I told her.

"Because you're a doctor, you think that gives you the right to tell folks what to do?"

"No. It's just that you have a nice smile. Why do you fight it?"

"I wasn't aware that I did," she said, frowning again.

"Tell me, why were you named after a poem?"

"My dad's a big Poe man. That's not all. I got a sister named Lenore, too," she added, shaking her head. "If he'd had a boy, he was all ready to name him Roderick after Roderick Usher from 'The Fall of the House of Usher.' My dad likes all that romantic crap."

"You don't?"

"I'm more of a realist."

A week later, under the pretense of bringing her sick father a volume of Poe's poems I'd bought in a used bookshop in Asheville, I stopped by her house, which was on Magnolia, a street of impressive Victorian homes. I also picked up a bouquet of flowers at Calby's.

"Isn't that nice of you," she said. "They'll brighten up his room."

"The book's for your father. The flowers are for you."

"For *me*?" she said, surprised. It turned out she wasn't used to receiving gifts from men. I'd later learn the locals thought the Brysons odd, though the older daughter, Lenore, pretty and elegant and demurely feminine, had had her share of suitors. Annabel, however, scared most men off.

Her father happened to be sleeping, but Annabel invited me to stay for a piece of pie she'd made. We talked there in the kitchen.

"I have something else for you," I said.

"You do?"

Then I launched into reciting Poe's "Annabel Lee," which I'd been practicing ever since I'd met her.

*It was many and many a year ago*
*In a kingdom by the sea,*
*That a maiden there lived whom you may know*
*By the name of Annabel Lee;—*
*And this maiden she lived with no other thought*
*Than to love and be loved by me. . . .*

When I finished she clapped, surrendering her mouth to an unconditional smile. "I'm impressed, Dr. Jordan."

"Call me Stuart."

"All right. Stuart."

We passed a pleasant hour talking. I asked about her work. Only after I'd pressed her did she relent and show me some of her paintings and sketches. She was shy about letting people see her work, but it was actually quite good, at least to my untutored eye. When it was time to leave, I asked if she wanted to go out sometime. I was a little surprised when she said she would.

At first, I didn't think anything would come of this. In many ways we were exact opposites. She was creative and rebellious and extravagant in ways frowned on in small towns, and she held passionate, often contradictory opinions about a wide variety of subjects, while I, on the other hand, was logical and plodding and fairly conventional. She hated hunting and fishing and most sports, while I enjoyed those things. She liked to go to art exhibits in Asheville, while I found that sort of thing boring. She was also of a mercurial temperament; she could be light and jovial and chatty one moment, glum and irritable and silent the next. I, on the other hand, had a calm, mostly phlegmatic disposition, hardly ever getting angry enough to raise my voice. As they say, though, opposites attract, and we fell deeply in love. I had never loved anyone the way I loved Annabel Lee Bryson. Our courtship was short but passionate. Her father passed away not long after I met her, and we got engaged a month after that.

Some people raised their eyebrows. They thought it was crazy. Too quick. That it wouldn't last. People I knew, friends and acquaintances from town, came up to me and asked if I was sure I knew what I was getting myself into. They tried to warn me that Annabel Lee wasn't the sort of woman who was likely to be happy in a place like Slade. Some alluded, usually politely and vaguely, to her being different, what they called "high-strung." Even her sister, Lenore, took me aside after we announced the engagement. "I love my sister dearly, Stuart, and I want more than anything for her to be happy. And I've never seen her so happy as she's been with you. But I feel it only right that you should know she has her, shall we say, blue moods." I didn't pay much attention to their warnings, well intended though some of them might have been. When you're in love as much as I was with Annabel, you see what you want to see and close your eyes to the rest.

After we were married we bought the old Mason homestead fifteen miles outside of town, up on Shadow Mountain. I thought it would give us some privacy, some distance from the censoring gazes and general nosiness of Slade. And it did; it was quiet and peaceful up there. Twenty acres with a large but rundown farmhouse. Slowly, we began restoring the place. Or rather Annabel did, and I helped when I had the time. It was mostly her project. Although we could afford to hire people, Annabel threw herself into the renovations: painting, wallpapering, stripping the woodwork, stenciling the walls. Artist that she was, she loved that sort of thing. She painted an incredible mural on one entire wall of the bathroom, a scene of the mountains in spring. Despite the warnings I'd received, our first years together up on Shadow Mountain were happy ones for the most part. Of course, like any couple we had our ups and downs. Anna complained I spent too much time away: at the hospital, tending to my patients. And she would have her bad periods, like when her mother passed away a few years after her father; Annabel stayed in bed for weeks. But that was before she'd been diagnosed as manic-depressive. After she began taking the lithium, her behavior, while occasionally rocky, seemed to level out. Then Will came along, and she threw herself into the role of being a mother. I remember that time, when we lived up on the mountain, first the two of us and then with our son, as the happiest period of my life. Though it ended long ago, in some ways I thought it was just coming to an end tonight.

● ● ●

The return address on Annabel's letter turned out to be a rundown tenement building down near the river. Across the street was a small park. I spotted two old men sitting on a bench, sharing a bottle in a paper bag. Standing off by himself, a young kid with spiky blond hair nervously smoked a cigarette and tried to pretend he wasn't interested in a Mercedes that slowed down going by the park. The driver went by, then circled around and came back. This time he stopped, and the young kid came over and leaned his head into the window. After a moment he got in and the Mercedes took off.

I sat in the truck for a moment, doing that little trick with the muscles in my stomach, firming them, getting ready to do something unpleasant. Like I said, I hadn't seen Annabel in more than a year and a half, and I was a little nervous. When she took off that last time, I told myself, just as I had so many times before, that that was it. The end. We both needed to get on with our lives. I even went so far as to contact a lawyer over in Crawford City, have him draw up the divorce papers. Yet I didn't go through with serving them on her. Like every time before, something had held me back. And as I sat there in the truck, I wondered if I could go through with it now. I'd promised I wouldn't leave her, but that was a long time ago, before I'd met Bobbie. Didn't I, as Bobbie was always telling me, have a right to be happy?

Finally, I got out of the truck and headed over to the building. In the entryway, I looked at the names above the mailboxes. Her apartment was on the third floor. The stairwell smelled of cat pee and cigarette butts. When I reached her apartment number, I took a deep breath before knocking.

"Yeah?" called a reed-thin voice from within. A voice that was only vaguely recognizable as Annabel's. My heart seemed to gorge itself on blood, like a flooded carburetor.

"Anna," I said. "It's me."

"Who?"

"Stuart."

Silence. Then, "What are you doing here?"

"I wanted to see you."

"It's not a good time."

I wondered if she wasn't alone. If someone was there with her.

"I just wanted to talk to you," I said.

"It's late. Not tonight. Come back some other time."

"I got your letter. About Will."

More silence. I could almost hear her breathing on the other side of the door.

"So?"

"I needed to talk to you."

Dead silence. Then finally, "All right, wait a minute."

I heard her footsteps move away from the door and then, after a moment, return. I heard the chain being removed, the lock being turned. The door opened and there stood my wife. She wore a beige wool sweater she'd obviously just pulled on over her nightgown. Her hair, a dull matte-black peppered now with gray, was tangled and wild, full of static and cut unflatteringly short. She wore the same wire-rim glasses as always, behind which the once striking smoky-brown eyes were agitated, flitting around like bluebottle flies over something dead. Her mouth was furrowed, hard-looking, her cheeks sunken. When she spoke, I saw that her teeth were in bad shape, worse than I remembered, and that she was missing a couple on the top left side behind the incisor. She'd lost weight, too, was thin even for her. The years hadn't been kind to her. Then again, she hadn't been kind to herself.

"I wasn't expecting company," she said. "But come on in."

It was the sort of place Annabel usually lived in. The apartment had a tiny eat-in kitchen with a small living area off it. The living area included a couch that must have pulled out into a bed, a single imitation-leather chair, and between them a coffee table with a pack of cigarettes and a paperback novel lying on it. There was a stand for a TV but no television. Annabel had never been much of a TV-watcher anyway. The place wasn't dirty, just spare, the furniture well worn from previous occupants. Everything was in its place. Annabel had always liked things orderly: the house, the garden, the clothes in her bureau. Except for when she was depressed and didn't care, she was always cleaning, picking up, arranging—trying to make the world conform to one or another version of her illness. I could recall waking in the middle of the night and finding her side of the bed empty. She'd be in the bathroom, down on her hands and knees scrubbing the tub. Or vacuuming or washing the windows.

"Have a seat why don't you. Could I get you anything?"

"No."

"You sure? I could make you some tea. Or coffee. All's I've got is instant. I think I might have some beer. You want a beer?"

She spoke rapidly, the words nervously spilling from her mouth in a torrent, as if she were afraid of the silence that might overtake us in their wake.

"I'm fine. Were you sleeping?"

"No. I was just reading." She sat opposite me on the couch, her bare feet up, her legs crossed in a zen position. I noticed her hands; I always noticed her hands first: a barometer of her health. They were twitchy. Not terrible, not the way they could sometimes get, but agitated. She rubbed the couch, pulled an errant strand of hair behind an ear, chewed on a ragged cuticle, tapped some vague tune on her thigh. Sometimes the business with her hands began when she went on the lithium; other times it was a side effect of some other drug, like Haldol, a heavy-duty neuroleptic; still other times her hands shook when she was just in a really bad manic phase. She saw me take notice of her hands, and then, as if to give them a purpose, she picked up the pack of cigarettes from the coffee table. "Mind?"

"Go right ahead."

"So what did you want to talk about?" she asked.

I wasn't ready to launch into my real reason for coming, so instead I said the first thing that came into my head. "You look good."

What I meant, of course, was that she didn't look quite as bad as I'd feared after all this time. And she didn't. Still, she didn't look good.

Far from it. She looked rough, seedy, like a street person who'd been cleaned up and off the streets for a little while. I could see her now in a way I couldn't when we lived together. I could view her the way I did a patient, with that doctor's clinical objectivity, appraising, making inferences as to her well-being. If I had to guess, I'd say she was drinking again, maybe doing drugs, just managing to keep things under control. I could picture her going across the street to the park to buy them. She looked just this side of a full manic episode, and I wondered again if now were the right time to try to talk to her. But then I thought, Yes, it has to be. I can't keep putting it off. It wasn't a kindness to avoid it, to pretend any longer that there was anything left to salvage of our marriage.

"Yeah, right," she scoffed. "Look at me. I look just great, don't I?"

"How are you doing?" I asked.

"All right. Why did you come?"

"To talk."

"About what?"

"Things."

"Things, huh? That sounds ominous."

"You working?"

"A couple of days a week at this bar over on Freemont. It's all right."

"How are you fixed for cash?"

"I'm managing right now. I still have some left from what you sent me last time." She took a long anxious drag on her cigarette. "You get any snow up in the mountains yet?"

"Nothing to speak of." I paused, glancing around. I tried not to let my gaze land on anything that would tell me something I didn't want to know. Her life was her business, and I didn't want to share in it. "So how have you been?"

"You already asked me that."

"Did I?"

"Yeah, you did."

Our conversation had the awkward feel not so much of complete strangers talking as of two people who'd known each other a long time ago and whose last shared memory was an unpleasant one, one which they now found themselves dancing around, avoiding, pretending it was forgotten. "You doing any painting?"

"Huh? I haven't done any in years. You know that."

"That's too bad. You were good."

"I was a hack."

"No, you weren't. People bought your work all the time."

"Yeah, who? Some tourist who wanted a picture of the mountains for his den."

"I thought you were good."

"Anyway, how have *you* been, Stu?"

"Busy."

"You take in a partner yet?"

"No, not yet."

"Still trying to do it all yourself?"

I smiled and said, "I guess so."

"Stella still with you?"

"Of course. She said to say hello."

"Say hi for me would you? So what's new in Slade?"

"A lot of building going on. Florida people buying summer property. The more it changes though, the more it stays the same. You know."

"They still have that dopey funeral hour on the radio?"

"Oh, yeah. 'This funeral hour is brought to you by Childress Funeral Parlor, a familiar face in your time of bereavement.'"

Annabel laughed self-consciously at my hill accent, turning her face girlish just as her laughter used to. As she laughed, though, she brought her hand self-consciously to her mouth. Her teeth, I thought. She's embarrassed by her teeth. Maybe it was the lack of sleep finally catching up with me or the roller-coaster ride I'd been on during the past twenty-four hours. But when I saw Annabel cover her mouth like that, I found myself nearly overcome by a deep and profound sadness. Here I was pitying a woman I had once loved and desired and respected, someone who had been my entire life and whom I was now about to leave for good. And I pitied myself, too, for having lost what we'd once had. It was almost too much to bear. I felt like sobbing, though I didn't, knowing as I did what it would mean—awkward apologies and inadequate explanations, a touch, a sympathetic hug, and, as it had on a couple of occasions when we'd met like this after a long absence, a pathetic attempt at recapturing the love we'd lost by resorting to lovemaking. No, I couldn't afford that. Not tonight. Not with what I'd come to tell her. So instead of crying, I did the next best thing: I laughed along with her.

"It has that same creepy organ music it used to," I added.

"You still doing that coroner stuff?"

"Some. I get help from Rob Neinhuis. The orthopedist."

"Never heard of him."

"He's been in town a few years. He'd like to take over. I think he could use the money. And to tell you the truth, I've been giving some serious consideration to stepping down anyway."

"Never understood your interest in the first place." She was about to say something else, then reconsidered. My working as ME had always been a sore spot between us. I saw it as a way to keep busy after Will's death, something to occupy the nights I couldn't sleep. She saw it, and I suppose with some reason, as my abandoning her.

"I had to go out with Cecil just last night, in fact," I said. "You remember the Pughs?"

"From over in Little Mexico? They were always a crazy bunch. What'd they do now?"

"They didn't do anything. One of them was killed."

I told her what happened. About Rosa Littlefoot shooting her common-law husband and her not letting go of the baby and then taking up the knife and threatening to hurt herself.

"It was pretty bad," I explained.

"Sounds bad. What happened to the baby?"

"That's the oddest part. The mother wouldn't give her up unless I promised to take her."

"What do you mean, promised to take her?"

"Watch her. Look after her."

"Why you?" Funny, but that was exactly what Bobbie had asked me, too.

"I don't know. There was just me and Cecil and a couple of the deputies. I imagine she was less afraid of me than them." I offered a smile.

"You didn't agree, did you?"

"As a matter of fact, I did."

"So the baby's with you?" she asked, looking toward the door almost as if I'd left the child out in the hall.

"Stella's looking after her now. But yeah, for a while anyway."

"Jesus, Stu," she said with a nervous little laugh, not bothering to cover her mouth this time. Her teeth were dull, long neglected. "Whatever for?"

"I don't know. That woman was right on the edge. I thought she might hurt herself or the baby if I didn't say I'd take her."

"Yeah, but you don't have to worry about that now."

"I know. It's just . . . I feel a little obligated."

"There are places for kids like that."

"Cecil couldn't find any empty beds this close to Christmas. So I agreed to watch her for a while."

"How long's a while?"

"Just until we see what's going to happen with the mother. Shouldn't be too long. A couple months."

"A couple of months! My God, Stu. How are you going to pull that off working all the hours you do?"

"I haven't worked out the details yet. I'll think of something."

"Then what?"

"If the mother's found guilty and goes to prison, which seems pretty likely, I imagine they'll place the child in some sort of long-term foster home. Maybe if she agrees, they'll put her up for permanent adoption."

Annabel took another tense drag on her cigarette, glanced down at the coffee table, and shook her head.

"I can't picture you tending to a baby."

"Why not?"

"I just can't. How you going to manage, with your schedule?"

"I figure I can find somebody to watch her while I'm at work. I was thinking of asking Kay."

"Kay Wallenbach?"

"Yeah. She used to watch Will for us, remember?"

Annabel's eyes seemed to wince with the mention of our son, and her once soft, pretty mouth turned hard and defensive, the way you'd hold your jaw if you thought somebody was going to hit you there.

"Yeah, but that was what, almost twenty years ago? Kay's got to be pushing eighty now."

"She's still pretty spry. I'm sure she'd love to watch a little baby. And if she won't do it, I'll find somebody else. Besides, it's only temporary."

"Just what the heck do you think you're doing, Stu?" she asked.

"What do you mean?"

"Taking in some kid you don't even know. I don't understand it."

"What's there to understand?" I said, my voice shaded with annoyance. Though I didn't want to start out like this, sometimes I couldn't help it with Annabel. Sometimes she seemed bent on goading me into saying things I'd later regret. "The woman needed a place for her baby to stay. I was just trying to help out. I felt sorry for her."

"You felt sorry for her? Some woman you don't even *know*?" she said, crushing her cigarette out in the ashtray. Then, rolling her eyes, she added, "It's your business, I suppose."

"That's right. It is."

"I just don't get the point, Stu."

"There is no point, Anna. I was just trying to help her out. Just forget it."

"Always playing the good doctor, huh? Trying to save the world." She paused for a moment, then said, "I'm sorry. I didn't mean that. It's just that . . . well, you know. Today and all. I've been in a lousy mood all day."

I nodded. Annabel picked a piece of tobacco off her tongue and studied it, as if on it were written her fortune. She was silent for a while.

"Did you pay a visit out there today?" We both knew what "out there" meant: the cemetery where Will was buried. It made it sound like some distant galaxy, something you'd need a telescope to see. For years she used to say, "I need to get out there and plant some flowers," yet she seldom visited. She found it too upsetting.

"Yes," I said. "I brought some flowers."

"That's good. I've been meaning to get out there."

"You should."

"It's just that I don't have a car anymore, and, well, it's not easy getting around without one."

"I could drive you, if you want."

"Maybe some time. Is that what you wanted to talk about, Will?"

I remained silent for several seconds, thinking of the best way of putting it.

"There is something else, Anna."

"Boy, this sounds serious," she said, raising her eyebrows.

"It is. Sort of." There was no good way to put it, so I figured just to say it straight out. That the kindest cut was the quickest. "I've been seeing somebody."

Her eyes didn't meet mine right away. Instead, she took a long drag on a new cigarette, blew the smoke slowly out, and watched it float up into the air. Finally, she looked over at me and said, "For long?"

"About a year."

"A year, huh? Knowing you, I'd say that *does* sound pretty serious."

"Yes. It is. I think it is, anyway."

"And you're only getting around to telling me now?"

"It just didn't seem like the right time, I guess. Besides, I wanted to be sure."

"And you're sure now?"

I nodded.

"Then I guess I'm happy for you."

"Do you really mean it?"

"I want to mean it. Nobody deserves to be happy more than you, Stu. It's just . . . "

She fell silent again. I leaned forward, reached out to lay a hand on her leg, but she shrank from my touch. Annabel's eyes misted over, turned a glossy black. She sucked in a mouthful of air and slowly exhaled.

"Jesus. Look at me. After all this time I should've been expecting it. I knew sooner or later you'd find somebody. I know it's only right. Still."

"I'm sorry."

"Nothing you got to be sorry for. You planning on marrying her?"

"I'd like to, yes. Eventually."

"And I suppose you'll be wanting to get a divorce."

"Well . . . yes."

"That would make sense," she tried to joke.

"It doesn't have to be right away, though. The woman I'm seeing, she's got some things to take care of on her end. She's still married. And her husband, well, he doesn't know about us yet."

"You're having an affair with a *married* woman?"

"Yes."

"Boy, you're full of surprises, aren't you? And here you were always so Catholic. So *proper*," she said, smiling through her tears. "I suppose that's why she can't help you with the baby?"

"She couldn't help anyway. She's got a full-time job. She's a district attorney. I had to work with her on some cases. That's how we met."

"Well, that's sure some news, all right. You getting a baby and then planning to marry some married woman. Seems like you got it all ass-backwards." She took another drag of her cigarette, held it in her lungs for a while. "I knew it had to happen sooner or later. I mean, what sort of life has it been for you? All these years, just baby-sitting me. Of course, there was that other woman. What was her name? Margaret?"

"Madeline."

"Right, Madeline. I just . . . didn't expect you to tell me tonight. Will's birthday and all. That's some timing, Stu. I was feeling a little down to begin with, and this, well, it sort of knocks the wind right out of me."

"I'm sorry."

"Would you stop saying you're sorry? I just wish you'd told me sooner so I could have had time to prepare myself. Get accustomed to the idea."

"Is there anything I can do?"

"No. I just want to be alone."

"You sure?"

"Yeah. Just go. Please."

"You'll be all right?"

"I said I'll be fine. Don't worry about me." She gazed down at the floor for a moment. Then she said, "You know I'd never hold you to your promise. You know that, don't you, Stu? I want you to be happy."

I looked over at her, uncertain whether she was releasing me from it or calling me on it. I stood up, leaned over, and tried to touch her shoulder.

"Please," she said, pulling away from me. "I'm barely managing to hold things together as it is."

"Sure. See you," I offered, as I turned and headed for the door.

Before I went out she said, "You always deserved better than you got, Stu."

Downstairs, I found her mailbox and slipped the envelope with the money into the narrow slot. I felt guilty doing it, as if I were buying my freedom. Then I left, trying not to think too closely on the mess I was leaving behind me.

# 14

*The week following* Christmas continued at the same hectic pace. I was busy with work. I had a couple of hysterectomies, a tubal ligation, a D&C on a twenty-seven-year-old woman who already had nine kids she could barely feed. That was in addition to the usual assortment of aches and pains and healthy checkups I saw in the office. Early in the week, I had two "normal" deliveries, where everything went smooth as silk, the sort of slam-bam, thank-you-ma'am births that obstetricians love. Then came Sybil Pettigrew. She was one of a group of neo-hippies who lived out in Baker's Cove, a progressive little enclave whose members made their own clothes and home-schooled their kids and used their own herbal remedies. Since the sixties, the locals called it that "damn hippie commune," and gossip had it that free sex, drug use, and strange, cult-like activities took place out there. Sybil had gone the natural route, with a midwife at home, and no doubt had planned to eat the raw nutrient-rich placenta afterward (another rumor). But after nearly two days of laboring on and off, her husband decided finally to bring her to the hospital. Despite a Pitocin drip, her water rupturing, and my trying every trick I had up my sleeve, she failed to progress. I recommended we go in and take the baby, yet they still weren't sure, especially the know-it-all husband, a tall lanky fellow with a long ponytail. He considered an operation both unsatisfying for the mother and traumatic for the baby. Sybil, however, was exhausted, and the baby started to show signs of trouble. The fetal heart tones and blood pressure began to drop alarmingly. I told the couple if we didn't do something, and quick, we were courting disaster. Finally, they acquiesced. They ended up with an eight-pound baby girl who had no visible signs of trauma. The mother seemed satisfied enough.

The same night I delivered the Pettigrew baby, I also had to go out with Cecil on a suspected OD. Life and death, side by side. A call came in that they'd found a body over in Hobbstown. It turned out to be Buster Hicks, Lakesha's brother, a well-known druggie. They found him out in the barn, a vial of crack and a half-empty bottle of applejack nearby. He had vomit all down his shirtfront, in his mouth and nose. Most likely an overdose. Then again, he could simply have frozen to death or aspirated on the vomit and cut off his airway. Take your pick. When we got there, Lakesha was comforting her mother. Cherise Hicks, whom I knew from the hospital, was crying.

"Oh, Dr. Jordan, what he wanna go and mess wid that stuff for? My baby boy. Now they all gonna know." I hugged her, told her how sorry I was. Though her son's problems were hardly a secret, she didn't want people to read in the *Slade Messenger* that her child had died of a drug overdose. I talked it over with Cecil, and we decided there was no harm done in leaving out the crack part, writing it up simply that he'd gotten drunk and vomited and choked on it. I couldn't see putting a fine point on the matter. He was just as dead either way, and nobody else had any part in it. Like bookends to his life, I'd ushered Buster into the world, and now, twenty-five years later, I was sending him out.

Like I said, it was a hectic week.

Now, two days before the New Year, I was looking forward to some well-deserved R&R. I had four days off. Rob Neinhuis had returned from seeing his folks and was handling the ME duties. Cheryl McClain was back in the office, and between her and Gladys I figured they could handle most things that cropped up. And for anything more serious, I'd arranged, as I sometimes did, for Dr. Chung to cover my patients. I hardly took any time off. Just a few days here and there, where I'd putter around the house or catch up on my reading. I couldn't remember the last time I'd had a real vacation. Stella was always getting on me to go away someplace. "Lordy, they been birthin' babies 'round here long before you come, Doc," she said, "and they'll keep right on long after you're gone, too."

On an overcast day for which they were predicting snow, I drove into Slade to do some shopping. I brought Maria along, figuring to let Rosa spend some time with her. I had her in Will's old carrier, the sort that wrapped around your chest and had become popular with baby boomers in the seventies. I'd found it up in the attic, along with some other baby stuff. It felt a little odd to have that thing strapped to me, I hadn't used it in so long. Still, the feeling wasn't unpleasant, carrying her around like that. Having that small, warm thing squirming and kicking and moving against you is probably the closest a man can hope to come to knowing what it's like to have someone growing as part of you. And that's from someone who knows his way around pregnancy, too. I always thought if men had to lug a child around for nine months, nurture a life and sleep with it, feed it from their own body, they'd be a lot less likely to start wars or raise a hand in violence to their fellow man. But then I thought of Rosa Littlefoot and realized I was just talking through my hat.

Now and then, say, as I was standing at the meat counter in the supermarket, I'd look down at Maria, and her earnest, molasses-colored eyes would glance up and lock onto my own. She might smile coyly, the little charmer flirting with me. I'd feel my pulse quicken, a sudden unexplained tightness in my throat. Looking at her, I couldn't help wondering what she was thinking. Who is this guy? Where's my momma?

During the day, Kay Wallenbach had been looking after Maria for me, while for the night I was called back to the hospital, Stella had offered to watch her. She lived only a mile from the hospital, so it wasn't too much of an inconvenience. In the morning, on my way to work, I would drop the baby off at Kay's and then pick her up on my return. When I offered to pay her, she wouldn't hear of it. She'd usually invite me to stay for dinner, too. "I made plenty," she'd offer. "Won't you please stay, Stuart? You know how John likes chewing the fat with you. It'll be like old times."

Old times. She used to invite us—Annabel and me, and later Will—for Sunday dinner. We'd walk down the path that cut through the woods to their place. Like a lot of mountain people, Kay and John were wary of outsiders at first, but once they got to know you they were warm and neighborly people. Kay was always bringing us vegetables she'd put up or jars of apple butter. Even now, worried I wasn't eating properly, she'd drop off a casserole or a plate of ham and "greezy-backs," string beans cooked in bacon grease. And each spring her husband used to arrive unasked on his old Massey-Harris tractor to plow a small garden plot for Annabel. They'd been like grandparents to Will, giving him birthday presents and watching him when Annabel was ill.

After I'd made my rounds at the hospital and had picked Maria up at Kay's, it would be just the two of us at home. I'd borrowed a crib as well as some other things from Kay's older daughter, Julia, whose children were grown. I set the crib up in Will's old room. Maria was really a good baby, especially considering everything she'd been through. She went to bed easily and slept straight through to morning. Though she'd been breast-feeding, she took to the bottle just fine. She didn't cry a whole lot, was mostly a quiet, curious, introspective child who stared out at the world with those dark enigmatic eyes of hers. You couldn't have asked for a more agreeable, good-natured infant. Still, while she adjusted just fine, it took some getting used to on my part, having a baby in the house again after all these years. Especially for someone who'd grown used to his routines, his privacy, the quiet of that big old house. The sounds and smells and constant needs of a child. Just the notion that there was under the same roof another life, one you were responsible for.

Before, when it had been just me, after work I might stay in town and grab a bite, have a few drinks. Or I'd come home and split some wood, watch a game on the television, maybe read a little. Now, however, I had a baby to think about, to feed and change and bathe; I had to cut her rubbery fingernails and comb her dark thick hair, pick her up on those occasions she did let out with a wail. And when I'd finished those chores, it wasn't as if I could simply ignore her. I'd have to get down on the floor and spend some time with her. I gave her one of Will's old toys, a ring of plastic keys, and she liked banging those around and putting them in her mouth. After I'd laid her down for the night, I found myself keeping one ear on the ready, listening for her. And when I heard nothing, I worried about that as well. Sometimes I'd get out of bed in the middle of the night and go in and check on her, make sure the covers weren't too close to her mouth, that she was warm enough and dry. I'd just stand there for a while and watch over her, as I had with Will.

One morning, just before daybreak, the house bathed in that bluish predawn light like that in a painting by Degas, I woke from a dream of my son. I lay in bed for a moment, trying to get my bearings. After a while, I became aware of an odd noise coming from what seemed to be his room, a frail sort of whimper. I thought, Will? Is that you? Perhaps he was talking in his sleep, having one of his dreams. The one about the wolves, maybe. I hurried out of bed and went to his room. Only when I opened his door did I realize my mistake. Maria lay there, staring wide-eyed up at me. But I didn't have much time to dwell on my error. Starting to cry, she insisted I put the past behind me and tend to her needs. Mornings were especially hectic. I'd have to get the baby up, change and feed her, get dressed myself, pack up her things, and head down to Kay's so I could be on time for my first patient. Funny how after just a few days, I'd begun to fashion new routines. Or perhaps the new routines had begun to fashion me.

• • •

My first stop was at the Bi-Lo, where I picked up what I needed for New Year's Eve dinner: a crown roast, red potatoes, and canned asparagus, and blueberries for the crepes I planned on making for dessert. In the produce aisle I ran into Lucy Ballard, the nurse who worked on the maternity floor. Lucy was a short, heavy woman, with an ever-present grin on her fleshy pink face.

"Why looky here," she said, leaning close and pinching the baby's cheek. "I heard tell you was tending to that woman's baby."

"It's just for a while," I explained.

"She sure is a sweet li'l thang, ain't she?" She looked at the baby for a moment and then at me, the way one might if trying to find a resemblance. "Well, I'd better shake a stick. They's talking a big storm. You have you a happy New Year, Doc."

"You too, Lucy," I said.

Afterwards, I went to the ABC store and purchased the most expensive bottle of champagne they had, spending $19.95. Then I headed over to the Wal-Mart and bought some new sheets, the ones I had being mostly threadbare and dingy. As I stood in line, I felt a vague, no doubt Catholic, sense of guilt, almost the way I had the first time I'd purchased a condom when I was going out with Yvonne Bottomley, a girl I'd dated in college. I pictured the cashier, a sober-looking woman with a cross around her neck, saying to me, "Y'all 'specting company?"

In fact, I was. Bobbie was coming over and I wanted everything to be nice. Her husband was still down in Florida, and so we'd have the whole night and all the next day together, instead of just a couple of hours in a motel room. I'd gotten up early that morning and cleaned the house, which was pretty messy seeing as Emmilou Potter hadn't been by for several weeks. I picked the clothes off the floor; I swept and vacuumed; I put out clean towels in the bathroom; I got the good china down from the hutch and set the dining room table. I couldn't recall the last time I'd eaten there, never had any reason to. Though Bobbie and I had been lovers for the past year, I still felt in my gut an adolescent nervousness in anticipation of the evening. Here I was, a fifty-seven-year-old man, yet I felt like a kid on his first date.

When folks who hadn't heard about me taking in Rosa Littlefoot's child happened to spot me in town with a dark-skinned baby, they didn't quite know what to make of it. I'd get double takes or inquisitive stares. And I could just hear the gossip now over at the Pancake Barn: *What in the world was Doc Jordan doing with that young'un anyhow?* some customer would say. Then Raylene Huggart would glance cautiously around, acting as if she were the model of discretion, before saying in a voice loud enough for the whole place to hear, *Well, I'm not one to spread rumors but what I heard* . . . . I happened to run into Mrs. DeForest coming out of the liquor store. She had a half gallon of Smirnoff vodka in a grocery sack, which she tried her best to conceal from me.

"How's the stomach, Mrs. DeForest?" I asked.

"Stomach? Oh, fy-on. Just fy-on," she said, staring at the baby. "And who's this?"

"This here's Maria."

"My word. What . . . is she?"

I wasn't sure if she meant what she was to me or what race she was or what I was doing with her.

"She's four months," I replied.

From my cell phone I called the hospital to check on Emmilou Potter. It wasn't that I didn't feel she was in capable hands. Han Chung was a good man, a skilled doctor, even if his bedside manner left something to be desired and his thick Korean accent made him sound as if he were always chewing on pork gristle. It was just that I didn't want Emmilou to lose another baby—or worse. During the week, her blood pressure remained elevated, and the lab tests weren't encouraging. Her proteinuria numbers were still pretty high. I was worried that if we didn't get things under control now, she'd get into serious trouble later on in her pregnancy; her condition could easily progress to full eclampsia or her kidneys could shut down and she'd go into renal failure. I'd warned her about trying to have another baby after her last miscarriage, but she said that her husband, Jack, was the last of his line of Potters, and she wanted to give him a son in the worst possible way. She was willing to risk dying to give him one, and I'd be damned if I was going to let that happen.

I stopped at the Cash-'n'-Go and picked up a couple of packs of cigarettes and some toiletry items for Rosa. Then I drove over to the courthouse.

The baby in my arms, I climbed the two flights to the DA's office to see if Bobbie had gotten back yet. My knees were acting up again, aching, so maybe it was true that bad weather was approaching. During the week I'd put in several calls to Bobbie's office, but each time Myrna told me that Mrs. Tisdale was still down in Florida. She seemed to take a certain pleasure in telling me that. Today when I stopped by, the secretary said Bobbie had called yesterday to say she was due back today, in the afternoon. I told her to have Mrs. Tisdale call me at home. Regarding the Littlefoot case, I added. Myrna glanced at Maria, then went back to typing. As I headed down to the sheriff's office, I wondered why Bobbie hadn't at least called me from Florida, to let me know if we were still on for New Year's Eve. Maybe she couldn't slip away from her husband. Or maybe something had come up with her mother-in-law and she'd forgotten.

"I brought you a visitor," I said, as Cecil unlocked the door to Rosa's cell.

Rosa Littlefoot, who'd been lying down, sat up on her cot and rubbed her eyes, squinting at us. "Oh, God!" she sighed, her hand flying to her mouth and her face momentarily clouding over, almost as if seeing her child was like gazing upon a light that was too brilliant to look at all at once. I wondered if I should've warned her I was bringing Maria. But then her expression changed again just as suddenly. Her face brightened. She stood up and put out her arms.

"How's mommy's little *ka-ma-ma*?" Rosa said, clasping her daughter tightly to her chest. She had a relieved expression, almost as if, after having momentarily lost her in a large crowd, she had just found her again. She held her baby silently for a long time, bouncing her gently. After a while she sat down, propped Maria on her knee, and unzipped her snowsuit, and took it off.

"Where'd you get the pretty snowsuit?"

"A woman in my office got it. I was never much good at picking out baby clothes. My wife used to say I couldn't tell pink from purple if my life depended on it," I said with a smile. "Here, I brought you some things."

"Oh, thanks. And I 'preciate you bringing her. Has she been good for you, Dr. Jordan?"

"No trouble at all," I replied. "We gave her a complete physical. She's healthy as a horse. What you call her, that Indian word. What does it mean?"

"*Ka-ma-ma*. It's Cherokee for butterfly. She's my little butterfly. Aren't you?" she said, kissing the baby's hands, first one, then the other.

"How's the eye?" I asked.

"Better."

"Let me have a look."

While she played with her daughter, I checked her eye. The swelling had come down some, though a shimmery bruise still blossomed beneath the eye. We didn't talk about her case.

Earlier in the week, Rosa Littlefoot had been arraigned in Superior Court for the murder of Roy Lee Pugh. Lewis Hunneycutt had surprised everybody by entering a plea of not guilty. Her trial was scheduled for late March. "It turned out that Bobbie was going to prosecute the case, though Bumgartner had handled the arraignment while she was away. He was still talking tough, at least in public, seeking a first-degree murder conviction against Rosa. When I happened to run into him in the Pancake Barn, however, he told me in passing that he'd offered Hunneycutt second degree, in which case Littlefoot could be out in as little as five years. "But the doggone fool turned it down flat, Stuart," Troy told me. "The stupid sum'bitch is going to get her life is what he's going to do."

"Is she been eating okay?" Rosa asked me.

"Why, she's eating me out of house and home," I said. Rosa smiled, the bones in her cheeks pushing hard against the delicate brown skin. "Hunneycutt fill you in about the custody business? How it's going to work?"

"Some," she replied.

•  •  •

Rosa's lawyer had drawn up papers giving me temporary custody of Maria. I had to show up at his cramped office above Shuster's department store to sign them. He had a tiny waiting room, in the corner of which sat his secretary, a big-bosomed older woman whose nameplate said Ernestine Grasty, one of the Grastys from Sugar Creek. Hunneycutt, whom I'd seen around town before, was lanky and tanned, a tall, rawboned fellow, with the largest Adam's apple I'd ever seen. It would jump up and down every time he spoke and go into spasms when he got excited; it made me think he'd swallowed a live ferret which kept trying to crawl back out of his throat. Nearly bald, he tried to cover this fact by marshalling the few stringy gray hairs he possessed from one side of his tanned skull all the way to the other. His eyes were a reassuring shade of light blue; they made you want to put your trust in him.

"You sure y'all know what you're getting yourself into, Dr. Jordan?" he asked me.

"To be perfectly honest, no," I said. "But she doesn't have many options. I'm willing to give it a shot. At least until we see what happens with her trial."

"I can't say I ever came across a case like this before. Normally, I wouldn't advise a client to place a child with a member of the prosecution team. But I've heard you're a straight shooter. So if it's okay by Ms. Littlefoot, I guess it's okay by me. Of course, I'll ask that in your dealings with my client you refrain from speaking about her case in any manner whats'ever. We clear on that?"

"Perfectly."

"Now you should know there are a couple of problems in your being granted custody. Even temporary custody." He had a plodding, pedantic way about him, as if he were explaining thermodynamics to a group of first-graders. He went on to cite the Indian Child Welfare Act, which Bobbie had already filled me in on. How he would have to contact the Cherokee tribal council to get their approval for the child to be placed with a non–Native American. Then he said there could be a conflict of interest regarding my testifying for the prosecution and at the same time assuming custody of the defendant's child. (Of course, he didn't know about the conflict of interest posed by the fact that I was sleeping with the prosecutor in the case.) More important, he said he'd just learned that the Pughs were going to fight my getting custody. They had their own attorney, Ennis Pugh, a kinsman who lived in town, and he'd petitioned the court, saying that the Pughs should be given custody as they were blood relatives. Ennis, Hunneycutt explained, often represented them in their various scrapes with the law.

"This complicates things considerable like, Dr. Jordan," Hunneycutt advised, his Adam's apple bobbing up and down. "First off, Ennis Pugh fights dirty. He's got mountain blood, which means scratching and biting's allowed. You got dirty laundry you don't want aired, you'd better think twice before you go up against Ennis."

"As medical examiner, I've faced tough lawyers before. I can handle myself."

"Good. The next thing, a judge might wonder what stake y'all got in all this. You don't even know her or the kid. I don't have to tell you, in these parts blood counts for a good deal. And say what you will about the Pughs, they are blood." Hunneycutt paused then, stared across his desk at me with his soft blue eyes, a stringy loop of gray hair falling down across one of them.

"I just want what's best for the child."

"One other little thing—my fee. I can't afford to do this for nothing. I'm already working pro bono for Rosa."

"I'll pay what it costs."

"I should warn you, Dr. Jordan, a custody fight, even to get temporary custody, can get awful expensive. I'll do what I can to keep the costs down, but it won't be cheap."

"I understand."

"Now, the judge is going to want to know how you're planning to care for a four-month-old while working full-time, without a wife in the picture."

"I already worked out child care arrangements. A neighbor's going to watch her for me."

"That's good. You belong to a church?"

"I'm Catholic. But I haven't been in a while."

"You probably already know being Catholic around these parts is a strike against you. But since you're not a practicing papist," he said with a long-toothed smile that drew his mouth into a simple-minded grin, "that probably makes you even with the board. Anything else I should know?"

"Like what?"

"About your character?"

"I can't think of anything."

"Have you had any contact with the Pughs?"

I told him about Tully Pugh and Glenn W. coming to see me and making vague threats.

"We'll get a restraining order to keep them away. If they come 'round again, I want you to call the police. Y'unnerstand?"

A few days later at something called a *pendente lite* hearing (it sounded more like a pasta dish than a legal maneuver), District Court Judge Lane Cobb listened as Ennis Pugh argued why the Pughs should get Maria and not a complete stranger. Pugh, a slight, fastidiously dressed man with boyish features, demanded a custody investigation be done on me, to see if I was, as he put it, "fit to raise a child in a loving,

Christian environment." The Pughs' lawyer spoke with an overly dramatic flair, like a student reciting Shakespeare badly. Hunneycutt countered, asking that the Pughs also be investigated and that they have no further contact with the child or me until the court made its ruling. Cobb agreed, and set a hearing date for late January. In the meantime, he granted me temporary custody of Maria. On the way out of the courthouse, Glenn W., wearing a too-large powder blue suit and white cowboy boots, hobbled up to me and said, "Looks like you won the first round, Dr. Jordan."

• • •

"You sure it's what you want to do?" Rosa said, smoothing a dark cowlick on Maria's head with a little spit. "Taking her in, I mean."

"I suppose. Why?"

"I just been doing a lot of thinking is all."

"And you're thinking it's not such a good idea after all?"

"It ain't that so much. It's just . . . "

"I thought that's what you wanted. Isn't that why Hunneycutt's petitioning for custody for me? I mean, for us."

"I know."

"Don't you trust me?"

"'Course I do. I'd trust you with my life. Soon's you come through that door that night, I knew I could trust you. H'ain't that."

"Are you worried I wouldn't take good care of Maria?"

"No, no. Not that neither. I can tell you got a way with children."

"Then what's the matter?"

"It's like this—I gotta think about down the road, Dr. Jordan."

"Down the road?"

"That Hunneycutt fellow said I could get life in prison. Then what? What happens to her?"

Rosa brushed her lips delicately across the baby's cheek, making Maria smile a lopsided, toothless grin. The baby reached up and grabbed her nose. I felt a faint tightening in my chest, like an artery clogging with plaque.

"You haven't even gone to trial yet. Who knows what will happen?"

Secretly, I wasn't holding out much of a chance for an acquittal, however. They had the murder weapon and a motive, the heroin they'd found in the suitcase. Plus the second shot, the one to the head. Any way

Hunneycutt played it, it was going to be awful hard for a jury to swallow that second shot as momentary insanity or self-defense or whatever he had in mind. They didn't get fancy around here. If every woman got it into her head she could go and kill her husband every time he beat the tar out of her, what sort of message would that be sending to impressionable young girls about the state of holy matrimony?

"I don't care what happens to me. I just want to know she's got a good home. What I got to think about is ten, twenty years down the road. With me in prison and all. What about her then? I can't hardly ask you to be responsible for her all that time. That wouldn't be right, now would it?"

She looked over at me, waiting for me to say something.

"I can see your point," I replied. She couldn't reasonably have expected any other answer, but I could tell she was nonetheless disappointed with it.

"That's what I mean then. And I don't want them yanking her from one home to the next. I grew up in foster homes, Dr. Jordan. I know what they're like. I don't want that for her. I want her to have one place she knows is hers. To have a family. Indian or white, it don't matter. As long as they love her and take good care of her."

I had to agree with her. She had to think long-term, not just what was good for Maria over the next few months. At best, I was just a temporary solution, a Band-Aid on a compound fracture.

"And I don't want her being raised by the Pughs. Filling her head with lies. Bad-mouthing me. Saying I didn't love her. And I know they'd never bring her in to see me. I don't want that. You won't let them have her, will you, Dr. Jordan?"

"No," I said. "I won't. What about your father then?"

"Him? Like I told you, he ain't likely to take her."

"But maybe if he knew your . . . situation. After all, it's his own grandchild." I thought of Glenn W. Pugh. Say what you would about the man, he had enough blood loyalty to want to take in his granddaughter. Maybe Rosa's father would feel a similar pull of kinship. "Has he been to see you? Call you or anything?"

She shook her head. "No. He ain't had a phone in a while. And he doesn't get around so good anymore."

I watched a black fat-bodied cockroach scurry across the floor and disappear behind the toilet in the corner. If her father agreed to take her, that would let me off the hook. Wasn't that what I wanted? To be let off the hook. And it might just be the best thing for Maria, too, to be with her own people, to grow up in her own culture. After all, that's exactly why they'd come up with the Indian Child Welfare Act, to keep guys like me from taking Indian babies and raising them white.

"If you want, I could drive over to the reservation and talk to him."

"Wouldn't do no good," she said, with a shrug of her thin shoulders.

"But what could it hurt?" I countered.

"I guess it's worth a try. If you don't mind."

"I don't mind. Listen, Rosa. However things turn out, I'll see to it that she's taken care of. That she has a good home. One way or another."

"You don't have to keep sticking your neck out for me. You ain't kin. You don't owe nothing to this young'un or to me."

"I know. But no matter what happens, we'll find Maria a good home. One way or the other. You have my word on that." There you go again, I thought, giving your word. When are you going to learn to shut your big mouth?

"Thank you, Dr. Jordan. You're a decent man."

"I guess I should be going."

She told me where her father lived over in Cherokee. Then, before handing the baby back to me, she kissed her one last time, nibbling her ear.

"You be a good girl now for the doctor, y'hear." Maria didn't fuss at all when I took her. She seemed more interested in the play of shadows on the wall behind me. I put her snowsuit back on.

"Lookit that," Rosa said. "How she goes to you. Hardly misses her momma no more."

"Of course, she misses you."

"Couple years she won't even know me from Adam. I'll be some stranger to her."

"Sure she will. You don't want to talk like that."

"Why not? It's the truth," she said, with the same sort of cool stoicism she had the night I first met her. "By the time I get out she'll be all growed up and I'll just be some crazy old lady who says she's her mother."

"Even if you go to prison, she can still visit you."

"Yeah, once a year," Rosa said, smiling ruefully. "She does take to you, though, don't she?"

"Babies can adapt to most situations," I said, zipping up her suit and pulling the hood up. "It's the adults who have a harder time."

"But you're good with a young'un, I can tell. Comes natural like. Not all nerves. Like you was afraid of dropping her."

"I've never dropped one yet," I joked.

"You must a had some of your own," she said. Then, recognition sliding over her eyes, she looked at me and added, "Sorry, Dr. Jordan. I forgot you said you had the one."

"That's all right."

"How old would he a been?"

"Twenty now."

"All growed up. How? I mean, how'd he die?"

I was about to tell her what happened, just as I had many times to many people. A story I'd told so often that the rough, once-splintered edges of it were worn down, polished and smooth to the touch as the banister in an old house, free from inflicting pain anymore. A story I could tell objectively, with a kind of cool, dispassionate distance, the way I might relate the specifics of a child's death if I were testifying on the witness stand. "Victim was a five-year-old male who succumbed as a result of hypothermia." Yet this time when I opened my mouth, nothing came. Not a word, not a sound. Nothing. Something seemed to catch in my throat, as if so much dirt. I sat there feeling a peculiar, burning sensation just below my Adam's apple. I started coughing.

"You okay, Doc?"

"Yeah, I . . . "

"Want a drink of water?"

"Please," I managed to get out.

The next thing I knew, I felt hot tears pushing out the corners of my eyes and trickling down my cheeks. They dropped onto Maria's pink hood, staining it dark. I couldn't even say why this was happening. It was the strangest damn thing.

"It's all right, Dr. Jordan," Rosa said, handing me a drink of water in a small cone-shaped paper cup. She stood beside me, her hand on my back, rubbing it in circles.

"I . . . "

"Don't you worry none. When did you lose him?"

"A long time ago," I said, after I'd had a chance to catch my breath. I took a drink, the water tasting like rusty metal. "Fourteen years. He was just five. He wandered off in the woods, and by the time we found him he was dead. Died from the cold."

"I'm sorry," she said again.

"I don't know what's the matter with me," I said. "I can't recall the last time I . . . this happened to me. I thought I was over it by now."

"Sometimes you never get over it." Rosa stared at her hands for several seconds. "I lost a baby when I was fifteen. Not lost. That makes it sound like I misplaced it or something. Killed it. You see, I had me an abortion. I went to this woman over on the reservation. It was the only thing I could think of at the time. No way was I ready to have a kid. I mean, I loved the boy and everything but I was too young. Even so, I sometimes still cry over that baby. I never even seen it. In fact, I can't even call it anything but *it*. Don't know whether it was a boy or a girl. Just an it. But I'll be settin' there and I'll get to thinking and all of a sudden I'll start crying like crazy. Over that *it* I never laid eyes on. You try to forget but it ain't easy."

We both fell silent. After a while I stood up. "I have to be going. I'll be in touch."

Out in the sheriff's office, Cecil was seated behind his desk with his feet up.

"You all right, Doc?"

"Yeah. Why?"

"Your eyes. They look a little fucked up."

"Oh, I got a cold."

"This damn weather. Hear we're supposed to get a good one. How are things working out with that little one?"

"I'm adjusting."

"Better you than me. Wouldn't want to change another diaper if you paid me."

"Has Rosa had any visitors?"

"Besides you and Hunneycutt? Nobody. Why?"

"Just wondering."

"Be good, Doc. And if you can't be good, at least be smart," he said, smiling cryptically. Our little secret.

# 15

*I drove the* thirty miles over to the reservation. A slushy snow was already collecting on the windshield, the wipers making their numbing *ca-thunka, ca-thunka* racket. The skies had darkened and closed in over the mountains like a cowl; the storm was coming in fast and low, burying the Smokies under a broiling cloud of gray. Now and then the overcast would momentarily break and a lone mountain peak would poke through the cloud-cover, hulking, surreal looking against the storm. On the radio they were talking heavy snow in the higher elevations, sleet and freezing rain in the valleys. Up in the passes driving would already be bad. Real bad. Snow didn't drop from clouds up there. It just appeared out of nowhere, without warning, blindingly quick and deadly as a copperhead's strike. It often caught people unawares and they paid for their carelessness with their lives. I was glad Neinhuis was covering. No doubt some business would be coming his way.

As I drove I thought about what had happened to me back at the jail. I couldn't explain it. I'd been in a real good mood, too, looking forward as I was to Bobbie coming over the next night. And it wasn't as if I'd been feeling bad about Will, thinking about him any more than I usually did. I missed him, of course. I would *always* miss him. The way you might miss an eye or the way a prisoner might miss the time he'd lost in jail. A day didn't go by that I didn't feel his absence in some palpable way. I thought, however, I'd come to terms with his death. I thought the wound had healed over into that smooth, touchable scar. Yet Rosa Littlefoot had said sometimes you never get over it. Maybe she was right. Maybe you never do. Maybe you just pretend to get over it, go about your business, act like the pain is gone, put as much distance as you can between it and you. Then it comes up and smacks you right between the eyes. And it was, I realized, the first time I'd cried. *Jesus,* I thought. *Fourteen years later.* I'd finally got around to crying for my son. I glanced over the backseat at Maria, who was staring out the window. Perhaps it had something to do with her, too. With her coming into my life, reminding me of just how much I'd lost when my son died.

I remember the night we found Will. They shipped his body to Childress Funeral Home, and Annabel and I drove home alone. She didn't say a word the entire ride back from Black Mountain. I was worried about her, what this would do to her. When we got home, I said, "I'll make us some coffee." She unpacked her art supplies and brought them up to her studio. I fixed two cups of coffee and waited at the kitchen table for her to come down. I remember telling myself, We just need to get through the next couple of days. Somehow or other, find a way to muddle through. We needed to take things one step at a time. After a while, when Annabel didn't come down, I headed upstairs. I opened her door and poked my head in. There she was, seated at her easel— *painting*! Quietly, calmly, yet with a certain intensity of concentration. I couldn't believe it. Our child was lying on a table at Childress's and here she was painting.

"Annabel," I said.

"I'm working."

"We need to talk."

"I don't want to talk," she said as she continued to apply brush strokes to canvas. "Leave me alone." I glanced at what she was working on. It was nothing. At least nothing I could make out. Just incomprehensible brush strokes, wild slashes of color—gaudy yellows, flaming ambers, bright reds—on a cold background of white.

"Stop it! Do you hear me? We need to talk."

"There's nothing to talk about. He's dead and we both know whose fault it is."

"Annabel, please."

"He's dead because of me. And you blame me for it."

"No, I don't. Don't say that," I cried.

"Yes, you do. You'll always blame me."

I went back downstairs and sat at the table. I poured myself a drink. I didn't cry that night, nor did I two days later at Will's funeral. I thought I had to hold myself together for Annabel. In fact, I didn't cry in the weeks or months following his death either. I don't know why.

Maybe I was too preoccupied with my wife. I spent the next fourteen years being preoccupied with her. Telling myself I was protecting her, trying to save her from her terrible guilt. When perhaps what I was really doing was saving me from my own.

• • •

In the dead of winter, Cherokee resembled a ghost town. During tourist season, June through Columbus Day, the main drag of Cherokee is a bustling, crowded place. It puts you in mind of a carnival midway and bears about as much relation to reality. Shop after garish shop peddling chintzy trinkets and hokey souvenirs: rubber tomahawks and plastic bows and arrows, velveteen pictures of Elvis or Dolly or Jesus, crummy oil paintings of beautiful Indian maidens or handsome bare-chested braves, as if taken straight from the cover of some cheap romance novel. Painted not to show how Indians actually looked but to conform to an aesthetically pleasing image whites have of the "noble savage." In front of every store stands a "real-live" Indian chief in full headdress, willing, for five bucks, to pose for a photograph. There are droves of old people bused in from Florida or Tennessee, Christian youth groups, newlyweds from New Jersey who've never before seen an Indian in the flesh. Even the odor makes you think of a carnival: the sickeningly sweet fragrance of cotton candy and fudge and toffee, the greasy smell of barbecue and french fries, the slightly bitter odor of roasted hazelnuts and pecans. Then there are the minizoos, where you can see rattlesnakes or mountain lions, or pathetic-looking black bears in eight-by-eight shit-filled cages. In summer it is a place that strikes anyone above the age of twelve as somehow depressing. Now, locked in the cold grip of winter, with most of the shops and restaurants and attractions closed down, it was irredeemably bleak. It was as if the Trail of Tears hadn't begun but ended here.

As Rosa instructed, I turned right just before I got to the Oconaluftee River. The road followed the course of the river for a while and soon began climbing, gradually at first, then more sharply, heading up into the Smokies. The slush on the windshield turned to a steady snow, which, as I went higher, began to accumulate at the sides of the road, collecting on the hemlocks and rhododendrons. By the time I reached Cady's Branch, the dirt turnoff where Rosa's father lived, there were a couple of inches on the ground. I decided I'd better put the truck in four-wheel drive. I drove up this road for a quarter mile until I came to a silver trailer with an unfinished wooden addition slapped together at one end. The addition was studded in and partially enclosed with plywood, but it had no roof, so that the wood was already weathered and beginning to rot. It looked as if the builder had stopped mid–hammer stroke and thought better of the idea. On a mailbox out front, a single word was painted: LITTLEFOOT. I parked, gathered Maria up in my arms, and walked through the snow to the front door.

It took a while before someone answered. A middle-aged Indian man finally opened the door. He was leaning forward behind a walker, a heavy-set guy with a morose, bloated face. He wore a cardigan sweater over yellowed long johns, sweatpants, and one hightop sneaker. He didn't need the other—he had only one leg.

"Yeah?" he said.

"I'm Dr. Jordan."

"Doctor! Hell, I guess I come up in the world. They sending out doctors now? Where's what's her name? The skinny-assed nurse."

"I'm not with the VNA. This child's your granddaughter, Mr. Littlefoot. Rosa's baby." He eyed me suspiciously for a moment, trying to make out if it were true, and if so what I was doing there.

"How do I know to believe that?"

"Why would I lie? Besides, you've heard about the trouble she's in?"

"I heard." He scratched his gray, unshaven jowls. "So what's this got to do with me?"

"I was wondering if we could talk."

"This about money? I don't got no money."

"No, it's not about money."

"About what then?"

"Mind if we came in? She's going to get wet out here."

He stared at me for a moment, then gazed at the child. I think he tried to see some connection in her face to his daughter, and thus to himself. Proof of what I was saying. Finally, he said, "Come on in, you want."

I followed him back into the trailer. The place was hot and had a bitter odor to it, almost like sulfur. A small TV set on the kitchen table was tuned in to an old *Honeymooners* episode. The Indian guy wasn't used to the walker, you could tell, and I was figuring he'd probably lost the leg fairly recently. He pulled out a folding chair as he went by the table and said, "Sit there." Then he negotiated his walker over to a sagging couch covered with a green army-issue blanket. He pivoted with difficulty, hopping on his foot, aimed his rear end at the couch, and straightaway dropped onto it. "Ahh, you dirty bastard, you," he cursed, rubbing the stump of his leg.

"Diabetes?" I asked, sitting in the chair he offered.

"Hell, yeah."

"When did you lose it?"

"A year ago. Damn thing still hurts like a bitch."

"It's pretty common. Phantom leg pain."

"Phantom, hell."

"It goes away."

"They keep telling me that. Seems like it's getting worse. You doctors should have to take your own medicine. So what kind of doctor are you anyway?"

"OB-GYN," I said. He frowned, uncertain, and I added, "I deliver babies."

"That's some way to make a living!" he said, offering up a phlegmy laugh. "Myself, I used to work construction. Before I lost the leg. I made good money, when there was work. I get disability now. It don't go far. Enough to keep me in butts and booze. Not much more than that. Interest you in something to drink, maybe?"

"I'm all set. Thanks."

"Suit yourself," he said, reaching down beside the couch and lifting up a pint of peach brandy. He removed the cap and took a long guzzle. He didn't change expressions when he swallowed. He could have been drinking water.

"So let me guess," he said. "Rosa gets her ass caught in a crack and I'm supposed to give two shits?"

"She could use a hand."

"Like I couldn't?" he said.

"She's in a lot of trouble, Mr. Littlefoot."

"That's got nothing to do with me."

"She's looking at a long stretch in prison."

"It's her own damn fault. Taking up with that feller. I warned her. You think she'd listen? She does what she damn well pleases, her whole life. Taking drugs and putting out for every man comes along. Never had a shred of decency, that girl. Now she goes and kills somebody. Jesus. She made her own bed, now she got to sleep in it."

"He was abusing her."

"She probably deserved it, knowing her. They was plenty of decent boys right here on the reservation she coulda took up with. But we wasn't good enough for her. Hell, no. Not for Rosa. Got her a taste for whites. And the needle, too. One's bad and the other's worse." He waited, as if for me to say something. When I didn't, he "humphed," then took another long swig of the brandy, wiping his mouth on his sweater sleeve.

"She was off the drugs," I said. "She was trying to get her life straightened out when she shot him."

"I heard that before. Plenty."

"I didn't come here to talk about her, though. Your granddaughter here is going to need a place to stay."

"And she expects *me* to take her in?"

"I just wanted to talk to you. That's all."

"I don't hear from her in years. Nothing. Worrying myself sick she might be dead with a needle stuck in her arm. Don't even rate a lousy call when I'm laid up in the hospital myself. And now she's in a mess of trouble, I'm supposed to take her kid in?"

"Otherwise your granddaughter's looking at a foster home. I don't have to tell you what they're like for an Indian child."

"That wasn't my fault. You can't lay that on me. I couldn't handle Rosa. Not by myself. She was a wild one. That's why they put in her those places. I did my best."

The baby, whom I had propped on my knee, started to fuss. She was probably hot, so I pulled her hood back and unzipped the snowsuit.

"You want her to wind up in one of those places, too, Mr. Littlefoot?"

"Ain't my responsibility," Littlefoot said, shaking his head. He was silent for a moment. "What is she called?"

"Maria."

"Figures."

"Why?"

"That was her old lady's name. My second wife. She took off on me, too. Like mother, like daughter. Screw the both of 'em." The man stared at the television for a while. The audience laughed at something Art Carney said, while Gleason's eyes bulged with their famous anger. "Even if I wanted to, and I'm not saying I do, how the hell am I gonna look after a kid? Lookit me. Can't hardly take care of myself no more."

"Any other relatives?"

"I got three kids from my first wife."

"They around here?"

"No, they hightailed it soon's they could drive. But I can tell you right now, they ain't likely to take on Rosa's mistake."

"Anybody else on the reservation who might take the child?" I asked. "There's a law that says ... "

"I know what the law says, Mister. I used to be on the tribal council. That's just to keep some white fellow from coming over here and paying cash and stealing our babies. This here's different. Somebody who thought she was too good for her own kind don't make a whole lot of friends, you know what I'm saying. Tell me, what's your interest in all this?"

"Just a friend."

"That *all?*"

"That's all. Listen, I'm sorry for wasting your time, Mr. Littlefoot."

"Ain't wasted my time. I'm just settin' here."

He picked up the remote and started flipping through the channels. He seemed to forget we were there. I put Maria's hood back on and zipped up her suit. She stared at her grandfather, almost as if she recognized him.

"You might could try a girl name of Blackfox," he said at last.

"Who?"

"Doreen Blackfox. Sister of a fellow Rosa used to go with. Before she got into the drugs and all that craziness. The three of 'em used to be pretty tight. If anybody might be willing to take Rosa's kid, I reckon it'd be her."

"Does she live on the reservation?"

"No. She got married and moved away. I don't know what'all her married name is. It was some half-Choctaw fellow from down Mississippi way. Least he's part blood."

"You know how I could get ahold of her?"

"I sure wouldn't. You could try her brother Lenny. Though I ain't seen him around in a while neither. Last I heard he took a job for the power company. Was living down in Farley. He'd most likely know where you could find his sister. The two of them were good kids. Him and Rosa used to be sweethearts in school."

I thought of what Rosa had told me, about the abortion at fifteen. How she loved the boy but was too young. Maybe it was Lenny. But her father said she'd been with a lot of men.

"Thanks for your help," I said, moving toward the door.

"You probably think I have a hard heart. Turning my back on my own daughter. And that little one there."

I didn't say anything.

"She hurt me bad too many times, that girl," he said, taking another sip from his bottle. "Rosa was the purtiest li'l thing you ever did see. I used to buy her presents, you know. Barrettes and stuff for her hair, things a little girl would like. You know how it is with your kids," he said, looking over at me. "You want the best for them. You put your hopes in them. When she got older, she started doing crazy things. Running with a fast crowd. Wouldn't listen to me. Her old lady had already flown the coop. I threw up my hands. After a while you learn to cut your losses. I did what I could for her, Mister. You tell her for me she can't lay any of this on my doorstep."

I opened the door, stepped out into the cold.

"I did my best," he called after me. "When you see her . . . "

I shut the door behind me and walked out to the truck. The snow had picked up, had taken on a certain violence. It was swirling now, coming from all different directions at once, stinging my face, pelting my skin. The mountains emitted a glassy stillness, save for the wind moving through the trees and the delicate *tckkking* noise of snow touching something solid, piling up, compacting itself on the ground. The world was rapidly being transformed, becoming something other than it was, covered by a sleek coat of white. I looked up. The mountains loomed above me huge and ghostly, glistening a slate-gray, shadowy as something from another world. The clouds passed quickly, visible to the eye, moving with the sinuous quality of a living thing: a catamount hunting for prey. You could almost reach out and touch its cool, luminous hide. The snow seemed not so much something apart from the mountains as an element *of* them, as much as the trees or streams or rocks. I thought of my son lost in these mountains, curled under some bushes as if sleeping, the snow gently covering him like a soft white blanket, soothing and comforting, protecting him, opening its arms to receive him. While I knew better than to sentimentalize these mountains, knew they could be cruel and harsh and unforgiving, I also knew they took care of their own, gave life to their children, fed them and sheltered them and nourished them, and, when it was time, accepted them into their still, dark bosom. I opened my mouth and let snowflakes settle on my tongue, cool and wet, forgiving as a host I had not accepted in years.

"We'd better get on home, little *ka-ma-ma*," I said, buckling Maria into her car seat. "It looks like it's going to be a bad one."

# 16

By *late on* New Year's Eve morning, the storm had about spent itself. Occasional gusts of wind continued to drive snow down through the Tuckamee Valley, yet the brunt of the storm had passed on toward the coast. Before leaving, though, it had slammed the mountains with a foot of snow in the valleys and two or more in the higher elevations. Nothing to get excited about for a native New Englander, I suppose, but enough to wreak havoc here. To the north, Painter Knob was wrapped in a hazy shroud of white, its mile-high peak lost behind a lingering cloud-cover. On the radio I heard they'd closed Balsam Gap as well as most of the highway west of Slade. Several hamlets were snowed in, many cut off from power. There would be a run on the stores in town, with folks frantically buying up canned goods and kerosene and batteries. I was glad I'd already done my shopping.

When I got home the night before from seeing Rosa's father, there was a message waiting on my machine: "Doc, it's me," came Bobbie's voice, sounding both tired and anxious. "I just got back tonight. Our flight into Asheville was delayed because of the storm." *Our?* I wondered. "We still on for tomorrow? I . . . never mind. We'll talk when I get there. See you." There was a long pause followed by an "Okay?" She sounded different somehow, as if something was wrong. While I didn't usually call her at home, I decided to chance it. I dialed her number, but nobody answered. In the morning I called again, and when I still got no answer I tried her at the office. No answer there either. I wondered where she was. I was worried she might be out in the storm, which had continued raging through the night and into the morning.

Jack Potter, Emmilou's husband, had come by earlier with his big Chevy dump truck and plowed my driveway. Though I knew he certainly could have used the money, I also knew better than to try to pay him. He was working off what he owed me, and offering money would have embarrassed him.

"Got us a good'un, eh Doc?" he said.

"Sure did," I replied, standing in the driveway near his truck. Jack Potter was a slight man, with a full orange-blond beard and impassive, ash-colored eyes. "'Preciate you plowing me out, Jack."

"No problem. How you fixed for wood, Doc?"

"I'm all set. Have you talked with Emmilou?"

"I been out all night plowing. I'm going to the hospital now to see her. She wants this one real bad."

"I know."

"She's got it in her head she has to give me a boy. I only want her to come home safe. With or without a baby, don't matter to me."

"She's tough, Jack."

"Tougher'n me. Hell, I don't know what I'd do if anything was to happen to her," he said, his voice trailing off.

"She'll be fine. Don't you worry."

"I hope so. By the way, Doc, I been a little strapped. Things's been slow at the mill. I can have you some money next week, more'n likely."

"Next week would be fine, Jack. Thanks for the driveway."

I'd just put Maria down for her afternoon nap, when I heard Bobbie's Volvo coming up the driveway. I'd gotten so I could recognize the sound of her motor from having waited for her in the motel room so many times. For some reason I always seemed to get there first.

"*Brrrgh*," she said, stamping the snow off her feet in the entryway. "I *hate* the damn cold."

"I wasn't sure you were going to make it."

"Almost didn't. The roads are lousy."

"You had me worried," I said, hugging her. "But I'm glad you're here."

"I would've been here earlier, but I had some work to do at the office."

"I called there. Nobody answered."

"You checking up on me, Doc?" she said, smiling.

"No. I just called to see if you were still coming."

"Nobody else made it in. It was quiet. I didn't want to be disturbed."

I took her overcoat and scarf and hung them up in the hall closet.

"You look nice," I offered. "Christmasy."

She wore a red blazer with a white silk blouse, black slacks. She'd just had her hair done, too. It wasn't frosted. It was all one color, a lighter shade of blond and falling loosely in her eyes. She'd gotten a tan, too, from being down in Florida. She looked lovely and ravishing as usual, but different in some way I couldn't put my finger on. Distant, I thought. She gave me a perfunctory peck on the cheek. Her skin was cool from the outdoors and I shivered at her touch. She carried a small overnight bag.

"What should I do with this?"

"I'll take that," I said.

"Well, what do you think?" she asked, turning her head from side to side.

"I like your hair like that."

"No, I meant the earrings. They're the ones you got me."

"They look nice on you. *You* look nice."

We headed into the den where she glanced around appraisingly.

"So this is Casa Jordan?" she said. She'd never been inside my house before. Here we'd been seeing each other for over a year and we'd never set foot inside the other's house, which only now struck me as odd. "You have a lovely place. And what a view. I don't know as I could take the drive up in the winter, though. By the way, where's the baby?"

"I just put her down for her nap."

"Shoot. I was looking forward to seeing her."

"She'll be up later. Can I get you a drink?"

"I'd love one. Bourbon if you got it. On the rocks."

"Make yourself comfortable. I'll be right back." From the kitchen I called, "So what was so important you had to go in the office today?"

"I had some catching up to do," she replied. "Mostly the Littlefoot case."

"What's going on with that?"

"How about we don't talk shop?"

"Fine by me."

"Who's the artist?" she called. She was referring, I knew, to the paintings Annabel had done, two of which hung in the den.

"Annabel."

"They're good. Really good."

I fixed our drinks. When I returned I found Bobbie over at the bookshelf looking at the framed photographs there. I knew they'd be a conversation piece, and I'd actually considered putting them away. But then I decided not to. I wanted all my cards on the table.

"Who are these people?" she asked, holding up a photo.

"That's my mother and father."

"Is your mom still alive?"

"No, she passed away a few years ago."

"And is this your son?" she asked, picking up another photo.

"Yes," I replied, handing her her drink. "Will was about four there."

"He was a good-looking boy. I can see the resemblance to you. And this must be Annabel."

"Yes."

She stared at the photograph closely. It was taken over in Gatlinburg, Tennessee, where we'd gone one summer for a few days. We'd ridden the chairlift to the top of the mountain. Behind us, the Smokies unfurled like a quilt stitched of various patches of blue.

"Your son's got her mouth, I think."

"Yes, he did."

"I didn't picture her looking like this."

"No?"

"When you talked about her, I don't know what I pictured her looking like. But not like this. She's pretty. She has beautiful hair."

"She was young there. Yes, she did have pretty hair."

I thought about the tense I'd used: *did*.

As if reading my mind, Bobbie said, "Funny how we've been seeing each other all this time and I hardly know anything about your past."

"Just some old pictures," I said. I took the photo from her hand and replaced it on the shelf. Then I leaned into her and kissed her on the mouth.

"*Brrrrr*. I'm still frozen." She slipped deftly away from me and walked over to the stove. Rubbing her hands above it, she said, "I just love a fire when it's cold out."

She inspected a painting on the mantel above the stove. It was called "Sunset over Painter Knob." Annabel had done it one summer, sitting out on the front porch. As I had after hearing Bobbie's phone message the previous night, I sensed something was wrong. There was a nervous restlessness in her I'd never seen before. She seemed committed to trying to hide whatever it was beneath a polite but cool formality that wasn't at all like Bobbie.

"Everything all right?" I asked.

"Yeah. Why wouldn't it be?"

"I don't know. You seem a little . . . funny."

"You know me. I'm always a little *funny*," she tried to joke, rolling her eyes and laughing that snorty laugh of hers. Now, though, it seemed forced, unnatural.

I wasn't sure I wanted to pursue this, so I asked, "Want me to put some music on?"

"That sounds good."

I went over to the stereo and put on the St. Paul's Boys Choir. Soon their angelic voices filled the room as if with morning sunlight. I sat on the couch.

"Want to join me?" I asked, patting the seat next to me.

But she didn't make a move. She stood there staring at the painting. After a moment, she turned and said, "Truth is, Doc, there is something the matter."

"You want to tell me about it?"

"I guess my coming here is what's the matter."

"You didn't want to come?"

"No. It's not that. It's just . . . I don't know. It's different from meeting you in a motel room."

"In what way?"

"Well, there we'd do our little thing. Have our fun. And then we'd go our separate ways. You know what I mean?"

"No."

"You'd go back to your life and I'd go back to mine as if nothing had changed. Because nothing had. *We* didn't have to change. But this, coming here," she said, turning back to stare at the painting, "it's like a big step all of a sudden."

"I suppose it is. But you're the one who wanted to."

"I know. And I did." I noticed her verb tenses, too. Past. "It's just that when I was down in Florida, Doc, I had a lot of time to think things over. Everything became a lot clearer to me. In some ways anyway."

"In what ways?"

"For one thing, I felt close to Paul. Closer than I had in a long, long time."

"You did?" I said, jealousy throbbing in my chest like an aneurysm.

"Maybe it was because his mother was sick and I felt so bad for him. Or maybe because he was acting really sweet to me, like he used to when we first met. I don't know why, but I felt this closeness to him."

I felt sick to my stomach when she told me this. I thought she was going to tell me we were through. While I knew I shouldn't, I couldn't help asking, "Did you sleep with him, Bobbie? Is that what you're getting at?"

"Geez Louise, Doc," she said, turning to face me again. "I really don't think that's any of your damn business. He *is* my husband, after all."

"But last time we talked you were all set to leave him. For us."

"I know. I know that."

"Now you're telling me how *close* you are to him," I said, my voice filling with both anger and fear.

"Don't get mad. It's actually good news."

"Good news! For who?"

"For us."

"You lost me, counselor. How is it that your feeling closer to your husband is good news for us?"

"Do you remember what you said, about jumping into one relationship because you're running from another?"

"I guess so. I just wanted you to be sure about why you were leaving him."

"And you were right, too. When I was down there, I kept thinking about that. If I really wanted *this*, you and me. What if I was just running from Paul and you happened to be there? Or what if I was trying to make him jealous and just . . . "

"Using me?"

She fell silent, looked down at the floor. She put her fist to her mouth, her index finger curled pensively along her top lip. I'd seen her make the same gesture before in a courtroom when she was grilling a witness, trying to figure out which strategy to use. I realized then how much I loved her, because I realized how much I feared losing her.

"Were you? Using me to get back at him?"

When she looked up, I saw that her eyes were moist with tears, her mouth pinched tight holding everything in.

"Maybe a little. At first, anyway. I still have feelings for Paul," she said. "I won't say that I don't. But that's just my point. I'm not running *from* him. I want to be with you because, well . . . because I love you, Doc."

"Are you sure?"

"Yes, I'm sure."

"Then what's the matter?"

"I guess that's why I was a little nervous coming here. Because I know I *do* want to be with you and that this isn't just some fun and games anymore. I haven't had the best of luck with men. It's a little scary to find yourself in love again at almost forty."

"That makes two of us."

"You're scared?" she asked.

"Petrified. I was afraid you might realize you were just running from a bad situation. And that sooner or later you'd come to your senses and wonder what in the hell you were doing with an old fart like me."

She walked over to me and sat down. She was smiling but tears were running down her cheeks. She wiped her eyes with the back of her hand, messing her mascara.

"Listen, you old fart, I'm here because I want to be. That is, if you still want me."

"Of course, I do." I said. And I did. I wanted her more, in fact, than I'd ever wanted anything before in my life.

She leaned into me and kissed me on the mouth, her tears wetting my cheek. She slipped her tongue into my mouth, forcefully, as if exploring for something she knew was there, some inner part of me she wanted to claim for herself. I took her hands in mine and kissed them.

"By the way, we didn't," she said.

"Didn't?"

"Make love. Paul and me. We slept in separate rooms at his parents' house. I'm looking forward to spending the night with you. So what are we doing now?"

"Nothing. What did you have in mind?"

She smiled coyly. "Where's the bedroom in this joint?"

"Upstairs."

"I just thought we might's well get rid of some of the tension I feel between us."

"Sounds good to me. I bought new sheets."

"You what?"

"The old ones I had . . . I mean, I didn't want you to think I was a complete slob."

We both started laughing.

"How's about we break those suckers in?"

Afterwards, we lay in bed for a long time, Bobbie's head resting on my chest, our legs intertwined. In the motel room we never allowed ourselves the luxury of just lying in bed together, at least not for very long. It was always the serious, calculated business of pleasure. Then hurriedly putting our clothes back on and getting back to our real lives.

"I'm so happy, Doc," she said.

"Me, too."

"Are you? Are you really happy?"

"Yes."

While that was true enough, somewhere at the back of my mind there was this nagging sense of . . . what? Sadness. An amorphous, detached melancholy that never quite seemed to leave me. I guess I was afraid to let it go, let *myself* go, afraid to give myself completely over to being happy. I was so used to denying myself, feeling guilty if I had a little fun, if I allowed myself even a small measure of happiness. It wasn't the first time I'd felt this way either. When I'd been seeing Madeline, in her arms, I would always think, What about Annabel? How can you let yourself be happy while she's so wretched? After everything, how can you turn your back on her? On your past? Even now with Bobbie, I couldn't help but think about Annabel, wonder where she was at that moment, what she was doing, if she was at all happy, or at least not suffering. I thought, too, how I'd never made love to another woman in this bed, before now. While it didn't seem so much an act of betrayal, it struck me as significant in a way I couldn't exactly describe. Perhaps, as Bobbie had said before, her coming here marked a change in things: that one part of my life was irrevocably over and done with, and another, strange and unfamiliar, was about to begin.

•  •  •

After we'd eaten dinner, Bobbie sat in the rocker in the den and fed the baby while I cleaned up the kitchen. The fire was roaring in the stove and Johnny Mathis's warbly voice was crooning about sleigh bells and chestnuts roasting.

"Will she take the whole bottle?" Bobbie called out to me.

"She's liable to," I replied from the kitchen.

"Then I'm supposed to burp her, right?"

After a while, I walked over and stood in the doorway, secretly watching the two of them for a moment. Bobbie had the baby over her shoulder and was patting her on the back. She wore a white terrycloth robe I'd got from Annabel's closet. She'd only brought a skimpy nighty, the sort she wore in the motel room—that is, if she wore anything at all—and she said she was cold. As I watched the two of them, I thought, *Don't do it. Don't let yourself think like that. You're just asking for trouble.* Then again, I thought, *Why not? Why couldn't it be like this? Was it so wrong to want a family again?*

"See," I said after a while. "You got the hang of it. It comes naturally."

"Not to me, it doesn't. This is virgin territory for me."

"Relax. You're doing just fine."

Maria started to fuss. Bobbie put the baby on her knee and bounced her.

"I'm not sure she likes me."

"Of course, she likes you. Why wouldn't she?"

"I don't know. I keep thinking about her mother."

"What's that got to do with anything?"

"Well, here I am feeding her and I'm prosecuting her mother for murder. Talk about ironic."

"And you think she holds that against you?" I scoffed.

"I don't know. I think there's something to kids being able to pick up on things. Something they can smell on you. A scent you give off. Maybe she can smell my guilt."

"You feel guilty?"

"A little, I guess. I'm going to send her mother away for the next twenty years, when I'd probably have shot the bastard myself. No offense to your daddy, little one, but he had it coming."

"So there's no doubt about that? I mean, about her mother being found guilty."

"Let me put it this way, Doc. I've been a prosecutor for fifteen years. This is the easiest murder case I've ever handled."

"Hunneycutt still going to plead her innocent?"

"As far as I know."

"Do you think he's got something up his sleeve?"

"Hunneycutt doesn't *have* sleeves. He's a wonderful man. A real champion of the oppressed and all that. Only thing, he's a damn poor lawyer. My guess is he's going to go the temporary insanity route. Maybe diminished capacity. Or say Littlefoot was suffering from Delayed Stress Syndrome or some such hogwash. Which ain't gonna fly in these parts. If he were smart, he'd get her to take our offer of second and we'd make a lenient sentencing recommendation. She could be out in five to seven. Still have a life. A shot at being a mother."

"I thought we weren't going to talk shop?"

"You're right. It's just that I know what it's like to grow up alone. And at least I had one parent."

The baby quieted down, found her fingers and began sucking on them. Bobbie lay her in the crook of her elbow.

"A kid like this doesn't stand much of a chance. She's got two strikes against her even before she's out of the gate."

"She looks pretty content right now."

"She does, doesn't she? She's just so perfect. Look at those eyes."

"Want to help me give her a bath?"

"Sure."

Bobbie carried Maria down the hall and into the bathroom. While I drew water in the tub, she hummed to the baby.

"Boy," she said, staring at the mural Annabel had painted on the bathroom wall. "Did she do that, too?"

"Yes."

"She's pretty talented."

"She doesn't think so."

Kneeling beside the tub we took turns soaping Maria up and then pouring handfuls of water over her to rinse her off. Each time the water dribbled across her skin, the baby offered up a toothless grin of pleasure.

"She likes it," Bobbie said.

"Yes."

"Sometimes I wonder if there's something wrong with me."

"What do you mean?"

"That I was never into all . . . *this*."

"All what?"

"You know—babies, giving them baths, feeding them. That whole maternal thing. I mean, I like kids. It's just that having one of my own was never a priority. Or at least I never let it be one."

"Funny thing is I don't remember much of when my son was a baby. I was too busy with my practice. Getting established. I didn't spend as much time around him, feeding him, bathing him, as I would've liked. Like a lot of men, I missed the boat on that. They're only babies once and then it's over. You look back and you have all these regrets."

"I know about regrets," Bobbie said, washing the baby's toes. "About six months ago I woke up this one night and I lay in bed alone. Paul was off someplace for his job. I thought how I'll never have grand-children. I'll be an old woman and Paul will be off screwing some young bimbo and I'll be all alone. No grandchildren will ever come visit me. It was like I'd skipped right over the having-my-own part."

"It's your biological clock kicking in."

"You think so? I'll be forty in May."

"That's still not too late to have a child. Especially these days."

"But what about birth defects and all that?"

"The odds increase a little after forty. But you're pretty safe until you hit forty-five. Then they go way up."

"I guess it's mostly that I don't like the door being shut and me not even having a say in the matter. How about you? Did you ever want another child?"

"I thought about it after Will died. I think I would've liked having another child. But things didn't work out."

"And now? Would you want another one now?" Bobbie looked over at me. "I don't mean us. I don't want you to get the wrong idea. I just mean hypothetically, could you see yourself being a father again?"

"I don't know. It takes a lot of energy. More than I have. Would you hand me that towel?"

I lifted Maria out of the tub, and Bobbie wrapped her in the towel and dried her off. Then we headed down the hall and into Will's room. Bobbie placed the baby on the bed, and I handed her a diaper and a T-shirt.

"This was your son's room?" she asked, looking around at his things.

"Yeah."

"Is it hard to be in here?"

I thought about how I'd cried when Rosa Littlefoot asked about him, there in the jail cell. Cried as if the tears were pent up inside me all those years.

"It used to be. It's not too bad now. Mostly."

"That must be the absolute worst thing. Losing a child. I mean to put all this time and emotion into something and then lose it."

"I used to think so, too. I'm not so sure anymore."

"What could be worse than losing a child?"

"Maybe not remembering how it used to hurt. Sometimes I think that's worse. You see, as long as you can feel the pain, as long as it hurts to touch his things and think about him, you tell yourself that he can't be too far away. You can still *feel* him there. It's when it doesn't hurt anymore, that's when you finally realize he's gone. Really gone and never coming back. I think that's why Annabel never wanted to let go of the pain. That was her way of keeping our son with her."

Bobbie pursed her lips and bowed her head, as if in thought. We both stared down at Maria for a moment. Then Bobbie slid the diaper under the baby and attached the flaps. She pulled on the T-shirt and then the sleeper and zipped it up. She scooped Maria up and held her against her shoulder.

"You're getting to be an old pro," I said.

"I have a good teacher," she replied. "Hunneycutt told me you're trying to get official custody?"

"Yeah. Just till the trial's over."

"Geez Louise, Doc, that's a pretty big step. Have you thought this through?"

"Some."

"I mean, what if you win temporary custody and then Littlefoot gets sent away for a long stretch. What happens then? To this one?"

"I don't know. Mostly I've been trying to take it one step at a time. What do you think the chances are I'll even be awarded custody?"

"Hard to say what Cobb will do. I know him a little. He's local. Has family back up in the hills. Pretty conservative. On the one hand, you're financially stable, well known in the community, a model citizen—except, of course, for certain indiscretions with a married woman," she said, winking at me. "But the Pughs are next of kin, and even if they are scumbags, I don't have to tell you blood counts for a whole lot around here. And then there's the fact that you put in long hours. That you're away at the hospital a lot. Not to mention the ME work."

"I've been thinking about giving that up anyway."

"Since when?"

"For a while now. I've also been toying with the idea of bringing someone into the practice. So I'd have more free time."

"And, of course, the court will have some concerns about your being a single parent at your age. You'd have a better chance if you were married."

"I am married," I said.

Bobbie, who was swaying with the baby to some soundless music, stopped and stared over at me.

"I mean, really married. I'm just wondering if you've considered what you're getting yourself into, Doc."

"Who's the one always telling me I think things out too much? That I should just jump in more?"

"This is different. You have to think about what's best for her, too."

"I gave that woman my word."

"You and your word. Is that what this is about—your *word?*"

"It may have started out that way. It's more than that now. I can't just wash my hands of her, can I? Let her go to some foster home. Or worse, let the Pughs get her. Maybe I could at first, but not now. I mean, look at her, Bobbie. Could you just give her up?"

Bobbie nuzzled her nose against the baby's ear.

"I admit it'd be hard. I just don't want to see you cause yourself a lot of grief for nothing. And there's one other thing to consider."

"What?"

"Ennis Pugh will get in there with a spade and dig up all sorts of dirt on you."

"Let him."

"Which also means dirt on me," she said, frowning.

"Oh. I guess I didn't think of that."

"I mean, at this point that doesn't bother me too much. I'll have to tell Paul about us sooner or later. But you ought to know Pugh'll pull out all the stops. I've come up against him in court. He's one nasty son of a bitch."

"Huneycutt's already warned me."

"Just so you know. What do we do with her now?"

"It's bedtime."

Bobbie lay Maria in her crib, and I wound up the mechanical mobile Kay had lent me. The mobile was made up of zoo animals: zebras, monkeys, lions, elephants. Maria watched with fascination as they spun about above her.

"Goodnight, sweetie," Bobbie said.

I shut the light off, leaving just the nightlight on, and we headed back downstairs. I popped the cork on the champagne and poured two glasses. Bobbie and I curled up on the floor in front of the stove.

"This is nice," Bobbie said.

"It was the best they had," I replied, sipping the champagne.

"I'm not talking about the champagne. I mean tonight. Being here with you and the baby. I can't remember being this content."

"Neither can I."

She leaned toward me, took my face in her hands, and kissed me tenderly on the lips.

"I love you, Doc."

"Marry me," I said.

"*What!*"

"Marry me, Bobbie."

"Are you kidding?"

"No, I'm serious. I love you and I want us to be together."

"I want us to be together, too. It's just that maybe we ought to take things a little slower. I've already botched up two marriages. Besides, there's the little fact that we're both still married to other people," she said with a laugh. "Or did you forget that?"

"I mean as soon as we're free."

"Did you tell your wife about us?"

"Yes."

"How did she take it?"

"She was a little upset. But I think she understood. How about you? Did you tell Paul?"

"I didn't have a chance. When he gets back, and things with his mother, well, resolve themselves, I will." She pulled back and searched my face, her green eyes scrutinizing mine. "Do you really mean it about getting married?"

"Yes."

"Are you sure?"

"Positive. I've wasted too much time. I want to be happy again. I want *us* to be happy."

"Shoot, Doc. I don't know what to say."

"Say you'll marry me."

"Boy, when you jump in it's with both feet. All right, I'll marry you. Just as soon as we can."

That night, we made love again, slowly, deliberately, exploring each other, sounding each other's depths. Afterwards, Bobbie fell asleep in my arms. I listened to her breathing, inhaled the fragrance of her hair, her skin. The sadness I'd felt before was still with me, would probably *always* be with me, yet it had receded off into the distance. I had a right to be happy. I was in my own house, beside the woman I loved. In the next room a baby was sleeping. It could be ours, I thought. Bobbie's and mine. And why not? Maria had come to me out of the blue, as if dropped from the sky. Was I to turn my back on her, on everything? Or should I grab hold of this chance and hold on for dear life? I let myself think these thoughts as sleep washed over me. Outside in the night, the wind whispered softly as it slid east through the valley, toward Wolf Lake, carrying with it a message that was just out of hearing.

# 17

*About a week* later, on a Wednesday, my free afternoon, I brought the baby in to visit with Rosa Littlefoot again. Before I stopped down at the jail, however, I decided to head up and see Bobbie. We hadn't spoken since New Year's Eve at my place. I didn't want to press her; I wanted to give her enough space to work things out with Paul. But at the same time I missed her, and I wanted to assure her I'd meant everything I said. As proof, I was going to tell her I'd already been in touch with a lawyer over in Crawford City, to discuss beginning divorce proceedings. I'd called Bobbie twice at the office, but each time she was busy and couldn't talk. I knew her husband was back; I'd seen him in the Pancake Barn, talking to Raylene, flirting with her in a casual way. Paul Tisdale had the easy, confident good looks of a man who knows women will make fools of themselves over him. I felt like going up to him and saying, *You don't need her. I do. So why don't you just let her go?* I asked Bobbie's secretary if I might have a word with her boss, but she said Mrs. Tisdale was in court.

"Could you have her call me at home? It's about the Littlefoot case." Myrna stared blankly at me, as if she'd forgotten who I was. "Tell her Dr. Jordan stopped by."

"I'll see she's gits the message."

Then I headed down to see Rosa. She was sitting on her bed, writing something, when Cecil told her she had a visitor.

"Hey, Dr. Jordan," she said, putting aside the pen and the piece of paper she was writing on. I noticed how she slipped the paper under her pillow so I couldn't see it.

"Look who's here." I told her.

"How's mommy's little sweetie?" Rosa asked, taking her daughter from me. Her eyes turned soft at the sight of Maria; the rigidity with which she held herself gave way and she allowed herself to smile. I sat in the folding chair Cecil had provided for visitors, that is, for Hunneycutt and myself. "Ain't she getting big?"

"She gained two pounds," I offered.

"She taking any solid food yet?" she asked, as if she'd not seen her daughter for months instead of only days.

"No, not yet." I watched as she cooed to Maria and played patty-cake. She nibbled on her daughter's fingers until the baby laughed out loud. It was a touching image, one that was hard to reconcile with the one I had of Rosa coolly blowing away Roy Lee Pugh's head.

"You think sometime you could bring in a bottle so's I could feed her?"

"Sure," I said. "How are you feeling?"

"A little better. My breasts is still hurting a little."

"You using the pump?"

"Yes."

"It'll pass," I offered. "By the way, I spoke with your father the other day. He's in no position to take your daughter in."

"I know."

"You know? Did you talk to him?"

"No. I just figured as much."

"He did mention a couple of friends of yours, though."

"Friends?"

"A fellow named Blackfox and his sister."

"Lenny and Doreen. What about them?" she asked, glancing over at me.

"He thought maybe Doreen might take your baby in. Said you used to be good friends."

"We were."

"You see, there's a law that says that Indians looking to get custody of Indian babies get consideration over whites."

"So?"

"What I'm saying is if your friend was willing to take her in, the court might give her custody over, say, me. Or the Pughs, for that matter."

"I ain't heard from Doreen in a while. Last I knew she married some fellow and was down south someplace. I don't know where all."

"Her brother would probably have her address. Any idea where I could reach him?"

She shrugged, stared down at her daughter.

"I ain't heard from Leonard in a couple of years neither."

"Your father thought he might be living down in Farley."

"Like I said, I ain't heard from him. And anyways, he wouldn't want to get mixed up in any of this. Can't say I blame him none."

"Maybe I could give him a call."

"Just leave him out of this. Lenny was a good kid. So was Doreen. They don't want nothing to do with me."

"I was just thinking . . . "

"*No*," she said sharply.

"You're the one who was worried about down the road."

"I know. I'm just tellin' you I don't want you troubling them with my worries."

"Then it looks like we're back to where we started from. Me. At least for the time being."

"Why are you so concerned what happens to me? You don't even know me."

"I'm not sure myself. And mostly it's not you I'm doing it for. It's for that baby there."

She seemed to chew on that for a moment.

"Do you reckon . . . what I mean is, Dr. Jordan, if I do get sent up, you think you could see to it that whoever's looking after her could bring her in to see me ever' once in a while. Just so she don't forget who I am?"

"I'm sure we could arrange something," I said.

"God bless you, Dr. Jordan."

When it was time to leave, I said, "I'll bring her in next week."

Out in the sheriff's office, Cecil asked, "Any more problems with them Pughs?"

"No," I said.

"It true you're looking to get custody of that young'un?"

"Temporary custody," I replied. "Just till the trial's over."

"And then what?"

"I don't know."

"She's going to prison; you do know that, don't you?"

"Yes."

Cecil raised his eyebrows so his glasses rode up his nose. He scratched around his beard as if hunting for something.

"You been feeling all right, Doc?"

"Just fine. Why?"

"Seems to me you're acting a mite peculiar, is all." Lowering his voice so Bryce couldn't hear him, he added, "First that business with Bobbie Tisdale and now this. Just worried about you."

"Thanks for your concern, Cecil," I said and headed out.

A couple of days later, during my lunch hour, I met with Lewis Hunneycutt. We went over some things regarding the custody business. The home evaluation. The sort of things they'd be looking for. And the hearing that was coming up in a few weeks. The kinds of questions Pugh would ask at the deposition.

"I know I'm not supposed to talk to you about Rosa's case," I said to him, "but does she stand a snowball's chance in hell of being acquitted?"

"I can't get into strategy with you, Dr. Jordan, seeing as we're on different sides. But I'm going to give her everything I got. Why?"

"Just wondering how long Maria might be with me."

Hunneycutt thought for a minute, tapping his chin with a pencil. "I'm hoping for the best. But I'd be less than honest, Dr. Jordan, if I told you that that child wasn't going to be needing somebody to look after her for the foreseeable future."

On the way out I thought, the foreseeable future.

• • •

One evening, I had to go out with Cecil on a case. I was making rounds at the hospital when I got the call. He asked me to meet him out at Piney Ridge, a small settlement about fifteen miles north of Slade. An accidental shooting. As I drove over, I thought about my father. I could recall once going out with him on a home visit. I was maybe nine and we were in his black '48 Buick, the one he would later drive into the garage and kill himself in. He had a slight tremor in his hands then, though he could still drive, still tend to his patients. I remember we drove out into the country someplace to see a man dying of end-stage lung cancer.

"It won't be pretty, son," he had said to me. "And he'll smell of the cancer."

"Can't you help him?"

"No. He's going to die."

"You can't give him *anything*?" I asked, outraged, the way children are outraged at the inevitability of death.

"No. There's not a thing I can do for him, except ease his pain. Sometimes the best a doctor can do for a patient is to make his going as easy as possible. Do you understand?"

I nodded.

"Do you really? Because what I'm saying to you, Stuart, is important. A doctor can do a lot, but even he has his limits. And when he reaches his limit and it's out of his hands, he has to know he's not God and he's done his best, and he has to be able to live with that. Death is not a doctor's enemy. And he has to recognize and accept this. Do you understand?"

I nodded again, though of course I had no idea what he meant. I think he knew even then that his own days were numbered, and in a way he was preparing me for the inevitability of his own death.

The shooting out in Piney Ridge turned out to be a couple of kids, brothers. They were fooling around with their father's handgun and one of them ended up dead. Which doesn't happen here as much as in cities because kids out here grow up around guns. But it still does happen. As I entered the house, Cecil came up to me. He was pale and sweating, so I knew it was a mess. I could smell the stench of blood spilled unnaturally, that inside-of-a-turkey rankness.

"How's it goin', Doc?" he asked.

"All right. What do we got, Cecil?"

"Same-old. The kid in there," he said, leading me into the den, "took a single 9-mm slug in the chest. My guess is he was dead before he hit the floor. Young'un over yonder done it." He pointed at a small, red-eyed, redheaded boy sitting on the couch with a woman I took to be his mother. Both of them were crying silently. "Dumb little fucker," Cecil whispered under his breath, but not in a mean-spirited way.

"Yeah."

"I'll be outside you need me, Doc."

The dead boy, who looked all of seven, had light brown hair and freckles. He wasn't a particularly cute kid, but death being the great equalizer, it has a way of making children look all about the same: fragile, delicate, and fine as expensive crystal. And pure, too, something unstained, untarnished yet by the world. He lay on his side, the front of his shirt soaked with blood, a puddle of it forming on the linoleum under him. I put on some gloves and checked him out. I would guess he'd been dead about an hour. The bullet had entered the middle of his chest, fracturing the sternum, sending bone fragments and lead slamming into his

heart, reducing it to something like pureed tomatoes. Cecil was right—
he probably didn't know what hit him, poor kid. At least it was quick
for him. I finished up my examination of the body and headed over to
where his brother and mother were seated. I squatted down in front of
them, my knees screaming like hell.

"I didn't know," the boy explained, sobbing. "I thought it was
empty."

They always do. They always assume that a gun doesn't pose any
danger to them. That it's a toy, something to be played with, like picking
up a snake. *Bang, you're dead.* And then, with that look of surprise and
terror in their now suddenly ancient eyes, they say, *I thought it was
empty.*

"It's all right," I said, patting him on the shoulder. Then I looked at
the mother. She was hollow-eyed, in shock, in a place momentarily beyond pain. Every day for the rest of her life, as she looked at this one,
her living child, I knew how she'd have to fight back the thought that
he'd killed her other one. Grateful yet bitter at once, trying to stifle her
hatred though every day it would seep out in little ways, every day she'd
have to beat it back, and every day she'd lose the battle. I leaned toward
the child and whispered in his ear, "You be a big boy for your mother,
all right? She's going to need you."

He stared at me with sober eyes, wiped the tears away, and nodded.

Outside, as the EMTs carted the body away, Cecil said to me, "He's
gonna grow up right quick, that one. Got time for one, Doc?"

"No," I said to his offer of a drink. "I should be going."

I got in my truck and headed home. I thought how Cecil was right,
about the boy, that is. Just as that kid's brother was now officially dead,
his own childhood was formally over and done with. When filling out
the death certificate for his brother, I might as well have made one out
for this one's innocence.

On the way up Mason Hollow Road, I stopped and picked Maria up
at Kay's. She wanted to fix me something to eat, but I begged off, saying
it was late and I was dog-tired and going to turn in early. The baby was
sleeping, so when I reached home I brought her right upstairs and put her
down. I was heading into the kitchen, planning on fixing myself a good
stiff drink and another after that, when I heard the noise. It seemed to be
coming from the den. A muffled cough. I grabbed the bottle of Scotch
from the cabinet, and clutching it weaponlike, I headed back toward the
den. I froze in the doorway, staring into the darkness of the room, my

heart pounding. The only light was that from the kitchen. Yet as my eyes adjusted to the darkness, I thought I could make out a form on the couch. My thoughts leapt immediately to the time Tully Pugh had tried to force his way into my house. I had a picture of him sitting in the dark with a gun. Maybe the death of the boy had spooked me, but I pictured him sitting there waiting to kill me. I held the bottle, ready to wield it.

"Who's there?" I called, my voice brittle with fear.

There was a pause, followed by a noise like someone yawning. Finally, a voice said, "I must've fallen asleep."

It was a voice I'd recognize anywhere.

"Annabel?" I asked.

"Hey, Stu. I used the key under the mat. Hope you don't mind."

"What . . . what are you doing here?"

"It's a long story. I had to get out of my apartment. You fixin' yourself a drink, you could be a sweetheart and make that two."

"Did you need money? I left you some money."

"No, it wasn't that. Let's just say I had to leave Asheville in a hurry."

"Are you in some kind of trouble?"

I went over to the end table to turn a light on, but Annabel said, "Would you mind not turning it on? My eyes hurt."

I figured she was high or drunk, or both, and didn't want me to see her.

"How did you get here?"

"I took a bus from Asheville. Then I caught a ride out of Slade from one of the Tarbell boys. One of Eunice Tarbell's kids. He gave me a lift as far as the church and I walked the rest of the way." It was four miles down the mountain to Highway 7.

"You still haven't told me why you're here."

"Mind if we talk about that later? I'm flat-out exhausted. You wouldn't happen to have anything to eat, would you?"

Now that my eyes had adjusted to the darkness, I could more clearly make her out sitting on the couch. Her legs were crossed, and she wore a bulky coat she hadn't unzipped. On the floor in front of her I saw something large and squarish. A suitcase? My heart tightened, not with fear this time but with something close to anger.

"I don't know what I have," I offered curtly. "I might have some eggs."

"That would be good. If it's no bother."

I didn't know what to say; my mind was awash with thoughts. So instead of saying anything, I headed into the kitchen. I went over to the stove and put the kettle on for tea. Then from the fridge, I took out some eggs and bread for toast. I grabbed a couple of pans from under the stove and started fixing something to eat. I wondered what she was doing back. What she was running from this time. What she wanted.

"You sure it's no bother?" she called from the den, her words distorted by another yawn.

"No."

"I hate to put you out."

"I said it wasn't any bother, didn't I?" I replied, a note of anger rising in my voice.

"Where's that baby you were telling me about?"

"She's sleeping."

"I was hoping I could see her. Maybe later, huh?"

"You should've called," I said.

"I figured you were too busy to come and get me."

"I mean you should've called before coming, Anna."

"You know me. I never won any awards for planning ahead."

"You can't just show up out of the blue like this."

"Did I come at a bad time?" she said, her voice shooting for girlish innocence and missing the mark, coming across instead as merely coy. I wasn't in the mood for coy.

"A little warning would be nice."

"I didn't think you'd mind."

"Mind. Jesus, Annabel."

"Look, Stu, I deserve whatever you're going to say. I'm just not in the mood for a lecture right now, okay? I'm starved half to death and I haven't slept in I don't know how long."

I fell silent. I was mad, so mad my right eyelid took to twitching. So mad I was afraid I'd say something I might later regret. I concentrated hard on making the food. I could tell she was in one of those in-between phases, exhausted, coming down from a long manic period. Played-out. Drained. Empty. I could just picture her eyes, heavy-lidded, glassy, the pupils fixed on some spot on the floor.

When the food was ready, I fixed a plate, poured her some tea, and waited for it to steep. I certainly wasn't going to give her any booze. I wondered what she would say and then what I would say. And I thought about offering to drive her into Slade so she could stay at the

Balsam Lodge. And then I pictured how she'd look at me when I told her that. Finally, I put the food on a tray and brought it into the den.

"Anna," I said into the darkness. "Your food's ready." Silence. "Let me turn the light on so you can see." I went over and flicked on the light. I found her curled up on the couch, sound asleep. Her thighs were drawn up to her chest and her hands lay between her knees, her jacket still on.

"Annabel?" I said, touching her shoulder. "Anna, your food's ready." She continued sleeping.

I took a seat in the rocking chair. Jesus, I thought. Jesus fucking Christ. I sat there for a long while, not saying anything. Just watching her. Then I began to eat the plate of food I'd fixed. I was hungry and there was no sense letting it go to waste. I watched her as I ate. She appeared small and insubstantial, like a child sleeping. She was pale and her cheekbones stood out. Her dark hair was unwashed, tangled. Her nails were dirty. Her clothes filthy, wrinkled, and giving off an odor of dampness and decay. She slept leadenly, without stirring, with only an occasional flickering of her shadowed eyelids beneath her glasses. I'd almost forgotten how soundly she could sleep at times, especially after those periods of acute mania when she hadn't slept for days on end. I could recall sitting by our bed, watching over her, the depth of her sleep something actually scary to behold, like looking down into a deep, black well. It almost seemed as if she were sinking further and further into her slumber and would eventually disappear altogether.

After a while, I went into the hall to get a blanket from the closet and threw it over her. As I removed her glasses, she cried, "No. Don't touch me," but continued sleeping. I turned the light off, headed into the kitchen, and poured myself a drink. I sat at the kitchen table for a long while. Damn it, I thought. Damn it all to hell. What was she doing back? Now especially. It couldn't just be a coincidence. What did she say? She had to leave Asheville in a hurry. I'd heard that sort of excuse before.

I poured another drink and went upstairs to my bedroom. It took me a long time to fall asleep, my thoughts occupied as they were with Annabel. I still couldn't believe she was back. How long this time? And what sort of shape was she in? Not good by the looks of it. In the middle of the night, I woke out of a sound sleep, and for a moment I thought Annabel was just a dream. I thought perhaps, like so many times before, I'd just dreamed she had come back. I had to get up and head downstairs to check. She wasn't a dream, though. She was still there, still sound asleep.

In the morning she slept right through my banging around adding wood to the stove and even through the noise I made shaking the grate and shoveling ashes into a bucket and carting it outside to the ash pile. Later, as I sat in the rocking chair feeding Maria, I watched Annabel on the couch. When it was time to head into work, I thought about waking her, but I recalled how exhausted she looked and decided to just let her sleep. Instead, I left her a note on the kitchen table: *I had to go to work. If you need anything, call me at the office. See you tonight?* I debated about the question mark. I dropped the baby off at Kay Wallenbach's and then headed into town.

At my office, Stella must've seen something was on my mind.

"You all right, Doc?"

"She's back," I blurted out to her. I shouldn't have said anything, because she'd want all the details, and I had none. But I had to tell somebody.

"Who?"

"My wife."

"Annabel Lee's home?" she said. "When did she get back?"

"Yesterday. She just showed up at the house."

"Well I'll be. What's she doing back?"

I shrugged.

"How is she anyway?"

"The usual," was how I left it.

Stella eyed me for a moment before saying, "I know it ain't none of my business."

"That doesn't usually stop you," I said.

"But what's this mean for you, Doc?"

I wasn't sure what she was getting at, if she'd heard about Bobbie and me.

"She's just staying for a few days."

I went about my work, tried to put her out of my mind as best I could. Yet all day long she sat in the middle of my thoughts, so that everything else had to detour around her. That night when I got home she was still sleeping. It looked as if she hadn't moved; she was curled up on her side in the same fetal position I'd left her. I had to get up close so I could assure myself that she was breathing. She continued to sleep all that evening, right through my giving Maria her bath and feeding her, right through my rummaging around in the kitchen getting something to eat. She remained sleeping when I turned in, and when I was leaving for work the next morning she was still out. In the past it wasn't unusual for her to sleep twenty-four hours straight, sometimes even longer. I left her another note. I said the baby was down at Kay's, to stop down there if she got lonely or needed anything. I said I'd be home around six, barring an emergency.

I saw patients in the morning, then drove over to the hospital in the afternoon to perform surgery on Mrs. Eblen, who had a prolapsed uterus. After that I made rounds. Emmilou Potter was doing well enough—blood pressure down, liver enzymes and other tests looking better—that I went ahead and discharged her, though I warned her to stay off her feet this time and said that I wanted to see her in the office early next week.

When I had a second, I put in a call to Bobbie's office. I wanted to break the news to her about Annabel showing up; I didn't want her to hear about it through the grapevine. But her secretary, Myrna, said she wasn't available. I told her to have Mrs. Tisdale call me at the hospital as soon as she got the chance. I was getting a coffee in the doctors' lounge when my beeper went off. I was thinking maybe it was Bobbie, but it turned out to be my office.

"Stella, it's me," I said. "What's going on?"

"Your neighbor just called. Kay. Had herself all worked up."

"What's the matter?"

"Says your wife showed up to her place this afternoon. Came walking right through the woods. She like to have dropped dead when she seen her at the door. Said Annabel was real peaked looking, white as a sheet."

"She called to tell you that?"

"That and to say Annabel took the baby."

"Took her? What do you mean took her?"

"When she left, she took the baby with her."

"Where?"

"Back to your place, I reckon. Where else would she take her? Kay says her husband offered to drive 'em, what with all the snow on the ground, but Annabel preferred to walk up the mountain. Oh, and she says Annabel told her you'd said it was all right to go ahead and bring the young'un with her."

"She said what?"

"That you'd said it was fy-on. I guess Kay was all in a tizzy-fit, on account of the way she looked and her insisting on walking home through the snow. So that's why she called. I told her not to worry. That you'd probably said it was all right, just like Annabel said. You did, didn't you?"

I hesitated, then said, "Annabel just wanted to see the baby."

"I figured it was okay. Just touching base with you, Doc. What do you want me to do?"

"Call Kay and tell her everything's fine. Not to worry. Tell her I'm heading home now."

I tried to believe that everything was fine. That Annabel just wanted to see the baby. But why had she taken the child home? What did she have in mind? And why did she lie about my saying it was all right? I didn't like the idea of her walking the half mile up through the woods in her condition, carrying a baby in her arms. What if she slipped? Or what if one of those Pughs came by? I called home but didn't get an answer, which worried me all the more. I found myself pushing the gas pedal harder than I normally would in that curvy section of Highway 7 north of my house.

When I got in the front door I called out, "Anna? *Annabel?*" Nothing. I headed into the kitchen. I could smell something cooking. The oven was on, but no one was there. Had she gone out again? She didn't have a car but given what she'd already pulled, who knew what she'd do? I walked back into the entryway and called again. After a second or two I heard her voice. "Up here, Stu."

I found Annabel in Will's room. She was sitting in the chair in the corner and feeding Maria a bottle.

"What are you doing?" I snapped.

"She was hungry."

"I don't mean that. I mean, why'd you pick her up? Kay was worried sick."

"I guess I took her a little by surprise."

"I guess you did. You told her I said it was all right? To take the baby?"

"Kay was acting a little weird. Like she didn't trust me. So that's why I said it."

She looked different. She'd cleaned herself up a little. She looked rested, not quite so worn out. Her hair was washed and pulled back off her face and held in place with a hair band. She'd changed out of the filthy clothes she'd been wearing; she now wore a pair of jeans, frayed but clean, and a T-shirt that advertised a bluegrass festival. Her slender arms were white as the flesh of a potato. Her complexion was still pale and her eyes tired, but her countenance wasn't as haggard as it had been. The sleep had helped a little, as it often did, reviving her spirits, clearing the haziness from her eyes. After going on little or no sleep for weeks on end, she would often crash and slip into one of her depressions, where she wouldn't get out of bed, sometimes for days. But when she finally did get up, she would suddenly be cheerful and buoyant and chatty. The change in her personality, though welcomed in most ways, would still be unsettling.

"She's a beautiful child, Stu."

"You should've called me first," I said.

"I didn't think you'd mind. What's the big deal?"

"The big deal is I'd arranged with *Kay* to watch the baby. She's an old lady and she got herself all worked up when you showed up like that."

"That's just it, Stu. She *is* getting on in years. She shouldn't be chasing after an infant. Not with me here now."

"What do you mean, not with you here now?"

"For the baby."

"The baby?"

"Yes. After you came to see me that time, I got to thinking. Figured you were in a bind and could use some help."

"What are you talking about, Anna?"

"With the baby and all."

"I didn't ask for your help."

"Not in so many words. I knew you being that stiff-upper-lip Yankee sort, you wouldn't ask. So here I am."

"Just like that?"

"Yeah."

"I thought you said you came because you were in some kind of trouble."

"Well," she said, her voice trailing off. "I figured I could help you out at the same time. One hand washing the other, like they say."

She looked over at me and smiled, her bad teeth making her look older than fifty. I didn't know what to think. Whether to believe her or not.

"What's the baby's name?" she asked.

"Maria," I replied, my voice growing a little calmer now. "Maria Littlefoot."

"She looks Cherokee."

"Her mother's a full-blood. Her father was a Pugh."

"She killed him? The mother."

"Yeah. Listen . . . "

"What's going to happen to her?"

"They're going to charge her with murder."

"And the baby?"

"There's going to be a custody hearing. The Pughs are contesting me getting her."

"What will happen?"

"We'll have to see. Annabel . . . "

"How old is she?"

"Four months."

"She's big for four months. You're a big girl, aren't you," she cooed to the baby.

"Annabel, we need to talk."

"Sure. Over supper. I hope you're hungry. I made meatloaf," she said. "I found some hamburger you had left over in the freezer. You didn't have any bread crumbs so I had to improvise. I made a list . . . "

"Wait. We need to talk—*now*. Right now," I cried.

"All right. Go ahead. Just lower your voice, Stu, you're scaring the baby."

I took a breath and asked, more calmly now, "Do you remember what we talked about last time we met?"

"We talked about a lot of things. About visiting the cemetery."

"Yes, we did. I also told you about me and . . . well, this woman I'm seeing. Remember?" I said, speaking slowly and deliberately, my tone patronizing, as if I were talking to some young mountain girl about prenatal care.

"Of course, I remember. Don't treat me like a little child."

"Then don't act like one."

"What's the problem, Stu?"

"*What's the problem!* You come blowing in here after being away all that time. What about me? What about my life?"

"Do you want me to leave? Is that what you're saying?"

"Annabel, it's just . . . if it's money, I could give you some. To help you get set up. If you don't want to go back to Asheville, you could go someplace else. I could help you find a place. Wherever you want."

"But I wanted to come back here for a little while."

I almost blurted out, *You can't come back here. Not now. Not ever.* What I said, though, was, "You think that's a good idea?"

"I just needed a place to stay till I figured out what I'm going to do next. I didn't think you'd mind. You never did before."

"Annabel . . . "

"And besides, I thought I could help. I thought I could be of some use. If you want me to leave, just tell me. I don't want to screw things up for you again. Like with that other woman."

"Annabel, just listen to me. I appreciate what you're trying to do. Really, I do."

"If you don't need my help, I'll leave tomorrow morning. Just say the word, Stuart. It's up to you. I just figured I'd stay a little while to help you out. And it'd give me a place to hole up while I was figuring out what to do next. But then again, if you want me out . . . " Her voice trailed off.

Annabel looked up from the baby and at me. I didn't know what to say. Actually, I *did* know what to say. The problem was I didn't know *how* to say it. I knew what I should do: Tell her straight out she couldn't stay. Or no more than a few days, a week tops, just till she caught her breath, had a chance to make other plans. I knew that's what I should say. And I knew, too, what she was doing, whether it was consciously on her part or not. Knew that that story about her having to leave Asheville suddenly, even if true, was only part of her reason for coming. She had an uncanny knack for drifting back into my life just when I was starting to put things in order, just when I was getting over her and learning to live on my own. And yet, how could I tell her to leave? How could I just kick her out into the cold? Finally, I asked, "How long you planning on staying?"

"That depends."

"On what?"

"On how long you need me."

I didn't say anything. The baby had finished feeding, and Annabel laid her over her shoulder and burped her.

"Oh, such a big burp from such a little girl," Annabel said, giving the baby kisses behind her ear. Maria grinned a toothless yet contented grin. "Whyn't you take a shower, Stu, and then we'll eat."

# 18

*After the baby* was down for the night, we had dinner in the dining room. Annabel had put out cloth napkins and the good china, and the white brocade tablecloth that had been her mother's. She'd made meatloaf, instant mashed potatoes from a box she'd found in the pantry, green beans, and buttermilk biscuits. She served the sweet pickle relish that Kay had put up and given me for Christmas. She'd even lit candles.

"You didn't have to go to all this trouble," I said to her.

"No trouble. Figured I'd surprise you. Go ahead and sit down."

It felt more than a little odd sitting across the table from her again. If Annabel felt odd, however, you could hardly tell. She was in good spirits, chattering away as if the nearly two years she'd been gone had been nothing more than an afternoon spent in Slade, and as if the last fourteen hadn't happened to us but to some people we knew. The way she acted, you'd have thought it was just another night that I'd come home from work. She asked about my day and who I had working in the office, how Stella was, what was new at the hospital. Occasionally she would add a nervous little laugh at the end of a sentence, her hand fluttering up to cover her mouth, and now and then she would look up from her plate and shoot a furtive, anxious glance at me.

"Is the meatloaf all right?" she asked. Of course, she didn't try any, as she'd been a vegetarian ever since I'd met her.

"It's good," I replied.

"It's not too dry?"

"It's fine."

"You need to go shopping, Stu. You're out of just about everything."

"I don't eat home much anymore. I usually grab something in town."

"Time was you liked to cook."

"I've been too busy. Besides, I don't like cooking for just myself."

"Oh," she said. When I glanced up at her, she quickly added, "I mean, no wonder you've lost weight, Stu."

She reached across the table and squeezed my bicep. "Look at that. I can feel your bones."

"I manage just fine."

"When was the last time you had a good home-cooked meal?"

"Kay has me down now and then. And I went to Stella's for Christmas dinner."

"Well, I made a list of things for you to pick up in town."

We spoke about the snowstorm and when the mountains last had been hit this hard. Annabel said she could remember a big storm from when she was a little girl. Several feet. How the people in the mountains still talked about it. Everything being closed down for days. She recalled Orel Pressley giving people rides in his horse-drawn sleigh right down the middle of Main Street.

"He was a nice old man. I remember when I used to go into his store to buy seeds, his little granddaughter would be on the floor playing. Tanya, I think her name was. She must be all grown up now."

"She's dead," I replied.

"Dead? How?"

"She and her boyfriend, one of the Ledbetters, they committed suicide."

"No!" she exclaimed. "When was this?"

"A couple of years back. Up at Miller's Landing. He shot her and then himself."

"God. That's just awful."

"Yes. It was pretty bad."

"I seem to recall you having a hard delivery with one of the Pressley boys?"

"Yeah. With Marty. Tanya's older brother. Dixie was in labor for hours. Last time I saw her she was telling me Marty's married and has a couple of kids already."

"Get out. He can't be more than, what, fifteen?"

"He's twenty."

"Twenty!"

"Don't you remember? He'd be around Will's age."

Annabel turned pensive, nibbling on a biscuit. "I guess that would be about right. I can remember bumping into Dixie in Green's and we were both out to here. We had a hot Indian summer that fall I was pregnant. Remember that, Stu? How hot it was?"

I nodded.

"I remember Dixie and me commiserating about being pregnant in such ungodly heat. Doesn't seem possible it was twenty years ago, does it?"

"I need to get some wood," I said.

"I'll make us some tea."

I put my coat on and went out the sliding doors, heading across the backyard for the woodpile near the barn. The night was cold, the sky clear and razor-sharp. I felt the cold as a pressure against my cheeks. Underfoot, the snow made a sound like a horse chewing on oats, and down through the valley a plaintive wind moved, knifing through the woods and rustling the fragile beech leaves still clinging to their branches. I didn't need any wood; it was just an excuse to get out and clear my head. The whole thing just seemed too odd, too strange. Having her back. Sitting there and talking like we used to when we lived together. As if nothing had happened. As if the past hadn't happened. Of course, she'd come back into my life many times before, suddenly and without warning. But this time she'd been gone so long. And this time things were different. There was Bobbie.

As I was heading back to the house, I spied Annabel washing dishes at the sink. I stood for a moment in the dark and peered in at her. *Twenty years,* I thought. Yet she was right; it didn't seem possible. I could remember when she was pregnant. She'd carried low, everything in front. Somebody had told her it meant she was going to have a girl, one of those old wives' tales, and until Dr. Bembry, her physician, did the ultrasound, that's what we thought, too. I could still remember what she looked like pregnant. Not all woman glow when pregnant; many times it's a struggle. The body robs from Peter to pay Paul. Take Emmilou Potter, for example. But Annabel did glow. She radiated with the life she was carrying. Her skin turned luminous, as if there was a fine light glowing under its surface, and when she smiled her entire face shone. I could remember how she moved about the house when she was carrying Will, slowly yet lissomely, like some large but graceful sea mammal floating in her own element. I could remember, too, holding her at night, my hand wrapped around her smooth belly, feeling Will's impatient kick, ready to get on with his life. Twenty years ago.

When I returned with an armload of wood, Annabel had just finished the last of the dishes. She dried her hands and took out her pack of cigarettes.

"You mind, Stu?" she asked.

"Go ahead."

She lit up a cigarette and gazed out the window. "My garden's really gone to hell, hasn't it?" she said. "I was out there today."

"You know I'm not much of a gardener."

"Imagine it would take a whole lot of work to get it back in shape."

"I imagine so."

"Probably better off just to have John come up with his tractor and plow the whole thing under."

I didn't say anything, didn't want to go down that road. I watched Annabel's hands as she smoked her cigarette. They weren't too bad. Not like the night I'd visited her in Asheville. I wondered if she were taking her lithium again. Or when she last had seen a doctor or had a blood test done to check her levels. I thought about asking her if she was on her medication, if she needed to see someone. If she wanted, I could make an appointment for her. There was a new psychiatrist I knew had just set up practice over in Crawford City. I'd referred one or two of my patients to him. I heard he was good. But I decided that could wait.

"How are you feeling?" I asked.

"Better than I was."

"Looks like the rest did you some good."

Later, as I was stoking the fire, my beeper went off. It was the hospital. I called and Lucy Ballard told me a patient of mine, Leola McGruder, was en route. Her water had broken and she was in active labor. It was her fourth baby and I knew things would progress quickly. I'd have to get going right away.

"It's the hospital," I said to Annabel. "A woman in labor."

"Just like old times, huh? Never a dull moment."

I thought about Maria, what I should do with her. I picked up the phone and dialed Stella's number.

"Who are you calling?" Annabel asked.

"Stella. She said she'd look after the baby if I got called in."

"What on earth for? I'm here."

"She doesn't mind."

"But that's why I came. To be of some use."

Howard, Stella's husband, picked up.

"It's Stuart," I said to him. "Is Stella there?"

While he went off to get his wife, Annabel whispered, "I'm all right. Really, I am. Look." She held out her hands as proof. They were pretty steady, not perfect but much calmer than I'd seen them in a long while. "I'm fine."

I stared at her, debating what to do. Stella came on the line then. "You need to drop the baby off, Doc?"

"Actually, I was wondering if you could do me a favor? Pull Carrie Blyleven's file for me tomorrow."

"Pull her file? Couldn't that'a waited till morning?"

"I didn't want to forget. Could you see the last time we did an ultrasound on her?"

"If I'm not mistaken, Carrie had one last visit. But I'll pull her file. Everything all right, Doc?" she asked, seeing through my deception.

"Fine," I replied.

After I hung up, I asked Annabel, "You sure?"

"Of course. I feel great. You go on. I'll hold the fort down."

I stared at her, debating with myself.

"That baby's going to be born without you, you don't get a move on, Stu."

Finally, I grabbed my coat and left. All the way to the hospital, though, I worried if I'd done the right thing, leaving Maria with her. I tried to reassure myself: What could happen? The baby was sleeping. She normally slept through the night. Besides, Annabel looked much better than she had that first night. Calmer. More in control. I decided if I was going to be any longer than a couple of hours, I'd call John and have him go up to the house. He was usually up late reading anyway. I'd have him check in on her. I'd make up some excuse: that she'd heard a noise, that I was worried about a chimney fire. Something. Though he and Kay were certainly no strangers to my wife's problems.

Yet all my worrying was for nothing. As it turned out, things went so smoothly with the delivery I was out of the birthing room by midnight and home by one. I peeked in the baby's room where I found Maria sound asleep in her crib. For some reason, I went over and touched the warm, silky skin of her cheek, gently stroking it with my fingertips. Then I headed down the hall and looked in the guest room, where I'd assumed, correctly it turned out, that Annabel had gone. She was in bed, lying on her side, facing the window. I couldn't hear her breathing.

"Anna," I whispered. "I'm home."

Nothing.

I closed the door and headed down the hall to my room.

• • •

When I came downstairs in the morning, Annabel was sitting at the kitchen table, holding the baby and feeding her a bottle. The sun was glinting harshly off the snow up on the crest of Shadow Mountain; farther down, light gathered together and then exploded off the flat whiteness covering the land behind the house. The day was boldly advancing, and I was running late.

"I made some coffee," she said. "There's no milk but I know you take it black anyway."

"Thanks," I said, pouring myself a cup.

"You want any breakfast, Stu?"

"I'll grab a donut at the Pancake Barn."

"That's not very healthy."

"I'm running late." I hesitated before asking, "What about the baby?"

"What about her?"

"Kay's expecting her."

"I thought we went over this last night," she said. She lay the baby over her shoulder and burped her. "Atta girl. How can I help you, Stu, if you don't let me?"

"I just thought maybe . . . you could get situated first."

"Situated?"

"You know. Get your feet under you. Rest up for a few days."

"I'm already plenty rested. Besides, it'll give me something to do. If I just sit here, I'll be bored out of my mind. You know me," she said, frowning, a veiled threat seeming to hang there.

"Well, if you're sure."

"I'm sure. Stop treating me like an invalid."

I still wasn't certain. It was one thing to leave her with the baby for a few hours at night. Another to leave her alone all day. But something told me that nothing would happen, that everything would be fine.

"All right. But if anything comes up, if you start to feel antsy or . . . whatever, you make sure you call me. Promise?"

"Scout's honor," she said, smiling. "Now go on. You don't want to be late. Here's that list of groceries to buy. Better get some more formula, too."

I headed to the front closet and grabbed my coat. Annabel followed me, carrying Maria.

I turned to her. "See you tonight then."

"That woman," she said. "The one you're seeing."

"What about her?" I asked defensively.

"God knows I don't have any right to butt into your life. Not again. I just wanted to know, is it . . . I mean, does she make you happy?"

I looked at her and nodded. "Yes."

She chewed on her lip for a moment, then offered up a wan smile, so I saw her missing teeth. This close and in the bright light of day, I noticed how gray her hair had gotten, the tiny furrows around her mouth, like fissures in pale marble, something that could shatter altogether. The delicate wrinkles at the corners of her eyes. How the years had eroded her looks, robbed her of her youth. Yet it was in her eyes that I saw, if not exactly the old Annabel, something that called her to mind. Like a not-quite-in-focus photo of a once pretty girl. Her brown eyes were clear this morning, and when she smiled they shimmered the way they used to.

"I'm glad for you, Stu. Really. And I don't want to be messing up your life. Not again. The last time I left I promised myself I wouldn't come back. That you deserved to have a life. One without me to fret over. I just thought you might need a hand with the baby is all. That's the *only* reason I came back. I swear to God. Anytime you want me to leave, just say the word and I'm out of your hair."

I thought how she was now making it easy for me. All I had to do was say it *would* be better if she left. That I wanted to start a new life and that she wasn't part of it. But instead I said, "You can stay," then added, "for a while."

"Are you sure?"

"Yes. Till you're ready to go. Besides, I could use your help."

"Tell you what. I'll stay until they decide what's going to happen with the baby. All right?"

"Okay. See you tonight," I said, heading out the door.

All the way into town, I kept wondering if I were making a mistake, letting her stay. But what else could I do? I couldn't just kick her out. I did make a decision, though: Whatever happened, however long she stayed, this would be it. The last time. The *very* last. I would make that clear to Annabel when she left. That she couldn't come back again. On my cell phone, I called Kay Wallenbach and explained that I wouldn't be bringing the baby after all.

"Annabel Lee be all right up there, just her and the baby?" the old lady asked.

"She'll be fine. Tell you what you could do, though. Would you mind stopping by the house? She could use the company."

"Sure thing, Stuart. How's she doing?"

"She's a little tired. Otherwise she's doing pretty good."

"I'll bring her up my blackberry cobbler. She was always partial to that."

Then I called Bobbie again. She hadn't returned any of my calls from the previous two weeks, and I was beginning to get a little worried. Maybe she was just busy at work. Or maybe she was having her own problems at home. But her secretary said she wasn't in yet.

"Tell her Dr. Jordan called," I said. "Tell her to call me at my office." As an afterthought, I said, "Tell her it's urgent."

When I got to the office, Stella wanted to know how things had turned out with Annabel and the baby.

"Nothing was the matter. She's going to stick around and look after Maria for me," I said.

"You mean permanent-like?" Stella said, raising one eyebrow.

"No. Temporary-like."

"That does my heart good, Doc. Maybe that's just what that girl needs. Something to get her going." Stella, I could see, was chomping at the bit to ask more, but somehow refrained. "Here's the file on Carrie you was wantin'. But like I said, we done an ultrasound last visit. Oh. Cecil called. Says that Littlefoot woman took sick."

"Sick? How sick?"

"I don't rightly know. He said she was throwing up."

"What's he want me to do?"

"I reckon he was hoping you'd come over and have a look at her."

"If he's worried about her, he should bring her to the hospital," I muttered.

"She wouldn't go."

"That's not my problem. Am I supposed to drop everything just because one of his prisoners gets sick? I have a practice to run."

"You don't have to kill the messenger, Doc."

"Well, I got other things to worry about."

"Your one o'clock, Mrs. Dills, called to cancel. Which means you got a free hour and a half counting lunch. I ain't telling you how to spend it."

Stella smiled at me. I shook my head, annoyed, but knowing already I would go.

"All right, tell Cecil *if* I get a chance I'll be over around noon. That's *if* I get a chance."

Around midmorning, I called home. A woman whose voice I didn't recognize at first answered. She was laughing, her voice sounding giddy, light as air.

"Annabel?" I said.

"Speak of the devil," she replied, giggling. "You checking up on me, Stu?"

"No. Just seeing how your morning's going? What's so funny?"

"Kay and John stopped up. We were talking about the time you tried to shoot that groundhog in the garden. Remember? Stuart, the big white hunter. How you nearly destroyed all my tomatoes trying to hit the darn thing?"

"Everything's all right then?"

"Everything's fine. Make sure you pick up that list of groceries I gave you. I'll have supper ready about six. If y'all are gonna be late give me a call."

After my last morning appointment, I told Stella I was going over to the courthouse, that I'd be back by 1:30 for my next patient. Checking on Rosa gave me an excuse to see Bobbie.

"She's in court, Dr. Jordan," Myrna in the DA's office told me.

"Did she get my messages? I must've left a half-dozen."

"I gave 'em to her. She been awful busy."

I was heading downstairs to the jail when I happened to run into Bobbie coming out of the door that led to Superior Court. She was with a heavy woman dressed in a waitress outfit and a surly-looking teenage boy with one black eye.

"Well, looky who's here." Bobbie said, surprised to see me.

"Hello, counselor."

"Gimme a minute?" she said. I moved off toward a window that looked out onto Main Street. The day was mostly sunny, a few straggler clouds cluttering up an otherwise clean blue sky. The confederate soldier in front of the courthouse gazed south, offering his verdigris backside to the conquering North, the way most Southern war memorials do. Off in the distance, the Plott Balsam peaks glimmered under a blanket of white. Bobbie spoke to the woman and boy for a little while, and when they left she walked over to where I was standing.

She had on a gray double-breasted suit. When she got up close, I saw that she wore a pair of diamond-studded earrings I'd never seen her wear before.

"What're you doing here?" she asked.

"Cecil said Rosa Littlefoot was sick. He wanted me to take a look at her. I've been trying to reach you."

"I know. Sorry. I've been flat out."

"I missed you, counselor."

"I missed you, too." She glanced around, and when she saw no one around she took my hand and gave it a firm squeeze. I leaned toward her to kiss her but she pulled back.

"What?" I said.

"We'd better not. I wouldn't want Troy to see us. I got a feeling he already suspects something's up."

"He say anything?"

"Not in so many words. I half don't even care. Still, it might cause some problems for me right now."

"Listen, I have to tell you something. Annabel's back."

"What do you mean back?"

"I mean, she showed up at my house the other day."

"But why?"

"Who knows why? I told you she has a habit of just dropping in out of the blue."

"How long is she staying?"

"I don't know. She doesn't usually stay very long." When Bobbie pursed her lips, I added, "I can't very well just tell her to leave, can I?"

She shrugged. "No, I don't suppose you would."

"It doesn't change anything between us, Bobbie. I meant what I said the other night."

"I know."

"Just for now I need to deal with her."

"Maybe it's a good thing, after all. That we cool it for a little while."

"Why?"

"For one thing, I've been swamped with work. And like I said, I think Troy may be onto us. The fat jerk's made a couple of cracks about you in my presence. Like the other day your name came up. He said how Doc Jordan was burning the candle at both ends and then he smiled at me. I ignored him but I think he knows about us."

"So let him."

"He could make things difficult. When I do decide to leave, I'd like it to be on my own terms. Besides, it just wouldn't be good timing right now."

"What do you mean?" I asked.

She hesitated for a moment. "Paul's mother has improved some. They took her off the respirator but she's still pretty bad. She could die tomorrow or last like this for a while."

"What does that have to do with us?"

"Paul's taking it pretty hard. He needs me right now, Doc."

I felt a pang of jealousy being drawn across my heart, raking my heart like a wood file. I recalled what she'd said on New Year's Eve, about how she still cares for him. How close she'd felt toward him when they were together down in Florida.

"What about me?" I asked, petulantly. "Don't I need you?"

"He needs me more right now. You know how you just said you had to deal with your wife right now. While I got to think of him."

I felt like saying he's an asshole who treats you like dirt, but I didn't dare, fearing it might only make her defensive and stick up for him, and I couldn't bear that.

"I just want us to be together."

"Don't you think that's what I want, too? But right now we both have other issues we have to deal with." She glanced at her watch. "Listen, I have to run. I'll call you."

"When?"

"As soon as I can."

"Can't we see each other?"

"I'll call you. I promise."

She turned and hurried toward the stairs, yet she stopped before she headed up. She looked back over her shoulder, winked, and mouthed the words, *Bye, Doc.* I told myself it was just a temporary sort of good-bye, not to worry about it. But something in her expression left me a little uneasy. *He needs me right now.*

I wasn't in a good mood when I entered the sheriff's office, and it sure didn't improve any when I saw Troy Bumgartner there. That comment he'd made to Bobbie, about me burning the candle at both ends, stuck in my craw.

"Just the fellow I wanted to see," he said. He had one fat cheek propped on the sheriff's desk. Cecil sat hunkered down behind it, looking as browbeaten as a student in the principal's office.

"Thought you were going in for surgery," I said.

"Had to postpone it. Why, I turn my back for two seconds and this place goes to hell in a handbasket," he said, giving Cecil a meaningful stare. "Stuart, how did the Hicks boy die?"

"What?" I said. Now it was my turn to look at Cecil. Behind Troy's back he screwed up his mouth as if to say, *Watch your step*.

"Buster Hicks. That nig—I mean, that dope addict from over in Hobbstown. How did he die, Stuart?"

"You read my report."

"I did and that's why I'm asking. Were drugs involved?"

"They may have been."

"Could death have been caused by an overdose?"

"I didn't think so."

"But it *was* a possibility?"

"I suppose it could've been a contributing cause."

"Then how come you didn't mention it in your report?"

"It didn't seem to make much difference."

"The hell it didn't."

"He was dead, Troy. Whether he'd OD'ed or just aspirated on his own vomit, it ends up the same thing."

"You know when you're not sure of cause of death, Stuart, you're supposed to request an autopsy. You know that as well as I do."

"He could just as easily have choked as died of an overdose. Why waste taxpayers' money when I don't have to?"

"But something like that gets around, it don't look good. Folks'll think we're hiding something."

"I'm not *hiding* anything," I said.

"I would certainly hope not," he replied, staring at me in that way a poker player does who's holding only a pair and yet wants you to think he's got a full house.

"I just didn't see any reason to cause the Hicks family any more suffering than I had to."

"But that ain't your call to make. You know that. In the future please follow departmental guidelines."

I'd about had it with departmental guidelines, with Troy Bumgart-ner, with deciding how people left this world. I was sick and tired of the whole damn thing.

"All right," I said. "I resign."

"*What?*"

"You heard me. I resign. I'm done as medical examiner."

"Don't be silly, Doc. You don't want to do that."

"No? Watch me. I've had my belly full of it for a long time. You want my resignation? Then you got it. Take it and shove it up your fat ass for all I care."

Behind him Cecil was silently shaking a fist in the air.

"*Whoa!* Now just hold on a minute, Stuart." Troy gingerly clambered down off the desk and came hobbling over to me. He put a hand on my shoulder. "Nobody wants you to resign. Least of all me. Hell, I need you. Don't we, Cecil?" he said, turning to the sheriff. Cecil nodded soberly, though he winked as soon as Troy looked back at me. "Neinhuis is a good fellow and all, but he can't handle this all by himself. I'm just asking you to follow standard procedure is all. C'mon, Doc. What the hell am I gonna do without you?"

I walked over and poured myself a coffee.

"You need you a vacation, Stuart. That's why you're all nerved up."

"I'm not all nerved up," I replied. "I'm *fed* up."

"Same difference. It's all that staying up late you're doing," he said. "Wears a fellow ragged."

"You mean, sort of like burning the candle at both ends?" I offered. If he remembered having said that to Bobbie, he didn't let on.

"I just meant you having to tend to that papoose."

"Jesus. Her name's Maria."

"All right, Maria then. What in the Sam Hill you doing with that young'un anyhow?"

"None of your business, Troy."

"Hell's bells, Doc. You're the ME. You're supposed to be helping *us* out. Not wasting your time with some junkie Indian murderer and her damn kid."

"Stay out of my personal life," I said, shooting him an ornery look.

"Your personal life is one thing. When it affects your professional judgment, it's another. If it was me, I wouldn't be putting my career on the line for some Indian whore, that's for sure."

"What career?" I scoffed. I took a sip of coffee, grimaced as the lukewarm, bitter-tasting stuff rolled over my tongue. "And since we're talking about careers, tell me, Troy, why in the hell are you so dead-set on a first-degree murder conviction anyway?"

"Why? Because she killed that Pugh fellow in cold blood, that's why."

"And it doesn't have anything to do with furthering your own career?"

"What?"

"You getting appointed to the bench and all that."

"I'm just representing the people who elected me."

"You're so full of shit, Troy, it's coming out your ears. I don't see how you get premeditated out of a simple family argument that escalated to a shooting."

"Number one," he said, counting off the reasons on his sausage-fat fingers, "the way she *dis*patched him. Number two, she had her escape all planned out. And number three, they's drugs involved. That equals murder in my book any day of the week. Want a piece of advice, Stuart? One old friend to another."

"Listen, Troy, let's get one thing straight right now. You and I were never friends."

He actually looked hurt when I said it, as if he'd really believed we were.

"Suit yourself, Stuart," he said, shuffling with his cane toward the door. He paused and turned around. "Here I thought we was buddies all these years. Live and learn."

When he was gone, Cecil said, "Never could stomach that asshole. I'll be glad when he gets that job as a judge and is outa my hair."

"Where did he hear about Buster Hicks?"

"Who knows? I didn't tell him. Hell, for a minute there, Doc, I thought you was actually going to quit."

"I thought I did." For a moment I wondered if I had quit or not. "You said Rosa was sick?"

"Yeah. Night shift said she threw up a coupla times. She refused to go to the hospital, though. When I come on this morning, she was looking poorly. She said it wasn't nothing, but I thought I'd better give you a call to be on the safe side."

"You know, I'm not the only person with a medical degree in Slade."

"Just figured you were taking such a personal interest in her case."

"You starting in on that, too, Cecil?" I snapped at him.

"Easy, Doc. I didn't mean nothing by it."

"Like I got nothing better to do than solve everybody's damn problems for them."

"I'll bring her over to hospital if'n you want."

I shook my head.

"I'm here already. I might as well take a look at her."

"Sorry, Doc."

"Don't worry about it, Cecil. It's just that I got a bug up my ass so far I can taste it. How's Ruth doing?"

"Last few days she been feelin' a mite better. Been up and about. Say, I hear tell Annabel is back."

"Where'd you hear that?"

"Around."

"Yeah, she came back the other day."

"How is she?"

"She's doing all right."

"How's that gonna . . . well, you know?"

"Don't ask, Cecil."

. . .

I found Rosa sitting on her cot, bent forward, her arms cradling her stomach. Her complexion was ashen, her lips blue-tinged. Her eyes were hollow and her hair was pulled back off her face and into that single long braid again.

"How are you feeling?" I asked, sitting down beside her on the cot. The cell gave off the stench of recent vomit.

"All right, I reckon."

"The sheriff tells me you were sick."

"I felt worse."

"What's the matter?"

"My stomach hurts. Not too bad now, though."

"Where does it hurt?"

"Right here," she said, pressing the left lower quadrant of her stomach.

"Any cramping?"

"No. Just kinda aches."

"Your periods regular?"

"Yeah. Sure."

"Since I'm here, mind if I check you out?"

"No need. Like I said, I'm feeling better this morning, Dr. Jordan."

"If I don't give you a quick inspection, the county won't pay me and I'm out my fee. I got bills to pay, Rosa."

"Well, in that case."

I removed a thermometer from my bag and took her temperature. Then, with my stethoscope, I listened to her heart and lungs. Next, I checked her pulse and felt under the angle of her jaw. I had her lie down and I felt her stomach. It seemed a little tender when I pressed. I finished a cursory examination, as much as I could do in a jail cell. She was running a low-grade fever and there was that tenderness in her belly. It was probably nothing. A virus. Still, given her drug history and the fact that she hadn't had regular medical care, I'd have felt a whole lot better if I could have done a thorough exam on her.

"Your breasts still tender?" I asked.

"A little. I stopped pumping them a while back though."

"Your milk should've stopped by now. You could have a mastitis. A breast infection. When was the last time you had a complete GYN exam?"

"Back at the clinic on the reservation, I suppose. Eight, nine years ago."

"You should have one. What I'd like to do is have you admitted to the hospital. I could work things out with the sheriff."

"I'm fine. I don't need to go to no hospital."

"You're going to be in jail for a couple of months. You need to be strong and healthy when you go to court. Last thing you want is to get sick. It might be a good idea to have you checked out now."

"I don't need to be checked out. I feel better this morning, Dr. Jordan. Really."

"It's up to you," I said, packing up my things.

"How's my little *ka-ma-ma*?" she asked.

"Your butterfly is doing just fine."

"Who's tending to her now?"

"She's home with my wife."

"Tell her thank you for me. For looking after my baby."

"I will." I got up and headed toward the door. "They're going to have the custody hearing in a couple of weeks. Hunneycutt said there's no guarantees how the judge will rule. He said this Cobb fellow is hard to predict. He might give me sole custody or he might give it to the Pughs. Or he might even place Maria with the state. There's no telling. I just want you to know that."

"I understand. And after that?"

"After that we'll play it by ear."

# 19

*We had our* usual late-January thaw, where winter suddenly seems to change its mind, grow listless and apathetic. In the daytime the temperatures rose into the high fifties, once even topping sixty. It confused the birds and made people skittish. The mountains sloughed off their covering of snow like a snake its whitish, feathery skin. The snow-melt gathered in tiny rivulets, which flowed into small creeks and branches, and then into larger and still larger ones, the runoff coursing down countless valleys and hollows before spilling into the already swollen, brackish Tuckamee River. Some of the low-lying pasture land out along Highway 7 had flooded, and the creek to the side of my house overflowed its banks. At night you could hear the water surging over the rocks, pounding like a heart in love or in fear, as it rushed down the mountainside: an ancient sound, at once comforting and disturbing in its power.

On nice days Annabel would take Maria out in the large old baby carriage she'd borrowed from our neighbor, what Kay referred to as a perambulator. She'd walk down Mason Hollow Road, stopping at the Isleys' barn to show Maria the cows. On the way back, she'd pause beside the roadside and gather wild grapevines, which she fashioned into wreaths and garlands she hung in the baby's room or about the house. Most days she would visit with Kay and John. The Wallenbachs' younger daughter, Sara, and her family had recently moved down to Charleston, and Kay missed having them nearby. So she liked when Annabel and Maria paid a visit. Sometimes Kay would invite us all down for supper.

"Wouldn't put no stock in this weather," John warned one evening.

We sat in the Wallenbachs' dining room eating ham steaks, grits and gravy, and greezyback beans Kay had put up from her garden.

"People were walking down Main in shirtsleeves," I said.

"Fool's spring. Won't last."

"I don't know, John. Drew Hazard told me he spotted his first Florida license tag the other day."

"That's surer'n a robin around these parts," his wife added, chuckling.

In her late seventies, Kay was slender and fair, with delicate features and a usually reserved manner, except when it came to her husband, with whom she liked arguing. John, on the other hand, had a sharp face like an ax and a ruddy complexion. He often said he must have had some Melungeon blood in him. The Melungeons were a dusky-skinned, mysterious clan that lived way back in the mountains and were variously described as descendants of Indians, shipwrecked Portuguese explorers, or even the lost colonists of Roanoke, who had intermingled with slaves and Indians. John could talk your ear off and held strong opinions on any number of subjects, especially about times moving too fast in the mountains. He favored the old ways and old traditions. When I first moved in up on the mountain and told him what I did for a living, he said he didn't hold with women having babies in hospitals. He said women should do their birthing at home. He thought hospital babies had weak blood.

"Those Florida birds'll be here soon enough," he said. "By the way, Doc, I'm reading me a book about the Great Wall they got over in China. That Shihuangdi was a real smart feller. Yessir. Built it to keep the northern invaders out. I think he was onto something. That's what we shoulda done. Built us a wall to keep out ever' durn fool with a camera around his neck."

"What on earth we need with a wall?" scoffed Kay. She was holding Maria and feeding her a bottle. "We already got the mountains. They're wall enough."

"It'd keep things like they are."

"What you mean is like they *was*," Kay said, winking at me.

"Just 'cause some folks in California and New York and ever' other damn place want all these newfangled things, hit don't mean we have to."

"You watch your mouth, John Wallenbach. I won't have cussing at my dinner table. He lives in the past, that one," she complained, looking over at Annabel and me.

"All's I'm saying is we got invaded first with Yankee armies—no offense, Doc. And now we're getting invaded again, only this time around it's with their dag-blame McDonalds and MTV and Victoria's Secret."

"Huh," his wife scoffed. "And just what would an old cuss like *you* know about Victoria's Secret?"

We all laughed at that, except for John, who looked sheepishly around the table. "I heard tell about it," he said, giving me a wink.

"He gets more cantankerous ever' year, I swear," Kay joked. "Can I get y'all seconds, Annabel Lee?"

"No, ma'am. I couldn't hardly eat another bite."

"It's so nice to have a little one around again," said the old woman, rocking the baby in her arms.

"Yes," Annabel agreed, shooting me a glance and then quickly averting her eyes.

"If I ain't mistaken, they's a box of baby clothes up in the attic. I'll have John fetch it down. Some things might fit Maria. Go and make yourself useful," she commanded her husband.

Later, while John and Annabel went through the box of clothes, I helped Kay with the dishes in the kitchen. She leaned close to me and whispered, "It's sure good to have her back, Stuart."

I took a plate from her, dried it, and put it up in the cabinet.

"She's seems a whole lot better."

"Yes," I replied. "A little."

"It's this clean mountain air," Kay explained, scooping some table scraps onto a plate for Milly, their dog. Then she added, "And that precious young'un's putting some spark back into her."

"I suppose."

"Suppose, nothing. Anybody with eyes in his head can see it." I followed her gaze into the living room where Annabel held up a small white outfit to see if it would fit the baby. "I ain't seen that gal look so good in years. Fit as a fiddle."

• • •

During the day, when Maria was taking her nap, Annabel kept herself busy with projects around the house. She took down the curtains, washed them, and hung them out on the clothesline to dry. (The line, which went from the back deck to the tulip tree near the creek, was so frayed I had to buy some new rope at Goody's hardware in town and put it up for her.) She brought the rugs outside and beat them with a broom. She washed all the windows, inside and out, so sunlight streamed in, filling every corner of the house, driving out the lingering shadows. She cleaned and scrubbed, polished and dusted, organized and rearranged. She went through all the closets, sorting and throwing things out. The house took on a new, almost alien smell; it lost the familiar odor of dust and staleness, the smell of a bachelor who'd grown too comfortable with his own slovenliness.

"Don't you have anybody come in to clean for you?" she asked me once. She was on her knees washing the shelves in the refrigerator. She'd taken all the food out and set it on the counters.

"Emmilou Potter used to come in once a week. But she's been having problems with her pregnancy."

"That woman pregnant *again*? Good Lord, you'd have thought she'd have learned."

"Some people never do."

Annabel shot me a quick look, then went back to her work.

"When are they coming for the custody evaluation?" she asked.

"Should be any time now."

"Well, you want everything in order. You want them to see a spotless house, Stu."

I was glad she was keeping herself occupied, staying busy. At the same time, the sudden change in her concerned me a little, too. There was, I knew all too well, a very fine line between her normal hyper self and her crossing over into the burning mania that would consume her like a moth flying too close to a flame. I told her she didn't have to push herself, but she said she wanted to keep busy, to have something to do. Yet there was another, not altogether altruistic, reason for my concern. I didn't want her getting too comfortable here, didn't want her assuming that things could go back to what they once were. Her stay this time around was only a temporary thing, and I didn't want her to think otherwise.

"I straightened out your bureau, Stu," she told me one evening.

A few days later, a Saturday, I was going out to split some wood and I couldn't find my ratty old Duke sweatshirt I liked to wear around the house.

"Have you seen my sweatshirt?" I asked Annabel. "The one that says Duke on it?" She was in the den, dusting around the pictures on the bookshelf. In her hand she had the photo of the three of us from that time we went to Gatlinburg.

"That old thing. Why, I threw it out."

Since I usually brought the garbage to the dump myself and she had no way to get around, I asked, "Is it still out in the barn?"

"Actually, John was going into town so I had him bring a bag of clothes to Goodwill."

"That was my favorite sweatshirt."

"It was coming out at the elbows. You can pick up another at Shuster's."

"But I liked *that* one," I said curtly. "Anna, please, just leave my things alone."

"I was only trying to help, Stu," she replied, sounding hurt.

"It's just that I'm used to things being a certain way. You can't come in here and change everything around."

"Sorry."

"Things are different now," I snapped. Annabel seemed visibly to flinch. I thought to myself, Tell her. Tell her she can't stay. Or at the very least give her a deadline. I'm sorry, Anna, but you have to leave by such and such a date. Right after the custody evaluation, say. Or by the middle of next month. Something clear-cut, providing closure. But I couldn't bring myself to utter the words that would in effect banish her. Calming down a little, I said, "I appreciate your help, Anna. I do. Just slow down a little. And just leave things the way they are. All right?"

"Whatever you say. You're the boss."

I went ahead and made an appointment for her to see the psychiatrist I knew in Crawford City. She resisted at first, saying she felt fine, that she didn't need to see anybody. She hated psychiatrists and hospitals, and with good reason. But I told her if she didn't see the doctor, I wouldn't let her stay alone with the baby. Since she very much wanted to tend to Maria, she finally agreed. The psychiatrist, Dr. Butler, put her on a combination of lithium and an antidepressant. He also wanted to see her once a week for therapy. I arranged the visits for Wednesday afternoons, so I could be free to bring her. She went, grudgingly, cynically, and I knew it was mostly just to placate me and not out of any sense that the sessions did her any good. The medication, however, did have an immediate effect. Right away she seemed more calm, less agitated. Her hands were quieter, and her eyes lost something of that frenetic gleam they sometimes took on, as if her skin was on a slow burn.

As always with her return, our first days together were awkward: fumbling for conversation, avoiding certain topics, negotiating the house in self-conscious and overly solicitous ways, moving around the other in a kind of clumsy dance whose steps we made up as we went along. It was as if each time she returned we had to start from scratch, get to know the other all over again. If I didn't have to stay late at the hospital, we'd have a late dinner. Annabel would ask how my day had gone and I would do the same. The polite, formal conversation of two patients sharing a hospital room. She would tell me what Maria had done—how she had grabbed her hair while she was feeding her, how she was starting to hold her head up, how she seemed to be fascinated by Milly, the Wallenbachs' dog. After we cleaned up from dinner, Annabel would tell me, "Why don't you go relax, Stu, while I give Maria a bath?"

"I'll give you a hand."

"But you must be tired."

"I *want* to," I said.

So together we'd give her a bath. It was good having Maria there. She gave us something to talk about; her needs occupied us and lent structure to our time. Before, when Annabel would return and it had just been the two of us, the silence of that big old house would stretch out between us like a rubber band pulled so taut that you kept waiting for the *snap*. But Maria's presence seemed to absorb the quiet, take it in and transform it, and all of her cries and laughter, her cooing and giggles and gleeful utterances gave the house—and us—a shape, an alternative to the claustrophobic silence that would normally have surrounded Annabel and myself.

"She's got gorgeous skin," Annabel said, soaping Maria's round belly with a face cloth. "It's so dark and smooth."

"Yes," I replied.

"It's been a while, hasn't it? Giving a baby a bath."

I nodded but didn't say more.

Later, when the baby was sleeping and the thick, palpable quiet of the mountains descended on us like the lid of a tightly mitered box, my wife would go into the den and read by the fire, while I headed into my study to peruse some article from one of my medical journals or catch up on some paperwork. She was careful not to disturb me, moved about the house with the unobtrusiveness of a cat. Since the time I'd told her to leave things as they were, it seemed she didn't want to upset anything, didn't want to make another mistake.

One night, after she'd taken a shower, she was sitting in the den in her white bathrobe, reading. I happened by, saw her in there, and asked if she wanted some tea.

"If you're having some."

When the tea was done I brought her a cup, set it on the coffee table, and turned to leave.

"Can you sit for a minute, Stu?" she asked.

"I have some work."

"Just a minute? Please."

I relented, took a seat in the rocking chair. She was smoking a cigarette and offered to put it out, but I said I didn't mind.

"I keep saying I should quit. But I figure something's got to kill you, right?" She was reading a slender dog-eared paperback she'd taken from the bookshelf. It was one of her books from college.

"What are you reading?" I asked, for something to say.

"Some Yeats. Remember how we used to read to each other?"

I nodded. We used to sit in this room on winter nights, the fire blazing, and we'd listen to music or play Scrabble, or read to each other. Without a satellite dish, the TV reception wasn't very good this far in the mountains; besides, Annabel didn't watch much television, and except for an occasional game, neither did I. So we often used to read to each other. Dickens, Shakespeare, Blake, Emily Brontë. Once we read the whole of *Wuthering Heights,* alternating chapters between us. I remember she cried when we reached the end, where Catherine's and Heathcliff's souls were said to wander the moors together at last.

We were quiet for a little while. She was thumbing through pages, seeming to be in search of something. I wanted to ask what her plans were, how long she thought she was going to stay this time, though I knew that was a little like asking a bird when it planned on flying south.

"Anna," I said.

"Yeah?" she replied, distractedly, not looking up.

"I want to ask you something."

"Sure. Listen to this first, Stu. I've always liked this."

*And bending down beside the glowing bars,*
*Murmur, a little sadly, how Love fled*
*And paced upon the mountains overhead*
*And hid his face amid a crowd of stars.*

"Isn't that beautiful?" she asked. "And so sad."

I said it was, both beautiful and sad. She held the collar of the robe pressed to her face, rubbing it, lost in thought. I watched her for several seconds. Then it occurred to me. The robe was the one that Bobbie had worn New Year's Eve, several weeks before. I'd forgotten to wash it. Could she have detected Bobbie's scent, her White Shoulders perfume, maybe even the scent of us?

"What did you want to ask me, Stu?"

I stared at her. I thought how she never stayed long in any event. Sooner or later she'd get restless, pull up stakes, and leave. It was only a matter of time. I wouldn't have to do anything.

"Nothing," I replied. "I'm pretty beat. I'm going to turn in. Good night."

"Good night, Stu."

Now and then, I would hear her passing by my room or moving about in the guest room. Sometimes in the middle of the night, I thought I could make out the muffled sound of her voice, as if she were talking in her sleep. Once, I got up to go to the bathroom, and on my return I heard a noise coming from the guest room. I paused outside her door, eavesdropping. She *was* talking in her sleep. Most of what she said was incoherent mumbling, but I could make out one thing clearly, a line she repeated several times: *It's up ahead. It's just up ahead a ways.*

Lying in bed, I thought how much things had changed in so short a time: Bobbie out of my life, at least temporarily, the baby and then Annabel sliding into it. For the longest time my world had revolved around Annabel's coming in and out of my life. When she was gone I waited desperately for her to return. I put things on hold. I threw myself into my work and tried just to get by. Yet I felt as if I were in a prison, counting the days to her return and to freedom. When she finally showed up at my door, I would find myself waiting again, this time watching for the signs that would tell me she was getting ready to leave again. I didn't want to go through that anymore. That part of my life was over. Besides, I loved Bobbie. I wanted us to be together and knew we couldn't as long as Annabel was here. The decent thing, I told myself, the painful yet necessary act called for me simply to tell her she could no longer stay. That this was no longer her home. That was what I needed to do, *should* have done when she first showed up. But how could I just throw her out, this woman I'd once loved, this fragile, broken, pathetic creature? And after all that had happened, all that we'd gone through together and apart, how could I send her away?

One evening I had to call from the hospital to tell Annabel I was going to be late.

"You'll be all right?" I asked.

"I'll be fine. You want me to keep your supper warm?"

"No. I'll grab a bite here."

"I made pork chops and roasted potatoes. Your favorite."

"It can't be helped, Anna," I said. "You know that."

"Of course."

Though she didn't ask, I volunteered anyway: "Dr. Chung wants me to assist on a breech. He thinks it might be a problem."

"Stuart, you don't owe me any explanation. Really, I understand."

I'd told her the truth, but even to my own ear the palpable note of guilt in my voice rang clear. I realized only after I'd hung up that I didn't want her to think I was seeing Bobbie.

For several days I was hardly home. I was extremely busy at the office and I'd had to stay late at the hospital a couple of nights in a row. Not only that, but I'd had to go out once to the scene of a death on the Interstate. A man had hit a wild horse crossing the highway. It was one of a small group of horses that had descended from those of the early settlers, turned wild, and continued to wander the hills. They usually weren't much of a problem. Occasionally they'd get into somebody's cornfield, or a stallion would mate with someone's prize mare. The guy had hit the horse broadside, and the impact flipped it up and propelled it crashing through the windshield. When I got there Cecil said, "Get a load of this, Doc." The legs of the horse were sticking out through the windshield, with the bloody, eviscerated torso lying on the surprised man behind the wheel. He had a broken neck. I pronounced him at the scene and they shipped him to Childress's.

On Wednesday, after finishing my rounds early, I headed home. I was dead tired and planned on grabbing a couple of hours of sleep and then bringing Annabel for her therapy session in Crawford City. The day was sunny, the sky the soft pastel blue of carpenter's chalk. Turkey buzzards rode the warm thermals above Shadow Mountain. The road up was muddy, with steam rising off the ground where the sun hit it. I stopped to get the mail out at the road. There was a letter from the court explaining that the person who would "evaluate" us for the custody hearing was coming two days from then in the morning. Before I got back in the truck, I spotted smoke rising up from behind the house, billowing as if from an explosion. I was a little concerned until I saw Annabel tending to a fire. Standing in the middle of what was left of her flower garden, she had raked leaves and kudzu vines, dead branches and sticks, into a pile and had set it all ablaze. But it was still wet, and thick clouds of blackish smoke tinged with green and yellow drifted lazily up the valley. Even from where I stood I could smell it, a pungent, grassy odor.

Inside, I poured myself a drink. I'd been good about not touching any booze, not wanting to set a bad example for Annabel. In fact, I'd tossed all the bottles out, save one that I hid way up in the cabinet over the refrigerator, out of reach. I watched her from the kitchen window. She had a hooded sweatshirt tied around her waist and wore an old pair of work pants she used to wear when tending the garden. She bent over and yanked at vines and dragged them over and dumped them on the fire. With a rake she'd gathered several years' worth of leaves and debris, and had set it all on the blaze as well. Her face was flushed from the heat and smoke. Yet I thought it was true what Kay had said, that she appeared healthier, fit as a fiddle. Better, in fact, than she had in a long time: some color coming back into her pallid cheeks, her short hair pulled back into a careless ponytail, her movements deft and assured. It was good to see her getting back on her feet.

She'd set the baby out on the deck in her yellow, plastic windup swing. The swing mechanism had stopped, and Maria was idly following the smoke as it drifted skyward. It might have been that I was tired or just the unseasonable warmth throwing me off balance, making me sluggish and out of sorts. In any case, watching the two of them out there, I felt, suddenly and overwhelmingly, the most peculiar sensation. It seemed as if I'd left the familiar contours of my life and were viewing it now the way a complete stranger might. Like one of those out-of-body experiences people say they have when near death. As I stood at the sink gazing out the window, it didn't seem as if *I* were doing the watching but someone else. Someone who could've been my twin, and I was watching *him* watch the two outside. And the scene could very well have been one from among those old photos on the shelf in the den, showing Annabel and Will and a person that looked like me but wasn't: a photo of three happy people, a happy regular family. And then I thought about what Annabel had said to me that night in Asheville: *Just what the heck do you think you're doing, Stu?* What *was* I doing? Did I think I could go back? Change the past? Recover the irrevocable? Was that what I had in mind when I'd agreed to take the baby in? It hadn't started out like that, I felt. It had begun just as a way to help that woman, and later to give Cecil a hand. But on some subconscious level, had I suspected, even on the night I agreed to take the baby, that it was something more, something other than just being charitable? Maybe Annabel knew me better than I knew myself. Maybe that's exactly what I was trying to do—recapture the life I'd lost. Bobbie had said living in the past was easy, and perhaps that was what I was trying to do. Is that what I saw out the window: my past recaptured?

Annabel must have seen me in the window. She waved broadly and headed down toward the house. I met her out on the deck.

"Whew," she said, wiping her brow. She climbed the stairs, went over to the baby, and picked her up. "How long have you been watching?"

"I just got home. What're you doing?"

"Some tidying up. What a gorgeous day, huh?"

"Yes," I replied.

She glanced over at me. "You look beat."

"I am. I think I'll catch a nap."

"Something the matter, Stu?"

"No. Why?"

"I can always tell when something's up with you."

"Am I that shallow?" Then to cover what I was really feeling, I held up the letter I'd received from the court. "Got this in the mail. It's the home evaluation. Somebody's coming day after tomorrow," I said.

"What will they do?"

"Hunneycutt says they'll just look around. Ask some questions."

"I could make myself scarce. Go visit Lenore for a couple days. Though she didn't sound too thrilled last time I asked if I could visit her."

"Unless, of course . . . "

"Unless what?"

"Never mind. Forget it."

"No. What is it, Stu?"

"I suppose you could stay."

Annabel cocked her head, looked at me at an angle. "Would that really be a good idea?"

"Probably not. Although Hunneycutt did say it looks better if there's a woman at home. But it's up to you."

"I don't mind. Question is, do *you* want me to be here?"

"You don't have to."

"I will if you want."

"Hunneycutt said a woman in the picture wouldn't hurt."

"Is that what you want me to be?" Annabel said, smiling impishly. "The woman in the picture?"

"You might as well stay. It can't hurt anything," I said, unsure I was doing the right thing. Unsure for two reasons. First, I wondered if having her there would help or hurt my chances of getting Maria. And second, Annabel had been home for several weeks already. Would this give her a reason to stay longer? And how would that complicate things even more?

Behind her glasses, her dark eyes were quick and playful, the way they once were. Despite her teeth, the furrows around her mouth, the strands of gray in her hair, Annabel looked youngish again. Or rather, she looked like something that had been dormant for a long time and was just now coming slowly back to life, stretching, sloughing off the remnants of her quiescence. She kissed the baby on the top of her head and then swirled her around on the deck, as if the two were dancing. When Annabel looked over at me again, her expression had turned introspective. As if she could read my earlier thoughts, she asked, "You sure this is what you want, Stu?"

I wasn't certain what she meant by *this*. Whether she was referring to the baby or my asking her to stay or what. Still, I replied, "I think so."

She turned her back to me and gazed up toward the fire in the garden, which was starting to burn itself down. I followed the trail of smoke upward. A trio of turkey buzzards circled gracefully about in the blue sky over the mountain, their long gray underwings catching the air currents, riding them. Their huge, distorted shadows skittered along the ground, spinning, wheeling, occasionally slashing right through the fire.

"Remember he used to help me in the garden?" she said, still turned away. I stared at her, at the hair stuck to the back of her neck. She, too, was following the dance of the shadows. "'My little helper,' I called him."

"Anna," I said, "what's the sense of going there? Bringing all that up?"

"I'm just remembering, Stu. It's the only place I have to go sometimes."

"I know. But . . . "

"We can't stop our memories."

"But it doesn't do any good."

"Remember, you brought up the idea of having another child? And I didn't want to."

"Yes."

"You thought it was because another child would only remind me of Will. That wasn't why. At least not the *only* reason." She turned to face me again. Her eyes had gathered moisture to them, though her mouth had a rigid smile plastered on it. "You know what it really was? I didn't want to bring another child into this world and then run the risk of losing it. I couldn't bear that."

"I know, Anna. I know."

"No, I don't think you do." She wiped her eyes with her hand and said, "Whyn't you go lay down? You look tired."

"Don't let me sleep too long. We have your therapy session."

When I woke, however, it was dark already, the smell of apple pie baking in the oven.

•   •   •

Two days later there was a knock on the door. It was early, and we'd just finished breakfast. I'd canceled my office visits for the morning so I could be home for the custody evaluation. When I opened the door, however, I was a little surprised to see an old woman standing there. She wore a bandanna over long, stringy, ash-gray hair, a red wool overcoat, a cotton shift that came down almost to her ankles. The skin on her face was a grayish-white and deeply etched with wrinkles; her bifocal glasses made her eyes look spongy and distorted. Out in the driveway I saw a vaguely familiar red Ford pickup truck with a cap over the bed, and a man sitting behind the wheel.

"Are you here about Maria?" I asked the woman.

"Why, yes. I am," she replied, seeming a little surprised that I knew the purpose of her visit.

"You from social services?"

"Why, no, sir," she said. "I ain't. I'm Ada Pugh, Dr. Jordan."

Pugh, I thought. Goddamn it. I looked out at the truck again. The man seated there I now recognized to be Tully Pugh, the same large, square, good-looking face, the sharp chin and delicate features. Behind him in the gun rack sat a rifle with a scope, though hunting season was long past. I wondered what they were doing here. Was this another strategy of theirs to get me to give up the baby to them?

"Hope I ain't disturbin' you," she said, glancing over my shoulder at Annabel.

"To tell you the truth, we were expecting company, Mrs. Pugh."

"I won't take but a minute of your time then. It's about Maria."

"You aren't supposed to come here, Mrs. Pugh. Not till the custody business is straightened out."

"I know. I jes' wanted to give her a little somethin'."

I stared at her, trying to make up my mind whether she represented trouble or not. The closer I looked at her, the more I realized she wasn't all that old. A little older than me, perhaps, say early sixties. The wrinkles and gray hair had aged her well beyond her years, like so many mountain women.

"You shouldn't have come here, Mrs. Pugh," I told her.

"Please, Dr. Jordan," she pleaded, wringing her hands. I heard the truck door open then and saw her son start to get out. "No!" she cried to him. "You g'won and git back in that truck. You hear me, Tully? I won't have none of that." Her son stood there for a moment, then got back into the truck. He sat behind the wheel, glowering at me. "I won't stay but a minute, Dr. Jordan."

"Where's your manners, Stuart?" Annabel scolded from behind me. "Won't you please come in, Mrs. Pugh?"

My wife showed her into the den. The woman glanced around the room.

"You got yourself a right nice place here, Mrs. Jordan."

"Thank you. Can I get you something to drink?" Annabel asked. "Some tea maybe?"

"No, I'm fy-on," the woman replied. Her hands, I noticed, were badly twisted with arthritis. "You think I could see my grandchild?"

"I don't know if that's such a good idea, Mrs. Pugh," I said. Hunneycutt had thought the Pughs were a high risk for abducting the child and making a run for it. If they got their hands on her, we'd never find her up in the mountains. "Legally, you're not supposed to come here."

Annabel glanced over at me and frowned. "Oh, why not, Stu? She just wants to see her granddaughter, for mercy sakes."

I finally relented. "I suppose it wouldn't hurt anything."

"I'll be right back," my wife said, and headed out of the room.

"I'm sorry about your son, Mrs. Pugh."

"Thank you, Dr. Jordan." She glanced down at her hands, lying broken in her lap like the mangled bodies of birds along the roadside. "I reckon *sorry* should be my middle name. The menfolk in our family always do seem hell-bent on destruction. With nary a thought to the consequences neither. It's the women and little ones end up paying for it ever' time. Like Rosa. I ain't condoning what she done to my Roy Lee. No sir. But I tell you, blood or not, he never treated her like he ought to've. And I feel bad about that poor little young'un, too. I just wanted to see her is all. I ain't agonna make no problems for you. If'n it was up to me, I wouldn't even've gone to court with it. But Glenn W., he don't see it like that."

Annabel brought the baby in.

"Oh, my Lord," the old woman said, her eyes welling up with tears. "Ain't she the purtiest l'il thing?"

"Would you like to hold her, Mrs. Pugh?"

"If'n you don't mind," the woman said, glancing at me. "How old she now?"

"Five months," I replied.

"I made her something." Mrs. Pugh reached into the handbag she was carrying and pulled out a paper bag. "Here," she said, handing it to Annabel.

My wife withdrew a small green and red crocheted sweater.

"That's real pretty," Annabel said.

"Hope it fits. I ain't never give her nothing when she was born. Glenn W. wouldn't allow it. He never liked Rosa, you see. He thought she was a tar'ble influence on Roy Lee. That it was her led him astray. And when she killed him, he near about went crazy with anger. That's the second son we've lost, Dr. Jordan. My husband is plumb filled up to his eyeballs with hatred. He can't see straight on account of it. When I married him, he had some tenderness and loving in him. But it all got dried up. The Lord says we should forgive our enemies, but Glenn W. don't want no part of forgiveness. It ain't so much the baby he's wanting as it is just plain getting even for Roy Lee's death."

"Even with who?" I asked.

"Ever'body, I reckon. Rosa. The law. People here'bouts who think we ain't nothin' but white trash and such. Yourself, too, Dr. Jordan."

"Why my husband?" Annabel asked.

"Because Glenn W. feels he ain't got no business in this and is just trying to shame him by taking his grandchild from him."

"I'm not trying to shame him, Mrs. Pugh. I got nothing against your husband. I'm only trying to do what's right for the baby."

"I know. I tried telling him that. I'm just saying that's how Glenn W. figures it. He's got his pride. He's a proud and stubborn man. If'n the court gives her to us, Dr. Jordan, I want you to know I'd love her like she was my own child. And I'd see to it that she had a good home." The old woman looked from Annabel to me, then to the baby. "I just want what's best for her, too. I reckon I should be going. Thank you for letting me visit with Maria."

"You're welcome," my wife offered.

When she was gone Annabel said, "She didn't seem so bad."

"I suppose not. But I don't trust those others."

Later that afternoon the court-appointed social worker finally showed up. Ms. Ensley was a plump woman with short reddish hair and small teeth that made her expression appear somewhat disappointed. She apologized for being so late, explaining that her caseload was already twice what it should be and that she'd been running like a chicken with her head cut off all day.

"So this must be Maria?" she said to Annabel, who was holding the baby.

"Yes. She just got up from her nap."

Ms. Ensley began by asking if she could see the house. We showed her around, with her peeking into rooms, nodding appraisingly or occasionally knitting her brows into a frown, almost as if she were considering buying the place. She was particularly interested in the baby's room, where she jotted things down in a small leather-covered notebook. Afterwards, we sat in the den. Annabel brought out a pot of tea and a plate of oatmeal cookies she'd made. The social worker said no thank you, that she was on a diet. She said she was going to ask us some questions. She explained that she didn't mean to pry but that her job required that she find out all she could about us. She began by asking whether we liked children. If had we any of our own. Why at our age we wanted to take on the responsibility of a child. How much money I made. Where we went to church. What we knew about Indian culture. Who fed and cared for the child. Who gave the child her baths and who got up in the middle of the night if she cried.

"As I understand it, Mrs. Jordan, until recently . . . , " the woman said, pausing to find the right word.

Annabel helped her out. "Yes, Stuart and I have been separated. I came back when my husband needed some help with the baby."

"Are you planning on staying put?"

"For as long as Stuart needs me," she said, glancing over at me.

The woman turned to me and asked, "So would it be safe to say that Mrs. Jordan here would be the primary caretaker for the baby?"

"She's helping me," I replied. "For now."

"But you work full-time, Dr. Jordan. As a doctor, you must be on call quite a bit, too."

"A fair amount."

"And in your absence, the primary caregiving responsibilities would fall to Mrs. Jordan then?"

"As I said, for now. I also have a neighbor who's willing to look after her while I'm at work."

"Dr. Jordan, the child's natural mother is on trial for murder. If she's convicted, which as I understand it seems quite probable, the child will need a long-term placement. One of the issues the court needs to consider is what will happen in that eventuality. While this custody hearing is only to establish a temporary placement, until the outcome of Ms. Littlefoot's trial, we will still need to consider the child's best future interests as well. In other words, wherever the child is placed now may turn into a long-term arrangement. Whether Mrs. Jordan stays or not, Dr. Jordan, are you prepared to accept responsibility for Maria in that case?"

I paused for a moment, then found myself saying, "Yes."

Ms. Ensley asked a lot of other questions, some of which seemed to have nothing whatsoever to do with our fitness as parents. For instance, she wanted to know who did the dishes most nights, who took out the garbage, who balanced the checkbook. She even asked what the sleeping arrangements were. Hunneycutt had warned me that they would get into some very personal and private aspects of our lives, first in the home evaluation but especially later at the deposition hearing. I said rather curtly that Annabel and I slept in separate rooms. Ms. Ensley explained she was only trying to do her job, which was to see to it that the baby's best interests were served. After she was finished, she shut her notebook and gathered up her things.

"I'll write up my report and submit it to the judge along with my custody recommendation. Judge Cobb will use it in making his final custody decree." She stood up to leave. "On second thought, would you mind if I grabbed a cookie for the road? I didn't eat lunch and I'm half starved to death."

"Of course," Annabel said. She wrapped several cookies in a napkin for her, then showed the woman to the door. Holding the baby, Annabel stood at the front window watching as the woman got in her car and drove down the mountain.

"You think it went okay?" she asked me.

"Yes."

"Why did she want to know if we were sleeping together?"

"I guess to see if we're a happily married couple."

# 20

*Several days later,* after dropping Maria off at Kay's, we drove into town for the deposition, which was to take place at Hunneycutt's office. The day was clear and cold. A hard frost etched the ground with silver designs. While we hadn't had any more snow, the temperatures, just as John predicted, had settled back to normal for this time of year. The higher mountains shone brilliantly in the chill morning sunlight, their white-capped peaks standing out in vivid contrast to the deep blue of the sky. However, back in the hollers lingering shadows and mists still prevailed, covering and obscuring and lending to things a nighttime murkiness.

I glanced over at Annabel. She wore a black wool blazer, plaid skirt, dark tights, a string of pearls I'd mistakenly bought her for our second anniversary and which she never wore. She wasn't the pearls sort. She must've tried on half a dozen different outfits before settling on this one. And for once she'd put on some makeup: eye shadow, ruby-colored lipstick, and some blush to give her cheeks a little color. She didn't know her way around makeup, and it showed, though of course I didn't say anything. From time to time she would inspect herself in the mirror on the back of the visor.

"Do I look okay?" she asked.

"You look fine."

"I don't look too-too?"

"Too-too?"

"Like I'm putting on airs?"

"You look nice, Anna." She was chain-smoking one cigarette after another. She had the window down a little and kept flicking her ashes out. I glanced down at her hands. She was tapping the fabric of her skirt. Occasionally she chewed on her nails, which were already ragged and bitten to the quick. "You take your meds?"

"Of course," she replied, annoyed with me for asking. "How long do you think this will take?"

"Hunneycutt said plan on a couple of hours if things go smoothly. Longer if they don't. He said Ennis Pugh will get nasty."

"I understand."

A few days before, Hunneycutt had me come to his office to go over the sort of things Pugh would ask. That's when he brought up the idea of having Annabel come to the deposition. I said I didn't think that was such a good idea. It would be too much of a strain on her. Hunneycutt explained, however, that the social worker's report had included Annabel as being one of Maria's primary caregivers.

"Technically, she needs to be there, Dr. Jordan."

"She won't be staying long."

"Doesn't matter. She's there now. Besides, like I already said, a maternal presence would be to our advantage," Hunneycutt added. "Judge Cobb is a pretty conservative fellow. A woman's place is in the kitchen and all that. He's going to wonder how this fellow who's working eighty hours a week is gonna take care of a little baby."

"I have my neighbor to watch Maria."

"Ain't the same. And besides, she *is* still your wife."

I thought of telling him about how she wouldn't be for long, how I was planning on starting divorce proceedings. I considered telling him about Bobbie and me. But for some reason I didn't.

"What about her . . . problems?" I asked.

He said he'd do his best to minimize any damage Ennis Pugh inflicted on our side. Besides, he said, the Pughs had their own character issues to worry about, and Judge Cobb was well aware of the sort of people they were. "He's not expecting either of you to be saints. Just be honest and forthright. Though don't volunteer anything either," he added with a smirk.

Now, as we drove along, I wondered if we'd made a big mistake.

Annabel asked, "How's my hair look?"

"Fine. Just relax."

"I *am* relaxed," she said, gazing out the window.

"You don't have to do this, remember."

"I said I would, didn't I? Sounds like you're having second thoughts about me coming."

"No," I lied.

"Then stop with all your questions. *You're* the one making me nervous." She glanced at her raggedy nails. "We're just going to go up to his office, do what we have to do, and leave, right? We're not sticking around?"

"No."

While she didn't say anything about it, I think she was also a little worried about having people in town see her. Since her return, except for getting off at the bus station, she hadn't been into Slade once. If she needed anything, she would ask me to get it. Though she'd grown up here, she'd never felt the ease of being in one's hometown. She used to say she didn't care what they thought of her, that they were nothing but a bunch of narrow-minded hypocrites; nevertheless, I think she was always hurt by the stares and whispers and gossip of the town. *That Annabel Lee Jordan sure is a strange bird.*

When we got to Hunneycutt's second-story office, old man Pugh and his wife, Ada, were already there. Glenn W. sat on one side of a long table next to his wife. To their left was Ennis Pugh, their kinsman and lawyer. Sitting across from them was Hunneycutt and another woman, the court reporter. As soon as we sat down, Hunneycutt said, "We might as well get started."

While Hunneycutt and Pugh discussed some technicalities relating to the deposition, I had an opportunity to glance over at Glenn W. and his wife. Glenn wore the same pastel blue suit he had worn to court. He sat there nonchalantly paring his nails with a jackknife, not acknowledging our presence in the least. Ada Pugh looked across at us and nodded demurely, then glanced nervously at her husband. I thought about what she'd said. How her husband was doing this mostly out of pride, thinking I was trying to embarrass him. That the baby was just something, a piece of property, he considered his, and he planned on getting it back one way or another. He looked up from his nails momentarily and met my gaze. He stared at me with his small, liquid-gray eyes, his expression haughty and full of contempt.

"Good mornin' to you'all," Ennis Pugh said to us at last, laying on thick his sugary Southern drawl. "Dr. and Mrs. Jordan, how are we today?"

"Fine," I replied.

"I'm glad to hear that." He had that exaggerated Southern civility I had learned to be suspicious of, especially when coming from the mouths of certain individuals, including Realtors and lawyers. He wore a red bow-tie and had recently had a manicure, of which he seemed quite proud. He held his hands cautiously, like precious ornaments he didn't want to harm in any way. His boyish face was unnaturally pink and well scrubbed. He gave one the impression of the prissy student in class who not only knew best how to manipulate the teacher but took a smug satisfaction in his talent.

"I thank you kindly for appearing here today. And I assure you I will try my utmost to make this as short and as painless as possible."

After I was sworn in, Pugh began by saying to me, "Y'all understand how this works, Dr. Jordan. It's just like testifying in court 'cept there's no judge and the rules are a bit more relaxed, shall we say."

"Mr. Hunneycutt has already explained it to me."

"Good. I'm sure you got patients waiting so I'll get right down to business. I can't say I've ever had the pleasure of meeting you, sir, but your reputation certainly precedes you. How many children have you brought into this world, Doctor?"

"I couldn't say."

"Hundreds?"

"Maybe."

"Thousands?"

"Perhaps."

"Now of all those children, there must have been one, prior to the Pughs' grandchild, that needed a home. Some unmarried mother who didn't want or couldn't take care of her child."

"I suppose."

"And yet, before now, did you ever volunteer to act in a custodial capacity for any child?"

"No."

"Humph," he sighed. "Why is that, I wonder?"

"I couldn't really say."

"And yet, now you've taken a very keen interest in this particular case. Why?"

"It just sort of happened."

"Just sort of happened?"

"I guess it was out of a sense of obligation," I replied.

"To whom?"

"Rosa Littlefoot and her baby."

"You felt obligated to a woman you didn't even know? A woman, I might add, you first met when you were investigating her for the murder of her common-law husband, my client's own son."

"She asked and I gave her my word."

"Your word, sir?"

"That's correct."

"So. You would consider yourself a man of your word, Dr. Jordan?"

"I would like to think so, yes."

"An honorable man," Ennis Pugh said, his expression serious, but the irony seemed to slip out the corners of his mouth like spittle.

"I wouldn't know about that. All I know is if I give somebody my word, I try to keep it. If I can."

"In this day and age that's a noble sentiment. Yes indeed, quite noble. Is your interest in my client's granddaughter still merely out of an honorable obligation to one's word?"

"No, it's more than that. I've been taking care of Maria for over a month now. I've grown quite fond of her in that time."

"Do you think that that fondness should outweigh the blood bonds of a grandparent's natural love?"

"That's for the court to decide. I only know what I feel."

"Do you believe you could provide a loving and nurturing home for the child?"

"Yes, I do."

"What sort of experience do you have with children?"

"I'm a doctor. An obstetrician. I've been around children my whole life."

"I was referring to raising children. Your own."

"I had a son."

"Had?" Pugh asked.

"He died."

"Oh, I'm sorry to hear that," he said, pursing his lips and glancing across at Annabel. She met his gaze and then looked away. "Now you just described yourself as a man who believed in keeping his word, correct?"

"Yes."

"Do you think that teaching a child the value of keeping one's word is important in his or her upbringing?"

"Of course."

"Sort of like teaching right from wrong, isn't it?"

"Yes."

"Do you believe you could teach a child the difference between right and wrong, sir?"

"I would certainly try."

"Do you yourself go to church, Dr. Jordan?"

"No."

"Don't you think that a child ought to have a strong moral foundation?"

"Yes. But I don't think you necessarily have to go to church to provide a child with good morals."

"I see. You're one of them atheist humanists, I reckon?"

"No, I'm a Catholic," I replied. "I just don't go to church anymore."

"Would you consider yourself a moral person?"

"I don't know. I try to be."

"You're being far too modest, sir. Most folks you talk to here'bouts consider Doc Jordan a decent, upstanding fellow. Why, a pillar of the community. Someone beyond reproach."

Pugh folded his neat little hands beneath his chin and smiled prissily. I wondered what he was getting at.

"I guess you'd have to ask them," I replied.

"But would you say you try to lead a decent, Christian life?"

"I try. I don't always succeed."

"Few of us do," Pugh said, nodding sagely. "Few of us do. That's why they put erasers on pencils. For instance, do you try to follow the Ten Commandments, sir?"

"In my own way, I suppose."

"In your own way? They's only one way to follow them, last I heard. By keeping them. Well, let's say we look at a few of them. How about the one, 'Thou shalt not kill'? Do you follow that one?"

"I've never killed anybody."

"Why of course not. You're a doctor. You've taken an oath to save lives. As an obstetrician, your very job is to bring life into the world, right?"

"I suppose."

He paused for a moment, looking over his notes.

"Have you ever performed an abortion, Dr. Jordan?"

Hunneycutt put his hand on my arm to stop me from answering.

"We're not going to get into that, counselor. Abortion is a perfectly legal medical procedure in the State of North Carolina. Next question."

"All right. How about the other commandments? Say commandment seven. Are you familiar with that one, Dr. Jordan?"

"I'm afraid I don't know them by the numbers."

"See, if you went to church you would," he said, chuckling. "That's the one concerning adultery. Do you know the one to which I'm referring now?"

How did he find out? I wondered. But of course, as Cecil had warned me, a thing like that didn't stay quiet very long.

"Yes," I replied.

"Have you ever committed adultery, Dr. Jordan?"

I looked over at Annabel, but she had her eyes on her lap. Then I glanced at Hunneycutt, who swallowed once, his Adam's apple bounding up and down his throat. He gave me a look that said, *What's he got on you?* I was wishing then that I had told him about Bobbie.

"No."

"No? Are you a married man, Dr. Jordan?"

"Yes, but . . . "

"Did you or did you not have an affair with a woman? A fellow physician, if I'm not mistaken?"

I paused for a moment, realizing he meant Madeline, not Bobbie. I mentally sighed with relief. "Yes," I said.

"There's no call to besmirch her reputation, so she shall remain nameless for the record. And yet, you *are* a married man, are you not, Dr. Jordan?"

"Yes. But my wife and I were separated at the time."

"You were still married, though, correct?"

"Yes, technically."

"Technically? You're either married in the eyes of the Lord and under the statutes of North Carolina law or you're not. It's like being a little pregnant. How long did this affair last?"

"Not long. A few months."

"And it's over now, I assume?"

"Yes. It's been over for several years," I answered.

"And this woman has since left town, correct?"

"Yes."

"Are you and your wife currently living together, Doctor?" Ennis Pugh asked, glancing at Annabel.

"My wife has recently returned home."

"And what is the current nature of your relationship with your wife, sir?"

"That's none of your business," I said.

"But it *is* the court's business," Pugh countered. "I'll ask Mr. Hunneycutt to direct his client to answer the question put to him."

"You need to answer," Hunneycutt said to me.

Without looking at Annabel, I said, "We're friends."

"Friends. You *are* living under the same roof?"

"Yes."

"As man and wife?"

"Do you mean do we sleep together?" I hissed at him. "No."

"But *technically* you are still married, correct?"

"That's right."

"Are you currently involved in any *other* extramarital affairs, sir?"

"No. I mean . . . well . . . "

"The question is really quite simple. Are you or are you not involved in an intimate and, may I add, illicit relationship with a woman? A woman familiar to the court as the assistant district attorney for this county. And let me remind you, you are under oath, Dr. Jordan."

I gazed across at Glenn W. He had the sort of cocky look a boxer must have when he hits an opponent and knows he's inflicted grievous damage, can feel the other fighter's knees begin to buckle, his eyes glaze over.

"We had an affair, yes."

"*Had,* sir?"

"Are having. But it's not like you're trying to make it."

"I'm not trying to make it anything. You're the one that committed fornication. That's adultery in my book. In the good book, too."

"I don't care about your damn book," I said. Hunneycutt lay a hand on my arm and whispered under his breath, "Easy."

"How long have you been . . . carrying on like this, Dr. Jordan?"

"About a year."

"How many times did you have intimate relations with *Mrs.* Roberta Tisdale?"

"I don't know," I snapped at him.

"Well, was it a single indiscretion? Everybody could understand one tryst with a pretty woman like Mrs. Tisdale."

"No, it was more than once."

"Was it five times? Ten? Once a week?"

I glared at him. I felt like lunging across the table and ripping his throat out. The dirty little bastard. "A couple times a month usually. I wasn't really counting. And I didn't consider I was doing anything wrong."

Raising his eyebrows theatrically, Pugh said, "You didn't consider you were doing anything wrong, sir?"

"No."

"Where would you go to fornicate?"

"Usually over to Crawford City. A motel there."

"So nobody would find out?"

"I suppose."

"But you didn't consider what you were doing morally wrong?"

"No."

"I would imagine such an affair would take a lot of planning and lying and covering up. A whole lot of sneaking around to keep it secret in other words."

"Some."

"Does Mrs. Tisdale's husband know?"

"No." I thought, he will now. Despite this being a closed-door hearing, I realized that by tomorrow what we'd said here would be all over town. I wondered how it would hurt Bobbie.

"Are you planning on continuing this secret affair with a married woman?"

"I don't know."

"You don't know? For someone who supposedly values his word, you do an awful lot of sneaking around and lying, Dr. Jordan. Do you think this sort of immoral behavior would be conducive to the proper upbringing of a child?"

"I don't know," I said.

"I have no more questions for Dr. Jordan," Pugh said, waving his manicured hand dismissively at me. "I would like to ask Mrs. Jordan a few, however. That is, if it's all right with her."

"Fine by me," Annabel said nervously.

I knew it was a mistake now, having her come. Probably the whole thing was a mistake. I should never have agreed to any of this. I should have stayed out of it, just like everyone had warned me. What was I thinking trying to get custody of Maria?

"Can I have a word with my wife?" I said. Pugh had no objections. "You don't have to do this," I whispered to her.

"I know. It's what you want, isn't it?"

I shook my head. "I don't know anymore."

"You don't want her going with those people, do you?"

"No."

"Then all right. I'm fine, really."

"We all set now?" Pugh asked. "Mrs. Jordan, do you consider yourself fit to take care of a child?"

"I think so."

"How would you describe your health?"

"It's all right."

"How about your mental health? Ever have any problems regarding that?"

"I've been diagnosed as being bipolar."

"How does your illness affect you?"

"If I don't take my medication, I can have mood swings."

"Would you mind elaborating, madam?"

Annabel explained about her manic episodes and then the depression that often followed. She described her illness as if she were reading from a psychology textbook, not as if it were something connected to her.

"When you are ill, would you characterize your behavior as erratic?"

"Sometimes."

"Isn't it true that you have often taken off from your husband for long periods of time? Leaving him without a word."

"That's right. When I was sick."

"Did you ever try to commit suicide?"

"A couple of times."

"Have you ever been arrested, Mrs. Jordan?"

"Yes."

"For what?"

"Some things."

"What sorts of things, madam?"

"For shoplifting."

"Anything else?"

"Driving while under the influence."

"How about for solicitation? In other words, prostitution." Annabel nodded, and Pugh said, "That's a yes, correct?"

"Yes. I was pretty sick then."

"Were you ever arrested for buying drugs?"

"Yes."

"Do you have a substance abuse problem, Mrs. Jordan?"

"I did."

"Not anymore?"

"No. Not now."

"How long have you been straight?"

"About a month."

"A little month?" Pugh said, proud of his allusion to Hamlet's line. "And that makes you ready to assume the guardianship of a little baby?"

"I want to get better. I really do. Having a child to care for gives me something to work toward."

"Would you say you're cured from your illness?"

"No. I'll never be cured. But as long as I take my medication and stay away from the bottle and drugs, I can do all right."

"In your current condition, do you really think you're capable of tending to the needs of an infant?"

"Yes, I think I am. I've been doing it for the past several weeks." She looked across at Glenn W. "I feed her and give her her bath. I bring her out for walks. Everything has been going just fine."

"But given your past history of mental illness and substance abuse, don't you think, Mrs. Jordan, it would be reasonable for the court to be skeptical of your ... *parenting* skills?" he said sarcastically.

"No."

"No?"

"Not now. I feel better now."

"Does your husband trust you home alone with the child?"

"I think he does," she said, giving me a sideways glance.

"Mrs. Jordan, you don't think he has *any* cause to worry?"

"No."

"I see," he said, pausing to write something down. "As your husband mentioned earlier, you had a child who died, correct?"

"That's right."

"How old was he?"

"He was almost six."

"I know it must be a painful subject to discuss, madam, so I'll be as brief as possible. But would you mind describing the circumstances under which he died?"

You bastard, I thought. You slimy, little bastard. I looked to Hunneycutt to object, but he just sat there taking notes.

"He got lost in the woods," Annabel explained, her voice calm, almost matter-of-fact. "He died before they could find him."

"And who was watching him at the time?"

"I was. At least I should have been," Annabel said. Her face didn't show any emotion. Behind her glasses, her dark eyes remained impassive, almost indifferent. The only thing I saw was the muscle in her jaw clenching and then releasing.

"Madam, do you feel your negligence was responsible for . . . "

"That'll be enough," I said to Pugh.

Hunneycutt put his hand on my arm again. "Just take it easy."

"I'm not going to sit here and let him do this to her. He doesn't know what the hell he's talking about. It was an accident."

"I'm all right, Stu," my wife said to me. "Really."

"Mrs. Jordan, do you feel your negligence was responsible for your boy's death?" Pugh asked.

Still looking at me but responding to Pugh's question, she said, "Yes. It was my fault. I should have been watching him closer. I've had to live with that the past fourteen years."

"And given your admitted culpability in your son's death, why should the court think you would make a suitable guardian now?"

"Because I want another chance," she said, looking straight at me.

"You want a chance to put some other life in jeopardy?"

"No. I just want a chance to make things right."

"Why should . . . "

"She answered your question already," Hunneycutt interrupted.

"I suppose we can leave it there," Ennis Pugh said, smiling at me. "Yes, I've heard quite enough. Thank you, Mrs. Jordan."

Next Hunneycutt had a chance to interrogate Glenn W. Pugh to drag him through the same mud we'd just been dragged through. He pressed Glenn W. pretty hard about his various run-ins with the law. About the drug convictions. About some unregistered guns he'd been caught selling. About the time he was convicted for assault for cutting the thumb off some guy who'd cheated him in a poker game. Hunneycutt, it turned out, wasn't as incompetent as people made him out to be. In fact, he did a good job of making Pugh squirm. After the deposition and the Pughs and their lawyer left his office, Hunneycutt took me aside, out of earshot of Annabel. "See, I told you they'd be vulnerable. I sure wish you'd a told me about Bobbie Tisdale, though," he said, shaking his head. "But that's water under the bridge."

"What will happen now?"

"The judge will review the deposition and the social worker's report and make a decision."

"How long?"

"A week or two. I'll be in touch," he said.

We drove most of the way home in silence. I guess neither of us wanted to say anything about the deposition. Annabel finished the last of her cigarettes and hunted around in the ashtray for one to salvage. "Damn," she cursed. We turned onto Mason Hollow Road and followed the Tuckamee River as it began to narrow and pick up speed slicing down through the valley from Little Bear Reservoir. The river surged a brackish gray, cluttered with flotsam: chunks of ice and trees limbs and detritus it had scavenged from up the mountain. I didn't think about the dream I'd had of that woman in the river, but of Annabel, that time she'd tried to drown herself in it.

"How are you holding up?" I asked.

"Oh, I'm fine."

"I'm sorry. He had no right to say those things."

"I said I'm all right."

"I should never have let you come. I don't know what I was thinking."

"Don't worry about it, Stu."

"You were always a good mother to him. Always."

She nodded and continued staring out the window at the river.

# 21

*The day after* the deposition, I was examining Emmilou Potter in my office. Emmilou, now about twenty-five weeks along, was holding her own. The fetus was on the small side but developing normally, and Emmilou's numbers—electrolytes, blood pressure, urine output—while they hadn't gotten any better, hadn't gotten any worse either. Sometimes in matters of pregnancy settling for the status quo was the best one could hope for.

"How's things looking, Dr. Jordan?" Emmilou asked, after she was dressed.

"Fine for now. Any more dizzy spells?"

"No. Well . . . I had me a bit of one a while back. Not bad a'tall."

"Have you been staying off your feet?"

"As much as I'm able. You see, Jack hurt hisself. He tho'ed out his back again and ain't been to work these past coupla weeks. So I been taking in extra laundry."

"Just go easy. We're going to try for another five or six weeks if we can squeeze it in. So I want you to continue to watch your salt intake and drink lots of water. And get as much bed rest as you can."

I turned to leave the exam room. "One other thing, Dr. Jordan," she said. "Me and Jack been talking over names. If'n it's a boy we'd like to name it Stuart. Long's it's all right by you."

I wasn't sure I liked the responsibility of having a child whose chances of survival weren't all that good named after me. It seemed like bad luck. But I told her, "That's real thoughtful, Emmilou. I'm honored."

Out at the receptionist's desk, Stella told me I had a phone call.

"It's that Mrs. Tisdale," she said. If Stella had heard the news already, she did a good job of keeping a poker face.

"I'll take it in my office."

"Doc?" Bobbie said when I picked up. "Looks like the shit finally hit the fan."

"You heard?"

"Yeah. That scumbag Pugh. I swear, they let anybody practice law in this state."

"Sorry for dragging you into this."

"I did my own share of dragging. It's probably for the best. Now it's out at least."

"How did you hear?"

"Troy called me at home last night. Like I said, I was pretty sure he already knew something was up. But I guess he was willing to turn a blind eye as long as it wasn't made public."

"What did he say?"

"Oh, that it made our department look bad. A married DA carrying on with the medical examiner. Said Slade was a conservative place and all that. And especially now with us prosecuting Littlefoot and you taking in her child, he thought it might make people think something was fishy. I guess that we'd go easy on her."

"Did you tell him you had nothing to do with me taking in the baby? That it was all my decision."

"Troy wasn't in a listening frame of mind. He said he'd already gotten several calls. Including from the Hubbard County morality czar, Reverend Stevens," she said, forcing a laugh. "I offered to resign."

"Why? You didn't do anything wrong."

"I don't feel like fighting it, Doc. I'm plumb tired of playing these silly games. Hiding things from him. From everybody. Most of all from Paul. The funny thing is Troy wouldn't accept my resignation."

"He wouldn't?"

"No. Though I'm not so sure I want to stay. I'm not real optimistic about my long-term job prospects in Slade. What it is, you see, with him laid up with his back, he can't afford to let me resign now. But as soon as he's on his feet, he'll be looking to run me out of town on a rail."

"And your husband?"

"He's been away on business. Won't be back till tomorrow. It'll give me a chance to make some plans."

"Plans? What are you going to do?"

"Leave."

"Leave?" I said, growing worried. "You mean Slade or your husband?"

"For now, just pack some things and get out of the house."

"So you've decided to leave him?"

I should have been happy at the news. Pleased that she was finally going to be free, and she and I could be together. It's what I wanted all along, wasn't it? Yet I felt oddly uneasy about it. The sort of feeling that always came over me when I should simply have been happy.

"No sense kidding myself. It's over. It's been over for a while."

"I'm sorry for messing things up for you."

"You haven't messed anything up. It's just what I needed to get my ass in gear and finally do it. Here I've been jabbering about leaving him, but when push came to shove, I guess I was still afraid to really do it."

"Where will you go?"

"I'll find a place in town for now. Leastways till I figure out what I'm going to do."

"Bobbie, I . . . "

"Don't worry, Doc. I understand. I wasn't going to hit you up for a place. Not with her there. Your wife *is* still there, right?"

"Yeah."

I could tell she wanted to ask me something else but decided not to.

"I've missed you," she said instead.

"I've missed you, too."

"Now what?"

"I don't know," I replied.

"Listen, I have to be in court. But I do want to see you. Are you free this evening?"

"No, I'm covering for someone at the hospital tonight. How about tomorrow?"

"Paul's coming back tomorrow afternoon," she said, sighing. "But I guess I can come up with something. Tell him I have to work late. In for a penny, right?"

"You want to meet at the Skyline?"

"Not there. I feel like they got spies watching that place. How about the Best Western down in Farley?"

We'd gone there once before. We agreed to meet at seven. When I got off the phone, I thought about what she said: *Now what?*

Then I went ahead and did what I should have done a long time ago: I wrote Troy Bumgartner a letter of resignation. I said that given the circumstances and the potential for a conflict, or at least a perceived conflict, of interest, it seemed best that I tender my resignation. I made it effective immediately.

• • •

The next day at noon I called Annabel from the office.

"Listen, something's come up," I explained. "I'm going to be late."

"How late?" she asked.

"Pretty late. I have something to take care of."

There was a pause on the other end. I decided I wasn't going to lie if she asked me why I was going to be late.

"Want me to keep your supper warm, Stu?"

"No, I don't think so. Don't wait up for me," I said.

"Whatever you say," she said in a way that made me feel guilty.

I told myself I had no reason to feel guilty. I wanted to see Bobbie. In fact, seeing her was something I not only wanted but *needed* to do. Like a breath of air after being underwater too long. My lungs burned for her. I missed her terribly, a physical ache that started under my ribs, proceeded upward, and lodged as a tightness in the back of my throat. Talking with her, touching her, breathing in her smell. These past several weeks I'd been miserable without her. Annabel's return had nothing really to do with us, I told myself. She was here for a little while, helping out; and for my part, I was just providing a place for her to stay till she got back on her feet. That's all it was. What I felt for her was more pity than anything else. Annabel knew how I felt about Bobbie. Hadn't she said she didn't want to mess anything up between us? Despite all these mental debates, there was a slightly sour aftertaste in my mouth that I could only describe as the taste of guilt.

I left the office at five after my last appointment and drove the forty-five minutes to Farley, a town to the southwest, on the way to the Georgia line. As if someone had taken a rolling pin to them, the mountains started to flatten out. The woods thinned, the hills became softer-edged, dotted by pastureland, peach and apple orchards, nurseries, cattle and horse farms. I pulled into the parking lot of the Best Western and headed in and got a room under my own name. Why not? The cat was already out of the bag. I was early, though, and the thought of waiting in a motel room for Bobbie wasn't very appealing. It seemed as if our relationship was taking a giant step backward. Instead of going up to the room, I decided to drive around for a while. I took one key and left the other with the middle-aged, balding clerk and told him it was for a friend who'd be arriving shortly. A conspiratorial smile played about his thin, jagged mouth.

Farley, situated on the Little Tennessee River, was more built-up than Slade. Right off the highway, a bright cluster of new motels, chain restaurants, stores, and car dealerships had sprung up, and just past the older downtown section was a new mall. I looked around for a Chinese restaurant. I was hungry and I knew Bobbie liked Chinese food. Sometimes we used to get some and bring it back to our room and eat it while lying in bed. I pulled into a convenience store and asked the plump young girl who worked there if she knew of any Chinese restaurants in town.

"I sure 'nough wouldn't," she replied. She was about seventeen with lank brown hair and a round, unformed face, which reminded me of an artist's preliminary circle face. "They's a new place out near the Western Sizzlin'. Don't know what-all they serve."

"Would you have a phone book?"

She hunted around behind the counter and handed me one. I found a place called Mandarin Garden listed in the mall. While I had the phone book open, it occurred to me that Farley was where Lenny Blackfox lived. Or had lived. So I looked up his name, too. There it was: Leonard Blackfox, 562 Oak Ridge Road. I handed the phone book back to the girl.

"Would you happen to know where Oak Ridge Road is?"

"Sure do. What you want is to go back yonder the way you come. About a mile up, you take a left at the third light. Don't count the blinking one. Some folks do and that'll throw you off. After the third light, take that left and foller 'er up a ways and when you come to the tire place you take the next right. That's Oak Ridge. Can't miss it."

"Thanks," I said.

It was only six o'clock, so I decided to take a ride out to see if I could meet this Leonard Blackfox. What could it hurt? I was figuring if

I found out where his sister lived, I'd give her a call. See if she'd be interested in helping out her old friend by taking Maria in. Perhaps going to stay with Doreen Blackfox, or whatever her name was now, might be the best thing for the child. For *everybody* concerned. Ever since the custody deposition, I'd been having second thoughts. All along, I guess I kept thinking that Rosa Littlefoot wouldn't go to prison. Or at least not for that long. I still considered it just a domestic that got out of hand. I felt that Troy Bumgartner would come around finally to that and reduce the charges against her to second degree, maybe even manslaughter. Worst case, she'd be out in a couple of years. I guess I'd been thinking, crazy as it seemed in retrospect, that Maria could stay with me in the meantime. Somehow, I could manage that. Yet it seemed more and more likely that Rosa would get a long prison term. While it was one thing to look after the child for a few months, even, if need be, a couple of years, it was something else again to take on a permanent commitment.

Sure, I had to admit I liked certain parts about having a child around the house again: feeding her, bathing her, getting down on the floor and playing with her. But I also had to face the stone-hard reality of the rest of it. I was fifty-seven years old. How in the hell was I going to take on the responsibility of a child for the next fifteen or twenty years? I'd be seventy-five when she graduated from high school. I was old enough to be her grandfather. And what if something were to happen to me? What would become of Maria then?

Besides, my own personal life was up in the air. A child needed a mother *and* a father, and half the time I wasn't even there. What was more, I wasn't Indian. What did I know about raising an Indian child? There was something to be said for a child being with her own kind. Would it be fair for Maria to get stuck with some old fart who knew nothing about Indian ways, the problems she would face in a white world? And what about me? Would it be fair to me? Here I'd been threatened, taken to court, had my placid bachelor's existence turned upside down with diapers and feedings and a baby's constant needs. And somewhere in the back of my mind, unspoken and indistinct but no less real for all that, another reservation had slowly begun to form, one more troubling than the others. When I finally gave voice to it, as I pulled into 562 Oak Ridge, it amounted to something like this: If the baby stayed on, Annabel might stay on, too. Maybe indefinitely. After all, she said she'd stay as long as I needed her. Was that what I wanted? For her to stay on? And what about Bobbie? What about our new life together? That couldn't happen with Annabel there.

In any case, I figured it wouldn't hurt to look up this fellow.

I pulled up in front of a small wood-frame house with peeling yellow paint. In the headlights, I saw a rotted-out blue Toyota pickup truck sitting beneath a bare willow tree at the side of the house. I parked and got out. The deepening twilight hung overhead, cool and quiet, broken only by the occasional *whuf-wooool* of a beagle from a couple of houses away. I climbed some sagging stairs and knocked on the front door. From the wall a small-watt lightbulb spilled a weak circle of light onto the front porch. After a while an Indian man answered the door. He had his mouth full of food.

"Yeah?" he mumbled.

"Are you Leonard Blackfox?" I asked.

He didn't answer, just continued chewing, his jaws working slowly, his eyes scrutinizing me for several seconds. He was tall and had a slight paunch. He wore a plaid flannel shirt over a yellowed T-shirt. Long shiny black hair tied in a ponytail hung down his back.

"What's it to you?"

"I'm looking for him."

"Why? Who are you?"

"A friend of Rosa Littlefoot's."

"You a cop?"

"No. I heard Rosa used to know him, that's all," I said.

He shrugged. "I ain't seen Lenny in a while."

"Phone book said he lives here."

"That ain't my problem." He kept his eyes trained on my hands, as if waiting for me to do something that might place him in danger. "He used to live here. But he's been gone a while now."

"You a friend of his?"

"Yeah."

"Would you know where I can find him?"

"You sure you're not a cop?"

"No, I'm a doctor." He looked up at my face, staring suspiciously at me. "I'm just trying to help Rosa. She's in a lot of trouble. You know where I can get in touch with him?"

"I sure wouldn't, Mister. You try up at the reservation?"

"I did. How long's he been gone?"

"I don't know. A few months maybe."

"He didn't say where he was going?"

"He didn't tell me."

"You knew Lenny and Rosa were friends?"

"More than friends. Rosa used to be his woman. Way back. Till she took up with that white fellow. I knew Rosa had her problems. The drugs and all that. She'd call here and tell him about that fellow she was shacking up with. What kind of trouble she in anyway?"

"That man, the one she was living with. She killed him."

"Killed him! Holy shit. Lenny said he was a mean one. Usta beat up on her pretty good I heard."

"You know when he last spoke to her?" I asked.

He put a finger in his ear and twisted it around. Then he pulled it out and inspected it. "I don't know. A few months back. She kill the sucker, huh?"

"Yeah."

"Jesus," he said, wagging his head. "From what I hear, he had it coming."

"She's being charged with murder."

"What's this got to do with Lenny?"

"Nothing. I was trying to get hold of his sister."

"Doreen?"

"Yeah. You wouldn't know where she is, would you?"

"No. What do you want with her?"

"I wanted to see if she might take Rosa's child in. They used to be friends. If Rosa goes to prison—and it looks that way now—we got to find a permanent place for her daughter."

"We?" the man said, smiling.

"I only meant . . . that is, Rosa doesn't have anybody else. I'm trying to help her. I was thinking it might be best if the child was placed with an Indian."

"I can't help you there, Mister."

"If I left you my name, you think you could have him call me if you saw him?"

"Like I told you, he ain't been around. And I don't expect him back. In fact, he owes me some money for rent."

"If he does come back," I said, handing him a business card, "have him call me. My phone number's right there." I thanked him and started down the steps.

"Fellow treats a woman the way Pugh did his, in my book he deserves what he gets," he called after me.

• • •

I stopped to pick up some food before heading over to the motel. I was starved, hadn't eaten since breakfast. But mostly, I was hungry for Bobbie. It was after seven when I entered the room, and I heard water running in the shower. I figured we'd eat later, so I got undressed and climbed under the covers and waited for her to come out. I felt the sweet rush of anticipation I usually felt when waiting for her. I pictured her emerging from the shower, like Venus from the ocean, her hair wet and darkly blond, her broad athletic shoulders narrowing to her slender waist, the small firm swelling of her breasts. I loved her body, the large yet graceful sweep of it. I wanted to fall into it, to seek comfort in it, to lose myself in it tonight. As I waited, my ardor growing by the minute, I realized I hadn't made love to her in more than a month, not since New Year's Eve. At the same time, that nagging sense of guilt returned and put a damper on things. I pictured Annabel home, waiting for me. Unlike any of the other times I'd been with Bobbie, I now felt as if I *were* doing something wrong. Not a sin so much in the Catholic sense but something nonetheless wrong. I knew it was silly of me to think like that, unfair to Bobbie, to me. Yet I couldn't help it.

"Doc?" Bobbie said, emerging finally from the bathroom. A towel was wrapped around her, while she used another to dry her hair.

"Yeah, it's me," I replied. "I bought some Chinese."

"I'm not that hungry." She stood at the foot of the bed, bent over at the waist, toweling dry her hair. Her face was mostly hidden and angled away from me. The firm pulchritudinous curve of her rear made me forget my guilt. Or almost.

"Bobbie . . . " I stopped in midsentence as she straightened and turned toward me, letting the towel drop away from her head. I felt the breath go out of me and a sour feeling turning in the pit of my stomach. "My God, what happened?" I cried.

Her left eye was swollen, the cheek beneath it a shiny, outraged pink.

"You should see the other guy," she joked stiffly, wincing with the effort of moving her mouth.

I went to her and put my arms around her. "What happened?"

"That asshole."

"Who?"

"Who do you think? Paul."

"*He* did this to you?"

From all I knew of Paul Tisdale, he wasn't a violent man. Of his many flaws, raising his hand to his wife hadn't been one.

"Yeah. Somebody had already told him about us. When I said I was leaving him, he called me a fucking whore. He said I shamed him in front of the whole town. After all his tomcatting around, he has the nerve to say *I* shamed him. The low-down dirty dog."

"He hit you because you told him you were leaving?"

"Mostly on account of I kinda hit him first."

"*You* hit *him* first?"

"Yeah. He made me mad. I didn't care what he said about me, but I wasn't going to let him get away with saying anything about you."

"*Me*. What did he say about me? He doesn't even know me."

"I guess he heard the usual rumors around town. Mostly he was just trying to get my goat. And it worked."

"Tell me what he said about me."

"Forget it, Stuart." She hardly ever called me Stuart.

"No, I want to know."

"He called you an old fart. Said you were . . . well, old enough to be my father. So I said you were twice the man he was. Especially in bed, which really got him riled."

"And that's when you hit him?"

"No. He said some other things."

"Like what?"

"Does it really matter?"

"Yes."

She gazed up at me. Her left eye was a little bloodshot from where he'd hit her. It made her look vulnerable all of a sudden, something I didn't normally think of her as being. She was always so tough and strong.

"He said I was crazy if I thought you were going to leave your wife for me. He said everybody knows Doc Jordan hasn't left her all these years and isn't going to either, and that he was just using me for a good lay. I should've known better but I couldn't help myself. That's when I lost it and started pummeling him. I got me in some good'uns before he hit me. He's a fair counterpuncher, I'll give him that." Bobbie tried to laugh it off, rolling her green eyes as usual, but she flinched with the pain and, instead, tears formed in her eyes and ran slowly down her battered face.

"Oh, Bobbie," I said, kissing the side of her face that wasn't bruised. "I'm so sorry, honey."

"I didn't care what he said about me. I wasn't going to let him get away with saying stuff about you, though."

"Did you have the bastard arrested?"

"No. What good would it do?"

"Why not? You *are* the district attorney."

"Not for long. Besides, I assaulted him first. But Lord-amighty, if I'da had me a gun," she said, slipping into her down-home twangy accent. She looked up at me and, through her tears, smiled. We were both thinking the same thing: Rosa Littlefoot. It can happen that easily. Recovering her prosecutor's pose, she quickly added, "But he ain't worth twenty-five years in jail."

"By the way," I said, "I resigned as ME."

"You did?"

"Yeah. I sent Troy a letter saying it'd be best if I stepped down before we got close to Littlefoot's trial. I said it was on account of the conflict of interest."

"That's probably a good idea. Besides, it's not like he needs your testimony to convict."

"I suppose not," I said. "Where are you staying tonight?"

"I don't know."

"Come on," I said, leading her over to the bed. We got under the covers and I held her naked body against my own. I felt her shivering, her body tense and rigid. For a long while we didn't say anything.

"I love you," I said finally.

"I know. And I love you, too."

"I want us to be together, Bobbie. More than anything. You have to believe me."

"I want to. I do. But sooner or later, Doc, you're going to have to decide. Is it me or her you want to be with."

"Please don't put it like that."

"What other way is there to put it? For mercy sakes, she's back living with you."

"She's just staying there for a while. That's all it is. It's not like we're living together."

"It's not?"

"No. We sleep in separate rooms."

"I can't say I understand it. Geez Louise. I mean, here I just left one crazy relationship and I find myself stepping smack dab into another."

"She's just helping me out with the baby. And I'm letting her stay there until she . . . "

"Until she what?"

"Gets back on her feet. It won't be for long, I promise."

"Then what?"

"She'll leave like she always does."

"Until she comes back the next time."

"No," I said. "This is it. I'll divorce her. I will. I promise."

"You've been saying that for a while. I can wait, Stuart. I'm not saying I'm going to wait forever, mind you. We've both wasted too much of our lives waiting for things that never panned out. But I can wait a while more. Just don't make me wait too long. All right?"

I promised that I wouldn't. Then I gently kissed the eye that was swollen. I turned out the light and we lay there in the dark. We stayed like that for a long time, not talking, just holding onto each other, warming each other, giving each other the only thing we could—solace. After a while I could feel Bobbie stop shivering. Soon she began snoring lightly, and I felt her body relax into mine.

# 22

*On a Wednesday* afternoon, I was sitting in my study catching up on some paperwork. Annabel had taken the baby and headed down through the woods to visit Kay. She'd begun to miss her weekly visits with Dr. Butler, coming up with this excuse or that—that she had a headache, that the baby wasn't feeling well, that Butler had called to cancel. She complained that she didn't like him and that he wasn't doing her any good. Besides, she thought she didn't need to go. She said her medication was working just fine, that her appetite and strength were back, that she was sleeping better. All of which seemed true. "I'm feeling great, Stu," she'd reassured me. "Really. Stop worrying. I haven't felt this good in a long time. And anyway," she said with an impish grin, "I'm too busy to be sick." I had to admit, she did seem healthier, more vibrant and relaxed, more at ease with herself than she had in years. She'd gotten some color in her cheeks from getting out and walking with the baby or working in the yard, and she was eating and sleeping better. Yet just beneath the radiant surface of her sudden health I kept looking for the lurking signs of her illness. The lost and distant gaze. The trembling of her hands. The quirky behavior. As long as she took her lithium, I told myself, she'd do okay. Each morning I would check her prescription bottle in the medicine cabinet, counting the little brown pills. I hadn't brought up the subject of her plans. I kept putting it off, waiting for the time when she was strong enough and healthy enough to make other arrangements. And I guess, too, I was waiting in the hopes that she'd make the next move.

Outside, the day was hazy with a muted brightness. The mountains were slathered in a weak, wintry light that spilled like sifted flour from the sky. Down at the Wallenbachs', I saw John driving his tractor, haul-

ing a cart filled with manure toward his unplowed fields. I could remember watching him give Will rides. My son sitting on the old man's
lap, steering the large, red Massey-Harris tractor, laughing. Will used
to get a kick out of that. I thought of how the house used to be filled
with his noise, with his light and airy laughter, with his footsteps and
cries, and how for the longest time it had been so deathly still, morning
and night, like a tomb. And how lately it was animated once again with
the sounds of life. I'd wake at night to Maria's cries, to her soft, watery
gurgles and moans, to her shapeless yet silky utterances. And even if
there was just silence, it was of a different sort, full, palpable, perhaps
the exhalation of breath, perhaps the sound of a barely perceptible
heartbeat other than my own. Mornings, I'd grown accustomed to the
sounds and smells of waking: breakfast cooking, coffee on, water running, the baby's shrieks and whoops and sudden, revelatory laughter.
Voices. Noise. Life returning to this big old house, a house too long
filled with death and thoughts of death, too long occupied by guilt and
sadness and, what was worse, far worse, the quiet, cowardly accep-
tance of it all. Mine. I was thinking about the peculiar change in my life
when the phone rang, as if an omen of something. I was almost afraid
to pick it up.

"Judge Cobb has made his decision," Hunneycutt told me. I felt my
stomach tighten, though now it wasn't a voluntary thing, something I
was trying to do. Part of me was actually hoping for bad news: that I
wouldn't be granted custody. I was half hoping they'd take Maria and
place her with some family, not the Pughs certainly, but some nice young
childless couple who wanted a baby. Then it'd be out of my hands. I
could say I'd tried—and hadn't I, hadn't I done my best? And then my
life could go back to normal, or at least return to safe, familiar territory.

"Pending the outcome of Rosa Littlefoot's trial," Hunneycutt continued, "you've been granted sole temporary guardianship of Maria."

I didn't say anything for several seconds as I tried to get a handle on
what he'd told me.

"Dr. Jordan?"

"Uh huh?"

"Did you hear what I said?"

"Yes. Did you expect it to go that way?" I asked, feeling the tightness in my stomach slowly begin to dissolve. There was a part of me that
breathed a sigh of relief. A part that very much wanted Maria to stay
here. A part that had grown accustomed to having her around, that

wanted my life *not* to return to its old ways but to remain exactly as it was. Or at least something to that effect.

"To tell you the truth, I wasn't sure. But the social worker recommended the baby be placed with you. Ms. Ensley thought you could provide a loving and nurturing home environment for Maria. All things being equal, the judge usually goes along with the social worker's recommendation. Besides, Cobb was fully aware of the Pughs' criminal history. He didn't even grant them visitation rights, as I was concerned about the possibility of flight."

"Now what?"

"Now I get ready for Rosa's trial. And you and I go back to being on different sides."

"Not really. I thought you would've heard. I resigned as ME."

"Did you?"

"Yes. I'll have to testify at the trial, of course. But that's about the extent of my involvement. Bumgartner wants to keep me at arm's length. Thinks of me as a traitor."

"Was your decision based on what came out about . . . you and Ms. Tisdale?"

"A little. I've also been pretty busy. Mostly, though, it's because I don't see the logic in trying Rosa Littlefoot for first-degree murder. That never made any sense to me."

"I'm hoping a jury sees it that way, too."

"How did the Pughs take the custody decision?"

"As you can imagine, Glenn W. wasn't none too happy. If Rosa goes to jail, he'll likely contest this placement and we'll have to go to trial for a full-fledged custody fight. Which will make the deposition seem like a picnic. In fact, I'd say it's a certainty. That is, if you're still interested in taking Maria in."

"I . . . I suppose so," I said. Glancing out the window again, I happened to spot Annabel heading up the path that cut through the woods from the Wallenbachs' farm. Maria was strapped in the baby carrier against her chest. Every once in a while Annabel would pause and put her face down toward the baby's, as if saying something to her, whispering a secret.

"One other thing," Hunneycutt added. "Old man Pugh called me after he heard the news. He was cussing me and the judge and ever'body else he could think of. And you, too. Said he'd get what's his yet. I don't mean to alarm you, Dr. Jordan, but I'd take precautions if I were you."

"Precautions?"

"More'n likely Pugh's just blowing off some steam. Still, it wouldn't be a bad idea for you to keep a close eye on the baby."

"Do you think he'd really try to grab her?"

"I don't know. I'm just saying better safe than sorry."

"I understand. Did you tell Rosa about the decision?"

"I'm driving over to the courthouse now. I'll be sending you my bill."

When I got off the phone I thought for a moment about what he'd said concerning Pugh. Was he really a threat? Should I take seriously his backwoods sense of outrage in righting what he considered an injustice. Mountain people sometimes had a different take on right and wrong, and legal niceties didn't always enter into the equation. And given the Pughs' penchant for violence, I guess I shouldn't have been that surprised. As an ME I saw violence all the time. But it always concerned other people. I was more of a referee, not an active participant. It might be a good idea to be careful, I thought.

I was in the kitchen making tea when Annabel came in. Her face was flushed from the walk up the mountain, her cheeks pink, ruddy looking. Small and slight of build, she could, from ten feet at least, have passed for someone in her twenties. A young mother with a child. She smiled, and despite the missing teeth she revealed the pretty girl she'd once been. I stared at her and the baby for a moment, thinking how easy it would be to imagine her just getting back from a walk in the woods with our son. How easy it would be to slip back into our old life.

"*Whewph*," she exclaimed, taking Maria's hat off. "What a day. You should get out and get some sun."

"I have work."

"You always have work, you old fuddy-duddy," she said, smiling. "Take a break and smell the roses, why don't you?"

"I didn't know roses were out yet," I joked. "I made some tea?"

"Sounds good. Kay asked us down for supper tonight. I said yes." Then she paused and looked over at me. "That is, if you don't have any plans."

"No, that's fine. Hunneycutt called."

"Really?" she said, her voice anxious yet fighting to be restrained. I told her the news.

"So what does that mean?"

"It means she stays here. For now anyway."

"That's great," Annabel said. She came over to where I was standing at the stove, put her arms around my waist, and hugged me awkwardly. The baby, still in her carrier, was squeezed gently between us. I could feel Maria struggling against her confinement, squirming. Annabel looked up at me, her eyes searching mine. "I mean that *is* what you wanted, isn't it, Stu?"

"What I wanted had nothing to do with it. I was only trying to help that woman out. And give Maria a safe place to stay. That's all."

"Of course," Annabel said. She stepped back and started extricating the baby from the carrier.

"Let me help," I said.

"I always have trouble with these damn things," she said. "What happens after the trial?"

"I don't know. If Rosa goes to prison—*when* she goes—Hunneycutt said there'd probably be a full-blown custody trial with the Pughs."

"They wouldn't win, would they?"

"I don't know. But first I'd have to decide if that's what I wanted."

"What do you mean?"

"If I could make that kind of commitment. I'm not a young man and, well . . . I'd have to think that over long and hard. By the way, Hunneycutt said we ought to keep a close eye on the baby."

"Why?"

"He thought the Pughs might be looking to take her."

"*Take* her. You think they'd try to do that?"

"I don't know. It happens all the time. You see those pictures of stolen kids everywhere. What people don't know is most kids are stolen by family members, not strangers. Some father who lost a custody suit. Just like this."

"Jesus."

"I don't mean to scare you. I'm just saying we should be careful is all."

Annabel cradled the baby in her arms. "Don't worry," she said to Maria. "We won't let anything happen to you."

•  •  •

For several nights in a row, Annabel had been up late in her room. When I got up to check on the baby or go to the bathroom, I could see the light spilling out from under her door. I figured perhaps she was reading. In the morning, before I left for work, she'd come down to breakfast, her eyes red from lack of sleep but still nimble and quick as small dark birds hunting for food in the snow.

"You've been up late again," I said.

"Yeah, I couldn't sleep."

Late on a Saturday afternoon, I was splitting wood. When I came in the sliding doors off the deck with an armful of wood, Annabel, who was at the sink cutting carrots, asked me if I'd drive her into Slade. I was a little surprised. Except for the deposition, she had avoided going into town.

"You sure you're up to it?" I asked. "Tell me what you need and I'll pick it up for you tomorrow. I have to check a patient at the hospital anyway."

"I want to go. I need to pick up some paint supplies."

"You're *painting* again?"

With a shrug she said, "A little."

"Is that what you're doing at night?"

She nodded.

"That's great. How about we go tomorrow then?"

"No, now," she said. "I don't want to wait. If you won't drive me I guess I'll just have to drive myself. Or walk."

"To Slade?" I said, smiling. It had been years since Annabel had driven a car. I don't even think she had a valid North Carolina driver's license anymore. But I could see she was serious enough to get in my truck and try driving, or to attempt walking the thirteen miles into town. "All right," I finally relented.

I put Maria in the car seat, and the three of us drove into town. Annabel tapped nervously on the seat and hummed some tune I didn't recognize. The last few days I'd noticed a slight change in her behavior. She'd become, I felt, a little more antsy, hyper, though things were still at a manageable level. A level that, for her anyway, was good and productive, fertile as bottomland soil. She was, I knew, in that state where she could coast on two hours of sleep, skip meals, forget the time, work all day painting or in her garden or cleaning. A place where she used to like to be, in a blissful frenzy of activity. As always, though, I worried about what lay just beyond that, over the horizon. Knowing, as I did, how quickly things could change.

"So you're painting again?" I asked as we drove.

"Just puttering around."

"That's good."

She didn't say anything.

"Will you let me see what you're working on?"

"If and when it's ready."

I parked in front of Goody's hardware store, a block down from Hunneycutt's office.

"How long are you going to be?" I asked.

"An hour or so."

"Tell you what. I'm going to bring Maria up to the jail to visit with her mother. I'll meet you here around five. You'll be all right?"

"Of course, I'll be all right," Annabel said. "Stop treating me like some doddering old lady."

Darryl Childress, the deputy on duty, led me down to the cell.

"I heard you ain't gonna be goin' out with us no more, Doc," he said, as if all of our visits to the scenes of death and destruction had been nothing more than a night out with the boys.

"Yeah, that's right, Darryl. Getting too old for that."

"What's Cecil gonna do without you there to keep him from gettin' sick?" he said, and we both laughed.

Rosa was sitting on her cot listening to a Walkman when Darryl opened the door.

"I didn't know you'd be coming, Dr. Jordan," she said, smiling when she saw us. She removed her earphones and lay them on her bed.

"How's my little *ka-ma-ma*," she cooed, kissing the baby's cheeks. But Maria began to fuss and arch her back in Rosa's arms.

"Boy. She's already gettin' strange with me, ain't she?"

"She's been a little cranky last couple of days. I think she's got a tooth coming in."

Rosa looked better today. Her cheeks fuller, not so drawn and haggard. Her hair was in that shiny black snake of a braid again.

"You gain some weight?"

"Gettin' fat. All that greasy food they been feedin' me."

"No, it looks good on you." She frowned, the way any woman might after a man said the extra weight on her looked good.

"Who brought you the music?" I asked.

"Hunneycutt."

"He told you about the custody decision, I suppose?"

"Yes."

I watched the two of them together, Rosa holding the squirming, fussy baby tight against her, determinedly trying to rock Maria into acquiescence, into accepting her back as her mother. Trying in that strange and pathetic way I'd seen women rocking a stillborn infant, hoping beyond hope, to resuscitate something in her child. In this case it wasn't life so much as closeness, the love she'd lost in the month and a half she'd been in jail—more than a quarter of her child's short life, I realized. As I watched them, I felt an odd upward pressure in my chest, recognized the sensation for what it was, a primitive form of possessiveness, and immediately felt terrible for it. It's her kid, for Christ's sake, I told myself. Not yours. Nothing will change that. Even if she goes to prison, it's still hers.

"I ran into some fellow who knew Lenny Blackfox," I said.

Rosa stopped her agitated rocking and stared over at me.

"Yeah?"

"Well, I didn't just run into him. I was looking for Lenny. Hoping I might be able to find where his sister lived."

"Doreen? Why?"

"See if she might be able to take Maria."

"I told you not to go bothering them, didn't I?"

"I know. I was just thinking that if we got in touch with your friend and she was willing . . . "

"*No!*" Rosa said, adamant.

"Just hear me out."

"I said *no.*"

"But why?"

"They got their own worries, that's why. They don't need this."

"She might want to help you."

"Believe me, she don't."

"Have you talked to them?"

"Not in a couple of years."

"Then how would you know? Maybe Doreen would take Maria. You don't know unless you ask her, right?"

"No offense, Dr. Jordan. But it ain't your concern."

"But if she knew what happened she might . . . "

"*No,*" she snapped, her eyes suddenly the same fierce black as on the night she shot her husband. Eyes hard and shiny and jagged as pieces of flint. Eyes, I thought, capable of almost anything, even blowing a man's head off.

"It's up to you," I said.

"That's right, it is," she replied, her eyes softening a little as she gazed down at Maria. "What's the matter, Dr. Jordan? You don't want to take her no more?"

"It's not that. It's . . . "

"What?"

"The truth is, Rosa, I don't know if I'm the best person to look after your baby. I mean, think about it."

"Why? What's wrong?"

"Look at me. I'm fifty-seven. I'm too old."

"That's not old."

"I *feel* old. Old and tired. I just wonder if I'd be good for her."

"What are you talking about?" she said. "Just look at her. Anybody can see how happy she is."

"*Now* maybe. But remember what you said about down the road? That you had to think about what was best for Maria, not just today but twenty years from now. I'm thinking Maria might be better off with her own people."

"Her own people? What are you talking about, Dr. Jordan?"

"You know, with Indians. It wouldn't be easy growing up with whites. What do I know about Indian culture? Your ways?"

"What's that got to do with anything?"

"An Indian child growing up white. It would be hard. I'm just wondering if we could do better."

She stared at me for several seconds. "You changed your mind, didn't you? That's what this is about, ain't it? You don't want to take her now."

"No, no. It's not that. It's just . . . I'm wondering if it might be better if someone like your friend took your daughter in."

Rosa angled her head, rested her ear on top of the baby's head, as if she were listening to her daughter's thoughts. Maria grabbed at her mother's dark hair and tried to put a strand into her mouth.

"If you don't want to take her in, Dr. Jordan, you just tell Hunneycutt and have him make other arrangements."

"I'm not saying I won't. I'm just wondering if we're doing what's best for Maria."

"What's best for her," she said. "Hell, if I'da been thinking of that, I would've finished things that night. We wouldn't even be having this conversation."

"Don't talk like that. You don't want to talk like that. Listen, she can stay with me through the trial. Let's see how things go. Then we can decide what to do next. One step at a time. All right?"

She lifted her shoulders and slowly let them drop. "Whatever you say."

"And I don't want to hear any more of that kind of talk. You hear me?"

As I drove back down to Main Street, I thought of what she said about wishing she'd finished things that night. I worried about her, her doing something foolish. On the surface she was all tough and gritty and hard as nails, but under that I thought she was scared, all alone as she was, facing a long stretch in jail, being forced to give up her baby. I probably shouldn't have said anything about Maria going to stay with someone else, at least not now. That could've waited till the trial was over. Probably shouldn't have brought up the business about Blackfox and his sister either. Then I wondered about something else. Rosa said the last time she'd spoken to Lenny was a couple of years ago, but that Indian fellow down in Farley told me Rosa and Lenny had spoken just a few months back. Was he simply mistaken? Or had Rosa just forgotten?

I parked, got the baby out of her car seat, and headed toward Goody's. Just as I was about to enter, who did I bump into coming out but Bobbie.

"What are you doing here?" I asked, surprised to see her.

"I had to get a few things for my apartment," she said. We hadn't seen each other for a couple of weeks, not since the night at the motel. Bobbie looked good, despite the fading but still noticeable bruise below her eye. She wore jeans and a short suede jacket. Her hair was recently done and her mouth glistened wet with a plum-colored lipstick I felt like taking a bite out of.

"Where you living?"

"I got an apartment over near the college. It's a dump, but it's all right for now. You want to come over for a drink?"

"I . . . Annabel's with me."

"Oh," she said, raising her eyebrows. "I filed for divorce."

"You did?"

"Yeah."

"Good for you."

She offered up a tentative nod and pursed her lips. She reached out to touch Maria's cheek. "How's this one been?"

"Good. I just brought her up to see Rosa."

I was going to say something when I happened to spot Annabel emerge from Green's Pharmacy, two doors down, and begin walking toward us. Great, I thought.

"I'm ready, Stu," Annabel said, a bit too loud, in a way I knew was meant to stake out ownership. She cast a sideways dismissive glance at Bobbie but kept her eyes on me. There was an awkward moment before Bobbie had the common sense to extend her hand and fill in the silence.

"Hi," she said, smiling. "You must be Annabel. I'm Bobbie Tisdale."

"Why . . . hello," replied my wife, cautiously accepting Bobbie's hand. Annabel gave her an icy stare. "You're the district attorney, right?"

"Assistant DA."

"Of course." My wife looked at me and then said, "Stuart has spoken about you."

"We worked together," Bobbie said, smiling. "When he was the ME."

We fumbled for conversation for a few moments but luckily were saved when the baby started to fuss.

"We should probably get going," I said. "She's getting hungry."

"So nice to meet a colleague of Stuart's," Annabel said in a voice clearly intended to be sarcastic, full of disdain. I gave Bobbie an I'm-sorry-about-this look and we turned and made for the truck.

It was getting on toward dark when we reached home. On the ride Annabel was quiet, staring sullenly out the window at the dark river snaking below us. She lit a cigarette, took one puff, then tossed it out the window. I was annoyed at her behavior, at the way she'd treated Bobbie. We were passing the Wallenbachs' farm before she finally spoke. "So that was her, huh? Your *lady* friend."

I glanced over at her, trying to read her mood.

"Yes," I replied curtly.

"Pretty. Blonder than I'd have pictured your tastes running to."

"What's that supposed to mean?"

"Oh, nothing. I suppose I shouldn't presume to know the sort of woman you'd find attractive now. Just that I can't picture you with someone like *that*."

"Like what?"

"With frosted hair and all made up just to shop at Goody's."

"Annabel," I warned, "don't start."

"I'm not starting. Just making an observation is all. She and her husband . . . "

"Yes, they're divorcing," I replied curtly.

"Just curious. No need to get your dander up, Stu."

"It's just that . . . ," I began, but thought better of saying what I had on my mind. "Forget it."

"Isn't that what you wanted?"

I didn't reply. I just wanted to drop it. But Annabel, I could tell, didn't. She was in one of her moods. Looking for a fight. Hoping to goad me into saying something I would later regret, feel guilty for.

"Well, isn't it?" she asked. "So you can marry her?"

"I suppose so. Yes. Is that what you wanted to hear?"

"The only thing holding you back now is li'l ole me."

"That's not fair and you know it," I exclaimed.

"It's the truth. If I wasn't around you'd be footloose and fancy free. Face it, you need a divorce from me so you can marry blondie."

"Just stop it. Please. Before we both say things we'll be sorry for."

"I *never* say anything I'm sorry for. Not like some people I know," she said, smiling coyly at me. I suspected she'd probably stopped taking her medication. I could see the signs of her rushing out of control again, her picking up speed like a car that had lost its brakes careening down a steep mountain road, going faster and faster, just waiting for disaster.

"Enough, Anna. Just stop it."

"I know that Catholic in you. You may not go to church anymore, but you still want to do it the *right* way. Walk down the aisle with blondie. Make an honest woman of her."

"Jesus Christ, Annabel. I'm warning you. Enough."

"What are you going to do, kick me out on the street like you did those other times?"

"What! I never did that. You're . . . "

"Crazy?"

"No, you're not being fair. When did I ever say you had to leave? Name one time."

"Maybe not in so many words. But I could tell when you were getting tired of me."

"Jesus," I said, glancing over at her. "That's a lie and you know it."

"What about those times you brought me to Cedar Crest? What about that?"

"That was different. That was for your own good. You were sick and I couldn't take care of you."

"If you want me out, Stu, like I told you, just say the word. Far be it from me to stand in the way of your happiness with blondie."

"Oh, Jesus. Just shut the hell up."

We happened to be turning into my driveway. I stopped the truck.

"I'm going to check the mail," I snapped.

I didn't want to get into an argument with her over this. Not now, anyway. I got out and headed over to the mailbox. The night was cool and damp, the darkness quickly gathering itself together like metal filings around a magnet. The coolness cleared my head a little. When I climbed back in the truck, I said, "Listen, Annabel . . . "

"Who's that?" she interrupted. I followed her finger, which pointed up the road beyond our house. In the growing darkness I could make out a truck parked along the shoulder, about a hundred yards away. Its lights were off and it was facing down the mountain. I couldn't tell if anyone was in the truck.

"I don't know," I said, reaching over and grabbing the flashlight from the glove compartment. "I'll be right back."

"What are you going to do?"

"See who it is."

"Stuart, what if it's *them*?"

"Lock the doors," I said.

"I'm coming with you."

"No, you're not. You're going to stay here with the baby."

"Be careful then."

I didn't recognize the truck. It wasn't the red Ford I'd seen Pugh get into in town, though that didn't offer much in the way of reassurance. The boxy shape looked like a Blazer. I recalled the threat in Glenn W.'s small, gray, deep-set eyes. Recalled him saying that someone who stuck his nose in where he had no business might get himself bloodied. Recalled the way he'd stared at me across the table at the deposition, his look of feral meanness. And I recalled Hunneycutt's warning that he was dead-set on getting the baby. With all this in mind, the prospect of confronting Glenn W. Pugh along some dark road was not something I looked forward to.

As I got to within fifty feet, the engine suddenly kicked over and the headlights caught me in their blinding glare, frozen like a jacklighted deer. The next moment the truck was moving, headed right for me, tires howling and kicking up dirt, engine screaming with a murderous rage. I didn't move, just watched helplessly as the truck bore down on me. I should've leapt out of the way but for some reason I simply stood there, my feet rooted to the earth, as if awaiting my fate. Yet just as it seemed about to plow into me and send me flying to kingdom come, at the last possible moment, it swerved around me and, tires screeching, flew hell-bent down the mountain. Only then did fear and self-preservation kick in, and too late to do any good, I found myself diving for the side of the road. As the headlights retreated down the road, I got another look at it: a Blazer or a Ford Bronco, I was pretty sure. When I thought about it later, I couldn't tell if the driver had been aiming at me or, like a cornered animal, just trying to get by and I was in his way.

"God, are you all right, Stu?" Annabel cried when I got into the truck.

"Yes. Did you get a look at him?"

"No, I was watching you. He almost hit you, that crazy fool. You sure you're all right?" she said, reaching out and taking hold of my hand, which was scraped from the dirt of the road.

"I'm fine. He just scared me a little."

My heart, I realized, was clunking noisily inside my chest like a piston without any oil.

"Did *you* see him?" she asked.

"The lights were in my eyes. There might have been two of them. I can't really say."

"You ought to call the police."

"What am I going to say? Some kids up here drinking."

"You *know* it wasn't any kids, Stu. We both know who it was. It's those crazy damn Pughs. That fellow tried to hit you. You ought to have them arrested."

I wasn't so sure it was the best thing to do. If it *was* one of the Pughs—and if I had to bet, my money would be on them—how was I going to prove it? I didn't actually see the man behind the wheel. And if I called Cecil and got him involved, they would know they'd succeeded in scaring me. They weren't the sort you wanted to admit a weakness to. They would try to intimidate me. Scare me into giving them what they wanted. I guess my feeling was that since no harm had been done, it might be better just to leave things as they were. Drop it and hope that they didn't come back. That's what I was figuring anyway. At the same time I vowed to be more vigilant, more careful.

As we drove up to the house, Annabel touched my arm and said, "I'm sorry, Stu."

"I'm all right."

"No, I mean about before. What I said. I don't know what came over me."

"Don't worry about it," I said.

"I want you to be happy, Stu. Really, I do."

# 23

*Spring pounced on* us suddenly and fiercely, like a catamount going for the throat of its prey. Each morning the sun rose higher in the sky earlier over Shadow Mountain. Throughout the hills, light made bold forays into winter-darkened hollows and mist-enshrouded ravines, bringing things to life. The mountains thawed, and from every fissure in the earth water oozed and then trickled and finally cascaded in torrents down into countless valleys. Early flowers such as bloodroot and larkspur bloomed on the lower slopes, while the dogwood and crabapple and tulip poplar down near the river began to form buds. The growl of chain saws resounded through the valley as loggers from the Nantahala Paper Company started cutting timber up near Wolf Lake. A few farmers in the bottomlands even plowed their fields and turned their cattle out to pasture, though John considered that just plain crazy, what with the flooding we were sure to get.

Rosa Littlefoot's trial was drawing near. Since I was no longer the ME, what I knew of it came mostly from what I read in the *Slade Messenger*. It was big news in town. Every week Drew Hazard ran something about it on the front page: "Defense Asks for Delay in Littlefoot Trial" or "DA Seeks First Degree in Pugh Murder" or "Littlefoot Trial to Open Next Week." The few times I spoke with Bobbie about the case, she seemed a little reluctant to talk to me about it. I wasn't sure whether Bumgartner had cautioned her not to discuss the trial with me or she just didn't want to bore me with details that didn't concern me in the same way. Or was it that she herself wondered if my sympathies for Rosa might make me an adversary rather than an ally? In any event, we no longer talked about it; we didn't talk about much of anything for that matter. I'd heard, from Cecil and others, that Hunneycutt was constructing some sort of battered-wife-syndrome defense, which still seemed unlikely to fly around these parts.

During my weekly visits to the jail, Rosa seemed to be holding up, at least physically. Her color had returned, the cut above her eye had healed over into a bumpy though fading scar, and the bones in her neck and face were softened by the gradual addition of flesh. She certainly wasn't wasting away to nothing. Yet while she seemed healthy enough physically, she had grown distant and withdrawn, preoccupied with her own thoughts. I tended to chalk that up to the fact she was going on trial for her life. Who wouldn't be preoccupied? The few times I did happen to bring up her case or something connected to it, she seemed uncomfortable talking about it. Beyond, say, mentioning that Hunneycutt had just been in, or how she'd met with some "shrink come all the way from Raleigh just to git inside my head," somebody who was going to testify on her behalf.

Mostly, during my visits, she was content to play with the baby, ask if Maria was sleeping through the night, eating solid foods yet. I didn't bring up the business about the Blackfoxes again, and she didn't ask. If she didn't want to seek her friends out for help, who was I to insist? Nor did we talk about what would happen to her daughter down the road. "Down the road" was something neither of us wanted to think much about. My impression was that Rosa had retreated into herself, hunkering down like a turtle, withdrawing to a place beyond where she could be hurt—or helped—by anybody or anything.

Fortunately, I'd had no more contact with the Pughs, if indeed the truck that night had been them. The more I thought of it, the more I convinced myself it was just some kids drinking or parking, and then spooking when they saw me. As crazy as the Pughs could be, that made more sense than thinking they would actually try to run me over. Still, I took the threat they posed seriously enough that I changed the front and back locks, and had a floodlight installed over the deck. I also persuaded Annabel to go down and stay with the Wallenbachs if I was going to be very late at the hospital. I even offered to show her how to load my shotgun, but she drew the line on that. She'd always been leery of guns, even when I used to hunt. Whenever I spoke of introducing Will to hunting when he was old enough, she would say over her dead body.

Bobbie and I hadn't seen much of each other in the past several weeks. We were both pretty busy with work, her getting ready for the Littlefoot trial and me with my practice. We managed to speak on the phone a few times, and once, a few weeks before, we got together after work for a drink. Yet that meeting only ended miserably.

"I really missed you, Doc," she said when I met her in Pancho Villa's. She was at the bar. She put her arms around me and kissed me sloppily on the mouth. Her lips tasted warmly of Jack Daniels. I could tell she'd had more than a few already.

"I've missed you, too, Bobbie," I said.

"Y'all got time to come over my place for a quick one?"

"You mean for a drink?"

"'Course I meant a drink. What'd you think I had in mind?" she said, with a deadpan expression.

"Well . . . "

"Why you horny old hound dog you," she said, rolling her green eyes before breaking into that snorting guffaw of hers. She leaned toward me, close enough that I caught the scent of her shampoo, and whispered in my ear, "Truth is, Doc, I been real lonely these past few weeks. What do you say?"

"I'd like nothing better than to come over, Bobbie. You know that."

"Then what's stopping you? Did you eat yet?"

"No."

"Tell you what. I could rustle us up some supper, though I can't promise it'll be up to your standards. And then we could fool around. I only got the pullout. But what do you say?"

"It sounds great. It's just that . . . "

"What?"

"It's just that I'm kind of busy tonight."

"Busy, my ass. Why don't you say what you really mean? You won't come over because your *wife's* around. That's the real reason, Doc," she said, turning angry. She stared pensively into her glass for a moment, her mouth sewn into a pinched knot. "I don't understand you sometimes," she said. "I really don't. You say you love me."

"I do. I do love you."

"Then how long are things gonna go on like this?"

"Like what?"

"Like what! Jesus Christ, Doc. With her there living with you, that's what."

"Not long."

"You been saying that for a couple of months now."

"It won't be like this much longer. I promise. And besides, I waited all that time while you were making up your mind to leave your husband."

"Hell, that's a whole different story and you know it."

"Why is it different?"

"It just is."

"I promise you she won't stay much longer."

"But what if she doesn't leave?"

"She will. She always leaves."

"But just say *this* time she doesn't? There's the baby now. And who's to say this time she doesn't want to try and patch things up with you?"

"There's nothing to patch up. It's over. It's been over for years."

"Doc, I'm not stupid. I saw the way she looked at me that time in front of Goody's. It was the look a woman gives another when she wants to say, 'Stay away, he's mine.'"

"That's ridiculous."

"Is it?"

"I told her I love you. That we wanted to get married. She knows that."

"*Does* she?"

"Yes."

"Are you prepared to tell her she has to leave?"

"Well . . . yes. If I have to."

"For pete's sake, Doc, you going to put us on hold every time she comes sauntering back into your life?"

"Of course not."

She finished her drink, snatched up her pocketbook, and started for the door.

"Bobbie, wait," I called. "Bobbie."

She stopped and came back over to me. "Answer me one thing. Are you sleeping with her?"

"What? No. Of course not."

"Don't lie to me, Doc. I'm sick and tired of being lied to by men."

"I swear I'm not."

"Do you still love her?"

"No."

Her eyes searched mine, hunting in every corner for deceit. I don't know what they found. Then she turned and left.

"Womens, eh Dr. Jordan," said Hector, the bartender. Then, pouring me another drink and himself one, too, he said, "Salud."

• • •

During the next several weeks, I, too, kept wondering how long Annabel would stay. I wondered if I'd wake up one morning and she'd be gone, her bureau drawers emptied, her lone suitcase removed from the closet. A note on the table that said, "So long, Stu. Thanks for everything." It had been years since she'd stayed on this long. I began to think Bobbie was right, that I *would* have to take things in my own hands and tell her to leave. I wondered, though, if I'd have the heart to put her suitcase in the truck and drive her to the bus station in Slade. Not counting those times she'd been ill and I'd had to have her committed, I'd never kicked her out before. Never made her leave. She'd always stayed as long as she wanted, left when she felt like leaving. In fact, I never wanted her to go. I was the one who always tried to get her to stay, to keep her here another week, another day, another hour. Even after all those years of her coming in and out of my life, of her wreaking havoc with my heart, even after I'd resigned myself to the fact of her eventual leave-taking, I never *wanted* her to go. But now things were different, I knew. She had something to hold her here—Maria—and I had something for which I wanted her to leave—Bobbie. That's what was different now.

Neither Annabel nor I said any more about the argument we'd had the night the truck nearly hit me. While we didn't openly fight, Annabel's moods, I noted, were slowly beginning to deteriorate, though not in obvious ways. Many days she actually appeared normal: cheerful and vivacious, in good spirits, full of pep, talkative, often singing some song by the Beatles or Dylan or Joni Mitchell. I'd come down to breakfast to find her sitting at the table, humming, feeding Maria with one hand while making a long list of things she wanted to do with the other. She'd already have done a wash as well as vacuumed the house and baked a pie.

"Did you mail those seed catalog orders I gave you, Stu?" she asked one morning, though I'd already told her a half-dozen times I had. "I want to get seedlings started inside before warm weather. John said I could use his greenhouse. Oh, and could you pick me up some more turpentine? I ran out last night."

Other times, though, her vivacity seemed to cross over into the wild, ungovernable territory of her mania. In the evening, when she wasn't tending to Maria or upstairs in her studio, on those few occasions she'd sit in the den with me, I'd notice that her hands were growing more and more restless, flitting around like bees near a hive. She had that glassy, strung-out look in her eyes, like somebody after a cocaine binge of several days. It seemed now and then she would jump right out of her skin. Sometimes when she talked the words would spill from her in an incoherent jumble. Other times she would say the oddest things. One night, for instance, I was reading and she was skimming through one of the picture albums. She looked up suddenly and asked, "Where did you put all his stuff?"

"Whose stuff? What are you talking about?"

"Will's. Where did you put his clothes? There's not a thing in his drawers. I looked."

I stared up at her. It wasn't so much the fact she'd forgotten I'd already told her I'd given most of his things away that concerned me. It was *why* she wanted to know where his clothes were. I had the feeling that it wasn't out of some sentimental notion that she wanted to see them once more. I was afraid it was that she was worried that he didn't have anything to wear. After a moment, I could see the recognition come sliding down over her eyes.

"Never mind," she said, covering her mistake.

"Have you been taking your medication?" I asked.

"Yes, yes, yes. Of course. Why wouldn't I?"

One morning she was sitting at the kitchen table when I came down. She looked as if she hadn't slept at all. She looked wired, manicky, her hands squirrelly as hell. I told her, "I think I'm going to call Kay and see if she can look after the baby today."

"Whatever for?"

"You don't look good."

"I'm fine," she replied. "Really, Stu."

"You sure you'll be all right?"

"I'm just a little tired is all."

"You stay up too late. You're pushing things again."

"I am not. I never felt better."

How many times had I heard that, that she'd never felt better?

But most days she remained just this side of pathological. Most days she was merely buzzing with energy—bringing Maria for walks, cleaning the house, potting plants, going down to visit with Kay. And painting. In fact, she painted furiously, with an intensity bordering on obsession. I hadn't seen this sort of interest in her in years, not since Will was alive. Mornings while Maria napped, she would take her things— her easel and paints, her brushes and sketch pad and palette—and go out onto the back deck. She'd set up her easel and spend an hour or two sketching or painting. And if the day were nice, she'd bring Maria out with her and put her in the windup swing or in her playpen while she worked. She wouldn't, of course, let me watch her, nor would she let me see anything she was working on. She'd always been reluctant to show others her work, especially before it was finished. I tried to take her renewed interest in her work as a good sign, a sign that her health was improving, or at least not deteriorating. But I knew better. It was never that easy, never that clear-cut. Sometimes her passion for art was just another symptom of her illness rather than a sign she was getting better.

One afternoon, I happened to come home earlier than usual from work. Annabel and the baby were out on the back deck. From the sliding door in the kitchen, I secretly watched the two of them for awhile. Annabel was drawing on a sketchpad with charcoal, while the baby, seated in her swing, played with a rattle. It took me a second to realize she was painting Maria.

"That's nice," I said, stepping out onto the deck.

"How long have you been spying on me?" she asked, quickly flipping a sheet of paper backwards to cover her work.

"I'm not spying. I'm just admiring your work."

"You know that makes me nervous."

"How's your little model?" I said, to change the subject.

"I'm serious, Stu," she snapped. "I fucking hate it when you spy on me like that." She gathered her work and stormed inside, headed up to her room.

Sometimes in the middle of the night when I'd get up to check the fire, I would see the light under her door. Other times in the morning, when I'd get up for work, her light would still be on, and I knew she hadn't slept at all. One night I woke, thinking I'd heard something. I got up, headed over to Maria's room, and poked my head in the door. But she was fast asleep. As I was going back to my room I happened to notice the light from Annabel's door. I walked quietly down the hall and stood there in the dark for a while. Silence. I was about to turn around and head back to my room when I heard what it was that had awakened me. A voice. Annabel's. Speaking in a normal-pitched tone, not a voice of someone talking in sleep. If I didn't know better I would've said someone was in the room with her. I leaned in, put my ear close to the door.

"Be patient," I heard her say. "Mommy's almost done."

Hearing her say those words sent a shudder coursing through me. I waited out in the hall for another moment or two but didn't hear any more. Then I turned and quietly walked back to my room. As I lay in bed, I couldn't help but wonder what it portended that she was talking to him.

• • •

Several nights later, a call from the hospital woke me around midnight. It was Lucy Ballard.

"Sorry to wake you, Doc," she said. "But Emmilou Potter's here. Her husband brung her in. She had herself a seizure at home."

I'd been afraid of that. Despite bed rest and the antihypertensive medication I'd had her on, she had suddenly though not altogether surprisingly progressed from preeclampsia to full-blown eclampsia, which was no doubt what caused the seizure.

"How's she doing now?" I asked.

"She's groggy but awake. They got her on Aldomet and IV magnesium sulfate."

I asked about Emmilou's numbers: blood pressure, platelet count, liver enzymes, urine output. They were uniformly bad. The fetal heart rate was low but not yet dangerously so. Of course, things could nosedive pretty quickly with eclampsia.

"Who's covering the ER tonight?"

"Dr. Chung."

Good, I thought. At least it wasn't some second-year resident with his thumb up his ass.

"Get her prepped. Ask Chung to assist me. I should be there in twenty minutes. But if things take a turn for the worse, tell Chung to go ahead and start without me."

"Will do, Doc. We'll handle things till you get here."

I got dressed in a hurry. Out in the hall I saw the light from Annabel's room. I headed over and paused there for a moment. I debated whether to tell her I was going or just leave a note on the kitchen table, as I usually did when I got called in. I knocked softly on the door. No answer. So I knocked again, harder. When I still didn't hear anything, I opened the door a crack and poked my head in. Annabel was lying fully clothed on the bed, curled up on her side, asleep. I decided then not to wake her, to leave a note instead. I was about to turn and leave, when I happened to look at the easel in the corner of the room, near the window. Sitting on it was a nearly finished charcoal sketch of a face. Everything was done except for the mouth, which remained a whitish-gray blur near the bottom of the face. It was obvious that Annabel had tried over and over with the mouth, wrestled with it, erasing and starting again several times, never quite getting it to her satisfaction. Though unfinished, the drawing was clearly that of a young boy. His hair fell loosely in his face, and even without a mouth you could tell by his eyes he was smiling. Or trying to. A tightness, like angina, filled my chest. For several seconds, I stared at the drawing of my son.

"Stuart?" Annabel said, stirring from sleep. "What's the matter?"

"I got called in for an emergency."

"Oh," she said, sitting up. "When will you be back?"

"I don't know. I may be gone a while." I saw her follow my gaze to the sketch on the easel. "I have to run. You'll be all right?"

"I'll be fine."

"If anything does come up, if you feel you need anything, you can always call Kay, you know."

"I know. See you in the morning then."

As I sped into town, I thought about the picture. I'd never known her to draw Will before, at least not since he died. What did it mean? And what about her talking to him like that? *Be patient. Mommy's almost done.* Done with what? The picture? Was that what she meant? It was almost as if he'd been sitting for her, right there in the room. Her little model. Jesus!

At the hospital I examined Emmilou. Her blood pressure had worsened, spiking to 180/115, and I worried about the possibility of a stroke. We had to move fast, before the baby or the mother went south on us. I dressed and scrubbed for the operation, with Dr. Chung assisting. The section went fairly smoothly, all things considered. Emmilou came out of surgery a very sick woman, but her blood pressure started to come down, and I felt confident she'd do all right in time. She was tough as nails. She might not be able to milk Janey for a while and she probably wouldn't be able to have any more children, but she'd pull through. Her baby, on the other hand, was a different story. It was a boy, Stuart Haney Potter. He was even smaller than I had guessed, barely three and a half pounds, with a low Apgar score, poor muscle tone, and a dusky-gray cyanotic color. Because of the poor respiration, Chung thought the baby had hyaline membrane disease—immature lungs—and I had to agree with him. We decided to transport the baby to Henderson Memorial over in Asheville, where they had a Level III ICU. His chances, I felt, were slim at best, but he'd have a better shot at a bigger hospital. I met Jack Potter out in the waiting room.

"How they doin', Doc?" he asked.

"Emmilou's going to be laid up for a while, but she should do just fine. Your son . . . well, we'd like to transport him to Asheville."

"He gonna make it, ain't he?" he said.

"It's hard to say right now, Jack. He's very, very sick. You'll have to sign some papers."

Rather than head home, I decided to lie down in the doctor's lounge. I wanted to be close in case something came up with Emmilou. I told Lucy to wake me if there was the slightest change.

I dreamed of my father. I was a young boy driving with him in the old Buick, on a country road someplace. Outside, there were woods and occasional fields with men cutting hay. The day was sunny, and the air coming through the open window smelled sweetly of hay. We must have been going to visit a patient of his because he had his black doctor's bag on the seat between us. He was smoking a cigarette and humming along to some big band song on the radio. As the dream progressed, I somehow became the man behind the wheel and the young boy seated next to me turned into my son. He looked exactly as he had in Annabel's drawing. Then, from a long way off, I heard a voice calling to me. For a moment I thought it was Will: *Dad, wake up. Wake up.*

"Dr. Jordan," another voice called. "Dr. Jordan, wake up."

When I opened my eyes, I saw the broad, fleshy face of Lucy Ballard.

"What?" I asked. "Is it Emmilou?"

"No, she's doin' just fy-on," she said. "It's Sheriff Clegg. He wants to speak to you."

Groggy, I stood up and went out into the hall. What the hell does he want, I wondered. After all, I wasn't the ME anymore. Cecil was standing there in his blue sheriff's jacket, looking fat and tired and very old.

"Sorry to bother you, Doc," he said.

I thought it might be his wife, that she'd had a relapse and was back in the hospital.

"Something up with Ruth?"

"No, she's all right. It's the Littlefoot gal, Doc. Thought you'd want to know they had to rush her over here to the ER."

"What happened?"

"Don't know all the details yet. I just got back from transporting a prisoner over to Asheville. From what I heard, Butch Slocum was making his rounds and he found her laying on the floor. They was blood all over the place."

"Blood?"

"Yessir. Butch said he found a piece of wire from her mattress. Evidently what she done was broke it off and used it to cut herself."

"She tried to commit suicide?"

"Looks like. She bled like a stuck pig, Doc. If Butch hadn't a found her when he done, I don't reckon she'd a made it."

"How's she doing now?"

"They been operating on her."

"Thanks, Cecil."

I rushed down to the OR, thinking I could lend a hand. By the time I got there, though, Chung was already coming out of surgery.

"How did it go?" I asked him.

"She lose lotta blood," he explained. "She very bad. Almost die."

"She's going to be all right, though?"

"Oh, yes. She do okay now, I think. If no infection."

"Was she trying to commit suicide?"

"No, no. No suicide," he said, taking off his surgical scrubs and tossing them into the receptacle at the end of the hall. "She have perforated uterus."

"A perforated uterus? I don't understand."

"She give herself abortion."

"An abortion! She's *pregnant*?"

"Was. Fifteen week maybe. No more pregnant."

I waited for Rosa to come out of the anesthesia. Cecil had posted a guard outside her room, and one of her wrists was handcuffed to the bed rail, though she wasn't in any shape to make a run for it. She was out for a long time. *Pregnant,* I thought. Jesus. So that explained the weight gain, why her breasts continued to be tender well after her milk should've dried up. Why hadn't I picked up on it? And why hadn't she told me? I thought she trusted me. She'd been pregnant all this time and hadn't told anybody. I poured myself a cup of coffee out at the nurses' station. While there, I checked her chart. Perforated uterus. Self-inflicted D&C with resultant termination of pregnancy. She was on heavy-duty antibiotics to prevent infection, and they'd had to give her eight units of Type O blood. Eight units! People died losing less blood than that.

I was sitting in a chair in her room when I heard her stirring. She opened her eyes and threw a weak glance in my direction.

"What are you doing here?" she said.

"I work here. I should be asking you that."

"Please. I don't need no lectures. How . . . I mean, about my baby?"

"You lost it. That's what you wanted, right?" I said, a bit too sharply I sensed, almost as if I wanted to be cruel.

Her expression didn't change. Instead, she looked out the window toward the town of Slade, just coming to life. Smoke poured from the smokestacks of the paper company. In the early morning light, Rosa appeared emaciated and otherworldly, like one of those gaunt German Christ figures, her face a mask of bony suffering. Her dark skin stood out in striking contrast against the white sheets of the bed, her long hair cascading wildly about her slightly feverish face. And those black eyes of hers—tired, weary, yet still filled with such startling intensity. A woman capable of great extremes.

"How do you feel?" I asked, my tone softening a little.

"Like shit."

"The doctor says you're gonna be all right."

"Hooray."

"You could've died, you know. You should be grateful."

"Grateful for what? So I can spend the rest of my life in jail?"

"You still have a daughter to think about. Or have you forgotten?"

"She'd be better off without a mother like this," she said, rattling the handcuffs. She closed her eyes wearily and drew in a shallow breath. Her tongue darted out and moistened her lips. "How she doing anyway, Doc?"

"Maria's doing fine. Why didn't you tell me you were pregnant?"

"I don't know."

"I could've helped. You didn't have to do this."

"I thought about telling you. But then I thought you'd try to talk me into having it. And I couldn't have another one. Not like this."

"The doctor who operated on you said you were about four months."

"I don't know. Maybe." Rosa fell silent. Her pupils flattened out, her lids fluttered, then closed again. She seemed to have fallen back to sleep. I waited for her to come back. When she opened her eyes in a few minutes, she glanced over at me. "Was it a boy or a girl?"

"I don't know."

"Any chance I could see it?"

"I don't think that's a good idea, Rosa. Not under the circumstances."

"Could you do me a favor, Dr. Jordan? Could you at least find out what it was?"

I remembered her telling me about the abortion she'd had as a girl, how she'd always wanted to know if it had been a boy or a girl.

"I'll see what I can do."

"I'd appreciate it."

"Listen, I have to get to work. And you need to rest. Tell me something, though. The night Pugh was shot, did you know you were pregnant?"

"Why?"

"I just want to know."

She stared at me for a moment, then slowly nodded.

"How about him? Did he know?"

"Roy Lee? Yeah, he knew."

"How did he feel about it?"

"I don't know. He wasn't too thrilled, if that's what you mean."

"He didn't want to have another child?"

"I don't see how it matters one way or the other now."

"I suppose not. One last thing. Hunneycutt, does he know you were pregnant?"

"No."

"He ought to. It could help your case."

"It's not his business. It's nobody's business but mine."

"But this might help you. If Pugh was beating you and you were pregnant and trying to protect your unborn baby, it might matter to a jury. They might see it as self-defense instead of murder."

"Dr. Jordan, I appreciate everything you done for me. I do. But it's not his business or yours or anybody else's."

"Rosa, I'm just trying to help."

"You can't help me," she said, resignedly looking out the window.

"Not if you don't let me. Is something the matter?"

She laughed hollowly. "They ain't nothing the matter. Nothing at all."

"Are you sure?"

"Yes, I'm sure. Just leave it alone, Dr. Jordan."

"But . . . "

"Leave it. Just leave it be," she said, wearily but with utter conviction. Then she turned her dark gaze on me. That same look she had that night in her trailer: fierce and vulnerable, scary and wounded all at the same time. I remembered that first time I'd visited her in jail. How when I'd asked her about the number of shots she'd fired, she said she wasn't sure. How I'd had the feeling then that she wasn't telling the truth. That's the feeling I had now.

"What's the matter?" I asked.

"I keep telling you, nothing. It's just that I don't care no more. I'm just plain tired. If they want to send me away for killing Roy Lee, let 'em. Don't you understand? I *don't* care."

"Don't talk like that, Rosa."

"I just want it to be over. The trial, everything. I'm tired. I'm so tired I could sleep for a hundred years."

"You've just had major surgery," I said. "You need to rest. I'll see you tomorrow. Promise you won't try anything else stupid on me, right?"

"Good-bye, Dr. Jordan," she said, closing her eyes.

I turned and headed out the door. I was waiting at the elevator thinking, not about Rosa but about Annabel and that picture she'd sketched of Will. How the mouth wasn't finished. I could suddenly see him, though, smiling, the dimples in his cheeks, his eyes gleaming the way they once did. The blond hair falling loosely in his face. I could feel the softness of his hand in mine. The smell of his breath when I bent to kiss him good night. The sound of his voice. Especially his laughter, thin and high and light as a spring breeze over the mountains. Everything about him came back to me in a dizzying rush that made my head spin with memory and with loss. That's when I thought about Rosa's baby, as if thinking about my own child was somehow connected to the one she'd lost. The two fused in my mind. And what came to me was something that would've explained why Rosa had been acting so defensive. I turned around and headed back for her room.

Her eyes were shut, her breathing inaudible. She might have been asleep, or she might have been just pretending. I walked over to her bed and leaned close to her. I could smell her hair, the sweat and sick odor of her body. I whispered into her ear. "Rosa?" Nothing. "Rosa, was it his? Was it Pugh's baby?"

If she heard me, she didn't give any sign.

# 24

*After I left* Rosa's room, I headed down to pathology, which was in the basement. A skinny, fortyish woman named Frieda Skillings was the lab tech who worked nights. She had brittle, teased blond hair, black at the roots, and eyebrows plucked clear away and penciled darkly in. I told her what I was looking for. She went over to a refrigerator and removed a small plastic container that looked like a piece of Tupperware.

"Here you go," she said flippantly. I took the lid off. There, lying on the bottom of the container, was a small, pale, grayish-blue thing, bloodied from the trauma, curled up like a bean sprout just beginning to unfold. Based on the size and the appearance of hair on the scalp, I'd have guessed more like seventeen weeks. And the sex was clearly differentiated, too. It was a girl. I'd seen my share of miscarriages and stillbirths and aborted fetuses. It usually didn't affect me. It was part of my job. Something you trained yourself to get used to. But for some reason, seeing this one bothered me a little.

"First she kills her fella, and now she does in his kid. She's a real Christian, that gal."

"I don't think either one was a choice she wanted to make," I explained. "I wonder if you could do me a favor and run some blood work on the fetus."

"I get off at seven, Dr. Jordan. What you looking for anyway?"

"Nothing fancy. Just blood type would be fine. Shouldn't take you long."

With a snort, she finally agreed to do it. I told her I'd wait while she ran the tests, and she snorted again. I had nothing to go on other than a gut feeling, which isn't like me at all. I was someone of science and logic, someone guided by reason and my head, and not by instinct or gut feelings. Still, something felt wrong here and I wanted to try find out what it was.

"The fetus has Type O blood," she said when she'd finished.

"You sure?"

"Sure I'm sure."

"Thanks, Frieda."

As I headed over to my office, I thought how the fetus had the same type blood as the mother. Which didn't come as a surprise. O was a fairly common blood type in American Indians. I had two out of the three pieces of the puzzle I'd need, though it was a little like a shot in the dark. Figuring out parentage from blood types wasn't particularly definitive, I knew. Not like DNA. But it was easy, and I wouldn't need a court order, which I wouldn't get now that I no longer worked for the DA's office. It was worth a try, I thought. Especially if I was going to stick my neck out, I'd need some evidence. The chances were slim, but if Pugh's blood happened to be AB, it would eliminate him as the father.

I got to the office even before Stella, who was always there first to open up and put coffee on. I called home to check on Annabel.

"You all right?" I asked.

"Yeah."

"Did you take your meds?"

"Of course. Long night for you, I guess."

"I'll say." I then went on to explain about Rosa Littlefoot.

"The poor thing. She going to be okay?"

"I think so. How's the baby?"

"Sitting here eating breakfast. Want to say hi to her?"

"Hello, sweetie," I said into the phone.

"She's smiling," Annabel said. "She recognizes your voice. I'll see you this evening then."

Next I called over to Henderson Memorial to check on the Potter child. He was holding his own, they said, which I took as good news. After I hung up, I went into the back and took a shower in the small bathroom there, then changed into some clean scrubs and a lab coat. I made coffee and ate an apple that was in the refrigerator. Stella was just arriving.

"You rose with the roosters, Doc."

"I was at the hospital. Emmilou gave birth last night."

"How did things work out?" she said, grimacing in expectation of bad news.

"She's recovering."

"And her young'un?"

"He was pretty sick. We had to transport him to Asheville."

"He gonna make it?"

"Hard to say."

"I'll say a prayer. By the way, I had to fit Mrs. DeForest in this afternoon. One of her usual complaints," she said, rolling her eyes.

I saw patients all morning. Around eleven I had a few minutes, and on the offhand chance I'd catch her in, I decided to call Bobbie.

"Counselor," I said, surprised to hear her voice.

"Doc? How are you?"

"Good. A little worn out. You hear about Rosa Littlefoot?"

"Yes. That was something. She didn't tell you she was pregnant?"

"She didn't tell anybody. Not even Hunneycutt. Could this have any bearing on her case?"

"Hunneycutt's already gone before the judge to ask for a postponement."

"No, I mean in her defense."

"He can certainly try to make it an issue. I know I would if I were in his shoes. He can say her hormones made her unstable. That she was protecting her child."

"Do *you* think it'll make a difference?"

"Might. There's still the drugs and the plan to flee, though. And the second shot."

"What if . . . "

"What if what?"

"Never mind. Can I ask you a favor? Do you have a copy of the Pugh autopsy handy?"

"Yeah."

"Could you tell me what his blood type was?"

"Why?"

"I'm checking for inherited birth defects," I lied.

"What on earth for? I don't think she needs to worry about getting knocked up again for a while."

"I'm just being a doctor looking after his patient."

"All right, hold on." After a few minutes she came back on the line. "It's A."

"You sure?"

"That's what it says here. Type A blood."

I'd known it was a long shot, and it didn't work out. Pugh might have been the father or he might not. His having Type A blood didn't prove it either way. Didn't prove that Rosa was lying to me. Didn't prove a damn thing.

"I'm sorry about the other night, Bobbie."

"No, I'm the one who should be sorry. I had no right to say what I did."

"I understand how you feel."

"It's just that I love you and I get jealous. And the longer she stays, the more I feel like I'm losing you to her."

"You're not. I love you, too. Listen, Bobbie, I got patients waiting. I'll give you a call."

"Bye, Doc."

After my last patient that day I was sitting in my office. I was eating a ham and tomato sandwich Stella had made me and sipping a glass of Scotch. I was thinking about Rosa. Maybe I was wrong about the child she'd been carrying not being Pugh's. Maybe I was barking up the wrong tree. A part of me just didn't want to believe her capable of cold-blooded murder. Yet another part sensed that she was. *Knew* that she was. You saw it in her eyes, in those cold, hard, dark eyes of hers. A woman equally capable of taking a gun and blowing Pugh's head off or sticking a wire up herself and ending the life she was carrying. Still, I couldn't help but wonder why she'd gotten so touchy on the subject of her baby. And why had she kept it a secret? Especially from Hunneycutt, who might have done something with it to help get her off.

· · ·

At home that night we had an early dinner. After we'd given Maria her bath and put her to bed, Annabel said she was beat and going to turn in early.

"Are you feeling all right?" I asked. She appeared exhausted, frayed, edgy. Her hair unwashed and scraggly. Though the surface of her eyes still glistened darkly, they looked unfettered, lacking focus, as if starting to lose some of their manicky intensity. For the first time they made me think of Rosa Littlefoot's eyes, the same unknowable quality in them, the same black depths and scary potential.

"I'm just a little tired. I haven't been sleeping very well."

"That's what I've been telling you. You take your meds today?"

"Yes. Would you stop asking me that. Every day it's the same thing. 'Did you take your meds?'"

"Do you think it might be a good idea if you went to see Dr. Butler?"

"So that bastard could put me in the loony bin? I'm not going to Cedar Crest, I tell you that right now. No fucking way."

"Nobody's saying anything about going there. How about you just go talk to Butler?"

"I told you, Stu, I feel fine. Maybe a little tired but fine. Now good night."

I stayed up till about eleven, had another drink, listened to some music. I kept wondering if maybe I should ask Kay to watch the baby, that it was getting too much for Annabel. Maybe I'd even give her sister Lenore a call and see if she could come up for a few days—though they hadn't been on good terms for some time and I doubted Lenore would agree. At the very least, I decided I would ask Kay to stop up during the day and look in on my wife. I knew she'd be more than happy to. Before going to bed, I checked the locks on the doors, though we'd had no more contact with the Pughs. Funny, but the place I'd lived in and felt safe in all these years no longer felt safe.

I fell asleep and soon found myself in the tangled clutches of several odd but interconnected dreams, one merging into the next like a collage done by a blind man. In one, I got something out of the refrigerator to eat. When I opened the plastic Tupperware container I found that it held the remains of a dead fetus, slathered with blood. In another, a man with half his head missing was asking what I'd done with his child. "She ain't your'n," he kept saying to me. "She ain't your'n." In yet another, I was going out with Cecil on a case. We were driving and driving, and when I finally turned toward him I saw it wasn't the sheriff at all. It was my father. Then, in the last dream, the one I had right before I woke, that woman was standing naked in the river, holding a child in her thin arms. Just before I could reach her, they both slid under the dark waters and vanished.

I couldn't say why, but as soon as I opened my eyes I felt the presence of someone in the room with me.

"Who's there?" I called, my heart still beating wildly from the dreams.

Silence.

"Who is it?"

Then a frail voice coming from the grainy darkness just inside the door said, "It's me."

"Annabel?" I said, making out finally the whiteness of her robe.

"Did I wake you?"

"That's all right. What's the matter?"

"Mind if I come in, Stu?"

"Why . . . no."

She walked over and sat on the side of the bed.

"I couldn't sleep," she explained. "I had a bad dream and when I woke up, I kept thinking about that poor woman."

"Who?" I asked, thinking for a moment of my own dream woman, the one who stood nursing a baby in the river.

"Maria's mother. Seems like one bad thing after another keeps happening to her."

"She brought some of it on herself."

"Some people can't help hurting themselves."

I didn't say anything to that. I sat up in bed.

"Can I get you something? Some tea?"

"No, I'm all set. I feel sort of like Will running into our bed after a bad dream. Do you remember how he used to have those dreams?"

"Yes. About wolves."

"That's right. He always seemed to dream about wolves. Why do you think that was?"

"I don't know. Maybe we read him something about wolves."

"I remember how his little heart would beat like crazy."

"Yes," I said.

"And he'd get in and snuggle between us. Only then could he go to sleep."

I heard her chuckle, then take a breath and sigh. I could tell something was up, more than just her concern about Rosa Littlefoot. I reached for the light but she said, "No, don't. I don't want the light on. It's better like this."

"Anna," I said, touching her shoulder. "What's really the matter?"

"Nothing," she said. Then, "Did you ever wonder what it was like for him, Stu?"

"What do you mean?"

"I mean how it was for him when he died."

"He died of hypothermia."

"But what was it *like*?"

"Why get into this now, Anna? It doesn't do any good."

"But I want to talk about it. I want to know how it would've been for him."

"He'd have become drowsy, cyanotic. When his core temp fell below 31 Celsius, he'd have lost consciousness. Drifted off to sleep."

"That's just biology. Just facts. I mean, what it was *like* for him out there all alone. Cold. Terrified. Have you ever wondered about that?"

"I suppose I have."

"I always pictured him calling for us. Waiting for us to come and rescue him. Me. Calling for his mommy. He was just five years old, Stu. Just a frightened little boy. All by himself up in those mountains."

Her voice cracked and she began to sob.

"Try not to think about it," I said.

"Hell, Stu, I don't want to *not* think about it. I've spent too much time trying *not* to think about it."

"But what possible good can it do now? To dwell on it."

"I don't know. Maybe nothing. Maybe you're right. Maybe I'm just being a masochist. It's just that you never wanted me to think about it. Never wanted me to talk about it. It was always taboo."

"I was only concerned about your health."

"I know. But whenever I'd want to talk about it, you'd always say try to forget about it. Don't let it upset you, Anna. Try not to think about it, dear."

"I didn't see the sense in tormenting yourself."

"I know you meant well. Only wanted to protect me. I know that. You were always trying to protect me from myself. But what if I didn't want to be protected? You ever think of that, Stu? I mean, our son was dead and it was my fault."

"Don't say that. It was an accident."

"See. You're still doing it. Protecting me. It wasn't any damn accident. We both know that. I should've been watching him and I wasn't. I was too absorbed in my work. My goddamned work! It was my fault. *My* fault. I've had to face that. Don't you see, all these years I've had to face that. That Ennis Pugh fellow maybe did me a favor after all."

"Don't pay any attention to what that jerk said."

"He was a jerk. But he was also right. I *was* to blame for Will's death. We both know that."

"Stop it."

"No, Stu. You know I'm right."

"Stop blaming yourself."

"It's true. If it hadn't been for me, he'd still be alive. Our son would be a young man right now and our lives, yours and mine and his, too, would have been something different. We've always known that. Why can't you admit it?"

"Because it's not true."

"Yeah? You even said it. Why wasn't I watching him? Remember, Stu?"

"I didn't mean that. You know I didn't."

"I know. But it *was* true all the same. I should've been watching him, instead of painting."

"Anna, it could've happened to anyone. Besides, I'm as much to blame as you. If I'd been there with you, he might still be alive."

"But you weren't there."

"I *should've* been."

"You had your work. But *I* was the one who was there, and *I'm* the one who let him wander off. We both know that. All this time you hated me for what happened."

"No, I didn't. I didn't."

"Yes, you did. You hated me. I don't blame you. I hated myself."

She continued sobbing, quietly, and I leaned toward her and put my arms around her. Her shoulders heaved and she put her head against my chest.

"I'm sorry," I said.

"It's not you who should be sorry. It's me. I'm so sorry for everything. For Will. For these last fourteen years of hell I put you through. Can you ever forgive me, Stu?"

"I forgive you."

"Do you? Do you really?"

"Of course I do."

We stayed like that for a while until her sobbing subsided.

"I know I don't have any right," she said, sniffling. "But can I ask a favor, Stu?"

"Sure."

"I don't want to sleep alone tonight."

"Anna, I don't know if that's such a good idea."

"Just for tonight."

"But . . . "

"I'm just talking sleep. That's all. Just to sleep. I'm dog tired and I can't sleep. I know if I slept for a little while I'd feel a whole lot better. Please, Stu."

I hesitated for a moment, knowing I shouldn't. Knowing it was wrong. Finally, though, I said, "All right," and lifted the covers, making room in my bed for her. She slid in and I put my arms around her. Her skin was cold as ice and she was shivering uncontrollably.

"I'm so coooold, Stuart," she stuttered, trembling.

"It's okay," I said. "It's okay. I'm right here."

# 25

*When I woke* the next morning, Annabel's side of the bed was already cool to the touch. The house was unusually quiet—no movement, no sound of footsteps or water running, no cries of the baby, none of those things which in the past couple of months I'd grown to expect.

"Anna," I called. The sound faded to silence. I quickly got up, threw my robe on, and headed downstairs, not knowing what I'd find. Annabel, though, was in the kitchen feeding Maria as usual. Her hair was still wet from a shower, and her face had a high flushed color to it. Though her hands still quivered slightly, her eyes appeared calm, even placid. She looked up at me and smiled; there passed between us some unspoken meaning.

"You hungry?" she asked. "I could fix you some eggs."

"No, I have to make early rounds." I bent and kissed Maria on the cheek. The baby grinned, her mouth encrusted with oatmeal. "*Gaa,*" she cried.

"How are you feeling?" I asked Annabel.

"Better this morning. I slept like a rock."

"Are you going to be all right with the baby?"

"Of course."

"You sure?"

"Don't worry, we'll be fine. Figure I'll do some work in the garden if it's nice out."

As I showered, I thought about the night before, what we talked about, her coming into bed with me. I wondered if she'd be all right to stay alone with the baby. She did seem better this morning. Rested. Calm and relaxed for the first time in days. She'd just been pushing it, that's all. Working too hard. Staying up late. All she needed was a good night's sleep. Before I left the bathroom, though, I opened the medicine cabinet and counted her pills. I knew she could have been throwing them down the sink, as she had in the past, but I counted them anyway. I brought one out, put it on the table, and said, "Here. Take that."

"Yes, Daddy," she said, pretending annoyance. I watched her swallow it the way you would a child to make sure she took her vitamin.

I got my coat from the closet and headed for the door. With Maria in her arms, Annabel followed me out onto the front porch. The day was warm and expansive, a bright spring day filled with untold possibilities. The mountains stood out clear and sharp as far as the horizon. You could even see the sun glinting off the radio tower on Hornyhead, four miles away.

"Looks like it's going to be a beautiful day," Annabel said.

"Now you're . . .  "

"*Yes,*" she cut in. "I'll be fine. Would you stop it? Please."

I nodded and was about to turn, when she touched my shoulder.

"About last night, Stu," she said.

"Don't worry about it. Nothing happened."

"I know. I just wanted to thank you."

All the way into Slade I kept repeating that: *Nothing happened.* Or did it? I called Kay on my cell phone. "I'm a little concerned about Annabel," I explained.

"She feeling poorly?" Kay asked.

"Just a little tired, I think. I was wondering . . . "

"What can I do, Stuart?"

"Would you mind looking in on her?"

"Be glad to. I'll take her up some sassafras tea. That's good for what ails you."

I made rounds at the hospital. I checked on Emmilou, who was doing better. Her blood pressure was down as was the edema. I'd put in a call to Asheville about her son; he was still critical, though no worse. Holding onto life. Fighting just like his mother always had. I was keeping my fingers crossed.

Rosa was awake when I entered her room. I looked over her chart. She was running a slight fever.

"How are you feeling?" I asked her.

"A sight better. How long will I have to be here?"

"That depends. You have a low-grade fever, but that's not unusual after major surgery. A couple of days you should be good as new." I wondered if I should say anything about stopping back in her room yesterday, about asking her what I'd asked her. Whether the child she'd aborted was Pugh's or not. But then I decided it didn't matter. And even if it did, short of a DNA test, which wouldn't happen, I'd never know. Just forget it, I told myself.

"Get some rest. I'll check in on you tonight," I said, turning to leave.

"Doctor Jordan," she called. "Did you find out . . . you know?"

"Yes. It was a girl."

"Was she . . . what I mean is, was she okay?"

"Everything was perfectly formed, if that's what you mean."

She nodded without changing expression. "Thank you."

As I drove over to my office I still couldn't shake the feeling that she was holding something back about the baby. What it was I couldn't say. Then again, maybe it was just my imagination. Or my penchant for order, for tying loose ends. Or perhaps it was simply the fact that having been an ME all those years, I'd grown suspicious of people, always suspecting the worst, forever looking beneath what folks told you for the ugly truth hidden in their hearts. I'd become cynical, which is no attitude for a doctor, and assuredly not an obstetrician, to have.

I had a pretty full schedule that day. We even had to squeeze in little Sue Ellen McCreadie, who wasn't so little now; she was in her ninth month and spotting, and still cranky as ever.

"I can't hardly sleep no more with this damn kid pressing on my guts," she complained when I showed her her baby on the ultrasound. "And I got to pee like ever' five seconds."

"It won't be much longer," I assured her.

"And *that one*," she said, meaning her mother, who was out in the waiting room. "She's drivin' me half crazy. Don't do this, don't do that. Drink up your milk. You want the baby to have strong bones, don't ya? Like I give a damn about the thing's bones."

"Your baby's doing just fine," said Cheryl McClain, the nurse.

"I ain't keepin' it. They can't make me."

After the exam, Cheryl said, "Emmilou'd give her right arm for a healthy baby, and this one can't wait to give hers up."

"Doesn't seem fair, does it?" I said.

At the end of the day I was in my office filling out insurance forms and sipping a well-deserved second Scotch. My knees were acting up again, a dull, throbbing ache, and the booze took the slightest edge off the pain. I was thinking about Annabel. About last night. About everything. While nothing had happened, I still felt funny. Guilty, I guess. As if I'd betrayed Bobbie. I tried to reassure myself I hadn't done anything to feel guilty about: You were only helping her. She couldn't sleep and you held her and comforted her as best you could. That's all it was. Nothing more.

Despite trying to explain it away, I continued to feel guilty. She was still my wife and we'd slept in the same bed; if Bobbie ever found out she'd skin me alive. Besides that, I didn't like what it boded. I knew that pretty soon, if she didn't leave on her own, I'd have no choice but to tell her to go. I knew I should have done it long before this. Knew putting it off all this time would just make her eventual going all the more painful. I tried to ease my mind by saying I could help her find a place, get her set up. An apartment close by. Perhaps a residential treatment facility or halfway house. Maybe even checking into a hospital for a while, that is, if I could talk her into it. I would call Dr. Butler and see what he recommended. But knowing that I'd eventually have to tell her to leave, I felt guilty for that, too. Hell, I felt guilty about nearly everything lately.

Stella poked her head into my office.

"I made you a cheese and tomato sandwich," she said.

"I'm not hungry."

"You eat this here sandwich, y'hear. You can't live on just work. And that poison there," she said, indicating the glass of Scotch.

I finally gave in and took it, more just to shut her up than out of hunger.

"Mind if I take a load off?" she asked.

"Actually, I have ... "

But she'd already plunked herself down in the seat across from me.

"Y'all all right, Doc?"

"Yeah, why?"

"I known you since you come to town. I can tell when you got something eating at you."

"I do have a few things on my mind right now, Stella," I said, hoping she'd take the hint and leave.

"How's things 'twixt you and Annabel?" she asked, almost as if she could read my thoughts.

"It's not like that between us."

"Like what? She's your wife, ain't she?"

"You know our situation."

"But she's never stayed this long before."

I nodded.

"So what-all does that mean?"

"I'm kind of busy right now, Stella."

She wagged her head. "Y'all got any more of that there whiskey, Doc?"

"Thought you didn't touch liquor?"

"I have me a drop now and then. Especially when I can't sleep."

I got the bottle out of my desk and poured her a drink. She took a sip, puckered her lips, and said, "Yee-who. Just like my grandpappy used to make. Lived out in Crooker's Branch. Ever tell you about him, Doc? Had him a still up in the woods. Used to sell it during Prohibition."

"I really have some work to do."

"You know I don't like to stick my nose into other folks' business," she said with an ironic smile. "But I hate to bite my tongue when I see someone I care about making such a royal mess of his life."

"You mean me?"

"Yeah, I mean you. Been doing it ever since your boy died."

"Stella, really. My personal life's not your concern."

"Hadn't you oughta make up your mind one way or t'other, Doc?"

"About what?"

"About *what*, he says. Lordy, it's no secret about you and that Mrs. Tisdale. It's all over town."

"So?"

"You love her?"

"That's my business."

"Well, *do* you?"

"If you must know, yes. I do."

"And your wife?"

I took a sip of my drink.

"I know how you loved Annabel. I don't think I ever seen a man love a woman the way you loved that gal. You still love her, don't you?"

"Of course not."

"The truth?"

"What is this, confession? No, I don't love her."

Stella took another drink, swished the booze around in her mouth like it was mouthwash, swallowed, then smiled at me. "I can read you like a book."

I was about to argue with her but stopped short.

"I didn't think so anyway," I said. "When she first came back, I swore I wouldn't let myself love her anymore."

"But you found out different, didn't you?"

"I don't know. Maybe."

"So what's it gonna be? Or should I say, *who's* it gonna be?"

I thought how that's what Bobbie had said to me. "I don't know."

"Comes a time a body's got to make up his mind. Like my grand-pappy used to say: Do your business, child, or pull up your britches and get the hell off the seat, they's other folks wanting to use it."

We both laughed at that.

"Thanks for that little piece of homespun advice, Stella."

"You're welcome," she said, finishing the last of her drink. "I'm heading out now. Howard'll be getting hungry. Anything I can do for you before I leave?"

"Yeah. Could you get me Maria Littlefoot's file?"

"What for?"

"I just want to check something."

She left the room and returned in a minute with the file.

"Don't stay too late. Get you some rest, Doc. You're looking awful peaked."

"Goodnight, Stella."

"Remember what I told you."

After she left, I poured myself another drink. I sat there for a while thinking about things. About Rosa. About Annabel. About Bobbie. Somehow all three women seemed connected in my mind. Their fates intertwined with each other's. And with mine, too. All of us linked in ways I couldn't begin to fathom. I sat there for the longest time trying to sort it out, realized I couldn't or didn't want to, and finally gave up.

I glanced down at Maria's folder, picked it up, opened it. I casually looked at the blood type. *B*, it said. I stared at it for a couple of seconds. My mind was so occupied with other thoughts, it didn't register right away. It was just an isolated fact, standing all by itself. *B*, I thought again. Her blood type was B. Only then did it sink in. Only then did I make the connection. I thought, Jesus. Then, Goddamn! I looked one more time to be certain, and then closed the folder and set it back on my desk. I took another sip of my drink, leaned back in my chair, put my feet up on the desk, and shut my eyes. What did it mean, I wondered. What? At the very least, it meant that Maria wasn't Roy Lee Pugh's child. She couldn't have been his. It was a genetic impossibility. I let that thought play around in my mind for a while, floating like a bobber in a stream, seeing where it went, waiting for something beneath the surface to yank it down. What followed, I wondered, from the fact that she wasn't his child? Maybe nothing. Then again, if it didn't mean anything, why did Rosa keep it a secret, which she obviously had? What was her reason for not telling anyone, just as she hadn't told a soul she was pregnant? What was she hiding? And were those two evasions connected somehow? There was only one thing I could say for sure: She'd had a lover. The father of Maria, whoever he was.

Then I opened my eyes and thought, What the hell do you think you're doing? Give it up, why don't you? Why make more trouble for yourself? What was it Rosa had said to you? *Just leave it alone.* She was right, too. You should just leave it alone. Back away. It didn't concern you anymore. You weren't the ME. And even if you were, you were trying to make this into something it wasn't. It was a simple case. They'd had a fight, maybe even over drugs like Bumgartner contended. Pugh hit her. She went for the gun. She shot him, and then to make sure he would never hit her again, she shot him a second time. Period. End of story.

And she'd never given me any cause to think it had happened another way. If this had been any other case, I'd have accepted that long ago. The problem was I'd become emotionally involved. I was thinking with my heart instead of my head, twisting facts around and letting my feelings get in the way. So what if Maria wasn't Pugh's child? So what if Rosa had had a lover? Ten lovers? What the hell did that prove? That she was unfaithful. That's all. Nothing more than that. I was just shooting in the dark, trying to come up with something because I didn't want to see Rosa go to jail.

Still, I thought, sipping my drink, the alcohol seeming to lure me into deeper waters. What was she so nervous about when I asked her why she'd concealed her pregnancy? What was that about? And there was something else, too, something even more puzzling: If she knew that Roy Lee wasn't Maria's father, why didn't she tell us, Hunneycutt or me, especially given the fact that she hadn't wanted the Pughs to get custody? If she knew Maria wasn't biologically related to the Pughs, there probably wouldn't have been a custody issue at all. So why had she concealed that? It didn't make any sense.

*Unless.*

Unless, of course, she were protecting the real father from something. That was a possibility. But from what? And why? Fear perhaps? I thought maybe I should call Bobbie and run my rambling thoughts by her. Then again, it was Rosa's secret, and whatever her reasons, she hadn't wanted anybody to know. She told me to stay out of it. Did I have the right to interfere? I chewed on that unpalatable morsel for a while, without completely swallowing it. It left a bad taste in my mouth. Finally, I told myself, yes, I did have the right. For Maria's sake if not for Rosa's.

I picked up the phone and dialed Bobbie's new number.

"It's me," I said when she answered. "Can I come over?"

"Now?"

"Yes."

"Why . . . sure. Gimme a few minutes. I was just about to jump in the shower."

After a while, I locked up and headed out. The night was cool and had a raw smell to it, like scorched rubber. Something over at the paper mill. I was nearing my truck when I happened to spot another truck parked on the street next to mine. It was a red Ford with a cap over the bed. I recognized it right away. A small, wiry man got out slowly and limped over to meet me.

"Evenin'," Glenn W. said. He was wearing grease-stained orange coveralls and a plaid hunting jacket. He was unshaven, and the gray stubble made his normally youthful-looking face appear old and grizzled. His liquid silver eyes squinted hard at me.

"What do you want?" I asked.

"Just wondering if'n you'd changed your mind about the child."

"No. I haven't."

"I was kinda hoping you had. Like I said, I'd prefer to settle this without having to deal with the law."

"Then why don't you give it up?"

"Ain't gonna give her up. She belongs with us. I lose in court, there's more'n one way to skin a cat."

"I have to go," I said.

"Some fellow steals something as belongs to me, I ain't gonna stand around and say thank you kindly. No sir. I don't give a damn who it is."

I thought of telling him what I'd found out, that the child wasn't his granddaughter, but I decided to hold off, at least until I found some things out.

"You stay away from me," I said, turning and heading for my truck.

"I won't let you just take her from me," he tossed after me. "Not without a fight. Count on that. Y'hear me?"

• • •

Bobbie's place was over near the college. The apartment complex, called Mountainview Manor, was where we'd found the kid who'd done too much coke and had gone into cardiac arrest.

"Hey, Doc," she said, as she opened the door to her apartment.

"Hello, counselor."

We both hesitated for a moment, an awkwardness having developed between us. Then she stepped forward and planted a kiss lightly on my lips. She smiled, said "C'mere," and added a real one. She wore a blue jogging suit, and she smelled of soap and hair conditioner. She had no makeup on, and her hair was wet and shone darker than usual, making her complexion appear pale, her eyes shadowy and tired.

"I catch you at a bad time?" I asked.

"Not really. Doing a little work. Come on in. Can I get you a drink?"

She poured me a Jack Daniels and we sat on the couch. I glanced around. Her place was cramped and outfitted with the sort of functional furniture I had out in my waiting room, but otherwise it was comfortable and neat.

"Least it's cheap," she said, screwing up her mouth.

"How have you been?"

"Busy. What with Troy laid up and me getting ready for the Littlefoot trial and everything. I was working on it when you called."

"Actually, that's why I stopped by."

"So this isn't a social visit, I take it?"

"I did want to see you," I said, taking hold of her hand. "But I came to talk to you about Rosa's case."

"What about it?" she asked curtly.

"Bumgartner hasn't changed his mind about first degree?"

"You know him. Stubborn as a mule."

"Even after he learned she was pregnant?"

"He doesn't think that makes any difference."

"And you agree with him?"

"Mostly. She still killed him, Doc. It doesn't change that. It might have an effect in the sentencing portion of the trial, but not in her basic guilt or innocence."

"But what if she *is* innocent?"

"You mean like temporary-insanity innocent?"

"No. I mean didn't-do-it innocent."

Bobbie let out a mocking laugh, then saw I was serious. "What?"

"I mean, what if she didn't shoot him?"

"Didn't shoot him? 'Course, she shot him."

"But I'm saying, what if she didn't?"

"Get out. If she didn't, who in the hell did?"

"Somebody who might have been there with her that night."

"What! Nobody's ever said anything about there being a *somebody* else. Even Hunneycutt concedes she was the shooter."

"I know. But what if there *was* somebody else at the trailer that night?"

"Doc, listen. There's not a single solitary shred of evidence to lead us in that direction. The gun had no prints on it but hers. She was the one called it in. She was the only one there when you arrived. Why, shoot, even she's never said there was anybody else. Maybe we ought to not talk about this."

"But there're some things just don't add up."

"Such as?"

"That third shot. The one in the ceiling."

"We've been over this before. You and I both know it could've been a warning shot."

"But think about it, Bobbie. If she were angry enough to do what she did to him, I don't think she'd warn him."

"All right. Then they were struggling for the gun. It went off. Simple. Why make it more complicated than that?"

"That's what I've tried to tell myself. Keep it simple. But Pugh was a big guy. Well over two hundred pounds. Rosa is hardly a hundred soaking wet. You're telling me she's going to be able to get a gun away from him? All by herself."

"It could happen. Stranger things happen all the time. You know how people can get when they're angry or afraid. Littlefoot could have had a rush of adrenaline. Besides, the autopsy report said Pugh had a blood alcohol count of over point two. He was shit-faced, they struggled with the gun, it went off. That explains the hole in the ceiling. Somehow she got the gun away from him and killed him."

"Does that make sense to you?"

"As much sense as what you're saying, Doc. What's this all about anyway?"

"I just have some questions. I mean all this time we're looking at this as a wife-kills-husband deal, in self-defense or cold blood—take your pick. But what if it wasn't?"

"This is getting weirder by the minute."

"No, listen. What if it wasn't? Or at least, what if it was *more* than that? A domestic, say, but somebody else was there with her."

"Jesus, Doc," Bobbie said, getting up and heading into the kitchen. She returned carrying the bottle of Jack Daniels. She refilled her glass and offered to refill mine.

"No, I've already had a couple."

"Suit yourself. This is starting to sound an awful lot like a grassy knoll to me, Doc. I never took you for one of those conspiracy kooks. Maybe the aliens beamed Elvis down and he shot Pugh."

"Funny."

"All right. For the sake of argument, let's say somebody else was there, and that that somebody did take Pugh out. Why? For the drugs? They left the drugs there. And what happened to this mystery man? If he took off, why didn't Rosa Littlefoot go with him? She had her suitcase all packed. Why did she stay behind?"

"I don't know."

"And most importantly, why didn't she tell us about this, quote-unquote, *other* person? Why would she go quietly off to prison, for somebody else, and leave her child? Explain that to me, Doc."

"I'm not sure. Maybe she's afraid of whoever it is. Maybe he threatened her if she told. Or her baby."

"Who?"

"I told you, I don't know," I said. "I'm just a hick doctor in way over his head."

She smiled, wanting, I could tell, to agree with me.

"Doc, you don't need to stick your nose in this anymore. You're not working for Bumgartner now. And you've already done everything humanly possible for that woman. Face it. You can't help her."

"That's what she said."

"She's right, too. As much as you don't like it, Rosa Littlefoot was all alone that night. The only other person there was the baby. Unless you're saying Maria shot her old man," Bobbie said with a smile.

"It wasn't her old man," I said calmly, evenly.

"What?"

"Pugh. He isn't Maria's father."

Bobbie knitted her brows and eyed me suspiciously.

"She tell you that hogwash?"

"No. The blood types don't match up. I checked. It can't be his kid."

"Really?"

"Yeah, really. It's not DNA, but it's pretty reliable." I explained about the blood types and how they didn't work out.

"So that's why you wanted to know Pugh's blood type? It wasn't about birth defects, was it?"

I shook my head.

"Well, I'll be."

"I don't know who the father is of the one she was carrying either."

"Does Hunneycutt know about this?"

"No. I just learned it myself. What do you think now?"

"Interesting."

"That all it is, interesting?"

"It might say something about her motivation. But it still doesn't change the basic facts of the case, Doc. Actually, it could even hurt her."

"How?"

"If a jury knew she was screwing around, unfaithful on top of being a killer. You could even make the argument that she killed Pugh in cold blood so she could be with her lover."

"You don't buy that, do you?"

"If you can speculate, why can't I?"

"Another thing to consider. She didn't want the Pughs to get custody of Maria. And yet she kept it a secret that the baby wasn't really a Pugh. Why would she do that? Unless she were afraid of something. Hiding something."

"You got me. Anyhow, that doesn't prove she *didn't* kill Pugh." She held her glass against her cheek, pensively staring off into space for a moment. "Still, Hunneycutt should know about this. You ought to give him a call."

"I wasn't sure it was my place to tell him."

"Your place? Geez Louise, Doc. You've been sticking your snout in this all along. Why stop now? Besides, this just might help her side. Only thing is, you didn't hear that from me, okay?"

"Sure."

We both fell uneasily silent.

"So how are things?" she asked finally. "At home."

"Annabel hasn't been feeling well lately. Actually I think it's more serious than that. I think she's getting sick again. I've talked to her about going to see her doctor. Maybe going into the hospital for a while. She wants no part of it."

"Is she a danger to herself?"

"No. At least not now anyway."

"Are you sure?"

"Pretty sure. I wouldn't leave her with the baby if I thought she wasn't safe." Bobbie stared at me, and I knew both of us were thinking the same thing: *Will.* "Besides, Kay Wallenbach, my neighbor, is looking in on her during the day."

"I'm not exactly an objective observer, Doc. But if you're asking my opinion, you could have her placed on a seventy-two-hour hold so they could check her out."

"I know. I've done that before. If she gets bad, I will."

"You know her better than I do." Bobbie set her glass on the end table behind her and leaned over and kissed me on the throat. "Can you stay for a while?"

"I'd like to. But I have to stop at the hospital."

"Oh, they won't care if you're a few minutes late," she said, starting to unbutton my shirt. She kissed my chest. I shuddered.

"I really should get going," I said.

"Jesus Christ, Doc!" she cried. She pulled away from me and stood up. She started pacing the room. "I've tried to understand your situation. Really I have. That's why I've given you plenty of space. Didn't make any demands. Figured I'd back off and let things with you and your wife sort of play out on their own. But like I told you, I'm not gonna sit around twiddling my thumbs forever. I got a life to get on with, too, you know. This isn't just about you and your problems."

"I know."

"Do you? I'm not so sure you do. You put everybody's damn needs ahead of your own. And ahead of mine, too. Your patients'. Annabel's. Why, even Rosa Littlefoot rates more than I do."

"You know that's not true."

"The hell I do."

I thought of what Stella had asked me earlier, about making a choice. And I thought about what had happened the previous night, letting Annabel sleep in my bed. I stood up and went over to her and put my arms around her.

"No," she said, trying to push me away. But I held her firmly to me and wouldn't let go.

"Listen to me. I love you," I said.

"Fuck you, Doc!"

"I do love you. You know that."

"*Do* I?"

"Yes."

She stared at me without blinking.

"Then start showing it, for Christ's sakes. Shoot, I got needs, too, you know."

"Don't you think I've missed being with you?"

"You sure could've fooled me. Here I am practically raping you and you gotta run."

"Did you want me to drop by, fuck you, and then have to leave?"

"I'd settle for just a little piece of you, Doc. That's not asking too much, is it? Just a little piece."

"I know. Look, I'm sorry. These last couple of months have been crazy. For both of us," I said. "Do you want me to stay for a while? I have a little time."

She shook her head petulantly. "I don't want you doing it because you're feeling sorry for me. I don't need your damn pity."

"I don't pity you. I love you. I do. And I'd love to stay if you still want me to."

She pursed her mouth and sighed. The anger in her eyes softened, was replaced by something like resignation.

"Dammit all to hell," she said. "My aunt was right. If only I'd learned to cook, maybe I wouldn't have had such problems with men. Why couldn't I find some average guy who loved just me. Is that asking too damn much? No, I had to fall in love with Don Juan. And now with Albert fuckin' Schweitzer."

"Is that who I am? Albert fuckin' Schweitzer?" I said, smiling. Bobbie, finally, stubbornly, gave in and smiled back. I kissed her on the mouth, which was cool and tasted of whiskey. I led her over to the couch.

"Wait. We got to pull this thing out first," she said.

# 26

*Noon on a* blustery Sunday a few weeks later. I was standing at the kitchen sink finishing my coffee and staring contemplatively out the window at a garishly bright spring day. Sunlight scorched the hills, and the wind was whipping the treetops and driving clouds scudding across a severe blue sky. A red-tailed hawk wheeled high over the mountain, riding the air currents. Annabel was up in her garden working. Yet it wasn't really a garden anymore, just a gaping reddish wound in the flesh of the mountain. John had stopped by the day before with his tractor and plowed everything under—the tangle of roses and azaleas, the half-dead burning bush plants and hostas, the insidious kudzu and bullying rhododendrons, even the slender saplings that had taken root in the years she had left the spot untended. All of it fell before the plow blade. Then he returned with his wheelbarrow and diced the large clumps of sod into smaller ones. And what he'd missed, Annabel was now smashing and pulverizing and bludgeoning with a hoe. She'd been at it since right after breakfast, working nonstop, fiercely wielding the hoe like some sort of weapon against an enemy to which she would show no mercy.

I was planning on bringing Maria in to visit with her mother. I hadn't been to see Rosa since she'd left the hospital. Her trial, which had been postponed while she recovered from surgery, was now slated to start in a week. I'd called Hunneycutt, as Bobbie had suggested, and told him about Maria not being Pugh's biological child. He didn't seem to think much of that. In fact, just as Bobbie had surmised, he thought it might do more harm than good.

"Last thing we need is for the jury to get wind of her fooling around on Pugh," he explained in his slow, pedantic way. "Her being a whore on top of ever'thing else won't help none."

I tried to get him to see the possible implications—of there being a lover, of her trying to protect the identity of the child's real father, and where such a line of questions, if pursued rigorously, might lead. He listened politely, made wet-sounding *uh-hum*s deep in his throat, and condescendingly thanked me for my concern.

"Hi-ever," he told me, "I think I know what's best for my client, Dr. Jordan."

"But . . . "

"And what's best at this late stage isn't grasping at straws," he said. "It's creating a solid defense based on her mental state at the time of the murder. Now if you want to do her any good, I'd appreciate it if you kept this under your hat. 'Course if it's true, we'll ask for a DNA and use that later, if and when it comes down to a custody fight with the Pughs. Good day to you, Dr. Jordan," he added, before hanging up.

Annabel worked relentlessly, attacking the ground, beating it with savage strokes of the hoe. Even from here I could see that her face was flushed, and despite the gusting wind, sweat matted her hair into thin black streaks on her forehead. Except for the night she spent in my bed, she'd continued not to sleep well. Most nights she slept hardly at all, an hour or two on a good night, some nights not at all. Yet at breakfast she'd be sitting there, full of nervous energy. Her hands, I noticed, began to tremble again. They shook as she lit her cigarette or sipped her tea. She'd sit across from me rapping her knuckles on the table or brushing hair back from her face or picking at a scabbed-over cut on her forearm she'd gotten from pulling out a rosebush. They made me think of my father's hands, when the Parkinson's was well advanced. And her eyes had that all-too-familiar unsettled look, darting restlessly about, as if nothing they lit upon was the thing she was searching for. At night, I'd hear her wandering through the house, shuffling about, occasionally muttering to herself. Other times, when I'd get up, I'd see the light under her door. I hadn't disturbed her again, hadn't bothered her when she was painting, or whatever it was she did in the room at night. Nor had she come back to my bedroom after that one time. In fact, we both pretended it hadn't happened.

It was clear, though, that she was getting worse, losing control bit by bit, her grip on things becoming more tenuous by the day. For instance, at supper one night she told me she and Kay had taken Will for a walk down to the river. I stared across the table, waiting for her to catch her mistake. When she didn't I said, "Will?"

"Yeah. The fresh air did him good."

"You mean Maria, don't you?"

She frowned and stared at me, momentarily lost. You could see the gears in her head turning, trying to mesh, but for several seconds they kept missing, slipping by each other. Finally, realizing her mistake, she said, "Of course. What did I say?"

"You said *Will*."

"No, I didn't."

"Yes, you did."

Another time I came downstairs in the middle of the night to get a drink of water. I found her in an old flannel nightgown, down on her hands and knees under the sink.

"Anna, what are you doing?" I asked.

"Setting up some traps. Do you know we have mice?"

"Mice?"

"You didn't hear them?"

"No. It's three in the morning."

"I'm surprised you didn't hear them. They were making such a racket, I couldn't sleep. But I'll fix their little wagon."

For a while at least, before she got bad, I felt comfortable enough having Kay come up here and stay with Annabel and the baby during the day. Kay was good with my wife, a natural nurse. Plus, having the baby around had seemed to have an ameliorative effect on Annabel's condition, to calm her and give her something to do, and I didn't want to deny her that if I could help it. But as her mental state continued to slip, I decided I couldn't take the chance anymore. So I called Kay and asked her if she'd mind watching Maria for a little while.

"She gettin' bad again, Stuart?" she asked.

"I'm afraid so."

"Oh, Lordy," the old woman sighed. "And she was coming along so good, too."

Kay agreed to watch Maria for me. The next morning I was packing the bag with the baby's things.

"What are you doing?" Annabel asked.

"I'm bringing her down to Kay's," I explained.

"Whatever for?"

"You're not in any condition to look after her."

"What are you talking about? I feel fine."

She tried to grab hold of the baby's bag, but I pushed her hand away.

"No, she's going down to Kay's," I said. "I think you need to go to the hospital."

"Like hell."

"Just for a while."

"I told you, I don't need any goddamn doctors poking and prodding me. Anybody can see that I'm perfectly fine."

"Anna, you're not fine," I said. "You're sick. And you need more help than I can give you."

"*You!*" she cried, suddenly and fiercely angry. She hissed at me, "I don't want your *damn* help. I don't trust you. You and that bitch you're fucking behind my back." I stared at her, both shocked and not shocked by this brutal outburst. I was well aware of how quickly she could change, turn mean-spirited, ugly. She smiled wickedly at me, her missing teeth dark, vicious holes in her pallid face, her eyes gleaming savagely. "Go to her if you want. Go fuck her. You think I'm stupid? You think I don't know?"

"Annabel. Please. I'm just thinking of you."

"Thinking of me! Huh! That's a good one. When have you *ever* thought of me?"

"You need to get some help," I tried to explain, though I knew there was no sense talking to her when she was like this.

"You think I don't know you've been with her? I could *smell* that whore on you. You just want me out of here so you can go back to her."

"Stop it."

"The truth hurts, doesn't it, Stu?"

"That's not why I think you need to go to the hospital. You need help."

"You're gonna stand there and tell me you don't want me out of here? That it wouldn't be convenient if I got carted off to Cedar Crest again so you could go back to screwing blondie."

"Stop it. For God's sakes, Anna."

She tossed her head back and laughed out loud, a high, shrill sound. "Put me away and then the two of you could fuck in our bed. That's what you want, isn't it? Me out of here so you can go back to screwing her."

"Why don't you just leave then?" I said, half regretting the words as soon as they were out of my mouth. She stared at me, a lingering smile about her mouth. But I could see that what I said had hit the mark. Her eyes appeared jolted, the anger replaced by surprise. I thought of saying

I didn't mean it, yet the truth was I did. I wanted her gone. Realizing it was pointless trying to talk to her, I picked up Maria from her highchair and headed out to the truck.

"Maybe I'll do just that," Annabel called after me. "Maybe I'll get out of your life permanent-like."

Part of me feared that she would do something drastic, maybe hurt herself. And yet another part didn't care. I'd had about all I could take. When I got home that night, though, she was still there. I could hear her moving around up in her room. For the next couple of days, she avoided me. I would bring Maria down to Kay's in the morning and pick her up in the evening. Annabel mostly stayed in her room.

One night, I was in my study doing some work; she knocked on the door. When she came in, she sat down and said, "I'm sorry, Stu. I didn't mean what I said. I was just in an ornery mood. I was really tired. But I'm feeling better now. Really, I am." She didn't look any better. She was hollow-eyed, and her face was drawn and pallid, except for the dark circles under her eyes. "Do you think the baby could stay with me tomorrow?"

"I don't think that's a good idea, Anna."

"Please. I swear I'm feeling a lot better now."

"No."

I kept wondering if I should have her committed. On the one hand, while Annabel wasn't nearly as bad as she could sometimes get, I knew enough about the course of her illness to be worried. The signs of her slowly spinning out of control became more unmistakable with each day. On the other hand, I didn't want to act hastily. I didn't like having her committed unless I was pretty sure it was the right thing. A last resort. I knew how she hated, even feared, going into the hospital. And I didn't look forward to having to do it, even if I felt it necessary: the crying and pleading that would ensue, the curses and recriminations. The raw, shameful ugliness of actually getting her from here to a hospital bed. I could still remember that time I'd driven her to the ER in Slade, how she'd tried to leap from the truck. And I suppose, too, part of me wondered if Annabel, in her own twisted way, was right about me trying to get her out of the way— if I wanted to commit her not so much for her own sake as for mine.

So I called Dr. Butler and talked to him about my concerns. After hearing how she was behaving, he said for me to try to convince her of the need to see him. If she was as bad as she sounded, he could have her committed, or at least placed in a halfway house that had twenty-four-hour supervision. We left it that I'd try to talk her into seeing him voluntarily, but that if things got worse I should call an ambulance and have her transferred to Cedar Crest. In the meantime, I'd wait, keep an eye on her, make sure she took her meds. I even called Lenore, to see if she might come up and stay with Annabel for a few days. But as I expected, she wanted nothing to do with her sister. "I feel sorry for you, Stuart. I really do. But I've done all I can for my sister."

I ended up arranging for Mrs. Mason, a woman who lived at the bottom of our road, to stop by a couple of times during the week, under the pretext of doing some cleaning but mostly to look in on my wife. And Kay said she'd drop in with the baby most days to keep her company. Perhaps, too, I thought if I just waited and didn't do anything, Annabel would, as she had so many times in the past, simply take off on her own. Then I wouldn't have to make the decision to have her committed. I knew that was selfish, not to mention gutless, of me. And as a doctor, I knew I was putting my own feelings and concerns and welfare ahead of those of a patient. But in some ways it seemed the better option to let her decide her own fate. Each morning when I woke up, I half expected her to be gone, to have vanished into thin air the way she usually did. Yet each day I still found her here.

Somehow I thought the upcoming trial connected in a way to Annabel's worsening mental state. She would read about it in the paper and ask me questions.

"Do you think she'll be convicted?" she'd ask, looking up from a front-page article about the Littlefoot trial in the *Slade Messenger.* "How long do you think they'll give her if she's found guilty?"

"I don't know."

"Will they give her life?"

"They could."

"That doesn't seem right."

•  •  •

When Annabel came in from the garden one day, she was carrying a bouquet of wildflowers: red-striped spring beauties, purple larkspur, snowy-white bloodroot.

"Look what I picked," she said, kicking off her muddy boots on the mat at the back door.

"I'm heading into town now," I told her. "I'm going to bring Maria in to see her mother. Do you need anything?"

"Mind if I come with you?"

"Are you sure? I might be a while."

"I can keep myself occupied. I feel like taking a ride."

We drove into town without exchanging a word. Annabel held the bouquet, wrapped in tinfoil, and stared out the window. Her hands, which were cracked and raw, the nails dirty from working in the garden, made the flowers quiver, as if in a wind. On her lap rested a manila envelope she'd brought along.

I pulled into the courthouse parking lot and started getting Maria out of her car seat.

"I'll be about half an hour. You'll be all right?"

"Here," she said, handing me the envelope. "Give that to her, would you?"

"What is it?"

"Just a little something."

When I got inside the courthouse building, but before I went down to the sheriff's department, my curiosity got the better of me. I opened the metal clasp and took out what was inside. It was a pencil sketch of Maria, similar to the one I'd seen on the deck that time, only smaller. It was actually pretty good. It looked just like her. The face was round and pudgy and dimpled, the gaze that earnest one of Maria's.

"What do you say, Cecil?" I said to Sheriff Clegg, who was mopping up something nasty looking on the floor when I came in.

He paused to glance at me and the baby, then went back to wiping up the floor. "Crazy Bob got sick on me," he said, by way of explanation. Crazy Bob, the town drunk, was a regular customer of Cecil's.

He took his sweet time, going back and forth over the same spot. After a while, I said, "I'm kind of in a hurry, Cecil. Do you think you could let me in?"

"Sorry, Doc. Can't."

"What do you mean, you can't?"

"I mean, I can't let you see the prisoner. Bumgartner's orders."

"You pulling my leg?"

"Nope. Them's his orders."

"Why the hell not?"

"I don't know. That's just what he said. Only next of kin and Hunneycutt. I guess with the trial coming up and everything, he's not taking any chances."

"Chances? What's he think I'm going to do, break her out of jail?"

Cecil scratched his beard noncommittally and went back to mopping.

"What's the real reason?"

The sheriff started to say something, then shrugged and fell silent.

"Cecil, it's me you're talking to. What did he say?"

"I reckon he thinks you might be on her side now."

"I'm just bringing her baby in to visit."

"I know. That's what I told him. But he said I wasn't to let you in. Sorry."

"C'mon, Cecil. I've been in a dozen times. Just a few minutes."

"Listen, I don't like that fat fuck any more'n you. But I could lose my job. Hell, I can't afford to be unemployed right now."

"Five minutes. I'll be in and out. I promise."

"Jesus, Doc. You're puttin' me on the spot."

"As a favor. It's Sunday. Nobody'll know."

"*I* will."

"Since when are you so damn particular? Besides, you owe me one. Remember?" I said, looking at Maria.

Cecil straightened up, rubbed the back of his thick neck, groaned, "*Goddammit!* All right, five minutes. That's all you get. And if anybody comes in, y'all are looking at her incision, y'unnerstand?"

Rosa was sleeping when Cecil let me in. She sat up with the clank of the keys in the door and rubbed her bleary eyes. She still appeared pale from the surgery, but she looked healthier than the last time I'd seen her at the hospital.

"Didn't know you were coming," she said, yawning.

"I figured I'd stop by. Look who I brought."

"Sweetie," she said, as I handed Maria to her. Right off, the baby started to arch her back and squawk. Rosa spoke to her softly, cooing and kissing and rocking her, but nothing she did would stop the baby's crying.

"Maybe you better take her," she said. "Till she simmers down."

I sat in the chair and took Maria's jacket off. After a while she slowly stopped her fussing and glanced around the room.

"Sheriff says we only got five minutes. Here," I said, handing the envelope to her.

"What's this?"

"My wife wanted me to give it to you."

She opened it and took out the drawing. She stared at it for several seconds.

"It's real nice. Tell her thanks, would you?"

"I will. How you feeling?"

"Better. I've got my appetite mostly back. What's it doing out? I never know being in here."

"It's sunny."

We fumbled for conversation for a few moments. After a while, she slid over so she was closer to her daughter. She took Maria's pudgy, silken hand and held it. The baby gazed at her mother warily. Then she pulled her hand back and looked up to me, before turning and burying her face in my chest.

"Oh. My little butterfly's afraid of me," she said, smiling sadly. The smile turned her face nearly pretty again, but mostly what it did was make her look emptied of something necessary, some essential thing she needed to keep on living. She seemed suddenly someone who was beyond being old or young, or anything in-between, someone ancient and ageless at once, the sort of Indian woman you might see over on the reservation pushing a shopping cart along the street, whose age you couldn't decide, the way you couldn't know the age of a tree unless you cut it down and counted the rings inside. "You remember me, little *ka-ma-ma*." But Maria kept her face buried, fearful of this now strange woman.

"Do you want that to happen?" I asked. "For her to forget you?"

"It's not like I can do much about it."

"It doesn't have to be this way."

"What other way can it be?"

"You don't have to go to prison and let him leave you holding the bag."

"Who? Her father?"

I looked over at her. She held my gaze for a second or two, then looked down at Maria. "Yeah," I said. "Her father."

"That one always left me holding the bag. Why should it be any different now that he's dead?"

"Pugh's dead. What I was talking about is this child's father."

She looked up from the baby and at me again, knitting her brows. She stared at me for several seconds, unsure what I was getting at.

"What in the hell you talking about, Dr. Jordan?" she said, forcing a gritty laugh out of her lungs. "You been drinking?"

"I think you know what I'm talking about."

"I can't say I do." She tried to ignore me, tried to pretend what I'd said meant nothing to her. She reached cautiously for the baby's hand again, and this time, still eyeing her suspiciously, the child allowed her to take it. In fact, Maria wrapped her small hand around one of Rosa's long thin fingers and wouldn't let go. "That's my little butterfly. My sweet little one."

"I know," I said.

"Know?" she repeated, not making eye contact. "What do you know?"

"About Maria. About her not being Pugh's child." For about five seconds neither of us spoke. Rosa continued to play with the baby. "Got nothing to say?"

"Hunneycutt already told me you said something to him about that. That's plain crazy."

"Is it?"

"Yeah. *Crazy.*"

"I checked the blood types."

"So?"

"Pugh couldn't be the father of this child."

"Well he is. *Was.* Whatever."

"He couldn't be. Either that or you're not the mother."

"Now I *know* you been drinking. I'm her mother, all right. Maybe somebody made a mistake. With the blood stuff."

"It's no mistake, Rosa. The blood types don't work out. This child couldn't possibly be the offspring of Pugh. Somebody else had to be this child's father."

"That's just a lot of bullshit, Doc."

"Is it? You know what I'm talking about."

"You're talking nonsense is what you're talking."

"What I want to know is why."

"Why what?"

"Why did you go out of your way to hide it from everybody?"

"I didn't hide nothin'."

"Yes, you did. Why? Was it another one of the Pughs?"

"What?"

"Was it Tully?"

"Tully?" she said with a fluttering laugh.

"You said he was nice to you. That he used to come around. Was he the father? Is he the one you're protecting?"

"I ain't protecting nobody from nothing. I don't know what the hell you're gettin' at."

"Or did he threaten you?"

"Nobody threatened me. Except Roy. And he's dead for it."

"Did Tully say he'd hurt your baby if you told on him? Is that it?"

"Why do you keep bringing up Tully? He's got nothing to do with this."

"No?"

"No."

"Who was it then?"

"Who was what?"

"Who was with you that night?"

"Jesus. You're talking through your ass now, Doc."

"Was somebody else there with you the night Pugh was killed?"

She released the baby's hand, got up, and walked away from me. She stood over near the sink, facing the wall, her arms wrapped around herself. With her narrow, bony back to me, she said, "I was there by myself. Pugh hit me, like he always did, and I wasn't going to take it no more. That's what happened. End of story."

"Then why did you hide the fact that this baby wasn't his? If you knew it wasn't and you didn't want her going to the Pughs, why didn't you just tell everybody the truth? The Pughs wouldn't have had any grounds for custody."

"I told you the truth. It was Pugh's baby."

"That's a lie."

"All right. Just say for a minute she's not Pugh's. So what? It doesn't mean a goddamn thing."

"So if it didn't mean anything, why did you lie about it? Why cover it up?"

"I didn't cover anything up."

"Just like you covered up the fact that you were pregnant. Was that one Pugh's baby, too?"

"Yes."

"Or was that just another lie? I should've seen it before, but I guess I'm a little slow. Did somebody threaten to hurt your baby if you told the truth? It that what this is about?"

"Hunneycutt says I'm not supposed to talk to you."

"I always felt something didn't fit. You calling the police. Your bags being packed. The fact that there was that third shot in the ceiling. Something rubbed me the wrong way from the very beginning. I just didn't see it till the other day."

"I'm not saying no more," she exclaimed.

"All right. Don't. Just listen then. Maybe Hunneycutt's onto something with this battered-wife defense of his. Maybe he'll pull it off and they'll set you free. But I'd bet dollars to donuts he'll lose and you'll end up in prison for a long time. A very long time. By the time you get out you'll be an old woman, and this little girl will be grown up and she won't remember you from a hole in the wall. Is that what you want?"

"It doesn't matter what happens to me. I just want her to be all right."

"She won't be, growing up in some foster home. Or with the Pughs."

"Pughs? But you said you wouldn't let that happen. You *promised,*" she said, her tone that of a small whiny child pleading against an adult's threat.

"Yes, I did promise. But I shouldn't have. I'm an old man and I had no business promising you that. I'm tired, and I just can't be responsible for her any longer. Do you hear what I'm saying?"

"You lied."

"No, I didn't lie. At least not on purpose. And not any more than you lied to me. Besides, you had no business asking me to take her in the first place. We both said things we shouldn't have. But that's neither here nor there now. Without me in the picture, the court more than likely will hand your baby over to the Pughs."

"No," she said.

"Yes, that's what they'll do. Unless you tell them the truth. That she wasn't Roy Lee's kid."

"It was his. It was."

"Stop lying, for Christ's sakes. It's getting too late. Tell me the truth. What really happened?"

"I told you."

"You want the Pughs to get custody of her? That's what will happen. That or they'll stick her in some foster home and she'll get handed around like an old penny."

"You promised you'd see to it she was looked after right."

"She'll end up just another Indian in some white foster home. But then, you know about foster homes, don't you? What happens in places like that."

"You promised me."

"Some half-drunk foster parent will take a shine to a pretty little girl like this."

"Stop it."

"And one night when his wife's at work, he'll come into her room with his greasy paws . . . "

"Stop it," she hissed, her shoulders starting to quake. "*Stop* it!"

"Who was with you?"

She finally turned to confront me, her eyes moist with tears yet contracted into tight dark orbs of anger, hard and deadly as tumors.

"I trusted you, you sum' bitch. I trusted you."

"I'm sorry."

She was silent for a while. Her body seemed to go slack; the fury drained out of her eyes and was replaced by a stony resignation that was something to behold. I shouldn't have been surprised anymore by what she was capable of, but the truth is I was. Jesus, I thought.

"If they want to send me away for killing him, let 'em. I'd do it again ten times over if I had the chance. Now take her and get the hell out. And don't come back—neither of you. She might as well be dead to me. G'won, get out of here."

Walking out of the courthouse I wondered if I'd done the right thing. If I'd pushed her too hard. Or then again, not hard enough, for I still didn't have any answers. Or maybe she *was* telling the truth. Not about Maria being Pugh's, that was a lie. But the rest—that it didn't matter if the baby was or not. And maybe it didn't. Maybe I was crazy, just like she said. Then again, maybe I just wasn't seeing something, something right in front of my nose. As I approached the truck, I realized Annabel wasn't sitting in the front seat. *Dammit,* I thought.

I drove around town looking for her. Glancing in the windows of stores, mostly closed on a Sunday afternoon; driving past the park, filled now with children playing. Past the green in the center of town. Past my office, thinking she might have walked there for some reason. Past the bus station. I crossed over the Little Addie and drove along Center, turned right on Highland, circled back on Mill. I then turned left onto Brevard and drove across Main and continued up until I reached Elm, the street Annabel grew up on. Nothing. No sign of her. Minutes passed.

A half hour. Then an hour. I wondered where she went. What she was doing? Was this just a momentary lapse? Or did it mean she'd taken off again?

Finally it hit me—the flowers. I should've guessed, but my mind was still half on Rosa Littlefoot. I drove out to Laurel Branch, turned onto it and started climbing the road up into the hollow. Just past the Methodist Church, I pulled in. Out in the cemetery behind the church, I saw a solitary figure kneeling near a grave under the big sycamore tree. I got out of the truck, unbuckled Maria from her car seat, and started walking across the grass.

"You had me worried," I said to her. She was on her hands and knees, pulling weeds from around Will's stone. The sound was sharp, guttural: *grrrpp, grrrpp.*

"Sorry. I just felt like walking. It's such a fine day," she said, looking up at me, shading her eyes against the bright sunlight. "She like it?"

"What?"

"The picture."

"Oh. Yes. She said to say thanks."

With a stick, she'd carved a hole in the ground, and she stuck the bouquet of flowers she'd brought in the hole.

"They don't do much in the way of upkeep, do they?" she said.

"No. I suppose not. Are you ready to go?"

She continued clearing around the stone.

"Twenty," she said after a while. "That's what he'd have been. Twenty years old."

"Yeah."

"What do you think he'd have been?"

"You mean like a career? Who knows? He was just five," I said, my voice sounding chilly and reserved even to my own ear. I was annoyed she'd ask such a question.

"Maybe a doctor? He had slender hands. Like yours."

"Maybe. Let's go."

"Wait. Just a few minutes more. It's been such a long while since I've been here. I forgot how quiet and peaceful it is."

"It's Sunday. During the week it's not so quiet. There are houses going in up the branch."

But she ignored me. She went back to pulling up weeds. Her movements were quick, desperate almost, as if she were picking ticks from a child's skin. I looked down at her, at the top of her head. In the harsh sunlight the whiteness of her skull beneath the dark hair made me think of something raw and exposed, vulnerable. A feeling welled up in my chest. I found myself hating her suddenly, hating her for bringing all this down on our heads, for opening the door and inviting in such sadness and misery and affliction. Even though I still believed Will's death *was* an accident, even though I knew she couldn't help her illness, help who and what she was—in spite of all this, I hated her. Hated her the way one does an inanimate object that brings about pain—a door that stubs a toe, a storm that wrecks a house, cancer that eats away at a life. At the same time I realized something else; I realized I still loved her, loved her in spite of everything that she did and was, in spite of everything that had happened. Loved her and would continue to love her, no matter what.

"Anna," I said, softer now. "Let's go home."

Without looking at me she said, "I know you're not the sort to believe in signs, Stu. But do you think this could be a sign?"

"A sign?" I said, wondering where this was going. "Of what?"

"For us. That all this happened for a reason."

"All what happened? What are you talking about?"

"A sign from God or . . . something. That that poor woman killed her husband and is going to jail, and we ended up with her baby. It couldn't just be pure chance."

"Anna . . . "

"I'm not wishing bad luck on her or anything. But since it had to happen, why couldn't it be that the child was given to us for a reason."

I started to speak, to say that was crazy.

"Just think about it, Stu."

"She's not ours, Anna."

"I know. I know that. But if her mother goes away to prison, somebody's got to take care of her. So why couldn't that somebody be us? And why couldn't we look at it like she was meant to be with us for some kind of reason?"

*Us,* I thought.

"Think about it, Stu," she said, getting up and coming over to me and the baby. She touched the baby with her hands, which smelled, literally, of the grave. I thought of that line from *Lear,* when the old king says his hands smell of mortality. "It would be like she was a gift to us."

"No," I said. "Don't think that."

"Why not? Like somebody was giving us a second chance. Like God was telling us, 'Here. You take this child and start over. I'm giving you another chance.'"

"No, Anna."

"But why?"

"Because it's not, that's why."

"Then why did she end up with you? Why did that woman ask you to watch her? And why did you say yes? Think about it, Stu. Why did you come to see me that night and tell me about it? Why? Unless it was for a reason. Hasn't it even crossed your mind?"

"No," I replied. A lie, I realized. I could remember thinking exactly the same thing that first night I'd brought Maria home and fell asleep with her in Will's bed. On his birthday she'd been dropped into my lap. How could it be anything other than a sign, I'd thought then and still thought now. "You mustn't look at it like that, Anna. You mustn't."

She was going to say something but held off. Tears started running down her cheeks. When she wiped her eyes, her hands left a streak of dirt, dirt from our son's grave, across the pale flesh of her face.

"We should go," I said, putting my arm around her. I felt her shoulders trembling as we walked across the cemetery.

# 27

*I was doing* an ultrasound on Joleen Pollard, an elementary school teacher who was a primigravida with twins. Everything was looking fine with her. She giggled as we watched on the monitor a pair of second-trimester fetuses moving about in the cramped, grayish confines of her womb. It had been like that the past few days, quiet and routine, just the way I liked it: the office visits predictable; the tests negative or positive, depending on the wished-for outcome; the deliveries going without a hitch, healthy full-term babies jumping into my hands like fish into a boat. That's when Stella poked her head in the exam room and told me Kay Wallenbach was on the phone. "Says it's important, Doc." I let Cheryl finish up while I went to answer the phone.

"I sure hate to bother you at work, Stuart," Kay said. "But it's Annabel."

"What's the matter?" I asked, fearing the worst. I could remember the time Kay had called me after finding my wife unconscious at home. I shouldn't have left her alone, I thought. I should've made her go somewhere for help. I was kicking myself that I hadn't and knew if anything bad happened to her it would be my fault.

"Don't you worry none," she replied, catching the panic in my voice. "She's right here with me. She's fy-on now. Just got herself all worked up is all."

"What happened?"

"I'm not altogether sure. From what I can make out, she was home and this feller come in the house."

"Somebody came in our house? Who?"

"Don't rightly know. Scared the living daylights outa her. She called down and John went up to check ever'thing out. He brung her down here."

"But she's all right, you said?"

"Yes. She's upstairs changing the baby right now. She didn't want me callin' and apesterin' you at work. But I thought you oughta know."

I explained to Stella something had come up at home. It was nearly four o'clock and I had only a few patients left, so I told her to have Cheryl and Gladys take over.

"Nothing serious, I hope, Doc," Stella said.

"I don't know."

When I got to the Wallenbachs', John took me aside and whispered, "I had me my shotgun when I went up to your place. Just to be on the safe side. Don't s'pose you need two guesses as to who it was, Doc." He looked at me, his dark, hawklike features tense with seriousness.

Annabel was sitting in the kitchen drinking a cup of tea. She looked paler even than usual, except for a redness around her eyes.

"What happened, Anna?" I asked.

"I was up in the garden and I thought I heard a door shut. So I went down . . . " Her voice broke and she started sobbing.

"It's all right," I said, my hand on her shoulder. "Tell me what happened."

"I came in the back way and I heard a noise, like somebody moving around upstairs. Then I heard footsteps come running down the stairs. I froze. In the hallway he stopped when he saw me. I guess I must've screamed. I was so scared, Stu."

"It's okay. Did you get a look at him?"

"Not very good. He had on some kind of dark sweatshirt with a hood up over his head. And he was big. Not tall so much as solid."

"Then what happened?"

"Nothing. He turned and ran out the front door. It all happened so fast."

"Was anything missing?"

"No. I don't know. I don't think he came to steal something," she said, pausing to put a fist to her mouth. "I think he was looking for Maria."

"You think so?"

"Yes. I got that feeling anyway. Why else would he be upstairs?"

"Dammit," I cursed. "Those sons a bitches." This time they'd gone too far. They'd crossed a line, and I knew I had to do something.

"You think it was one of them?" Annabel asked.

"Who else would it be? Kay, can Anna and the baby stay here for a while?"

"'Course."

"I'll be back," I said, starting for the door.

"Where are you going, Stu?" my wife asked.

"I'm going to pay them a visit."

"Don't you be going out there, Stuart," Kay cautioned me. "Them Pughs're crazier than bedbugs. And ornery, too. Always was."

"Stu, listen to her," Annabel pleaded.

"Call the *police*," Kay said. "You don't want to go tangling with that bunch."

"No. I've had my belly full of them."

"You want I should come with you?" John asked.

I told him it was better that I went alone. It was between me and Glenn W. The old mountain way of settling a feud, face to face, archaic, adhering to primordial laws.

"You want my shotgun?"

"No, he *don't* want your shotgun!" Kay said harshly. "For heaven's sakes, John."

"Stu, don't go out there," Annabel said. "Please. Call Cecil."

"I'll be back."

I got in the truck and headed north on Highway 7, gunning the gas, taking my anger out on the road. I knew what I was doing was probably foolish—no, not probably, *was*. Perhaps even dangerous. I knew that Kay and Annabel were right, that I should just have called the police and let them deal with it. But given the fact that she hadn't had a good look at the man, that we had no proof beyond some vague threats, I knew nothing would come of it. It would be their word against ours. Glenn W., or whichever son or cousin he'd sent, would deny it, thumbing his nose at me, just as they'd been doing all along. Laughing at the gutless Yankee doctor who was afraid to protect what he'd begun to claim as his own. Thinking they could push me around and I'd just take it. And I knew I'd be looking over my shoulder, playing their game, waiting for whatever they'd try next, for things to escalate, turn violent, feeling afraid and vulnerable as a mouse being toyed with by a cat.

No, I wasn't going to live like that. I was mad enough and fed up enough, and I guess afraid enough, too, that I wasn't going to just sit quietly by and let them intimidate me. Not this time. And this time I'd tell Glenn W. the truth. That Maria wasn't Roy Lee's child. I'd promised Hunneycutt I wouldn't say anything for now, that I'd wait for the custody trial, but I was going to break that promise. I'd tell him, and maybe that would be the end of it. He might be a pigheaded, vain, and violent man, but he wasn't a stupid one. He wouldn't want to fight for a child that wasn't even related to him, that wasn't his blood. That damn blood he seemed so ready to spill some more blood over. Then again, he probably wouldn't believe me. Still, I'd tell him. And what was more, I'd warn him to stay clear of me and mine, if he knew what was good for him.

I'd reached a point beyond desperation, the point a person reaches where he just doesn't give a damn anymore what happens to him. A point that makes someone a person to be reckoned with. I suppose the point Rosa had reached when she went for that gun or when she stuck that piece of wire up inside herself. Or the point my father had reached when he drove the Buick into the garage and shut the door and waited for his hands to stop shaking. The point Will maybe had reached when he was no longer afraid or in pain, when he quietly curled up under that bush and just let himself go. I didn't care that the Pughs lived by a different set of rules, that they were criminals, that they were violent and dangerous. I was dangerous now, too. My fear had made me that. I wondered for a moment if I should've taken John's gun and then realized just how stupid that would have been.

Annabel hadn't gotten a good look at the man, but she did say that he was big, solid. Tully Pugh was built like that. And he'd come by before. If I hadn't stopped him that time, he'd have pushed his way into my house. If he did it once, he may have tried it again. Maybe he was looking for Maria. My mind was revving up, spinning like a motor with a stuck throttle.

When I reached the post office just past where the bridge crossed the Tuckamee, I turned right onto Little Possum Road and headed east. For the first few miles, the road offered a gradual climb up into the mountains, into the heart of the Nantahala National Forest. But near Wolf Lake, the road turned to dirt and the ascent grew steeper. I shifted into four-wheel. Though I hadn't been out to Little Mexico in years—and never to the Pughs' place—I had visited that part of the county a few times before, back when I used to make house calls to pregnant women. It was close to twenty miles up in the Blue Ridge, along a narrow, winding road that had washouts in spring and proved nearly impassable when it snowed. A couple dozen other families, all related in one way or another, lived out there, descendants of the earliest settlers in these hills. Before the county regionalized things, like a lot of small settlements Little Mexico had been self-sufficient, with its own school and grocery store, its own church and cemetery.

After driving for half an hour, I came to the tiny center of Little Mexico. It amounted to a general store with a single, humpbacked gas pump in front, a whitewashed cinder-block structure called the First Baptist Church of Little Mexico, a cemetery out behind it, and a tar-papered one-room schoolhouse that was now the senior center. I stopped at the store and went in to ask directions to the Pughs' place.

"Whatcha want with them?" replied the heavy, blue-jowled man behind the counter. Probably a second cousin, I thought. He spat tobacco juice into a paper coffee cup, as if he were trying out for a part in a movie about hillbillies.

"I'm a doctor," I said. "One of them is sick."

He stared suspiciously at me for a moment, then must have decided I had an honest face. "You want to drive up yonder a piece and look for a big ole walnut tree on the left. Got struck by lightning. Cain't miss it. Their mailbox ain't but a quarter mile beyond."

It was getting on toward dusk when I finally spotted the blackened walnut tree and then a little ways after that a mailbox that said *Pugh* in startling red paint, as if issuing a challenge. I turned onto the road before the mailbox and drove for a ways, following the course of a creek swollen with spring runoff. The road was narrow and muddy and mostly climbed upwards, though there were a couple of steep declines, and I had to take it slow as it was nearly washed out in one or two spots. The woods were thick, clotted, dense with spruce and rhododendrons and mountain laurel. I wasn't sure what to expect, or what I was going to do when I got where I was going. My anger had had time to cool, and I was now having second thoughts about the whole thing. *Just turn around*, I kept telling myself. Yet I didn't, in part because there was no place *to* turn around. After driving for about fifteen minutes, the woods opened up all at once and I came upon a clearing. Several out-buildings were arranged around a large, white clapboard farmhouse, well maintained, with a wraparound front porch that had potted plants hanging from the ceiling. A neat little flower bed was laid out in front. To the side of the house stood a huge satellite dish. It wasn't what I'd expected. Then again, the Pughs weren't your regular dirt-poor mountain folks. A newer Chevy pickup and a late-model Ford car were parked in a cinder-block garage that had recently been constructed to the left of the house. I looked around for a Bronco or Blazer but didn't see one. Yet there, sitting in front of the flower bed, was Glenn W.'s red Ford truck with its huge tires.

I parked, got out, and headed for the house. An old dog with a gray muzzle had been asleep on the porch. It got slowly to its feet, limped toward the steps, and began to bark at my approach. I stopped in my tracks and waited to see what it would do. But after a few seconds the front door opened and old Mrs. Pugh stepped out onto the porch.

"Hush up," she cried at the dog. When the thing added a growl, she cuffed it on the muzzle. "Now g'won, git." Reluctantly, the animal turned and lay down again.

"Why, Dr. Jordan," she said, surprised to see me.

"Is your husband here?"

"We're 'bout to set down to eat. Would you care to join us?"

"Thank you. No."

She paused for a moment, then said, "I'll fetch him for you."

Before she'd taken a step back into the house, Glenn W., aided by a cane I'd not seen him use before, came hobbling up to the door. He was followed by Tully and two other men, both appearing to be in their early twenties. They stood behind the old man, looking at me over his shoulder. He stared at me for a moment with those shiny metallic eyes of his. Then something struck him as funny and he smiled.

"*Shee-it.* What you want anyway?" he asked.

"Stay away from us," I said, my voice flat but firm.

He turned his head slightly to one side, as if he hadn't heard me, and frowned so that the smooth skin around his mouth became deeply furrowed. "What?"

"You heard me. Stay the hell away from us. I mean it."

"Don't know what-all you're talking about."

"Like hell you don't. You," I said, then glanced over his shoulder at Tully, "or one of yours was just out to my place. Scared my wife half to death. She saw you. She can identify you," I bluffed.

"And just what was we supposed to be a-doing out to your place?"

"You know damn well what. Looking for Maria."

"I told you, I don't know what you're talking about."

"You're a goddamn liar then."

The smile came back to the old man's face. It made him look like a mean little elf.

"You come on to my land, interrupt my dinner, and call me a liar. Mister, you either dumb as dirt or one crazy fuck, I tell ya."

"Ask *him* then," I said, pointing at Tully.

"Ask him what?"

"If he was out to my place."

Glenn W. looked at his son. "I ain't been over there," Tully said. When his father's gaze remained on him for a while, he added, "I ain't."

"You heard him. Now turn around and git your ass outa here 'fore I lose my temper."

"I'll protect what's mine."

"Your'n? That young'un ain't your'n."

I looked at the old man, then at Tully. I figured I'd take a chance. "Is it you?" I asked.

"Was it me what?" the son exclaimed.

"Is she yours?"

"Is who mine? What in the hell you talking about?"

"Maria."

"What's this all about?" Glenn W. asked me.

"Ask *him,* why don't you?" I said, pointing at Tully.

"I tole you to git your ass on outa here."

"Ask him. Go ahead."

Glenn W. turned to look at his son again.

"I don't know what he's talking about," Tully said.

"Were you Rosa's lover?" I asked.

"*What?* The hell I was!" he cried.

"You used to go and see her when Roy Lee wasn't there. I know about that."

"That's bullshit."

"You didn't stop by now and then? Rosa told me."

"What'd she tell you I done?"

"She didn't tell me anything. What *did* you do?"

"Nothing! Not a damn thing! That whore say I touched her? Did she?"

Glenn W. looked from his son, to me, then back to his son again.

"Did you go over there?" he asked Tully.

"A few times maybe. But it's not like he's making out. I was just trying to hep her out."

"Hep her?"

"Give her a little money. See if she needed anything doing around the place. That's all I done."

The old man continued looking at his son. "So you don't know nothin' about what he's saying?"

"No. I swear to God."

Glenn W. turned back to me. "You bes' explain yourself and damn quick, Mister."

"Maria isn't Roy Lee's child."

He leveled his gaze steadfastly on me. "What?"

"It isn't his child. The blood doesn't match up."

"You're lying."

"No, it's true. I checked."

"You must think me pretty damn stupid to swallow that."

"No, it's the truth. The blood doesn't match. It isn't Roy Lee's child. Maria's not your grandchild."

"That's a goddamn lie."

"If you don't believe me, we can have DNA tests done. I'll give permission to have Maria's blood tested. Talk to your lawyer if you want. But it'll come to the same thing. It's not Roy Lee's child."

"Then whose is it?"

"I don't know," I replied.

"This is just your way of trickin' me into dropping my custody suit," Glenn W. said.

"It's no trick. It's the truth."

"Well, it ain't agonna happen. I'll do ever'thing in my power to see to it that child gets to stay with her rightful kin. *Ever'thing,* you hear me?"

"Have the tests done if you don't believe me. DNA will tell you it's not Roy Lee's child. And it just might tell you whose it is," I said, glancing over Glenn W.'s shoulder at Tully. He had some indefinable something in his eyes, though I couldn't tell if it were guilt or fear or what. The irony, of course, was that if Maria *did* turn out to be Tully's, it just might help Glenn W.'s case for custody. But to help Rosa, I had to take that chance.

The old man stared at me from under his deep brows, his liquid gray eyes hardening slightly like molten lead beginning to cool. Eyes that were still angry and fierce, but now shaded a little with doubt. I'd managed to put some doubt in him. As much as he didn't want to, he now at least wondered if I was telling the truth.

"G'won, git your ass on outa here."

I smiled at him. Then I turned and headed down the steps. The dog cast a halfhearted bark at my departure but didn't bother getting up. It was dark as I pulled out onto the main road that led back into Little

Mexico. At that point, I ran into Cecil in the cruiser about to pull up to the Pughs' road.

"Annabel said you'd be here. What in the Christ you up to, Doc?"

"Had a little talk with Glenn W."

"A little talk, huh?"

"That's right."

"You got you a screw loose, Doc? You know what it sounds to me? Like you're goin' through one of them midlife crisis deals. Having affairs. Adopting babies. Coming up here and gettin' in Glenn W.'s face. Whyn't you go stick your prick in a 'lectrical outlet and be done with it?"

"I'm getting too old not to start living dangerously."

"You keep it up, you won't have to worry about getting old."

"Take care, Cecil."

On the ride home I thought about how old man Pugh had looked at his son, as if he knew more than he was letting on. I wondered if Tully had been the one who showed up at my house looking for the baby. If he had been Rosa's lover, Maria's father. And if he was the one who'd been there that night with Rosa. Maybe Roy Lee had caught them and there'd been a fight, and Tully had killed his brother. Maybe it wasn't out of fear that Rosa was covering for him. Maybe it was something else, like love. It would make sense, I thought. Or if not quite sense— nothing to do with this case made sense—at least it wouldn't be any crazier than anything else.

# 28

*I was in* my study late one night, a few days before Rosa Littlefoot's trial was to start. I was looking over an article in a medical journal, trying to catch up on my professional reading, something I'd been remiss in lately. Yet my thoughts kept wandering, couldn't stay on oxytocin augmentation or the connection between epidurals and intrapartum fevers. Earlier, I'd given Maria her bath, put her in her sleeper, and sat in the den feeding her. She was getting big, changing, becoming more aware of the world around her. She might smile or grab hold of a button on my shirt, or she might just stare soberly up at me with those dark, bottomless eyes of hers, eyes you could slide right down into and stay there forever. When I held her like this I could actually feel my pulse rate slowing. I tried to remember holding Will in the same way, but his image in my mind kept being replaced by Maria's.

Mostly I was thinking about Annabel. She hadn't come down for supper, had remained in her room. For the past several days, in fact, she'd been spending nearly all of her time up there. She hardly came out, and then only to grab an apple or nibble furtively on something, like a mouse wary of a trap, before going back up and shutting the door. I couldn't tell if she was working or sleeping or what she was doing in there. She hadn't said more than two words to me over the last few days. She was acting different. I don't know if it had anything to do with her being frightened by the man who came in the house, but ever since then I'd noticed a definite change in her behavior. A gradual slowing, a tentativeness, as if the bright, confident intensity of her mania had spent itself and was replaced by a fearful hesitancy, a looking-over-the-shoulder expectancy, as if she were waiting for something bad to overtake her at any moment. I picked up on the familiar signs that she usually exhibited at the end of a long manic cycle, which indicated that she was about to enter the flip side of her illness, depression. Several times when I'd called home during the day to check on her, she answered groggily, saying I woke her from a nap. And once or twice when I got home from work, I found her asleep upstairs in her bed or on the couch in the den. The house a mess, dishes in the sink, no supper made. I didn't care about that, only what it boded. I noticed the change in her eyes, too. They lost that wild, agitated gleam. They were now dull, a lusterless surface, as if something had cracked and the vital force behind them had drained out. If she got up for breakfast by the time I left with the baby, she would stare listlessly into her cup of tea, her face drawn, dark circles under her eyes, her skin beyond pale: colorless, almost translucent, the bluish veins standing out at her temples. A few evenings before, I came into the kitchen late and she was standing at the sink, looking out the window. She was crying. "What's the matter?" I asked.

She shrugged.

"Anna?"

"What?"

"Talk to me. Please."

She said she was tired, and headed past me and up to her room.

While her mania was chaotic, a fierce and frightening thing, her depression was more subtle and, therefore, usually more dangerous, especially to herself. In the past it was when she was depressed that she would try to hurt herself. I couldn't put it off anymore. I knew I had to do something, so I brought up the question of her of going to see Dr. Butler again.

"Just to look you over," I had explained to her only the day before. She was riffling through the refrigerator, looking for something to eat.

"Do we have any peaches?" she asked, serious. "I know there were some in here."

"I don't know. Just let him check your meds. See if he needs to adjust them. Maybe that's all it is."

This time, instead of fighting me, telling me how she was fine and didn't need to see a doctor, she surprised me by saying, "Maybe you're right."

"Really?"

She shrugged, then nodded.

"I'll call him? Make an appointment for you."

"Whatever," she replied. "I suppose that means I'll have to go to the hospital again?"

"Not necessarily," I said, knowing it wasn't the truth. Knowing she probably *would* have to be admitted.

"Well if I do, I want a private room. I don't want to have to make conversation with some crazy fat lady. Remember that woman from Brevard?" she asked, smiling with forced gaiety.

I nodded, despite not having a clue what she was talking about.

"And afterwards?" she asked.

"Afterwards?"

"When they have me all tuned up and flushed out and doped up? What happens then?"

"I'll get you a place."

"Where?"

"Wherever you want. Asheville. Even Slade if you want."

"I wouldn't want to live in town with everybody gabbing about me. I can't come back here?" It was part statement, part question. I started to answer, but she answered for me. "No, I understand, Stu."

I called Dr. Butler and made an appointment for her to see him two days later. He suggested I bring her things. That way if he thought she needed to be committed, we could go right over to Cedar Crest. He said if she suddenly got worse, however, to have her brought to the ER. Though there was no predicting precisely the course of her illness, I figured she was still well enough that we could wait the few days. Besides, I thought it would give her a chance to get used to the idea. Used to the notion of leaving here. While she was in the hospital, I would arrange for a place for her to stay once she left. A halfway house or her own apartment somewhere. And I would wait till she was feeling better to bring up the subject of a divorce again. But I would do it this time.

It was near midnight when I heard the knock. At first I thought it was something Annabel was doing, but when I followed the noise I realized somebody was knocking on the back door. Who the hell could it be at this hour? And coming to the back door, too? Then I thought of the last person to do that, Tully Pugh. Jesus, I thought. My heart did a little dance in my chest. Was he here to cause trouble about the baby? Perhaps threaten me to keep quiet about my suspicions that he was Maria's father? And no doubt my suspicions about the rest? Before I answered the door, I went into the den and picked up the poker near the stove.

Then I headed back into the kitchen, flicked the floodlight on, and peeked out from behind the curtains.

A man stood on the deck, one hand shielding his eyes from the brightness of the light. He was of average height, but heavyset, thick through the waist and chest. He wore a dark sweatshirt with a hood pulled down low on his head, so I could only see a small circle of face. What was visible was dark, with rough, pitted skin. Though I couldn't see much of him, I could tell that, whoever it was, it wasn't Tully Pugh.

I pulled the curtains back. Through the sliding glass door, I said, "What do you want?"

"You Dr. Jordan?"

"Yes. What do you want?" I repeated.

"I need to see you."

"It's late," I said. "You need medical assistance?"

"No. I need to talk to you."

"You come back at a reasonable hour."

I was about to shut the curtain when he said, "It's about Rosa. Rosa Littlefoot."

I paused and stared out at him.

"What about her?"

"I'm a friend of hers," he explained. "I'm Lenny Blackfox."

Leonard Blackfox. Though I didn't have anything more to go on than his word, I decided to take a chance and let him in. But I held onto the poker for insurance. He glanced at it when he stepped into the kitchen.

"I don't usually get callers at midnight up here," I explained. "I thought you might be somebody else."

"That somebody else wouldn't be a Pugh, would it?"

"How did you know about that?"

"I heard about them causing you trouble over the baby."

I wondered what his interest was in all this, what he wanted to talk about.

"Have a seat," I said. He sat with his back to the door. "Can I get you something?"

"No," he replied. He took off his hood. He had a squarish head, with a broad face, high cheekbones, a thin, limp mouth that looked like a dead worm. His neck was thick, fleshy. His black hair was cropped close and he had a scar that skittered across his temple and under the hairline. He appeared to be full-blooded Cherokee, though his eyes were lighter than most Indians', almost a khaki brown, as if he had some white blood in him. He wore a serious, meditative expression, like someone considering a head-first plunge into water whose bottom he couldn't quite make out and therefore was taking his time, mulling it over.

"Well, I'm going to have a drink."

"In that case."

Deciding he wasn't a threat, I leaned the poker against the stove, went over to the cabinet above the refrigerator, and got down the bottle I'd been hiding up there. I poured two glasses. I sat opposite him at the table. His hands were blunt and callused, curled naturally into meaty hooks. "Here you go," I said.

"Thanks."

"Rosa's father told me about you and your sister. I looked you up down in Farley. Spoke to some fellow where you used to live?"

"Yeah. That've been Charlie. He told me you stopped by."

"He tell you what I was interested in?"

"Yeah," he said. "Listen, I'm sorry about the other day."

"Other day?"

"About scaring your wife."

"It was *you?*" I said. "You came in the house?"

"Yes."

"I've a good mind to crack you over the head with that poker. You scared the hell out of her."

"Like I said, I'm sorry. I came by and saw her up in the garden. I thought . . . "

"And was that you almost hit me with the truck that time?"

He nodded. "I just wanted to see Maria. That's all. I didn't mean no harm. Really, I didn't. I just . . . "

The words flew out of my mouth even before the thought could completely register in my mind, instinctive and right as a hand jerking away from a flame. "It's *you*. You're her father."

He looked over at me, blinked once, and without the least change in his expression said, "Yeah."

"Jesus Christ Almighty," I cried.

So it wasn't Tully Pugh after all. I was dead wrong in that. And yet, when I had a chance to consider it a little, it made perfect sense. Why Rosa hadn't wanted me to find him. Why she'd gotten nervous when I even mentioned his name. And then just as quickly, the next piece snapped into place, definite and clear and with the perfect logic of another round being chambered into a gun.

"*You* were with her that night, weren't you? It was you."

Leonard Blackfox drew in a long breath and, nodding slowly, said, "Uh huh."

"Son of a bitch. Why the hell didn't you come forward before this? Why did you wait? She goes on trial on Monday."

"I know. It's a long story."

I stared across at him for several seconds, waiting, letting him take a sip of his drink. Letting him get up the nerve to tell me his long story, what he'd come for.

"So?" I said at last.

He bunched his thick callused hands together and brought his wormlike mouth into an expression of both resignation and relief, the sort of expression I've always thought must come over people in the moment when death becomes a fact to them, a fact that is no longer up for debate, can no longer be challenged or questioned, has become just a clear, hard, irrefutable actuality they accept the way they would the sun coming up in the morning.

"First off, he deserved what he got," he explained. "Though I didn't mean for it to happen that way. Neither of us did."

• • •

He told me how he and Rosa had had a plan. She was going to take Maria, and the three of them were going to run off together. That's why she'd packed the suitcase. Why she'd squirreled away some money. The heroin, Leonard Blackfox explained, wasn't for herself but only to help them get started once they got to where they were going. He said she'd promised to stay off the dope. That's the only way he'd agreed to go with her. They were heading out west, to Arizona. She wanted to get as far away as she could from Pugh, from the drugs, from this life she was leading here. She wanted to make a new start, he said, and I could recall her saying the same thing to me in the jail cell. Blackfox had a friend out in Tucson, somebody they could stay with for a while. The friend was going to line him up with a job. Their plan called for Rosa to phone him down in Farley as soon as Pugh left to go out drinking that night, which he often did. She had her things all packed, ready to go. The only thing they didn't count on was Pugh returning early, before Blackfox could get there. Roy Lee was drunk, and when he was drunk he got mean. He got into a fight with Rosa. Started hitting her, as he often did. Only this time he seemed bent on killing her. When Blackfox showed up, he could hear them fighting inside the trailer, could hear Rosa screaming, *Stay away from me, you bastard. I'm warning you.* But he kept it up, kept hitting her. Blackfox said he worried that Pugh would kill her, so finally he went into the trailer.

According to Blackfox, there had been bad blood between the two men. Pugh knew that Blackfox used to be Rosa's boyfriend, and the two men had had some run-ins before. She'd stayed with Blackfox once when Pugh had beat her up, and Pugh had threatened him, told him he'd kill him if he ever saw him again. Blackfox tried to tell Pugh to stop, that they didn't want any trouble, just wanted to leave. Pugh told him she wasn't going anywhere and for him to get the hell out, if he knew what was good for him. But Blackfox said he wasn't going anywhere without her. Pugh got mad and hit him, knocked him to the floor. He picked up a chair and started beating him with it. Rosa tried to help him, but Pugh punched her in the face and then stormed off toward the bedroom. *He's gonna get his gun,* Rosa had cried. *Run,* she called to him. But instead of fleeing, he ran at Pugh and grabbed for the gun. They struggled for it. One shot went off. Somehow he managed to get it away, but Pugh lunged at the barrel and another shot was fired, this one hitting Pugh in the belly.

Blackfox told me how for a long while they debated what to do. He wanted to call for help. Maybe Pugh wouldn't die, he said. Besides, it was an accident. They could explain how it happened. That it was self-defense. But Rosa thought that was crazy. She said they'd be accused of murder. Two Indians killing a white man. And if the law didn't get them, there were the Pughs to contend with. They'd come after him. No, she said, you go on. He begged her to come with him then. That they could run off together just like they'd planned. But she said they'll come after us, and we'll both go to jail. Or the Pughs will kill him. He said he wasn't afraid of them, but she pleaded with him, *No, you go on.* She didn't want him getting mixed up in this. Getting tangled in her troubles. It wasn't his concern. *Go on,* she'd urged him. *Go on and don't look back.*

And so, reluctantly, he did. He got in his truck and left. He drove out to Arizona. Stayed with his friend. Tried to forget about it. He'd heard from someone back on the reservation that Pugh had died after all and that Rosa was being tried for first-degree murder. For a while he tried to put that night and Rosa behind him. Tried not to look back. But after a time he could no longer stay away. He couldn't let Rosa take the blame. He loved her, he said.

When he finished his story, he picked up his glass and polished off the rest of his drink.

"You took your damn sweet time," I said.

"I was afraid, I guess," he replied. "Anyways, I'm here now."

"What are you going to do?" I asked. Before he could answer, I heard something behind me in the kitchen.

"Stu," came Annabel's sleep-parched voice, "I thought . . . "

She stopped when she saw Leonard Blackfoot. Her eyes widened in fear and surprise. "My God, it's *him*!" she cried. "He's the one who was here the other day."

"It's okay, Anna," I explained. "This is Leonard Blackfox. He's a friend of Rosa's. He was just here to see Maria. He didn't mean to scare you."

"I'm sorry, ma'am."

"What's he doing here?"

I didn't know how to answer that. It was Blackfox who spoke next. "I wanted to see Maria. You think it would be possible?"

"I don't know," Annabel said. "Stu?"

"I think it would be all right."

We headed upstairs and quietly opened Maria's door. She was sleeping on her stomach. "Ssh," said Annabel to the man, holding a finger up to her mouth. Blackfox bent over the crib and peered down at his daughter. He reached one large gnarled hand down and touched her back. He sort of patted her, almost as if he wasn't sure she was real. He stood there looking at the sleeping child for a while, then turned to leave.

"I'm grateful to you," he whispered to Annabel.

He headed down through the kitchen and to the back door.

"What are you doing to do?" I asked again.

"Don't have much choice. I want to thank you, though."

"For what?"

"Taking care of them. For doing what I should've been doing."

He started down the steps.

"Did you know she was pregnant again?" He stopped, and just by the way he turned and looked at me I could tell that he hadn't.

"She is?"

"*Was.* She lost it."

"She hadn't said anything to me about it."

I didn't ask if it was his.

"One other thing. You said it wasn't until you were out in Arizona that you heard Pugh had died?"

"Uh huh. It didn't surprise me. He was gut-shot pretty bad. Near'bouts dead when I took off. Why?"

"No reason."

He turned and headed up through the garden and into the woods. After a while, I heard a truck start and take off down the mountain. I looked up at the sky. It was a clear night, with stars like sequins on a black dress. Jesus, I thought. It was certainly a night of revelations.

Annabel came back into the kitchen as I was locking up.

"You believe him?"

"Yes, I think so."

"What if the Pughs sent him?"

"No, they didn't."

"Why's he so interested in Maria anyway?"

"He's Maria's father," I said.

"Her father!" Annabel said, staring at me. "But I thought Pugh was her father."

So I told her about Leonard Blackfox and what happened the night Pugh was killed and where he'd been and why he'd come back. I didn't tell her I'd known for a while about Maria not being Pugh's.

"And what does that mean now?"

"I don't know," I said. "I don't know."

• • •

That night it took me a long time to fall asleep. My mind just wouldn't shut down, kept running on and on like a car engine dieseling long after the ignition was turned off. I kept thinking about it, everything. About this Leonard Blackfox. About Rosa willing to go to prison to protect him. About Maria being his. About him being there that night and fighting with Pugh and the gun going off. About her telling him to run and him coming back because he loved her and couldn't see her taking the blame. And I thought about Annabel and Bobbie and Maria. I thought about all of it. Everything that had happened these past few crazy months.

When sleep finally came, I had all sorts of odd dreams and half dreams, and things that were little more than bright images in my mind. The last dream, the one that woke me, was the one where Will was being chased by wolves. As he always did, he ran into our bed and crawled in between Annabel and me. *A wolf was after me, Dad,* he cried. He seemed so real to me, as he always did in the dream, and I held him and kissed him and comforted him. I could feel him against me, warm, his skin flushed with fear, his heart pounding in his small rib cage. But the funny thing was when I opened my eyes in the darkness, I could still feel the warmth against me.

"Will?" I said.

"*Ssh,*" a voice replied, a finger against my lips. "It's okay."

"Annabel?"

"I'm here," she said. "You were dreaming. It's okay now." I felt her arms around me, her naked body warm and inviting, unfolding itself to me like a flower to the light. I started to say something, but she covered my mouth with hers and she lifted herself and was over me. She felt so light, so frail and childlike in my arms. "Don't talk," she said. "Don't talk."

When I woke in the morning, the house was strangely quiet. Sunlight poured into the room. I reached out for the other side of the bed, but it was cold. I got up and headed into Annabel's room only to find it empty. The bed hadn't been slept in. All of her art things were packed away, the paintings rolled into tubes tied with pieces of twine and stacked in the closet. I looked in her drawers. Her clothes were gone, too. For a moment I felt a ball of panic rise in my chest: *Maria.* I hurried into her room. She was there, though, still sleeping soundly.

I saw something on Will's bed. A note, and beside it a piece of paper, rolled up. I picked up the note and began to read it.

> *Dear Stu,*
> *Sorry it had to be like this. You know me though. A rolling stone and all that. Thanks for putting me up—or putting up with me (ha, ha). I thought things might work out this time around. I really did. You and me and the baby. But I know now that was just wishful thinking. I've decided to get out of your life once and for all. I know I've said that before but I mean it this time. I do. I realize you'd probably never have the heart to tell me to leave for good. What I wanted is what we had—you and Will and this life*

*up here on the mountain. Oh, well. You can't hate a girl for try-ing. We both need to move on though. As for me, I CANNOT go back to the hospital. I'd rather be dead than do that again. When I get someplace I'll send you my address so you can forward the divorce papers for me to sign. I'm serious. I want you to go ahead and marry that woman. She seems right for you. I want the two of you to be happy. Don't feel sorry for me, Stu. What we had no-body can take from us. I love you. I've always loved you. Good-bye and good luck.*

    *Anna*

There was a P.S. "By the way, don't forget to put some flowers on his grave now and then. It seemed so barren when I was there."

I thought how she'd taken off because she didn't want to go back to the hospital. Then again, maybe it had something to do with that man coming last night, telling us he was Maria's father. It couldn't have been just a coincidence. But it really didn't matter much why she left. I knew it could've been anything. For a moment I considered getting in my truck and taking off after her. It was just after seven o'clock. She couldn't have gotten far. Even if she'd hitched a ride into town with one of the first-shift mill workers, the early bus to Asheville didn't leave till eight. I had time to catch her. But what if I did? What would I do? Grab her and force her to go with me? Have her committed again? Is that what I wanted to do? What she wanted? No, I thought. I had to let her go. It's what she wanted. It was the right thing—for both of us.

Then I remembered the rolled-up paper on the bed. I untied the piece of twine and spread it carefully out on the covers. It was a paint-ing. A watercolor of Will. He seemed to be looking at me, his eyes glit-tering a pale blue the way they used to, his soft blond hair falling loosely in his face, his mouth beaming with a smile. He looked happy. Safe and relaxed and, above all, happy. I started to cry. For Will and for Annabel. For my father, too. Mostly though, I cried for myself.

# 29

*Bobbie called me* at the office that afternoon.

"Y'all sitting down, Doc?" she asked. "You're not gonna believe this."

And then she told me how this fellow named Leonard Blackfox came into the sheriff's department and turned himself in for killing Roy Lee Pugh.

"Just like that," she explained. "Said he was the one that shot Pugh." When I didn't say anything, she asked, "Did you hear me, Doc?"

"I heard you."

"Well?"

"Well, what?"

"You don't sound too surprised."

"He stopped by here last night. He told me all about it."

"Geez Louise, Doc. Were you just planning to sit on that?"

"I'm not the ME anymore. And besides, I was pretty sure he was going to turn himself in."

"Son of a gun. Want me to say you were right after all?"

"Only partly."

"Did you believe him?" she asked.

"Yes. Why would he lie? Did you buy his story?"

"I suppose I do. Though Troy's having a conniption. He thinks it's some eleventh-hour trick of Hunneycutt's. He's going to have Blackfox take a polygraph."

"What will happen now?"

"We'll have to investigate. But if he passes the poly and his story checks out, he'll be arraigned on murder charges."

"What's he looking at?"

"He says he was only trying to protect her. That it was an accident. If Troy buys that, he might be amenable to offering him man-one. At this point I think Troy just wants the damn case over with. Of course, the sticky point still is that second shot. Did he talk to you about that at all?"

"No. What will happen to Rosa?"

"Well, if Troy wants to be an asshole, there's still the heroin possession. And being an accessory after the fact. But given everything she's been through, she'll probably get off pretty light."

"Will she have any problems regaining custody of her daughter?"

"I don't imagine so. I mean, she might have to enroll in a detox program. Prove that she's a fit mother. But no, I would imagine she'll have her daughter back in pretty quick order. So you're off the hook."

"Yeah, I'm off the hook." I paused for a moment, then said, "Annabel's left."

"Left? When?"

"This morning."

"Where did she go?"

"I don't know. She didn't say. I just woke up this morning and she was gone." Funny, but I didn't feel guilty about what happened the previous night. Not at all. It was just something that happened, something that didn't have anything to do with Bobbie or me. "She did leave me a note, though. She said she wants us to be happy."

"Really?"

"Yeah."

"What do you think she meant by that?"

"That she wants us to be happy."

Now it was Bobbie's turn to be silent.

"I don't know what to say, Doc. You all right about it?"

"I suppose it works out for the best."

"I know how . . . "

I interrupted her to ask, "You free tonight?"

"Yes."

"Want to come over here? I'll make dinner."

"You sure it's not rushing things?"

"I'm sure."

"Sounds good to me."

After I hung up, I happened to pass Stella out at the front desk.

"It true, Doc?"

I wondered how she could have heard about Annabel so soon. "Is what true?" I asked.

"That Indian woman didn't kill that Pugh fellow?"

"Oh. Yes, it's true."

"Well, I'll be."

I thought of telling her about Annabel, about her leaving, but I didn't want to get into that right now. I knew that, to Stella, it would have meant I'd made a decision, when in fact I hadn't. It was just something that had happened and I'd gone along with it, though I didn't fight against it.

"By the way, don't forget you got the Tibbetts woman this afternoon. Her first. You're suppose to induce her. But my guess is you're gonna have to section her. Got them slim hips, just like her momma."

"Thanks for the advice, Stella."

"You're welcome to it, Doc," she added, giving me a wink.

Stella's prediction turned out to be correct. At the hospital, I tried every trick to get Leola Tibbetts, four days overdue, to go into labor. I ruptured her waters and put her on Pitocin, which intensified her pains some and shortened the interval between contractions, but her cervix still refused to cooperate. I watched her through the night. Around five, with her resting comfortably, I caught a few winks myself in the doctor's lounge. When I woke at seven and learned that she still hadn't progressed at all, I decided we'd given Mother Nature her chance and now it was my turn. I sectioned her and went in and took the baby. She had a healthy baby boy. Afterwards, I stopped in the pediatric ward where the young Potter infant was. Jack Potter and Emmilou sat around an incubator watching their son take food through a gavage tube. The baby had spent nearly four weeks over in Asheville and they'd transferred him back here when he was well enough, though not quite ready to go home.

"Why, hello, Doc," Emmilou said to me.

"How are you, Emmilou?"

"Fy-on. Say hey to li'l Stuart Potter."

The child was still tiny, frail and unfinished looking as a baby bird. But he looked strong enough that he was going to make it.

"What do you say, Stuart," I said, feeling funny about using my own name.

"I reckon he'll have big ears like my side, Doc," Jack kidded.

"He does have a pair of ears on him," I agreed, laughing.

"They said he can go home purty soon."

"That's great."

"What days y'all want me to go out there and clean, Doc?" Emmilou asked.

"I'll give you a call," I said. "You folks take care."

Out in the hall, however, Jack caught up with me. Looking sheepish and embarrassed, he said, "Here you go, Doc." He handed me a wad of cash. Thinking they needed it more than I did, I tried to give it back but Jack wouldn't let me.

"G'won and have it, Doc. They's two hunnerd there. I'll get you the rest by and by."

I told him there was no rush, thanked him, and stuck the cash in my pocket.

When I left the hospital, I drove downtown, parked on Main, and headed up to see Lewis Hunneycutt. His secretary, Mrs. Grasty, told me he was with a client, so I sat in the closet-sized waiting room. When Hunneycutt came out, he looked at me with surprise.

"Just the fellow I wanted to see," he said.

He took me back into his office and we sat down.

"You heard by now, I suppose?"

"I heard. What's Rosa saying?"

"At first she denied that Blackfox was even there. Said he was lying. But I finally talked some sense into her and she came around."

"How long do you think she'll get?"

"Hard to say. She could be out in a year. Maybe less."

"What about the baby?"

"Do you want to keep her till we straighten out things with her? I doubt if the Pughs will contest custody now."

"I will if you can't find anybody else."

"You don't sound too inclined now."

The truth was I wasn't. I didn't want to have her for another six months or a year and then have to give her up. If I had to give her up, I'd rather do it now. Make a clean break.

"I think it would be better if she went to stay with somebody else. You could ask Leonard Blackfox's sister. She might be willing to take her in till Rosa's problems get settled."

"I guess you were right, after all."

I stood up, remembering then the cash in my pocket.

"Would you hold onto this for Rosa? It ain't much but it's something."

"Sure."

Before I left Slade, I stopped at the Bi-Lo and picked up some things to cook for dinner. I was in the dairy aisle when I saw Paul Tisdale pushing a cart toward me. He eyed me for a while, like he was going to come up and say something, maybe punch me in the nose for having an affair with his wife. But as he got close he smiled at me and offered a wink, whose meaning I wasn't quite sure of.

# Epilogue

*An unseasonably cool* afternoon for late May. In the distance, beyond Painter Knob and Doubletop, beyond Coward Bald, perhaps as far away as the Smokies, a looming bank of dark clouds gathers over the mountains. A front is moving in, though it's been a pretty dry spring and we can certainly use the rain.

I'm working up in the garden. I'm wearing only a T-shirt, and I find myself having to move fast to stay warm. Even so, I feel goose bumps sprouting roughly on the backs of my arms. Like Candide, I've taken up gardening. Since bringing in a new man to my practice, a Dr. Jim McClellan from Emory, down in Atlanta, I've been able to cut back on my hours. Sometimes I even take a day off in the middle of the week and let Jim, a young hard-working fellow though a little too cocksure of himself, handle things. I still can't help worrying about my patients, thinking Jim is sometimes too quick to resort to sectioning or that he'll jump to a conclusion I might have mulled over a while longer. But he's a fine young doctor with a good future ahead of him, and I'm lucky to have him. With him there, I now have time to putter around in the garden. The funny thing is, I've found that I actually enjoy it. It's relaxing and it gives me something to do in the evenings.

The garden is mostly vegetables now, though I've planted some roses along a new trellis I put up, and I've placed marigolds around the perimeter, which John—Pangloss to my Candide—tells me will keep varmints and deer away. He's also instructed me about cold-weather crops and warm-weather crops, about what to plant while there's still a chance of frost and what to save for after; he's taught me to cover vulnerable seedlings with milk cartons, to pinch the suckers on the tomato plants, and to use the ashes from the stove as well as coffee grounds as fertilizer. I've put in rows of radishes and carrots and beets, alongside pepper and tomato plants John gave me, two kinds of beans, romaine lettuce, pumpkins and honeydew melons and cucumbers, and asparagus, too, which won't mature for a couple of years, but which I'm looking forward to with hollandaise sauce. I wanted to put in some corn, but John advised against it. Said you need at least four rows to cross-pollinate, something he's surprised that I, being a fellow whose job deals with pollination, didn't know.

The other day John stopped by with some rose plants he dug up from Kay's flower bed. He helped me put them in along the trellis at the bottom of the garden. He's been spending more and more time up here, helping me with the garden, offering advice or seedlings, and he often stays for supper. Ever since Kay passed away suddenly last fall from an aneurysm, he doesn't know what to do with himself. He confided to me not long ago, "Never knew the day could be so damn long, Doc." At night when I get called to the hospital, I'll sometimes see the light on in his kitchen. He's down there reading about Augustus and Pompeii, about the Great Wall of China, about the Egyptians. I know what it's like to have trouble sleeping alone in a house. So on many evenings we'll have him stay for dinner, and we'll sit around the stove afterward while he tells us stories about the "olden days" growing up in the mountains. Sometimes he dozes off and we just let him stay there.

Later this evening, we have to go into town. There's a class that's being offered at the community center. A Lamaze class. *Me,* going to a Lamaze class! At first I objected. What do *I* need with that? Yet Bobbie thinks it's good for us to go through it together, that being a patient and a doctor are two different things, and I have to admit she's right. So I gave in and let her sign us up. Jessica Helms, no relation to our senior senator, runs it. She's one of those hippie types from out in Baker's Cove. Thinks everything should be natural. Doesn't believe in epidurals or forceps, or in guys like me for that matter. If it was up to her, Bobbie would just go out into the woods and squat down and drop her baby like a foal. In class, I'll be on my hands and knees, huffing and puffing along with the rest of the novices. But I guess it's a good thing. Bobbie is seven months pregnant and worries like any primigravida, especially those past forty. I tell her not to worry, that everything is fine. I show her all the articles, at least the good ones, about how safe it is to have a baby at forty-two. She goes to Dr. Chung, whose English is still as bad and bedside manner still as blunt as ever. When I ask him how everything's going with her, he tells me, "Good, good. She too fat, though."

After the Lamaze class we'll go out to eat at Pancho Villa's, where she'll get the combo platter and eat the entire thing plus whatever I can't finish. Lately Bobbie is eating anything that's not tied down. It's become a joke between us. Yet to my mind the added weight only makes her seem more desirable. Her breasts, before on the small side, are swollen and ripe as the honeydew melons I've planted will be in August. When she takes a bath at night, I love soaping the sensual bulge of her stomach, scrubbing the graceful curves of her back and thighs, the places she can't reach, the places that are now my responsibility.

She also wants to stop by her office and pick up some files to work on over the weekend. She plans on working right up to her due date, which is August 12. Not for Bumgartner anymore, though. She quit her job shortly after the Pugh case. Troy begged her to stay on, even offered her a raise, but she was tired of him and of prosecuting people. So she went into private practice, joined Lewis Hunneycutt, of all people. She has developed an appreciation for him. She tells me that if more lawyers were like him, half as bright as most but twice as honest, the law profession would be better off for it. She and I sometimes have lunch together at the Pancake Barn. She plans on continuing to work even after the baby is born. I'm thinking of taking a leave and staying home, at least for the first few months, to get to know Rebecca Sarah Jordan, whose name we chose for no other reason than we liked how it sounded. We'll probably call her Becky, though Bobbie thinks we should wait and see. She might not even seem like a Becky to us. And she's right. A name should be flexible enough to fit the wearer.

About a month back I was returning from having lunch with Bobbie, when I almost bumped into a small, wiry man coming out of Goody's Hardware. We glared at each other for a second like a couple of gamecocks, as if waiting for the other to make the first move. It was Glenn W. Pugh. I hadn't seen him since that last time in court, nearly two years before, at Leonard Blackfox's sentencing. He sat in the back, wearing that same powder blue suit of his and scowling over the fact that Blackfox got off with a light sentence for manslaughter.

"I 'spose you're looking for an apology," he said to me now.

I told him I wasn't looking for anything. He continued staring at me with those glistening gray eyes of his. Finally, he said that was good, as he wasn't about to give me one. Then he brushed past me and hobbled down the street. That was the last I've seen of him.

I saw Cecil about two weeks ago, at the hospital. His Ruth was in again with pericarditis due to her lupus.

"She was doin' so good, too," he said to me.

"Who's looking after her?"

"Doc Percival."

"He's a good man. She'll do fine."

"I hope so. How you and the Mrs. been?"

"Can't complain."

"Heard tell you're about to be a daddy again."

"Yes."

"Got to hand it to you, Doc. Old fart like you, I'da thought you'd be shootin' blanks." He winked at me and we both laughed.

"Give my best to Ruth," I said and left.

One Saturday morning last fall, I was outside near the barn, stacking a pile of firewood that Jack Potter had dropped off. Bobbie was in town working out at her fitness place. A car pulled up the driveway, a green Toyota with one brown fender. When it stopped, a woman and a child got out, came walking toward me. The child was holding the woman's hand. It was Rosa and Maria.

"Hey, Dr. Jordan," she said to me.

"Why, Rosa," I said, a rush of feelings sweeping over me. I gave her a hug, then bent and gave Maria a kiss.

I invited them in. I made us some coffee and we sat in the den. I hadn't seen Rosa in a long while, not since that last time in court. She looked good. Her hair was cut shoulder length and she'd gained a little weight, wasn't so skinny. Maria, about two then, was shy, not wanting to let go of her mother's leg. She'd changed a lot. Her face and body had stretched out, lost that baby look. When she laughed, I could see she had a mouthful of teeth. She was a pretty little girl, still looked a lot like her mother, though now I could see something of her father in her, too. The broadness of Leonard Blackfox's face.

"How are you doing?" I asked Rosa.

"I'm doing all right."

"Where you living?"

"Over in Raleigh. Got me a job and a place there. So I can be near Leonard."

"How is he?"

"He's fine. He could be out in two years if'n ever'thing goes right."

"Glad to hear that."

Leonard Blackfox had pleaded guilty to manslaughter and was sentenced to five years in jail. Rosa got a suspended sentence but had to agree to go into drug rehab in order to get Maria back.

"She's getting big," I said.

"I reckon she is. She's not my little butterfly anymore."

We both smiled. We talked for a time. About what she was doing, where she was working. She said she was saving up. She said when Leonard got out they were going to leave North Carolina and go out West, just like they'd planned. She said they wanted to try to start fresh someplace else. While we talked, Maria, losing some of her shyness, moved over to the bookshelf and started pulling things off, knickknacks and books.

"You get away from that," her mother scolded.

"She's all right." I thought of that night two and a half years ago, the night I brought her home. How much things had changed.

"I just wanted to thank you for everything, Dr. Jordan," she said. "I don't know what I'da done without you."

"I'm just glad I could be of help."

After a while, Rosa said, "Well, I guess we should be going. I'm heading over to visit my old man."

"That's good," I said.

She shrugged. "He's sick again. Figured I'd see him before it was too late."

Maria had pulled one of the framed pictures off the shelf and it crashed to the floor. Somehow the glass didn't break, though.

"Put that back, you little stinker," Rosa said, taking the picture away from her daughter. She looked at it. "This your son?"

"Yes," I said.

"He was a fine-looking boy."

"He was," I said.

I walked her to the door and saw her out. We stood awkwardly on the porch for a moment. I thought about asking her something I'd been meaning to ever since Leonard Blackfox told me what happened that night. Something that had been bugging me ever since he confessed to shooting Pugh. It was, of course, that second shot, the one that blew half of Pugh's head off. But then I thought, hell with it. Just leave it be. Some questions were better left unasked, for there were no good answers to them.

"Good luck," was all that I said.

"*Ga-li-e-li-ga,*" Rosa replied. "Thank you." She and her daughter headed over to the car and got in. Before they took off down the mountain, Rosa waved one last time.

I haven't had any word from Annabel. In some ways I'm surprised but in others it seems perfectly in keeping with her character. A day doesn't go by, though, that I don't think of her. Worry about her. Hope and pray that she's doing better. Getting along somehow. Coping with the day-to-day business of living. Every time the phone rings late at night, I think it'll be her—or *about* her. Somebody calling to say they have an Annabel Lee Jordan in their ER. Some cop saying they found a body, could I come and identify it. But mostly, when the phone rings, I imagine it will be her. In fact, several times in the past two years someone did call me, late at night, and when I picked up there was this familiar silence on the other end. "Annabel?" I would say, my words falling into that dark well on the other end. "Anna? Is that you?" No one answered, though in my heart I knew it was her. And every time an unexpected knock comes on the door I open it, half expecting it to be Annabel, wanting a place to stay. And if she did come back, would I be able to turn her away? Would I be able to say this wasn't her home any longer? Luckily, I haven't had to do that. There are some choices we make and some that are made for us, and either way we got to live with them.

• • •

Bobbie comes out onto the back deck. She moves slowly, tenderly, with that graceful awkwardness of late pregnancy, as if she were carrying a priceless glass object down icy steps.

"You need to get your ass in gear, Doc," she calls up to me. She still calls me Doc. "We don't want to be late."

"I'm coming."

"So's Christmas," she says, an expression she picked up from Troy Bumgartner and probably doesn't even know it.

"I'll be right there."

I stand, wipe my dirty hands on my jeans. Before heading down to join my wife, who's eager to practice our daughter's entrance into the world, I stare for a last quiet moment out over the mountains. Dark blue beneath the rolling clouds, unfurling as far as the eye can see. Almost like a painting.